The Truest Son of France

The Last Favorite's Page: Book Three

Patti Flinn

Gilded Orange Books

Copyright

This is a work of fiction. All incidents, dialogue, and characters are products of the author's imagination and are not to be construed as real, with the exception of some well-known historical figures and quotes publicly attributed to them. Where real-life historical figures appear, the situations, incidents, and dialogue concerning those persons are entirely fictional and not intended to depict actual events or to change the entirely fictional nature of the work. In all other respects, any resemblance to actual persons, living or dead, events, or locales is purely coincidental.

The Truest Son of France
(The Last Favorite's Page, Book Three)

Copyright @ 2025 by Patti Flinn

All rights reserved.

No part of this book may be used or reproduced in any manner by any means, graphic, electronic, or mechanical, including photocopying, recording, taping, or by any information storage retrieval system without the written permission of the author or publisher except in the case of brief quotations embodied in critical articles or reviews.

Ebook: ISBN: 979-8-9860600-8-8
Print ISBN: 979-8-9860600-9-5

Gilded Orange Books
P.O. Box 625
Blacklick, OH 43004
United States of America
https://gildedorangebooks.com

ADDITIONAL HISTORICAL NOVELS BY PATTI FLINN

Véronique's Journey

Véronique's Moon

The Greatest Thing

(The Last Favorite's Page: Book One)

The Devil's Berries

(The Last Favorite's Page: Book Two)

Dedication

This trilogy is dedicated to Louis-Benoit Zamor (~1762-1820).
May it keep his name alive until his true story comes to light.

Prologue

February 1820

Paris, France

Lying on my deathbed, the room cold and lit only by a single, sputtering candle on the table beside me, it occurs to me that I've become a cautionary tale. An example of a life lived—wrongly.

Having always been a person for whom life's ironies give sick amusement, the notion that I may have lived badly as only a possibility, and not an inevitable conclusion, makes my lips twist in ironic mirth. I stare at the water-stained ceiling of my room, pain wracking my body so that my head feels disconnected from the sack of torturous agony I have become. Only one other time in my life have I felt pain this complete.

"Did I do it all wrong, then?" I ask the ceiling. It remains silent in stubborn cruelty as I lie in the twisted, sodden sheets.

Where did I err to end up dying alone and in poverty? Barely a livre to my name, though my cupboard shelves are lined with empty caviar tins (*you can take the page out of the Palace, but you can't take the Palace out of the page!*). I croak with laughter.

Dying and hell-bound, for sure. Where did I go wrong? was a stupid question. "Was it before... or after that big thing? One mistake, or a thousand?" I mumble to the air, blinking the perspiration pouring from my forehead out of my eyes.

My vision fades in and out of clarity as the sound of death, hooves of a horse-drawn carriage with the royal emblem delivering me to my enemies in hell, is a storm raging in my ears. Me, the one whose mother called "The greatest thing God put on earth." Me, the poisonous devil's berry growing steady and deadly among the roses of the House of Bourbon. Me, the self-proclaimed son of France.

In the end, after everything, it turns out my feeders aren't enough to save me now. I blink as the stone fox (my savior and torturer) glares at me to come along, like a good boy. *Come along and don't fight me anymore,* I imagine it says. And with that fox comes all that I've vanquished and all that I've betrayed. All of us, to where we deserve to be. I imagine, if I were to wake up in hell, I'd better do so with my fists up and prepared for my enemies to attack on sight. I raise my shaking arms with weak, trembling fists to the ceiling.

En garde!

But then again, it wasn't *all* bad.

Once again, my lips twist with sick humor as my arms give way and drop. My vision finally fails me, completely. I imagine I am in that familiar silk and velvet-lined golden carriage that brought me to the Palace of Versailles at ten years old. I can almost feel the embroidered fabric beneath me as the horses take me and the carriage, away...

My face contorts into a grimace of a death mask as my life plays out in the dark space behind my eyelids, one last time.

It is a fitting end, I think. *C'est la justice poétique.*

Poetic justice and all that.

Part I
THE BEAST WILL BE FED

Gilded Orange Books

Chapter One

*D*ear Citizen,

My name is Louis-Benoit Zamor, and you have found the last pages of my journals.

I was the page and personal servant to the deceased Madame Jeanne du Barry, or Citizenness du Barry as she's called in the year 1793. Hopefully you've read these pages in order but, if not, I will make quick work of bringing you up to date.

By spring of 1793, King Louis XVI had been put to death, the Queen Marie Antoinette was in prison, and our country was now truly being run by the laws of man, and not by antiquated rules of a monarch. France was fully a republic!

As for me, I had lost the poker game against time. You see, I thought I had more time to get away from du Barry. As a faithful Jacobin, I thought I could convince George Grieve and Max Robespierre to free me, and I agreed to give them all the evidence I had secretly gathered against Jeanne du Barry. Unfortunately, they were annoyed by my hesitance to turn her over. And spending so much time away from Madame roused her ire. Angered by my lapse in adoration, she set her dog, Gaspard, upon me to make me never want freedom again. She gave him what he had been lusting for since I arrived at the Palace of Versailles as a child–freedom to attack me without punishment. His beating was bad enough by itself, but the cure almost took my mind.

The cure... bah!

I didn't know when I was lying on a table being sliced from stem to stern that I was one of the very first patients of what would become called "internal surgery". Until me and other unfortunates who had the displeasure of being guinea pigs, the world didn't imagine a body could be cut on and the insides moved around, all while a person still breathed. It is now thought to be one of the greatest advancements in medicine in all of history. At the time it happened to me, all I knew was I was being held down and cut open like a pig to slaughter. I had no choice in the matter. Left to me, I would have gladly gone to my grave and allowed someone else to be part of that particular advancement.

I apologize for my penmanship. The memory of that pain makes my hand shake, even today.

I now see my life in terms of before and after the physical calamity set off by the brutal beating Gaspard laid upon me. If he hadn't beaten me, I still would have turned in Jeanne du Barry—and had offered to do so—on principle. But the beating and its cure changed me. Sobered me to the reality of my existence and the stakes of gaining my freedom. It reminded me that death was not an impossibility if my existence was an inconvenience to Madame.

If they had been smart, they would have let me die because, once healed, I was determined to have justice. The beating and the surgery left me forever unable to make my own babies, so I had nothing left but my anger and resolve to gain my freedom. And even more anger on top of it from what I was going to have to do to my relationship with the woman I loved.

My apologies for this tremor in my hand that won't let up. I'll explain it all, after I've had a glass or two of Chartreuse.

In 1793, after the death of the king, the worst should have been over. The Révolution was won! We had a new government, by the people and for the people. But, somehow, the trouble persisted. I didn't realize at the time that it would get even worse. Much, much worse.

—Zamor, 1820

Chapter Two

"What day is it?" I asked the woman who came in to bring me creamy eggs and baguette for breakfast. Sun streamed through the window as she set the tray down on my bedside table. When she mentioned the date, I grimaced. Of course, Josephe and Thomas were long gone by now.

My friends, Josephe Bologne and Thomas Dumas, had long marched off to battle. And with them leaving, I'd lost my chance to be a part of the first army of black Frenchmen.

I swung my legs over the side of my bed and picked up a shiny silver fork, flashing a glint of sunlight as I loaded its tines with smooth, creamy eggs. Putting the fork to my lips, I tasted the pudding-like concoction, so laden with sweet butter and cream it tasted like delicious, edible sin. Tiny bits of fresh tarragon gave it subtle flavor, and sprinkles of fleur-de-sel allowed it to linger on my palate. Salanave was wicked in the kitchen.

I scooped it up with torn, crusty, still warm, bread and washed it down with a tiny sip of deep, rich café in the little white, handless cups, setting it back down on its saucer. I tasted brandy in the coffee. Bless her.

I'd been in the room for weeks, though Madame had come to see me once. The visit was unlike the very first time after the surgery when I was as weak as a baby and she laid her head on my chest. When she—smiling sweetly—explained why she'd sent Gaspard to beat me to within an inch of my life. She didn't touch me the next time she came to visit. Instead, she pulled up a chair some distance away and busied her hands with embroidery, jabbering on about nothing; nervousness made her chatter even more. She'd sneak quick glances at me under her lid as if wondering if I would make a sudden movement or pounce on her. I looked through her, as if she didn't exist at all, until she became uncomfortable and left.

Now, my only visitors were the servants who came to feed me or clean me or empty my chamber pot. Occasionally, the doctor. Never anyone I *wanted* to see.

At first, I was angry. Where were my friends? I grew crankier every day with their absence. Where was Salanave? Where was Henri? Where was Véronique? Why was I alone? Why was I *always* alone?

I had taken to walking in incomplete circles around three sides of my bed at night. Sometimes I heard talking outside the door and once or twice, very late or very early, there'd be a knock at my door. A second later, the knock was a little louder, then nothing. I couldn't get to the door fast enough to see anyone other than the guard sitting in a chair outside my door, lounging to the point of falling asleep. Before he could sit up and wipe the drool off his chin I was back in my room. That explained why none of my friends had visited me. Fucking guards.

Three times I caught him lounging. Then, he must have been thinking of me as well because the next time I opened my door, he straightened quickly.

"Monsieur Zamor." He nodded. I took in the empty hall and then looked at his face again. His neat dress and shaved face were in stark contrast to how I must have looked, dressing gown hanging and my tightly kinky hair and beard having grown up and over my face in abandon.

He was one of the ones who held my arms so Gaspard could beat me. He was one of the ones who held me down when the other madman went at me with his knife. When the madman plunged his hands inside of me. My eyelid ticked.

I could tell he knew I remembered the night because his face flushed red.

"Monsieur Zamor, I-I wanted to express my regret for having partaken in what must have been a horrific episode for you. Had I known what Monsieur Gaspard planned to do I would n—"

I had already stepped back into my room and slammed the door in his face. I didn't want to hear that nonsense.

In the mornings, I opened the window to allow a breeze in the room. It was getting hot outside and no matter how many times I wiped myself down with the stagnant water in my washbowl, by noon I was awash in sweat. And yet, I could feel myself getting stronger every day. The words of my old friend, Fabien, came to me. Fabien was a street fighter and had taught me how to wrestle. Years of fighting for money had made his scarred body strong. At silent times in that room, I remembered his words:

"Pain is the first doorway, Zamor. Pain is where your head tells your body—it's time to stop. You can't handle this! Most people will leave a fight the second real pain kicks in. But it's a lie. You can handle it! And if you don't stop, there's a good chance you'll beat your opponent who will.

Winning a fight isn't about being smart enough to know when to stop—it's about being mad enough to keep going after the pain, even if it kills you! It's the madness that other people will see. It's your willingness to embrace it that will win the battle of the mind."

I did what Fabien used to do to build strength. I squatted down like I was relieving myself until my thighs burned and only allowed myself to stand ten seconds later. And then I did it over and over again.

My torso still hurt, too, on the inside. But on the outside my stitches and skin held together. So, I didn't worry about the pain. I lay down on the floor and used only my arm strength to rise me up. My arms were weak at first, but over days and weeks they built back up. My arms were always the strongest thing on me. When they came back, I began to feel like myself again.

When I wasn't trying to pain myself back alive, I looked out the window. The servants had sent along only two books: the Bible and Voltaire's play, from which I was named after the enslaved man turned devoted servant. Madame was nothing if not persistent in her effort to remind me of my place. I hurled it against the wall.

Chapter Three

I dreamt of little Jean Amilcar, the little black child who, like me, had been gifted to a noble person. In his case, he had been given to Marie Antoinette. Like me, he had been educated, named, and baptized. Unlike me, he had been given his freedom papers and was, officially, adopted.

Everyone had thought him safe, but the school where he had been living put him out onto the street when the King and Queen's accounts were frozen. Asked by the Queen to track him down, I found him in a pile of unburied bodies at a mass grave. I took him back to the place he thought of as home—I buried him in the rose garden at the Palace of Versailles.

The King tore down the palace's Labyrinth when I was fourteen to build Marie Antoinette's little pretend farm hamlet, with its miniature water wheel and farm animals. It was a grown woman's dollhouse, designed for the sheer entertainment of noblewomen who thought it fun to pretend to be peasant farm girls. But underneath the Hamlet, the Labyrinth was still there, in my head. I had my own special memories of the Labyrinth. So, it made sense that little Jean should come to me in that place in my dreams, the space having meant so much to both me and the Queen for different reasons...

***

He stood in front of the little farmhouse in his silk short pants and well-embroidered coat with a lace shirt underneath, smiling up at me. He came to me as he was at five, when we first met each other, his cheeks fluffy as he quivered with delight to see me. He was always happy to see me.

"Bonjour, Monsieur Zamor," he said. "My maman used to tell me this was a special place for you."

And just like the piece of merde I was, I snapped at him again, just as I had in life. "She's not your mother, I told you!"

Jean's smile faltered and his eyes grew large as his body tried to decide if he should still be happy or if he should burst into tears. But I was still filled with regret for doing this the first time, I had yet to make it right! I kneeled down before him.

"I'm sorry, little Jean, I didn't mean to scare you. I'm not angry at you."

His face relaxed and now at his eye-level, his brown eyes seemed impossibly large and sweet. He reached for my hand.

"It's alright, Monsieur Zamor, Mademoiselle Véronique told me that sometimes you feel so much it bursts out of you without thinking. She says you have a good heart. I know she's right. Monsieur Zamor is family. That's what maman says, too."

It hurt me to hear him refer to the Queen as his mama, knowing that he'd been torn from his true mother's arms. Like me.

"I'm glad you know. I've never been angry at you, Jean."

"I know."

"I-I even like you a little."

"I know. You love me." The child looked at me, his cherubic face gentle and patient with me. He tugged on my hand. "But Monsieur Zamor, I came to stop you from doing what you plan to do."

He pointed off behind us. The hamlet disappeared and suddenly we were in the middle of the Labyrinth, standing in front of the stone fox fountain, its head cocked up to the sky and spewing water from its mouth. The fox's stone body transformed into a live one, its coat red and shiny. The water stopped spewing, and it closed its mouth. It looked over at Jean and me, and then its eyes slit. It began to back away from us into the tall, tall shrubs, giving little yips as if warning us not to come any closer.

"It's scared. It thinks it's trapped," Jean said. Then, the child took a step toward the fox, and it hissed, looking behind to see a wall of greenery and nowhere to go. Trapped on all three sides, Jean moving toward it.

"Leave it alone, Jean," I said, growing worried about the child. He was too innocent. He didn't understand danger; he never had. And still, he stepped forward. The fox slunk back as far as it could go, its hisses devolving into whimpers. It was petrified of the child. "Jean, step away."

The boy was crouching down, his chubby little hands reaching out towards the animal. He looked over his shoulder at me, and he was no longer the little Jean I'd first met. Suddenly I was looking at the older, taller Jean, at around eight. He still squatted but was higher off the ground. His jacket was stained with filth and frayed. His hands poked out of the sleeves, the wrists, delicate. He wore no shoes, of course. Having been taken from him at the time of his murder, his bare feet were clean. Looking up past the open neckline of his coat, with his lace cravat hanging loose, the skin of his neck was purple instead of brown, where the life had been wrung from it.

And yet, though I knew he was gone, when I looked at his face, it didn't reflect the horror of his death. At eight, he was simply an older version of himself, happiness and light shining through him. He smiled sweetly.

"It's alright, Monsieur Zamor." He reached toward the fox without looking, still smiling at me. "It's just scared." He didn't see the fox suddenly lunge at him, but I did. I pitched forward, lurching and reaching out.

"Jean!" I yelled...

I was sitting up in bed, my heart pounding in my chest. Twice. Twice I was unable to save him.

Chapter Four

D *ear Citizen,*

I think of it now as the beginning of my dreams. Stuck in that little room, all that time on my hands, caused my imagination to work frantically. All that time with nothing to think about and plenty to regret.

Dreams of Véronique returned as if the stubborn sans culotte woman from Burgundy had some control over them. And maybe she did. Today, I'm much more inclined to believe in such things than I was back then.

It was impossible to prevent thoughts of her from creeping in. Impossible not to wonder how she was and what she was doing. She, being the love of my life... and all that.

—Zamor, 1820

***

Summer 1793

Chateau du Barry, France

"Bring me something to read," I told the guard outside my door after jerking it open and surprising him into standing straight.

"Madame says you're not allowed to have anything to read but what you've got."

"The Bible? That piece of fluff about the obedient slave? She can kiss my ass. Bring me something good to read."

"But I—"

"You heard what I said!" I shut the door on his sputtering.

I was going crazy in that room, and thoughts of Véronique Clair were coming hard and fast. Every time I ate something I wondered if she was eating enough. Every time I napped, I remembered a time or two when she and I napped together on a blanket under my tree. I remembered holding her as my chest rose and fell, with the gentle sun laying over us like a silk sheet. We would have to scramble later to get our chores done, but it was worth it for those moments with her, softly snoring in my arms with the breeze blessing us with its kiss.

I maneuvered down to the floor of the room, lay down on my front, and began raising myself with the strength of my arms. As moisture began to drip from my head from the effort, I squeezed my eyes shut and, immediately, she was there.

***

"You do a decent enough job," she said, an expression of slight amusement on her face as she looked down at me from where she stood behind me as I sat on my chair. She held a straight razor and dipped it into the bowl of water beside her before raising it again. "Chin up, please."

I raised my chin without hesitation and felt the razor brush the skin of my neck.

"You just miss some spots under here sometimes," she said. "But it's okay. I'll take care of it."

I smiled. I knew she would. I trusted her with a razor at my neck as if I was as innocent as little Jean, as if I had not a thing to fear. And I didn't. Not with her.

***

I stood up off the floor and wiped my forearm across my wet forehead. It occurred to me that the guard could be of some use. Then, I walked over and jerked open the door again. I looked at him sideways under my hooded lids.

"Stop me," I told him, seconds before I barreled into him, carrying him across the hallway with surprise and brute strength. His back slammed against the wall and an *"oomph"* escaped him. But seconds later he pushed himself away from the wall and we were struggling with each other in that hallway. When he pushed back, pain streaked through my thigh and torso, and I held back a scream. But, taking in deep gasps, I kept going, remembering Fabien's lesson. *Madness over pain.*

So much at the royal court happened in the hallways. Lovemaking, fighting, arguing, begging... the hallways of the Palace of Versailles were prime locations for the juiciest information. No different here, even though this house was a fraction of the size. The rules of royal court remained, no matter the size of the domain. What happened in the hallways stayed in the hallways.

I grunted, trying to get his legs from under him, thinking about how sometimes in the hallways, if Véronique and I crossed paths while walking in the opposite direction, we had taken to a small bit of communication. Because no one was supposed to know we were together we were careful not to show any outward signs of affection. But at some point, we began to brush our hands or knuckles together as we passed. Just a tiny touch so we could feel each other during the day. So tiny, no one ever noticed. But those touches in the hallway could turn a full day of nonsense into something special.

I tried to shake her out of my mind.

To stave off thoughts of her, every day after breakfast... after enough time for my food to settle and not come up... I opened the door and barked the same order at the guard. He didn't even ask me why I was making him fight. It just kicked in; someone attacks you, you fight back. Day after day after day, we tussled longer and harder. The pain no longer made me want to squeal.

One afternoon a knock at the door brought a young servant girl. I yanked it open and looked down at the girl who collected eggs every morning. She and her brother—the cow milker—were the children of a woman who worked the laundry. She was a good enough sort. Her children, tolerable. The girl was maybe in her teen years now.

"Bon Aprés-Midi, Monsieur Zamor. Madame told me to tell you there's a visitor here to see you. He says his name is Sebastien. Madame told him you are ill and cannot possibly receive guests, but he says he won't leave until he knows you're all right. He says he'll yell the house down if he doesn't hear from you. Madame sent me to ask you what to do to calm him."

My lips quirked in an almost smile as my insides warmed. My Jacobin friend, Sebastien, came all the way out to the Chateau from Paris. That was quite a thing for him since I knew he was intimidated and, dare I say, frightened by anything close to the Palace. For him to come all the way out for me made me soften with affection.

I wanted to stay silent and allow him to rescue me, but Gaspard would use any excuse to hurt Sebastien, if he could. And might still if he didn't leave soon.

"Tell Monsieur Sebastien that I am on the mend and that he should ready the green drink for me. That I'll see him in Paris, soon. Ça Ira." *It's all good.* Sebastien would know the green drink was my favorite liqueur; no one at the Chateau knew that. And Sebastien would know the rallying cry of the revolutionaries: Ça ira.

The girl left and I heard no more from her which told me my friend had gotten my message. And now I knew Madame was telling people I was sick. Being so close to Sebastien and not allowed to speak with him made me cranky, but also more determined to come out of this room in better health than I went in. I opened the door and stepped out.

"Stop me."

***

The next night there was a new guard I wasn't familiar with, so I took the evening off to recuperate. But two days later, the sun beat furiously in my room. Perspiration dripped from me like I was under a waterfall. I opened the door and was happy to see he had returned. He must have heard me walking to the door because he was already in position, one leg behind him to brace himself. I liked to see that he had to do that. It meant I was even stronger than I felt.

When I came at him, he pushed me back against the opposite wall. Slamming against it almost took the air from me and I grunted. "Stop me, I said!" I growled, coming back at him, as he fell under the weight of me. Then we were grappling, and I was pulling his leg up so I could hook my arm under his knee and secure it with my hands clasped behind his neck. He made a noise like a whimper.

"*Stop me, I said!*"

***

Sometimes when we were in one of our rooms together, Véronique would remove her headwrap so I could touch her springy soft hair, smoothing my cheek in it. Sometimes it would be braided underneath.

"Why do you always cover your hair?" I asked as we lay in bed. I knew it wasn't for religious reasons; she was Catholic and there was no such rule in the Bible. I vaguely remembered women in my childhood wearing scarves, but my homeplace was India, where it was common. Even Indian visitors to the Palace were draped in them.

The true thing I wanted to know was if she saved the beauty of her hair for me alone, like a gift. It was a deep-seated desire of men, the world over, that pure love of us drove the actions of the women we loved. We could not be happier than to believe the very air they breathed was due to their love for us. I held my own air in anticipation, mildly disappointed when she told me the truth.

"It's bad enough I have to do the laundry, I don't want to have to wash the smell of it out of my hair every night. I uncover it when I'm safe."

When she was safe. That made sense.

Well, though it was not a gift for me, I understood. It was what I had done with my real name so many years ago, putting it away so no one knew it. So long ago I thought I'd forgotten it myself.

"One day, you won't have to worry about all that," I promised. "You'll be able to wear what you want, do what you want, and live how you want," I declared.

She laughed softly. "I don't think even in the best of worlds that anyone has that much freedom."

"We will set the rules for our world. Zamor and Véronique. You and I together; free to be as we choose. Free to be as God intended."

She cocked her head to look at me. "You believe in God, now? This is truly a miracle."

"It's just a figure of speech."

"Mhmm." She lay her head back on my chest and I could feel the smile, her cheek pressing into my skin and prompting me to hold her even closer. Closer. Closer...

***

"Stop, I can't—!" the guard cried out. I came out of my reverie, and I had him pinned. We were both breathing hard and sweating like two pigs, but I had him pinned on the ground. I didn't even remember doing it, so lost in my thoughts. He gasped for air. "I can't. Please. You win. You win."

I barely registered his words at first, I so wanted to keep at it. But then, they sank in. I won. My legs were burning, and I knew most of the pain would kick in soon enough, but still, I did it. I did it!

I released his leg and rolled away from him while he slowly stood like an old man, red with exertion, getting to his feet. He reached out an arm to me and I clasped it, letting him pull me off the ground.

"We don't have to do this anymore, d'accord?" *All right?* "You've taken your revenge?"

Revenge? I thought about it, giving him a once-over. That night flashed before me again.

"Well, almost," I said. Then I moved forward, quickly, to leap up and put all my energy into punching him across the jaw." Once again, he slammed against a wall. You would have thought he'd have learned by now. "D'accord, *now* I've taken my revenge. At least, all I plan to take from you."

He was working his jaw with his hand when I went back into my room. My chest heaved as water poured off me. I walked over to my wash basin and dipped a cloth into it, feeling good to wipe the sweat off. This time in captivity wouldn't be for naught. Yes, the guard was bearing the brunt of what had happened because he was the only one I could punish... at the moment.

The next day he brought me a novel that I lost interest in two pages in.

The bad thing about beating the guard was that I had no more reason to grapple with him and nothing to divert my attention. Now, all I felt was pain inside. Now all I wanted was to punish someone else for what I had lost. What *she* had lost. Someone had to pay for our destroyed future.

A week later the doctor came by and did the best examination he could from across the room without touching me, as I called him every foul name I could think of and threatened his life on at least two occasions. He must have reported to Madame that I was well enough to return to duty because, two days later, a servant informed me that I was being transferred back to my room, and I was to wake bright and early to deliver Madame's morning chocolat.

My last night in the back room, after a simple meal of soup and brioche, I sat on the bed and stared out the window, hugging my knees to me. I was going back different. My face was a mask, the only movement being an odd twitch that would happen involuntarily when a pain would streak through me. The pain came at odd moments, with or without a reason. And then, as if a switch, a corner of my face would twitch with the sudden streak of agony and then disappear just as quickly the second the streak was gone. Just when I'd thought I couldn't get more handsome...

While I hated being imprisoned in the room it suddenly felt safer than being out among people again. I knew what it was that Jean was telling me not to do in my dreams. *I knew it.* But Jean was a child frozen in time, alive only when I slept. What did he know?

The next morning while waiting for the guard to escort me back to my room, I sat on the edge of the bed. Suddenly, my stomach decided to unload itself. I lurched up and over to the washing bowl just in time let loose all that was in my stomach into the bowl, heaving with the turmoil of what was to come, I was sure. It would be the first of what would soon become almost a daily event, as much a part of my morning routine as toilette or breakfast.

Though gaining my strength and not thinking about Véronique were at the top of my mind while imprisoned in the room, I never stopped thinking about the best way to get justice. While I surely wanted to punish Jeanne du Barry, if I murdered her, I would follow shortly after.

The wrath of the revolutionaries was still the best option on the table. Sometimes the smartest thing was to do what one could to set things into motion... and then stand out of the way.

CHAPTER FIVE

Fortunately, I didn't pass anyone on the way back to my room the morning of my relocation. Closing the door behind me, at an initial glance, I was pleased my things were as I left them. When, finally, I ventured out and walked into the kitchen, the cook, Salanave, looked up and her eyes caught mine.

"Zamor! Merci á Dieu!" *Thank God.* "What did they do to you, petit?" she whispered. Her question made me feel pricks on the back of my eyeballs. It also reminded me of not so long ago, when she'd hurt me almost as badly. I wasn't going to give into any of it.

I pushed past her, taking a platter off the wall and sitting a bowl on it. "Is the chocolat ready?"

"But, Zamor," she whispered. "What happ—"

"What does it matter?" I said, pointedly holding the bowl up to her. She used pot-holders to pour the steaming hot chocolate from a saucepan into the bowl. I put the bowl back onto the tray and groused. "You did nothing when they took me away. You've been out here living your life like I never existed, even though I was locked away in a room for months. Months! You're not my friend. I'm not your child. You told me. 'We can't even speak', you said. I'm nothing to you. You made that very, very clear."

She looked stricken and her flat eyes filled with tears, which satisfied me. Salanave never cried. The fact that she almost did at that moment filled me with something I thought was joy. My feeders flared to life.

She wouldn't make the mistake of asking me again. I didn't care about her tears.

I delivered Madame's chocolat to her bedside table.

"Ah, there you are. My lovely, lovely Louis-Benoit, looking so strong and handsome today." She smiled and clapped to see me, going silent when I didn't respond. I straightened, turned, and walked out as her friend Chon eyed me, silently, from across the room, her dark eyes taking in everything. Then I went back to work as normal, dusting and taking coats at the door and clearing dishes from tables.

Throughout the day, when Madame smiled at me with her innocent, guileless face and blue eyes, I hated her with a fervor with which I had never hated anyone or anything. I wanted to destroy her. I wanted to burn the Chateau to the ground. My stomach bubbled inside.

And so it went. During the day, I did my chores. Then, I went to my room and imagined the best way to kill Jeanne du Barry. I even jotted down some ideas, throwing them into the fire before going to bed. It was summer so that became impractical, and quickly. I relegated myself to keeping my ideas in my head. Much like fighting with the guard had taken my attention, thoughts of her demise diverted my every waking moment.

The other moments were spent keeping an eye out, and avoiding Véronique. I didn't even visit my tree, knowing she would find me there. And when knocks rapped on my door in the evenings, I ignored them and kept my door locked.

"You look so much better, and stronger, my dear Louis-Benoit," Madame said one day as I was bending over to pour her tea as she sat in the parlor. "I know you're still angry," she said, softly. "But when that gentleman saw how distraught I was when you didn't come home, he promised his methods had worked before. Takes away your obstinance and aggression. I can't have that, Louis. You understand?" She held her cup in both hands and looked at me over the rim with innocent eyes as she sipped. "I can't live worrying when you might try to leave again, not now with so much going on. You do hold some responsibility, too. You were becoming more disagreeable every day. Now I understand it wasn't your fault; it was the aggression in your blood. I know you're upset but you'll see in time I'm right?" But the way she said it, in question, let me know she already doubted her part in it. She should have doubted it much, much sooner.

I didn't respond. I saw her clearly and felt not an ounce of affection for her. And I never would again.

My thoughts and ideas, my focus on them took my attention away sometimes. Once, at dinner, I lost focus in the middle of pouring her a glass of wine. I was staring at the wine one second and the next, the sound of gasps brought my awareness to the glass, now full to overflowing, red wine pouring onto the table and spreading over the white lace tablecloth. It was fascinating, the way that cloth soaked up all that red. It was equally amazing how such a raucous group of diners had quieted down. I righted the bottle and took a step away as a servant rushed forward to press cloths to the stain. "Anything else, Madame?" I asked.

She excused me.

Of course, I couldn't avoid Véronique forever. One afternoon she caught me in the hallway.

"Zamor," she whispered, her face brightening on seeing me up close. "They wouldn't let me visit; they had a guard at your door, even. I've been so worried. And I've been knocking and knocking, where have you been since they let you out? It's as if I always miss you. Please, speak to me. What happened?"

"Come with me," I said, leading the way into a small work room and closing the door behind us. I was twitchy and discomfort rolled through me. She was, sweetly, anxious and excited. She continued, as if having stored up weeks of the need to talk.

"They said you were ill, how are you, my love? They wouldn't let me see you and then when you came out there were so many people around, I could never find a time to speak to you alone and you always seemed to be disappearing. I am so happy you are all right." She put a hand on my cheek and stroked it gently. It felt so good I wanted to lean into it but, instead, I caught it and gently pushed it away. "Zamor, say something."

Alas, true life is not a romance novel. There is no place for romance during a revolution.

My voice came out hard and even. "I was sick, but I am stronger now, you needn't worry. But the time away was good for me. I realized while I was sick that a relationship between us is impossible. We cannot be. You have been very special to me but it's over. It's done."

"You've been ill. You're not yourself."

"I am."

She laughed a bit. "Your humor is back so you must be feeling better. I—" my lack of answering her laughter and something in my eyes finally caused hers to die down. Her gaze lost all mirth. I continued now that I had her attention.

"I..." My voice faltered looking at her. It was one thing to rehearse, another to look her in the face and not kiss her. "I... just listen. You and I will never be. We have no future, not ever. My life is devoted to the revolution. I don't have room for anything else."

The muscles in her face grew still while her lips quivered, slightly. Then, a frown sprouted between her eyebrows, and she spoke to me gently. "Salanave told me about that day Gaspard and his guards dragged you from the room. They've hurt you, somehow, but you are still here. Maybe, if I didn't know you, I would believe that you have lost all care for me, but I know better. I know your heart. No matter what they did, you are still *you*, and I am still me. And we still have each other."

My eyelid twitched at her condescension and stubbornness. I wanted this to be easy. I *needed* it to be. Why couldn't she let it be? Anger took fire in me at the false hope she represented.

"And who am I, brilliant woman?" I seethed. "A piece of nothing that lives to entertain? The boy dressed as a doll and mocked as court jester? Look at me, dressed like a fool, still! I'm nothing more today than I was then. Holding my chin up, uselessly, while I'm ridiculed and demeaned... I can't even stand up straight for all the years of being beaten. I'll be curled like a crab from a lifetime of beatings, even *before* one I just took."

Her eyes clouded even further. "They'll answer to Jésus-Christ for what they've done."

"Sure, they will," I mocked. "Stop it with your precious faith in God, it's tiresome and ridiculous. In this world innocent people are murdered and children starve in the street; and I've yet to see God smiting anyone. But you'd have me believe He cares about me more than them? Well, Gaspard and Madame will get their punishment, all right; God-willing, from *me*. It'd be the greatest blessing to have a hand in sending them to hell. A miracle! Pray to your precious Jésus-Christ for *that*." I snorted, mirthlessly.

"What they've done to you is *their* wrong, not yours. Don't fight their sin with your own. You're still the man I love," she insisted. "To me, you are *everything*. It's been your sense of knowing who you are that has carried you this long. The greatness within you, I see it! Just like you mother saw it. Your name is known throughout the kingdom because of your pride and dignity. Your strength of spirit. *Everyone* knows. You're more intelligent than any noble or any royal and most of the people who walk through this door. The only thing that has ever held you back is the circumstance they put upon you because of the color of your skin. You are brave beyond your circumstance. You are courageous beyond your size. You have earned your name and fought to be the person you are. Will you give up now? Will you let them win now?"

My eyelid twitched again, furiously, her complimentary words burning like holy water on a sinner, fire and brimstone scalding me. They made me angry. How dare she regale me with praise when I felt none of it?

"Don't stand there and lecture me, you spoiled, pampered, *free* woman."

"Pampered—?"

"—with your fancy home and two parents..."

"Fancy?"

"And rosy outlook on everything. You, who have never seen what's done to those of us who aren't free. A gilded cage is still a cage. Don't presume to tell me..."

"You *know* I'm a peasant. You *know* my papa is a freed enslaved man. Let me tell you something, a gilded cage would be a *blessing* to our enslaved brethren. *Neither* of us has it as bad as any one of them. Don't you dare talk down to me as if I haven't faced my own difficulties. Strange men pawing at me since I was a little girl, knowing they could get away with it because I'm poor and black. My entire future at the mercy of men; my value determined by them just the same. I keep going for the same reasons that you do. I want something more and I hope for more."

"Ah yes, following your moon," I mocked. She had told me once that she had been driven to follow her own moon, taking an unfamiliar path for a woman in her position. I admired it. But today, I mocked it. "I have no moon, Véronique. And my hope is to be the absolute best monster I can possibly be. That's what they've made me. *And I'll enjoy that life*! It's clear to me now. My purpose has only ever been to do my part to overturn this vile, putrid way of life or die trying. The age of kings isn't dead until the people at the head have served justice. And I can't do what I need to do with you around lecturing me... and all that. You're a burden around my neck. An anchor. Well, I release you. Live your life, free woman, and leave me to live mine."

Her eyes darted a bit.

"You just need a little sleep."

"I slept on it, I told you. I did nothing but sleep and think and it's over."

"Zamor... it's *me*..." She pounded her hands on my chest as if willing heat into it. I watched the hope dying slowly in her eyes; a smile of incredulity fading into lips thinned and losing color. Her next words were barely a whisper.

"*Fight for me... for us.* You read the Lord's book, now is the time to practice what it says. When all seems lost you must have faith. I can see you are in a valley of darkness now but it's temporary. Be with me and together we will find the light."

My eyes rolled up with frustration. Why must all Christians invoke God in every word and every thought? Why she imagined it would sway me was a mystery. Still, I felt my body begin to quiver.

That little room with its walls lined with shelves and containers of dried beans and grains suddenly felt too small. Too hot. And she was too close. Her eyes were too large and searching, too warm and familiar. Any moment now she would wonder how I could be so near and my body not stir for her. Not when, before, simply a glance or look from her could rouse me, even in inconvenient places. She didn't need to know what happened in that room. I would die before I told her.

I licked my dry lips, quickly, looking into her eyes and willing my own not to fill. Willing myself not to bend.

Mon Dieu, I wanted her more than anything I'd ever wanted in life. I wanted everything she was and everything that had made her. I wanted her smell, her sound, her touch. I wanted her past and her future. I wanted her smile and her sarcasm, her faith and her anger. I wanted to spar with her and to talk with her. I wanted to hold her and to support her. I wanted to curl up with her on cold nights and run with her on hot summer days. I wanted to hold her hand in mine for eternity. I wanted to ball up at her feet and kiss them. At her very worst, I would take her a thousand times over because I loved her. I loved her. I loved her!

But what would she get? A man eaten up with anger and resentment, dedicated to destroying Madame? A man who would deny her the one thing she wanted, children? A man who could no longer give her a beautiful future? Tethered to a soon-to-be murderer?

I was a selfish man, but it would kill me a little every day to watch the light fade from her eyes living beside me. She deserved to follow her moon, and more. I knew she loved me. But in that instant, I knew I had to kill that love dead.

"You've weakened me like Eve weakened Adam," the words were hesitant as my mouth didn't want to say them. Stolen bunk I decided to use because why not blaspheme the religion she loved? I firmed my voice and picked up speed. "I was fine with who I was until *you* came along..."

Don't you see? my heart screamed. *I might hate you if I can't be what I want for you! I might want to destroy you as I've been destroyed. Can't you see that?*

I looked into her brown eyes, and she seemed suddenly too good, my Véronique of the East. Still too loving.

"You stand here with your hope and faith and childish innocence," I all but spat at her. "Foolishness! Searching for freshness among a basket of rotting fruit is a fool's errand. For a moment I was a fool, too, but no more. These people are exactly as dangerous and cruel as they've always been; nothing's changed. It was only me. I changed because of *you*. I was surviving just fine until you came along and you're worse than all of them put together" My words caught her by surprise and her eyelashes fluttered.

"You don't mean that…"

"You come with your happiness and peace and all that nonsense. Bringing it to this place where only the most decrepit souls can survive. Véronique of the East! You liked that, didn't you?" I mocked. "The thrill of moral superiority, looking down your nose at us. Our first conversation, you talked about me like I was a dog and you didn't even know me. I let that go. And then you hit me!" My voice rose in indignation over the long-forgiven event.

I knew she hadn't forgiven herself for the slap. She was a person who punished herself for causing pain even if she was hurt herself. She wasn't wired to do harm without it hurting her. I saw it on her face now. Yet I went on.

"A piece of trash servant empties a vat of filth over you and nothing." I swiped my hands in demonstration. "But me? I make one poor comment, and you slap me across the face like I'm dirt on the bottom of your feet… good Catholic woman that you are." Her face was still but her eyelids fluttered with each word, a tiny ripple that said it hit its mark. "Chloe was right! When did I become special to you, Sainte Véronique? Let me see, oh that's right, after I started listening to your nonsense. It must have been wonderful for you, taking Zamor, the heathen, to church. Looking down on me. Like all those people spreading religion to the heathen Africans, telling them everything they believe is ignorance but you… you're the light and the way, right?"

I knew what I was doing. I said the ugly words that I knew would tear her hands from around my heart.

"Little did I know you're more dangerous than any of these demons in this place. Preaching virtue, but you didn't have a problem spreading those pure Christian thighs for me. I should call you Véronique from Hell for the pain you bring to others in the name of good."

So, I said those words. I said those words that my throat was now spasming on, working hard to take back. The warmth in her eyes chilled with every word until her gaze was cold on me. As cold as it had been the first time she called me vile. As cold as a frozen stone fox in the middle of winter.

A small part of me felt satisfaction at being able to cause someone—anyone—mortal pain. A part of me wondered if I would feel it later, like the after-effects of those hallway grapples with the guard or another bad beating. Maybe I would feel it later, but now this felt too good and evil to stop. Someone had to suffer for what I was giving up. What did it matter if it was the woman I *was* giving up who bore the pain?

"Whether it's Madame or the new republic, they'll destroy you," she said through tight lips. "When the dust clears, it's you who will be to blame if anything goes wrong. They will put the worst offenses on *your* back. They'll march you to that horrible machine and take your head as easily as if you were a goat. You're disposable to them. You can't fight for anyone or anything if you're dead."

"You don't need to teach me anything about French people, I already know what they'll do. You forget, I'll do the same. You ask me to fight, oh, I *will*. I'll fight to overthrow this corrupt system my way, like I should have been doing all along. Like I would have been if you hadn't come into my life. If it weren't for you, I would have been free of this place months ago." I nodded, pointing a thumb behind me as if she could see what I saw in the past of my fever dreams: Josephe and Thomas walking forward into battle and leaving me behind. My voice hitched. "I would have joined an army of Black men to fight for the republic! I had a chance to be a decent and honorable man fighting alongside them, but I was afraid to leave *you*. And now here I am, *stuck*, a shell of who I was. So, if I can never be the man I thought I'd be then my only purpose now is to take as many of my enemies down as I can. Someone will pay the price for each and every stolen, abused little Black child. I will make someone pay."

"Little Jean wouldn't want this for you."

"I'm not talking about Jean!"

No, Jean was a tragedy, but he was gone and safe in heaven. I was speaking of the little boy who'd tried to take me under his wing when I was first enslaved. I was speaking of the little boys and girls whose names I didn't know who were used, mercilessly, on the journey to even surer suffering. I was speaking of the child who taught me to speak French so I wouldn't be beaten. And, yes, I was speaking of a little boy named Zamor who was now good and surely dead after a lifetime of trying to fight the great monarchs. And I was speaking of the children he would never have.

"Don't say it's for them," she mumbled so softly I almost couldn't hear, her eyes glassy. "Don't say you're choosing evil for their sake. Don't put that on innocents. This is for you. You're choosing suffering over hope."

"Yes! Yes!" I gestured to heaven that she'd finally gotten it through her head. "You're right! I don't want to find the light! I want to be the highest, brightest beacon of the republic." I'd hit my mark and now was time to drive it home. "Go away and stop trying to tempt me with your childish dreams. Even if I were free, I could never have stayed with a woman who was too ignorant to marry a man above her station and whose greatest dream is to live in a shack by a river. A shack!" I shook my head like she was asinine, laughing mirthlessly. Just to be mean. "I want better things than a servant woman could ever give me. Véronique of the Dining Room, that's who you are. Ha-ha! Véronique with the hands as rough as any farmhand," I said, almost wincing myself.

I knew how self-conscious she was about her hands. Day in and out, plunging them into lye and scalding hot water to clean the clothes and bedding. All the rest of the time, those hands were gripping a needle to pull through fabrics as soft as silk and as tough as leather. It all showed on hands which she still hid from me, sometimes. As if her working hands would repel me. They were beautiful to me, but her sensitivity to them made them fair game now. And I continued to pile on the pain.

"Y-you're nothing more than a child of a slave who doesn't know her place. Just something to be had, not anything I ever intended to keep. I've had women from the lowest to the highest—*noblewomen*, even—and you think I'd want to keep *you*?" I laughed like she was ridiculous.

It's a lie! the voice in me screamed. *When we lay together and I press my nose to the skin at your neck it smells like warm, spiced honey—filling my nose with musky sweetness and earth. I've been with many women but not any one of them meant to me a fraction of what I felt with you. I'd give them all up to keep you! Mon Dieu, how I want to keep you!*

My thoughts were at odds with my words, but my words were all that mattered. My cruel laughter filled the little room. As someone who hated to be laughed at, I knew the laughter would rankle most of all.

"Stop it! Stop it!" she burst out, bunching her fists and closing her eyes to take several deep breaths. I hated myself, then. Hated what I was doing to her. Knowing it was still the right thing.

When she opened her eyes, they were glassy with standing water. She smoothed her skirt with her palms. Her face settled into the stern determination that I had seen on her that very first day. She took a moment to swallow before speaking, her voice firm and steady as I allowed my sick laughter to die down. She looked at me straight in the eyes.

"No more insults? Are you quite finished trying to hurt me, mon amour?" Shame filled me and blood flushed my cheeks. "I don't have the energy to fight for the both of us. If you expect me to say something equally foul to you so that you can tell yourself that what you are doing is right, you'll be waiting forever. I won't lower myself to wallow in the filth with you."

"I knew it." I cackled. "You always thought you were better—"

"—All this time, claiming you would do anything for me and now, the one time I finally ask for what *I* need..." She dipped her head and seemed to shake herself to. She exhaled, deeply, rubbing her forehead like it hurt. "Oh, my heart, how you disappoint me. You're a liar and a coward after all..."

I snuck a resentful look at her. "I thought you just said you wouldn't lower yourself..."

"It's not an insult if it's true, Louis-Benoit; it's just fact." That stung. "The 'republic' this and the 'republic' that, as if you have some grand scheme for saving this country. Now I see this has only ever been about your own ego. This has only ever been about you proving yourself worthy to these people and *that woman*. You choose them over me and what we have? Well, I won't beg you. I may be a servant girl with modest dreams, but I know one thing for sure: you'll be sorry for this. You'll regret it for the rest of your life. You're right, I *am* still a child of God. I will pray for your damaged, sorry soul."

My lips were tight, bunched against the rawness of her words. They stung, on top of the hurt. No matter that I knew I deserved them, they made me feel small. I lashed out, of course. "Save your prayers for someone who wants them, *Sainte* Véronique. Maybe your prayers will keep you warm at night."

"I hate you. I hate you!" she hissed, but the water in her eyes said differently. She turned on her heel and jerked open the door to leave, and I simply had to cause one last hurt. I had to get in the last word.

"That makes two of us, Mademoiselle, but I hate you *more*!" She hesitated for barely a moment and then walked out of the room with her head held high.

The door closed behind her, and my gut clenched like it was caught in the jaws of an angry beast. My body shook as if I was standing naked in a winter storm. An hour later, I waited for the beast to let up, but it stayed with me, my stomach a constant tight fist refusing to release. I waited. Days passed and I waited. But it seemed this pain would never die. Soon, I realized it was another permanent part of me, having settled into my body like the ache in my bones on a rainy day.

CHAPTER SIX

*D*ear Citizen,

Later, I would wonder if I should have been open to her words. Maybe, allowed a sliver of possibility in their veracity. That maybe my depression was blocking my ability to think rationally and hear her.

Hindsight... and all that.

—Zamor, 1820

***

Once our relationship was over, thoughts of Véronique came rushing at me all the time.

The pain came in bits and pieces as the moments she occupied my life came in fits and starts. When I woke and she wasn't by my side. When I wanted her opinion and couldn't turn to her for it. When my hand waited for the feeling of hers sliding into it. When I passed by a closet where we used to sneak into for a quick kiss or when I lunched behind my favorite tree where we used to hide.

Standing in a room like a statue and trying to forget how she used to smile at me from across a room. When a draft blew her scent my way. When the sun shone down on the grass and the breeze billowed sheets on a line. When one of the servant children ran through the house or when bread was baking in the oven or when the horses ran over the lawn. When the sky opened up and when it was quiet. All of it—any of it—reminded me of her. And the pain came in bits and pieces, shockingly deep and sharp.

Still, she was there. And in between these moments of missing her were the even worse moments when I was forced to see her and pretend like nothing had happened. Pretend we were strangers.

One day, we were preparing for dinner. I was going back to the cellar to get more wine. She was headed to the dining room with a stack of freshly ironed napkins in her hands. I saw her at the end of the hall and my body went on full alert, just as I would if Gaspard was about to hit me. I braced myself and raised my chin. Her face was expression-less and she barely looked at me from under hooded lids. We walked towards each other as if we were strangers, but with every step my body began to betray me. It was the hallway, you see. The magic hallways where memories lived. Every step was like walking through mud, harder and harder.

My gaze picked up a tiny movement from her, one hand freeing itself. One hand, casually, drifting down, down, down to sway slightly by her side. Freeing itself for me.

She forgave me! My heart leapt. My mouth went dry, and my forehead suddenly became clammy with excitement and fear. I could see in the stiffness in her face that hardened with each step, it was torture for her to release that one hand. Torture for her to let it hang there beside her as she walked toward me. She still loved me? She still cared!

You fool, the voice inside me screamed. Things hadn't changed, after all. The reason I'd ended us was still the same. I still had nothing to offer. I still knew that any relationship between us would only lead to her heartache.

I still knew the most decent, human thing for me to do would be to leave her alone. I'd caused all the pain already.

And then there was the dream I'd had when I was sick with fever after being cut open. The dream where she was running towards me and the ground opened up underneath her in a sea of mud. It clutched at her skirts and pulled her under. The harder she fought to get to me, the deeper she sank. The harder she tried, the more horrifying it was to watch the quagmire pull her under. I was the quagmire. I would be her doom, if I allowed it.

My heart began to gallop in my chest and my own hand on the left side of my body began to tremble. My head swirled as if a storm raged within it with every step. Already by my side, the tremble grew, and my hand began to shake ever-so-slightly, my body revolting against me. My eyes were riveted to her free hand.

Don't do it! something in me screamed. My eyelid ticked as we came within arm-length. My hand was shaking as if I'd caught a chill by now. And when I once would have gently brushed the back of her knuckle with the back of mine, I pulled my hand away, back just an inch. Just enough to miss hers.

Though my stomach roiled, you wouldn't have known from looking at me. No one would ever have known that it was at precisely that moment I broke us for good. That I changed the course of my life, forever. That I died inside.

Instead of going to the wine cellar, I walked through the kitchen to the door outside, walked over to the side of the house, turned, and emptied the contents of my stomach onto the grass.

***

Later that evening, I was in my place standing behind Madame. Gaspard was across from me. Véronique stood in a third corner.

"Is that the infamous Zamor, Madame?" a visiting duchesse asked, a smile on her face. "I told my friends I was coming to meet him and they're jealous."

"Yes, well, he's always here," Madame said. "I have to keep him... No one else will have him."

She'd said it a thousand times before, but this time when her guests laughed and I failed to follow up with a joke or playful barb, the laughter trailed off, discomfort spreading through the room. I think perhaps the lack of humor in my face soured the mood. Madame fiddled with her water glass.

"Please, eat everyone."

I looked up and Gaspard was glaring at me, angry I'd made Madame uncomfortable. I glared at him back. I think something in my face made him uncomfortable, too, because a muscle flexed in his jaw. And then he looked away.

I looked over the room and Véronique was standing quietly, her hands clasped in front of her and her eyes down. She looked up, no doubt feeling my eyes on her. We glared at each other. I looked away.

Now I knew that she really meant it when she said she couldn't go back home because she was still here. But I *needed* her gone.

Chapter Seven

Two nights later I borrowed the carriage and driver and, finally, took my body into town. I would have rather taken a horse, but I didn't want to ride, not yet. The carriage driver parked at a tavern, and I slipped out of view, walking two blocks to the Jacobin Club. Sebastien wasn't there but Grieve sat at a table with his quill in hand, mapping out his plans alone, his face fevered and manic with a tinge of insanity. He looked up as I approached, his eyes red-rimmed from the poisonous cocktail of lack of sleep, too much wine and obsession.

"I'm moving to your town of Louveciennes," he said without preamble, looking down to continue writing. "I'll gather information from the people in the community." He looked up at me again. "What's happened to you? You look terrible."

That statement made me smile with irony which brought on a brief episode of laughter. My laughter didn't inspire answering laughter but looks of concern.

"Here." A bartender handed me a small draft of brandy. "I'll add it to your tab."

I took it down in one spell and my body settled down, but still I felt hot from the ride into town. I held out a hand for someone to fill it again.

"Are you alright?" Grieve asked.

I swallowed my drink in one gulp, coughing so I had to clutch a chair as the pain wracked me with each exhalation of air. Finally, when I could speak again, my voice was hoarse but clear: "My offer still stands. Give me five hundred livres and citizenship papers. I will deliver you Madame Jeanne du Barry on a platter."

"We've gone through this and nothing's changed since you took your little vacation. As I said, I'm moving into your town. I'll take care of it myself."

"Are you refusing me, then?"

He looked at me, strangely, no doubt surprised by my tone. "Yes."

I strode away from him and out of the tavern. I didn't have time for this. If he wouldn't strike a deal, I knew someone else who would.

I walked through the streets until I reached Robespierre's townhome. Once there, I was allowed inside but there were guards in the hallway outside his study. Seeing me, the third seated man closest to the door stood up.

"I need to see Max. Now."

"Get out of here." One of them gave an obscene gesture.

"Tell him Zamor is here to see him. Tell him, now."

"You don't give orders around here. Leave before I give you a beating you won't soon forget." Two of them began walking my way, but I was in no move to be ignored today.

"Max! Max!" I yelled. "It's Zamor, I need to speak with you, now!" Two of them had grabbed me, one arm each. "Max, I can deliver what you asked for. Max!"

They were shuffling me down the hall when the sound of a door opening stopped us. We all looked behind us to see Robespierre poke his head into the hall.

"Are you mad, making such a racket in my home?"

"You asked me for something I wasn't ready to give but I did, finally, agree. Grieve turned me away. Did he tell you that? Did he tell you I was ready to give you what you need months ago?"

"He told me he'd finally had enough of you. He's taking care of things on his own."

"Does Grieve have a list? Does he have a ledger of her accounts? Does he have a list of her properties and all the people who've come through the Chateau? Or is he hoping he might get lucky once he moves to Louveci-ennes? Why hope he can solve your problem when I can get you what you need? I just need a few minutes with the Incorruptible, Citizen."

It might have been my appeal to his reputation as the most incorruptible man in France. Max was annoyed with me, I knew, but he wanted Jeanne du Barry more than he wanted to disregard me. He looked me over and then gestured to his guards. "Let him in."

***

For three days I did my best to avoid everyone. I busied myself with a new sandy-colored young horse. The man in charge of horses told me he hadn't seen my friend, stable-hand Henri, since well before I was attacked. Henri had been my only friend at the house not so long ago. I was sad he was gone, and even sadder I hadn't been able to say goodbye.

The man in charge of the horses told me about the new sandy-colored horse. It wasn't as beautiful or smart as Lightning, my horse that Gaspard had murdered, but he was strong and trainable. For days on end, I worked with him, training him to obey me. Then, when I was comfortable with him, I rode him into Paris to, finally, knock on Sebastien's door.

His face was a mask of relief when he saw me. "Mon Dieu, I thought they'd killed you and buried you on royal ground," he said, grabbing me in a hug. His wife yelled in delight behind him, waiting for her turn to give me two kisses. "Are you all right?"

"I will be," I told them. "I will be now."

Three days after that I had my five hundred livres and the promise of the papers once I testified against my benefactress to the committee. Max promised to send word when the arrest date was set so I could prepare myself and threatened me with every horror if my evidence wasn't sound.

The money would set me up nicely for a while. Once free, I'd likely take an apartment in Paris, but first I needed to gather even more evidence and prepare for my leaving.

I took more notes, going through papers, paying attention to the names of people who came and went. And it occurred to me that after I left, I might not have access to the things I loved. I began stealing little tins of caviar from the storeroom. Madame didn't drink Chartreuse so I made do with stocking bottles of fine cognac under my bed.

That was the plan.

Chapter Eight

Of course, three long, sleepless nights later the plan had changed.

It was too difficult to be what I needed to be and see the woman every day. *The woman.* That's how I referred to Véronique in my head—so much easier than the lovely sigh of her name.

I wrapped three hundred of my five hundred livres in a small potato sack and hid it away until one quiet evening. So much money and yet it still fit in the palm of my hand.

Madame was out of the country again, traveling to England to continue building her social base under the guise of assisting in the prosecution of the jewelry thieves. Fortunately, she took the dog, Gaspard, with her. When he wasn't traveling with her, he was skulking around the Chateau looking less triumphant than he should have been, having finally gotten out his hatred towards me.

So it was that I took that three hundred livres in its wrapped bundle in my hand. The night gently ruffled the flame of the candle I carried in its holder. I walked through the servant's quarters as quietly as I could and laid the packet down on the ground outside her door. Then I knocked and dashed quickly to hide around the corner outside so she couldn't see me.

I needed every bit of money I could get for when I was free. But I could only think of one thing once Grieve delivered it to me. I had stayed at the Chateau for my love for her. She had stayed for the same reason. Now, I was ready to destroy the place, and it was no longer a safe place for decent people.

There was no candle in her window. The candle in the window had been another symbol, a silent communication to me. I noticed it was gone right away.

Véronique opened the door, saw no one and then noticed the package at her feet. She bent down to pick it up, looked around, and then took it inside. At that point I moved to spy in through the window, watching as she opened the package and looked inside, flipping her fingers through the sheaves of money.

I prayed in earnest. I genuinely prayed to God. I knew the type of woman she was, and she might get caught up concerning herself with where it came from. I worried she might feel the need to ask questions or find the person of the lost funds. So, I prayed to God she would take the damned package—that was how much I wanted this to go the right way.

I also worried she would understand *who* the money came from and take it either as an insult or as a sign of renewed affection. So, I prayed for God to put a little hardness, a little selfishness in her. At the same time, knowing her to be as intelligent as she was good, it was on that I hoped she would lean.

She sat on the thin, threadbare cot, still as a statue. She sat and I prayed. She sat for a long moment; even at my distance I could see the fluttering of her eyelids as her brain calculated the options before her. She took a deep breath and stood. Pulling a few sheaves, she plunged them down the front of her bodice in that way women have of finding spaces to hide things around their breasts. Then, she reached down to pull off her thick, ugly shoe, putting the bundle in the bottom. She put her foot back on top and moved up and down a bit, testing how it felt underfoot.

Apparently, deciding it was acceptable, she then began pulling clothing out of the rickety dresser and shoving her meagre items into one of the burlap bags she used to carry her things. My heart lifted as she stuffed all of her things into that bag with increasing speed. A second bag was filled with materials and scraps of her sewing. And, when done, she looked around the room and found paper on the desk. Grabbing a quill and ink, she wrote a quick note and then left them both down on the table.

Véronique stood, clutching one bag, with the other over her shoulder, and looked at the room as if she was remembering it. Her face held a look that was a combination of fear and excitement and sadness. Then, at her quick pivot to the door, I moved as quickly as I could to run back to my hiding space behind a corner.

Opening the door, she looked to and fro and began walking quickly down the path to stables. Though I couldn't hear her, I saw her speak to the man in charge. He shook his head in the negative. She reached into her bosom and showed him a bit of money. That did it. Pocketing the paper, he pulled a horse by the reins from the stables and climbed atop it, helping her on behind him. Once settled, with her sacks held closely and tightly, she clutched him from behind as he guided the horse away from the Chateau in a trot.

She got away.

I wanted to shout with happiness even as I wanted to cry. She was safe.

Véronique's back was straight and stiff, slightly turned as if she felt something there in the darkness watching her leave. But she didn't turn around. She wouldn't have seen me if she had. I had melted into the darkness, into the fabric of this place, my eyes glassy and gut clenching from holding in unexpected sobs.

And soon, they gained in speed and disappeared into the dark night, leaving only the sound of hooves behind them.

CHAPTER NINE

"What did you do to make her go?" Salanave asked me when I came in for morning chocolat two days later. The kitchen oven was already spitting hot, pieces of lardon sizzling in large skillets over the fire. Her face was glazed with a sheen of perspiration from the heat as she wiped her hands on her apron, spearing me with an accusing glare.

I held up the bowl to her where it sat on the tray. "Chocolat, please. Make it quick, Salanave, Madame doesn't have all day."

"She's the best thing that ever happened to this place. Just the sweetest, sweetest thing. I asked you a question. Louis-Benoit Zamor, you answer me, now!"

I glanced up at her from the empty cup. "You can't talk to me like that. You're not my benefactress nor my mother." I raised the cup at her, a prompt she ignored.

"I might as well have been! It's me who's been watching out for you since you were a child. All your life I've been looking out for you."

"And look at how well that turned out."

"Don't you stand there and deny—"

"Until it became an inconvenience, that is." I nodded. "Because when it became inconvenient for you, you cut me loose without a second thought, didn't you? Told me to stay away from you. Took your friendship from me as easily as if it had never been."

"You know I didn't want to. Gaspard..."

"Yes, I know, Salanave. Gaspard's an asshole, like he's always been. It's nothing new. It was *you* who disappointed me. You, who cut me off as quickly as if I was a stranger as soon as he snapped his fingers. When I needed you, where were you? When he murdered Lightning? When he was dragging me, kicking and screaming, where were you?" She was quiet for a moment. "Don't come to me crying over Véronique. You knew damned well how it would end. You know how terrible this place is, and you pushed her on me and filled her head with nonsense when you know, better than anyone, who I am. When you knew how dangerous it was for her here. So yes, I got rid of her to help her. She's no longer in danger here, no thanks to you. She can hate me all she wants but at least she's safe. Now, once again... may I have Madame's chocolat? Please."

Her lips wobbled as she and I looked at each other for a long moment. Then she turned curtly, picked up the saucepan with her two potholders and poured the steaming drink into the bowl. Her lips were bunched like she had more to say but knew better than to.

We had known each other for a long time, she and I. She'd let me down. I was damned if I was going to listen to her whine about somebody else's feelings.

I put the bowl on the tray and turned to leave the kitchen to hear her voice behind me.

"She didn't deserve to be run out of here without a plan. Now that poor girl is God-knows-where, all alone during a revolution." Her voice was muffled as though she mumbled with her head down, wiping the table. Almost, as if to herself, with unbearable sadness.

"Oh, stop it, she'll go home, of course. She'll be fine," I said gruffly, without turning around to look at her as I left.

Of course, Véronique would go home. She was a bit naïve, but she was smart. Where else would she go?

***

Grieve, having been living in town, was now emboldened. I was outside brushing the horses one day when Madame's giggling ladies swept by and I heard them inform each other.

"He moved right in and said he's a member of the Committee for Public Safety here to do research. This Grieve fellow. The second he came in I wrote a letter to Madame in England telling her to stay there. This Grieve man seems suspicious to me."

That was how I knew Grieve had moved into the Chateau. Two days after that I was eating bread and reading by the tree near the Pavilion when I looked up and there he was.

He was walked the grounds, looking around both overwhelmed and enraptured by the beauty of the place. The grass so green and well-kept it looked like emerald velvet. The trees sculpted and controlled. The many rose bushes with only the perfect roses spared from pruning all along the border of the area. The fountain. The little shaded seated area covered with a wooden cross-hatched piece studded with flowers that gave their scent to the air around them. The royal statues that studded the paths and peaked out from the surrounding wilder trees like watching sentinels.

And that was just the grounds of the house. The Pavilion was even more stunning. Not to mention the horses, the tennis court, the other buildings and stretch of property from the Seine River to the main road.

While not as majestic and opulent as Versailles, the Chateau de Lou-veciennes and its Pavilion had a quiet intimacy and picturesque version of being a little piece of heaven on earth. I was used to the place but for others who were used to the poverty and ugliness that plagued most of the country, this was stunning.

Grieve wore clothes more formal than I had seen him wear in town and had pulled his hair back and tied it in a ribbon behind his head. He kept adjusting his coat with his hands as if uncomfortable and unaccustomed to the finery, nodding to nobles who walked by awkwardly. He had stopped to gaze around at the perfect green grass, green trees, and the view when, finally, he noticed me sitting under the tree.

I took a bite of my apple.

We looked at each other for a long moment. Then he pretended he didn't see me, adjusted his coat again and kept strolling along.

After that first time I seemed to see him everywhere—walking through the halls, talking to servants and guests, always jotting down his notes.

One evening, I was passing Madame's bedchamber and heard movement in the room when I knew she was still in England with Gaspard. I pushed open the door to see Grieve rummaging through her wardrobe, the drawers open. I glanced behind me to make sure no one was in the hallway, then stepped inside and quietly shut the door. Still, he didn't even notice me until I spoke.

"What on earth are you doing?" I asked as he jumped slightly upon seeing me. Then, he shrugged in discomfort.

"I'm looking for evidence, of course," he said.

"I'm already gathering evidence. I'm her social organizer, I know who's coming and going and I keep a log of everything. In fact, I don't even know why you're here. Or, did you just need an excuse to sniff her undergarments? I have to say, seeing you here makes me wonder about that rumor that the two of you know each other. That you and she cooked up the jewel theft. Did you help her smuggle those jewels to England? What happened, did she cut you out at the end? It's starting to make sense.

I always wondered why an Englishman cared so much about a French noblewoman. Did the two of you plan to set me up to take the fall?"

"Stop your nonsense. That theft had nothing to do with me, and I caution you not to defame me. Or should I remind everyone that you were considered a very strong suspect at one point? Max hates a thief."

My lip quirked at that. This one was a piece of work.

I grasped my hand behind my back and began to pace, watching him grow in discomfort as he still held her clothes in his hands. I motioned toward them.

"All those months of hounding me so you could do this?" He allowed the clothes to fall back into the drawer, looking caught and embarrassed. "It's not about the republic at all; it's about you wanting *her*."

"Don't make this into more than it is. I was only searching for evidence under her clothes," he straightened. "I'm not the only person in this room with an ulterior motive. Do you think I don't know she allowed that degenerate piece of filth to give you a beating? Word has it he was bragging about it in Parisian taverns until he realized it only made him look like the animal he is. If someone had done that to *me,* I would want to destroy them. It had to remind you of those years at the Palace when she let the nobles do whatever they wanted to you, all over again."

My eyelid twitched.

"I don't judge you for it," he continued. "I'd be driven by rage, too, if I'd spent years dealing with that."

"I've been studying and planning to work for the republic for years. Whatever did or didn't happen recently isn't the reason I became a Jacobin or joined the Committee. I'm just a man who wants to be a man in every sense of the word. A man who wants to make his country better."

"But this isn't your country, either. Why do you care what happens to France?"

"This is the only home I remember... *and all that*," I said, feeling myself getting riled up. "By doing what they did, they made this country mine. These people who think it's acceptable to buy other people. Well... they bought this trouble. They claim me; I claim France right back." I nodded. "And I want it to be a better place, run by people who don't believe it is right or just to enslave other people. That's bigger than you or I. Bigger than my hatred of that despicable piece of filth. If I gave this country to people like him now, it would all be in vain. I haven't lived this long by giving into the impulse for revenge. His time will come. First, I will get what I want."

Grieve had remained silent and now he smirked, pantomiming a long, slow clap. "You do have a way with words. And you might convince some, but I just don't believe you're above pure, simple vengeance," he chided me. "I mean, you didn't make the deal with Max until *after* her guard dog beat you within an inch of your life."

"No, that's not true. I came to you..."

"...You came to me because you suspected what was about to happen, I'm sure. Why fight it, Zamor? Just admit it. You may want your freedom, but you want revenge *more*. You're a base human being like the rest of us."

I gave a self-deprecating smile and humble shrug. "Maybe so. But at least I didn't devote the better part of two years to getting myself into the bedchamber of a dead king's mistress just so I can sniff her underclothes. Me being like you? God should strike me dead right now if that is true."

"Get out of here," Grieve said. "It wouldn't do for us to be seen talking. We need you to be known only as her loyal, trusted servant until the last. I will let you know when the arrest is scheduled. Go. Go, play the supplicant, as you do so well. *Traitor*."

Traitor.

The word rang in my head as if it could never be un-rung. Visions of Judas and his pieces of gold floated through my head, the correlation repulsive to me.

I left the room, then, with him standing beside her dressing drawers looking like he couldn't wait for me to leave. This new world of ours was slowly revealing its cast of characters and the essence of their souls. I only hoped when it was all over, I would be able to stand taller than he stood at that moment.

We continued to pretend not to know one another and two days later, heaven shined down on me: Against the advice of all, and for no discernible reason, Jeanne du Barry returned to Louveciennes. She could have stayed in England like everyone told her. She could have enjoyed the nest she'd build for herself among the English sympathizers and all the French noble émigrés who were already there. She could have been the belle of the ball in a new home.

But she came back.

Upon stepping foot into the Chateau, she was immediately informed of the charges against her by Grieve and taken away.

I wasn't there to see it. I had done my morning regurgitation before going to my tree to have bread and read my book. I thought about Henri and Véronique and Lightning and felt so alone. I was walking back, returning to the Chateau when I passed Madame's three ladies on the path, one of them with the audacity to be wearing a dress with Véronique's unique embroidery on the bodice.

"Oh, Louis-Benoit, the most horrible thing has happened."

Madame's lead lady, Chon, looked me in the eye. "They've taken her, Louis-Benoit. They've taken the Comtesse Madame du Barry…"

There was more talk but when they'd finished sharing their news they dissolved in tears, holding each other up as they continued down the path. I continued to the house, in a daze as the fog slowly lifted from the dreariness that had become my life.

It was finally happening. I smiled, but it wasn't one of ease or pleasure. There was no mirth. Only satisfaction. I'd done what I had to do, and I smiled the grimace of the justified. I smiled the smile of the vindicated. No one ever said vindication was worthy of joy.

It was September 1793.

CHAPTER TEN

I dreamt of Jean Amilcar.

***

I walked the grounds of the Palace at Versailles, straight to the final resting place of the child Jean Amilcar, as if we had an appointment. He stepped out from behind the nearest group of trees as if he'd been awaiting my arrival and walked over to me. He appeared as his young self of about five, a smile on his face...

"Hello Monsieur Zamor," he said politely, as always. A tiny version of me with a cleaner spirit and happier disposition. "I've been trying to speak with you for so long. But you've been blocking me in your dreams," he said, his young face wrinkled with worry.

"I have no viennoiseries to share with you, Jean." I deflected his question, deftly, with the excuse that I had no pastries to offer. "The kitchen is closed."

"But I came for you, Monsieur," he said with a hint of indignation. He was young but just old enough to be able to pick up on mild, subtle underestimation of his intelligence. I owed him at least a bit of truth.

"You came for me, did you?" I gruffed. "Why? To blame me? I'm sorry I couldn't save you. But I tried to harden you up, you know. I did try."

"I know." He shrugged. "But I can only be me, Monsieur Zamor."

"Yes, and I am who I am, however I got this way. Though... I won't blame Him for what I am. God didn't make this." I gestured towards myself. "I don't even believe in God."

"If you insist, Monsieur." He smiled softly with pity in his eyes.

I detested pity. I frowned.

"I've done horrible things, Jean, and I'm about to do more. I will do whatever I need to do to have my freedom. You may not understand, yours being handed to you on a silver platter, as it was."

"I understand. Your maman wouldn't give you your freedom like mine gave me."

"She's not my maman, Jean, I've told you about that—"

"—Now you want to hurt her like she hurt you with her anger and jealousy and spite. You want to make her eat all the poisonous berries of your discontent. You want to cause her pain, real bad. Vraiment?" Is that true?

"I want justice!" I sputtered.

"And... to cause pain real bad..."

I wasn't ashamed to admit it to myself, but to this little boy–that was a different story.

"I will leave this earth being called a man, Jean. You don't understand because you are just a little boy; sweet and innocent and all that."

"But I would have grown up to be a man, maybe like you. That wouldn't have been so bad."

I shocked me, a bit. What might have he grown up to be, if he'd had a chance? Maybe a flawed man like me, or maybe a good one. His life cut short meant we'd never know. He'd be forever, in my eyes, a child without reproach. An angel on earth. But me... I'd grown up.

"I will leave this earth a citizen," I vowed to him. They will call me Citizen Zamor before my life is over."

"What does it matter, Monsieur?"

"*My freedom matters!*"

"*What they call you and your freedom are different, non? I want you to be happy, Monsieur.*"

"*I'd be happy to call myself the truest son of France. This republic will birth me anew and give me a different life. This new republic will allow me to be the man I was meant to be.*"

"*It doesn't matter, so long as you love and are loved.*"

"*What is this love nonsense? I have things to do Jean, and love has nothing to do with it.*"

"*I know what you're planning. You'll make both of them eat the berries for the feeders inside you that grow strong when someone else hurts instead of you. Like she did. I know Madame made you eat the devil's berries—she caused you pain so she could feel strong and powerful again. Now you want to do the same to her. But the feeders inside of you will eat* everything *if they're hungry enough. Yours are very hungry, Monsieur. And when they run out of things outside of you to feed upon, they'll eat whatever they can. Even you. They'll eat you up from the inside. They'll feed on all the greatness and goodness and love inside of you until there's nothing left.*"

"*Shows what you know. There is no love left inside of me now. And whatever they feed on deserves to be fed upon because it's weakness. I had too much weakness, too much softness, to allow what happened to me to happen.*"

"*It wasn't your fault what was done to you. And it wasn't your fault when you were a boy, either.*"

"*Why are you haunting me from the grave?*"

"*I'm not haunting you,*" he smiled. "*This is your dream, you brought me here. I wanted to say hello, Monsieur. I know why you try to block me from your dreams. You think I'm part of the weakness, but you're wrong.*"

"*Why do you care?*"

"Mademoiselle Véronique asked God to send me to watch over you. She prayed it over my grave. You turned away when she began to whisper over me that day, but you heard it, all the same. When you were hurt, she prayed for it every night. Every day she didn't see you she prayed for God to keep you in His care and for me to watch over you. So, I come into your dreams, and I remind you what you know and pretend not to."

I didn't want to think about the day we buried him. I didn't want to be reminded of him or her.

"Listen, child, I sent Mademoiselle Véronique away, so maybe you should watch over her. *Yes, that's your new assignment. Besides, if you knew what I truly dream about in my waking moments, you would be horrified..."*

He shrugged his small shoulders. "Those are your feeder's desires, not your dreams. And it doesn't matter, I know what's in your heart."

"You know nothing. You're just a boy I used to give croissants to. They weren't even my croissants to give, they were yours! You were too young and foolish to realize I was stealing pastry from your own kitchen and handing it back to you like I had a right! Like it was a gift!"

"It wasn't my kitchen. I'm not foolish, Monsieur Zamor. I let you give them to me like they were yours to give because I knew doing it made you feel good. Because you felt you had nothing else to give me. Because you felt guilty that I might have been there because you were there first and I was adopted to undo the wrongness of you. But you weren't wrong, inside. And it was never your fault that I was there. You were my friend. You gave me love with every croissant."

I swallowed the lump in my throat. I sneaked a sideways glance at him from under hooded lids and all but hissed at him. "I don't know what love is, child!"

"You do. You love and you are loved, Monsieur Zamor. I love you. And you love me."

"What does it matter if you're dead?"

"Love never dies. It is forever and forever." At my dubious look, he went on. "Madame Véronique said, 'Watch over him, little Jean, his heart is even more delicate than a new little baby's.' She was right." He let out a small giggle. "You are an innocent."

"There's nothing innocent about me. Stop it!"

"She was right. You don't understand life. Not really. Life is more than fighting and surviving. The most important part of life is love. You don't understand life if you don't understand love. Love is like water."

I wanted to roll my eyes. It was like listening to Véronique wax poetic about the dirty Seine river behind that house she dreamed about in Crois-sy-Sur-Seine.

"Water gives life, you know," the child continued. "It can cover everything. It can fill anything. It can move you through the harshest time like a river moves a boat. Even though I know you plan to force your enemies to eat their own poison—all the devil's berries—you don't have to enjoy it. You don't have to let your feeders revel in their pain and grow strong from it. It's harder to grow strong without feeding on pain, but it's possible. Don't let your feeders take over. They are only there to keep you alive, not sustain you. Hatred doesn't sustain; it's like fire or poison, and it will eat all the way through if it can. Use love to grow instead. Love can keep you afloat in difficult times and it can deliver you to places you could never even imagine. It can wash it all away, Monsieur Zamor... even that."

"That, what?" I asked.

He gestured towards my front, and I looked down at myself to see the front of me, and my hands held out before me, covered—dripping, practically awash—in blood. The scream that tore from me came from somewhere deep inside and ripped me from my sleep.

***

I sat up in bed and looked around the room. I was still at the Chateau du Barry. And there was no little dead child anywhere to be seen.

CHAPTER ELEVEN

Dear Citizen,

Grieve left Louveciennes quietly after her arrest, which I attrib-uted to our last, less-than-pleasant conversation. I kept to myself and spent a lot of time out by the Pavilion and in my room. A few days later Jeanne du Barry returned.

I was still at the house.

Until I had my freedom papers there was no point in leaving, especially with her gone. I was only waiting for a note or letter, anything from Max telling me that a trial had been set or that the act was up. Anything to tell me it was time to go, as he told me there would be.

Instead, I was blindsided by Grieve. I should have seen it coming.

—Zamor, 1820

***

I watched from the landing above as Madame's maids swarmed her the second the carriage opened, like bees buzzing at her as she walked through the front door of the chateau. She kept walking over the shiny, polished floors towards her study, head held high.

What did she know? If Grieve was smart he would keep my confidence until the trial. I could still gain valuable information in the house just from listening to gossip or gathering more evidence from her study. But I had offended Grieve so there was no telling what he would do.

Walking downstairs and through the house I found myself stepping quietly, feeling eyes on me the whole way. It might have been my imagination, but I isolated myself in my room anyway.

Fortunately, it was after dinnertime, so I did not have to stand or sit beside her at the table, but I normally checked in to see if she needed anything. I prepared to feign illness if she sent someone to find me. She did.

"Please tell Madame I'm not feeling well this evening," I told the servant boy.

"Madame says you are to come to the study and no excuse will be tolerated, Monsieur Zamor," he said.

My mind went in a thousand directions. What did she know? What was happening? How was she feeling?

"D'accord," I told the boy with a nod. "I'll be there momentarily."

It means nothing, I told myself, stepping into the study shortly thereafter. She'd been released, after all. Maybe she was about to tell me she had decided to move to England permanently! Gaspard stood in the room already, like a wraith, holding still and silent. He didn't meet my eye.

It was a pleasant evening with the slightest bit of chill in the autumn air. The light from the fireplace glinted off the polished bits of the desk and tables, making the room warm and cozy. The only sound was the crackling of the fire.

I stepped forward towards where stood in front of the desk, her hands clasped before her as she looked down demurely. Calm and composed. That wasn't a good sign. Even worse, I felt Gaspard moving behind me and turned to see him stepping over to close the door, standing in front of it to block the exit. Not a good sign either.

Madame wasn't looking at me. That distance was a certain sign of trouble. I squared my shoulders. She was quiet a long time, and when she spoke it was with a careful tone.

"Bonsoir, Louis-Benoit." It was a statement.

"Bonsoir, Madame." I gave a quick, brief nod. I clasped my hands before me, looking down just as demurely. I knew better than to be impatient.

I waited.

She waited.

I waited.

We both knew the game. We were as still as the pieces on a chessboard, each waiting for the other to make a move or be moved. Gaspard cleared his throat, uncomfortable with the silence. But Gaspard never played with us; he didn't know this game. He didn't even understand we were playing.

We continued to stand there for another ten or fifteen seconds, which is forever when in the middle of a conversation.

She took a deep breath, releasing it in a long sigh. Then, she looked at me and spoke again.

"As I'm sure you know, I was taken in by the Committee for Public Safety on nonsense. But I understand that while I was gone the staff decided to sign their signatures to a petition to set me free, but everywhere they went to find you, you were away or unavailable?"

Yes, they'd come around. No way was I going to put my name on anything that might contradict my testimony. When I saw them coming, I always made myself unavailable. Or my hand was injured and couldn't write. Or I'd get to it when I could, please leave it... I'd used every excuse in the book. I was relieved.

"Ah, what a shame. I do recall hearing of it but never had a chance to actually sign," I said, false regret on my face.

Silence. Her eyes were steady on me. I stared back, keeping an amiable look on my face. One second. Three seconds. Ten seconds. She was trying to make me sweat.

"I would have thought nothing of it," she continued as if there had never been a pause. "But then we came across *this* in town. It's all over Paris." She was holding a paper which she put up to her face to read. "'I was working with Madame du Barry's very own page, Louis-Benoit Zamor, who accuses her of all sorts of crimes against the republic.'—Citizen George Grieves."

Fils de pute! *Son of a bitch*! I plastered innocence on my face as if I had no idea what she was talking about. And she was watching, closely. She continued.

"I knew that couldn't possibly be true. My dear sweet Louis-Benoit would never do something so duplicitous. So, then Gaspard tracked down one of the stable boys that used to work here and pressed *him* for information. What was his name?" she asked Gaspard.

He cleared his throat. "Henri, Madame."

"Oui, Henri! He confirmed that you've been working with the Jacobins," she stated.

Fury crept into me, and I felt my face turn to plaster. I turned to look at Gaspard. "What did you do to Henri?" The man had the nerve to go red about the ears, though he still didn't look at me. He looked at the air, the walls, the furniture, but not me. "Tell me! People don't speak to you unless you are hurting them, I know that much."

"You should be more concerned about yourself," he said through gritted teeth. "Explain yourself to Madame, and you'd better make it good, blackamoor."

I knew she only needed the tiniest glimpse of an explanation to go about weaving a tale of my innocence in her head. It wasn't even about feeling for me; it was about her control and how desperately she wanted to keep it.

Six months earlier I might have denied any allegation, but what was the point? Everything was different now. Gaspard had managed to kill a good portion of my fear when he took my future.

"Oh…" I said, allowing my shoulders to fall and a mischievous, light tone to enter my voice. "…All right, then. No excuse, it's true. Working with Jacobins… I *am* a Jacobin. Can you imagine?" All in good fun, and all that.

Surprise flashed across her face. I glanced over to see a similar response on Gaspard. I shrugged and he averted his gaze, staring straight ahead. It was almost as if they expected me to deny it. Or maybe…

"Oh my." I laughed a little. "You were bluffing, weren't you? Henri told you and you didn't believe him, did you?" I slipped my hands into my pockets and shook my head at my own slip up in falling for the trap. "You just wanted to frighten me into doing God knows what, and here I go revealing myself. Were you hoping to have something else to hold over my head like the jewel theft you were about to pin on me? Stockpiling crimes to pull out when you needed it."

"I don't understand, you admit it? That you betrayed me?" she asked.

"Oh, oui, Madame, absolutely. I betrayed you to them all: Jacques Brissot, George Grieve, Georges Danton, Max Robespierre…" I counted them off on my fingers. "They all know about what you've been up to. You know how I like to be thorough, and all that."

"But why?" She walked toward me with an incredulous look on her face. I didn't respond. "I asked you a question! You owe me answers, Louis-Benoit! After all I've done for you, all I've given you, how could you betray me?"

"All you've done for me?" My smile of amazement quickly changed as heat flared inside me. My face curled with disgust, anger, and fury. "All you've done for me?" I worked up a wad in my mouth and spit on the beautifully polished parquet floor beside me. "That's what you've done for me."

"Batard...!" *Bastard!* Gaspard stepped toward me fast, his fist raising

I put a palm up quickly, speaking softly. "Don't you lay one hand on me, dog. You got away with it once but now that the investigation has started, if anything should happen to me before I testify, Grieve will draw and quarter your filthy, wine-filled body in the street. That's how much he wants the pleasure of prosecuting..." I twirled my finger in the air until it pointed to Madame, "...*you*. Oh, look at that expression on your face." I laughed. "I've never seen that one, before. It must be real, because I've seen all your pretend faces—there are so many of them—and this one is different. Is this what true surprise looks like on you, Madame? Anger? Desperation?"

Gaspard's fist had dropped and now his mouth quivered with the effort not to touch me.

"How dare you!" Madame's voice came out like a hiss on a tea kettle, her yellow curls falling so prettily in her face vibrating from the fury growing within her. Her tone rose with each word. "I. Gave. You. *Everything*!" She growled. "We treated you like a son!"

"You walked me on a leash like a pet! You stole my innocence! You took away my name!"

"What name? You never had a name! My Louis told me, when he asked you, wretched creature that you were, you didn't even have so much as a name. Say it, if it's so important to you. Say your name."

My lips bunched as my satisfaction disappeared under my soul's effort to find it. I knew I spoke it not so long ago to Véronique. But I couldn't pull it up now for the life of me. Sweat began to bead on my forehead as my mind searched for it. And like the predator she was, she noticed my weakness and sneered.

"You came here a nameless, homeless, soulless beggar child. Uncivilized and uncouth! Without a pot to piss in and smelling like it. You might as well have been crawling on your hands and knees. And don't flatter yourself you were anything like my pets; they were all clean and washed and lovely. But you, you were nothing. I *gave* you a good Christian name so you could be baptized, that's how much I loved you!" Her eyes watered. "Named you after my beloved Louis. And if you are foolish enough to believe your family was ever looking for you then you deserved to be deceived. I gave you a better life than they ever could have had. I gave you a life that any nobleman would beg for. All because of my endless depth of love for the downtrodden and miserable wretches of the earth."

"You don't know how to love! The Queen was right."

Her chin tipped up, side-tracked by the subject of her nemesis. She hesitated, and then... "Right about what, what did she say?"

"That's all that matters to you, isn't it? Marie Antoinette is sitting in a cell and you're still competing with her. She said that you don't have the capacity to love; all you know is how to buy and sell and trade." Her eyes filled with tears. I knew it was less about the words than the fact that Marie Antoinette said those words to me... that we had that secret conversation together. I went on to cause more pain. "She said that you can't feel love for anyone but yourself. Damned if she wasn't right. You claimed to love Brissac and another man was in your bed not two weeks after the Duc's head rolled under your feet. You say you loved me and allowed your animal here to make sure I will never have children. Everything *you* love is destroyed."

"What? I didn't know." She shook her head desperately, tears flying. She speared Gaspard with a searing look. "Gaspard, what did you do? What did you do?"

"Oh, yes." I clapped, as if excited. "Do that innocent act, it's so fun to watch, Madame. Show me the innocence mask. You use it so well to make everyone want to save *you*. Even *I* tried to save you. Time and again, warning you over and over. I don't know, I suppose a small part of me was always that little boy that I was when I was brought to you. The one that wanted to believe you could be anything like a mother to me. Even when you showed you clearly didn't care what they did to me—hurting me in any and every way possible—you just didn't want to know because it wasn't convenient. You did what you always do, you closed your eyes and let me suffer for your benefit or your amusement—I don't know which. That isn't love."

Her lips pinched as her eyes hardened back on me. "Suffer? Oh, Mon Dieu." She put a hand to her head as if overcome with pain. Her tears dried on her hot skin. "I let you live a lavish life when *everybody…*" she strung out the word like a drunkard, sweeping her arm in an arc to encompass the world, "…*everrrybodddy* told me you were a miserable leech. I clothed you like a prince. I fed you from my own plate. I put jewels on your head and satin on your feet. Oh, how you *suffered*!"

This was the real Jeanne, now. The one that came out when she was cornered or angry, or both. The one I saw when she was most vicious. Her words came quick, full of hate and spite. "They told me you were no good. They told me you were as worthless as a bug on the ground. They told me you were no better than a rat in a corner of the deepest dungeon. No better than poison in your own garden, they said. *He's a devil's berry, Madame!* they said. Get rid of him, they said, and I…" She laughed mirthlessly and pointed to her own chest, nodding. "I *defended* you. I told them you were my family. I should have listened."

"Oui, Madame, you should have." I nodded vigorously. "They were right! I was miserable. I begged you to let me go. All I ever asked for was my freedom. All these years watching you help to pay for the escape of your noble friends and generals so they could go where they wanted with all their riches and money intact. Half of them already criminals themselves, stealing from sans-culottes and calling it their due. Noble after noble after noble... coming here to be wined and dined. Setting them up for a comfortable life! Harboring criminals trying to avoid prosecution. Shifting piles of assets from one place to another to make sure your wealthy friends could be safe to live their lives of privilege. Shuffling money to build yourself a new home in England all while denying me the most basic freedom!

"And still, I *warned* you that people were watching. I *warned* you that with every activity you put us all in danger! I even warned you not to come back from England. And what were you doing for me? You kept me trapped here, never intending to allow me my release. Kept me here to be a scapegoat, to pin that theft on me, to be punished in your stead!"

"I trusted you with my home, is that so wrong? Everything isn't about you, Louis-Benoit!"

"And after all those years and all that time, protecting you, my reward for being such an idiot was you siccing your dog on me for missing your damned morning chocolat." I gestured at Gaspard with disgust. "This piece of trash, so pathetic even his own son was ashamed of him. Handing me over to him like a consolation prize for the ridiculousness of his life."

"Don't you speak on my son!" Gaspard bellowed. I ignored him.

"So now, I feel nothing for you. It's a new world, Madame, one where all men are equal. And you don't just get to live a life of privilege because you are a noble. Or have you forgotten what it feels like to be someone with nothing? The people's queen... hah! The people's committee has spoken and decided all men deserve to *eat*. Let us all eat cake, and all that! And no one, not even Citizenness du Barry, is above justice."

The use of the term *citizenness* set her cheeks on fire as the blood rushed into them. She hated any reminder of her loss of title. Stripping her of her title was something no one in this house dared to do, but it was the law in this new republic. And the republic was here, today.

Her lips bunched. She picked up her skirts, shook her head as if to shake me off, and walked across the room towards the windows. Once there, she grabbed the drapes. "Well." She sniffed, having found her composure again. "I think I have what you want." She pulled at two sides of the drapes. The sound of the fabric tearing sounded in the room. The fabric separated at the seams as I watched, confused. When she had separated the front from the lining, she plunged her hand in between and pulled out a handful of papers.

She had papers hidden in the drapes? I'd looked all over the room; I never even thought of the drapes.

"This what you want?" She shook the papers at me with a mean little smile.

"What is that?" I asked.

She shook the papers in the air then began to read from the top as she paced: "'I, Louis XV, of sound mind, do hereby petition for the freedom and citizenship of the child known as Louis-Benoit Zamor...'"

What was she playing at? Could it be...? It wasn't possible. They weren't real. She was surely playing games. Playing chess, again. Cold dread began to seep into my bones.

"'I denounce any suggestion that the child was enslaved by me. I am unaware of any arrangement of slavery; I only take consideration in case a nefarious source, unbeknownst to me, might have taken the child against his will. I have no prior knowledge of this and only know the child came to the Palace voluntarily, as there are no slaves in France. In addition to his freedom, I, duly and of sound mind, bequeath Louis-Benoit Zamor an annual allowance for expenses befitting the station of the Governor of Louveciennes and, consequently, the property of the Chateau of Louveciennes upon the death of my love and Maitresse-en-Titre, Madame Jeanne du Barry, being that we had no children together. Upon filing, Louis-Benoit Zamor may be considered my adopted son and gain all the privileges of a child of nobility, short of any claim to the throne. As a full citizen, he is thus rightfully, and lawfully, able to own property. This decree is to be filed when it is proven the child is, and remains, good and humble, as determined by his godmother—or, adopted mother—the Comtesse Jeanne du Barry.'"

By the time she'd finished reading, her face had settled into a soft, content smile. She came to a stop before me, looking at me with that sweet, almost smile of hers; eyes sharp with flint. Her smile so sweet and calm, counter to my frozen expression and fidgeting fingers.

It couldn't be, my brain screamed. It wasn't possible! It was a lie, and she was baiting me. But my heart was galloping, and my eyelid was twitching madly. "Let me see."

"I just read them to you," she said teasingly. She shook the pages again playfully. "When he wrote these up he told me that they only needed to be filed with Parliament, but then he got sick so quickly. And when he did you were a hateful, hateful child to him and me. You didn't deserve your freedom at the time. You didn't deserve the goodness he gave you. But still, he gave them to me, and I *would* have filed them. I was only waiting for you to show yourself to be the gracious man I raised you to be."

I had to see them. I had to see if she was telling the truth or lying. To play with me on something so important, that would be cruel. I had to see.

I took a step toward her, and she stepped back. I stepped forward again and made a quick grab to snatch the papers, but she was quicker, pulling them out of my reach. I relaxed, as if giving up, and tried to snatch them again. A look of mischievousness came over her face as her eyes widened with the game. The third time, after I missed, she began walking backward, shaking them at me.

"What? Want these? These are what you want?" She sauntered backwards as I followed, mocking me, waving them before me. "These what you w—"

My feet propelled me towards her, but she was fast, even with the wide skirt, and took off running behind the desk and then around the outside of the room, knocking over glasses—and anything that wasn't solid—from the surface areas and onto the floor. I heard Gaspard curse, and his plodding footsteps followed behind me as he, belatedly, realized this was a chase.

She picked up her skirts, clutching them along with the now-wrinkled papers as she ran around the room again, behind the desk, around the settee, around the tables and back to the desk again. I tried to step on the hem of her skirt to bring her to a halt and, instead, missed and crashed into a chair, stumbling over it but staying on my feet. I heard Gaspard crashing into the sideboard behind me trying to avoid the over-turned chair.

The sound of the door opening brought a stranger's voice—a guest—to ask, polite but troubled: "Madame, is everything quite all right—"

"Get out!" she screamed as she panted, running. "This is a family matter!"

I only caught a glimpse of his wide eyes as I sped past him.

"But—"

"Get out! Get out!" Gaspard shouted, panting, as he jumped over the chair behind me again. The door slammed shut. By that time, we'd made at least four cycles through the room, all of us breathing hard. Then, suddenly, when Madame was behind the desk she skidded to a stop. Several paces away Gaspard and I did the same, stopping in our tracks, gratefully. My knee began to throb.

"I waited," she breathed, catching her breath. "I waited for you to show you were deserving and it turns out I was right." She panted. "You have never been deserving. Never. So, here you go."

The fireplace was behind the desk. As easy as you please, with a flip of the wrist she turned slightly and tossed the papers on top of the crackling fire. Then, she clapped her hands as though she'd just released a handful of rubbish as a sound like a crashing wave rushed through my head.

I ran over to the fireplace, sending her dashing out of my path as I dropped to my knees before the fire. The papers were curling as fast as the beating of my heart and when I reached in to try to snatch a page that, as I lifted it, burst into a pile of embers from the edges in. I barely saw the signature of the dead king before the paper seared my skin and then fell into ashes onto the polished floor while I panted. I had landed on my sore knee, and it screamed in pain while I sat there, heaving with exhaustion.

Could it have been real? Or could it have been any pile of papers she used just to punish me with a lie? I was going to get my freedom anyway. But the thought that they might possibly have been real was a searing pain inside of me. The fact that she knew that simply the question of it would torture me forever. She was playing with my emotions.

I was down on that floor on my knees, mumbling incoherent words of panic as the answers fell onto the ground. My eyes burned from the smoke of the fire and glazed with tears.

"All that I taught you," she said from above and behind me as I stared at that pile of ash on the floor and on my empty hands. "You and I, we both came from nothing. You and I were the last of our family. To see you fall for the lies of the revolutionaries...? Disappointment is an understatement. They are using you. I didn't raise you to turn on me or be used by commoners, Louis-Benoit. I raised you to be a proud representation of your family. I raised you to use *others*. I taught you better!"

I looked up at her standing there, hands on her hips. Her foot was tapping, impatiently, a tendril of blond hair loose in her sweaty face. She looked at me expectantly. Disappointment and anger on her face. Ready for me.

"Why would you do that?" I asked. "Why would you burn it before I could see it."

"I told you what it was," she said, patting the back of her hair into place. "Stop being a whiny little boy and think about why we're here. Why do you think good Louis XVI let me out of the convent? His bitch of a wife would have left me there to rot until I died, you know that. *You* were his grandfather's unfinished business, and you were making a nuisance of yourself at the Palace. If my Louis hadn't loved you so much his grandson would have shipped you off to the Bastille, never to be heard of again. But the Bourbon men are sentimental. And there were too many people at the royal court and in Paris who knew you existed and knew the rumors that you were enslaved. The whole thing was too messy. So, Louis XVI and I made an agreement. He'd give me back my properties and money if I would take you off his hands. He gave me those papers and told me it would be up to me to file them when I saw fit, as you were always meant to be a gift for me."

I thought back to the time when I went to Louis XVI myself and he swore his grandfather left no such document. Was he lying? Or was she? Or were they both? Playing with me... the two of them.

"It's always been in my power to file those papers, you know, and I would have if you'd shown an ounce of gratitude. Just once acknowledged what I wanted without me having to force you."

"Acknowledge what?"

"That you are *mine*!" She screamed at me with her face in mine, her head shaking, face red. "Mine! *He gave you to me*! And what did you do when they sent me away? You rubbed it in my face. You laughed at me. You had fun while I was in that convent, and you didn't care a bit about me. Thinking you were better than me. You proved to me you didn't understand gratitude and there hasn't been a day since that you've proven any better. And it's clear you never learned a thing about loyalty. So, no, you don't deserve something you haven't earned." She straightened and swiped her hands down her skirt.

"Besides, this whole business just proves you wouldn't have survived a day on your own. Look at what's happened. The Jacobins are making a fool of you. Laughing at you. You think you're a revolutionary? They're ready to use you up and spit you out, and for what? I have friends in Paris. I'm not an Austrian, I'm French! Whatever information you thought you had on me wasn't enough. Four hours later and I'm back in my home."

I was seething and raised up, slowly. "Not for long."

"Is that a threat, my Louis?" She cocked her head and smiled. "You've exhausted my patience. You think you're such a big man, you're about to find out. You're going to leave this house. I'll even give you three days to find someplace to stay. Go join those regular poor men you love so much. Then, you'll see. I've *been* poor; I know what it's like. You never have been poor in all your time in France, you've forgotten how it feels. You want your freedom? You are free to join the poor. Let's see how far you get with no money and no papers. According to official lists you don't even exist! One week out in the real world, surviving on your own, and you'll be back! You have no skills, Louis-Benoit! Let's see how you plan to survive. Then you'll remember how much you love me—oh, oui, you'll remember then."

I frowned, weary. "I haven't been in this place all these years because I love you. I've been here because I couldn't figure out how to get the hell away from you."

"It doesn't even matter, you'll come back crawling on your knees. Then, maybe I'll think about how to forgive you."

I got to my feet, slowly. "I think you forget, Madame, the republic has promised me my freedom. And citizenship, too. Maybe they are as big liars as you. But if not, I will soon be a citizen. Why, that's the same status as you. Imagine that!"

She stopped then and stared at me. It was as if she'd forgotten how the conversation started. Her hands bunched into fists like she would hit me. "How?"

"Did you forget? I'm a Jacobin and a member of the Committee for Public Safety. Did you think I became a Jacobin for nothing? You taught me better than that. I had something to give for something to get. And there are other forms of payment beyond money. Quid pro quo, and all that. I've only ever wanted one thing. You've taken a great deal from me in my life, but you've finally given me something of value to trade. *You.* The Madame Comtesse Jeanne du Barry, Mâitresse-en-titre to good King Louis XV, the Well-Beloved. You, who revolutionaries have been begging me to hand over for years and I, foolishly, felt some kinship towards you. I didn't hate you quite enough then. But now, for better or worse, you will earn me my freedom."

She had been listening to me, eyes sharp but with a nervous tick in her cheek as she took in my words. Then, her face relaxed into the cold numbness of acceptance. "Well then, we'll both see who comes out on top—the home-town French woman with a history of giving to charity, and whose entire staff petitioned for her release, or her thankless personal servant, the disloyal nègre, known to be the most unpleasant individual in all of France. We shall find out how unimportant you are when they laugh you out of the Club. Goodbye and bon chance, Louis-Benoit."

My body felt something at hearing those words. It was a strange combination of sadness and indescribable happiness. It was anger and relief. I'd been waiting to hear some version of these words my whole life so that now, I hardly believed it was real.

"If you send the guards after me..." I started to warn her.

"I wouldn't lift my finger to demand anyone chase after the trash you are. I can't stand the sight of you. You're a scourge on the House of Bourbon and on my dear Well-Beloved. You're a scourge on this Chateau and on me. But no more. You're about to find out what it's like to be alone on the hard streets. And when you die, I want the last thing you think of to be the love that you lost here today. Or, you will do the smart thing and beg for my forgiveness. I'll be placing bets on how long it takes you to crawl back with your tail between your legs."

No more needed to be said. I straightened my lapels, lifted my chin, giving a quick bow for fun. For sarcasm. For the last time. "Bonsoir, Madame."

She patted the hair on the back of her head, her eyes off looking at anything but me—I was no longer worthy of eye contact. "Bonsoir," she said nonchalantly.

I shut the door behind me and left.

Chapter Twelve

O utside the study, I leaned back against the door jamb while my eyelids drifted shut.

It was done. Finally, after all these years, it was over. I opened my eyes and was about to walk down the hallway when I heard Madame and Gaspard continue the conversation inside. I pressed my ear to the wood.

"M-madame... Jeanne... you said something, about the three of you being a family. I hope you know, you have always been like family to me. I mean, not like mother and son, of course, but..."

She laughed. "I certainly hope not, considering what we've done together. Don't be silly, you've always been a valued member of the household, but my relationship with Louis-Benoit is different. I really don't have the energy to deal with your petty jealousy tonight, Gaspard."

"Well, I would have liked to have known he was a free man. Or that he could be free."

"What?"

"Those papers, Madame..."

"Oh..." She made a sound as if he was saying something ridiculous. "Why are both of you going on about papers? What difference does it make if there were papers or not?"

"It's the difference between paying a fine for being brutal to a slave or going to prison for almost killing a man..."

"Oh, please. You already know there's no such thing as brutality against a slave because, legally, there are no slaves in France. At least, not without special permission and only temporarily. He's lived with us all his life so even suggesting you thought he might have actually been a slave could be used against you and me. Besides, *you* said you would only hit him a few times and, instead, you almost killed him. Whose fault is that? I had to clean up your mess and now he hates *me* for saving his life."

"I had to do something. He made you cry. That morning, you were so upset over the chocolat."

"Listen to yourself, you sound mad. Do you truly think I was upset over the chocolat? Am I a child? Am I stupid? I was upset because my Louis-Benoit was slipping away from me, little by little. My Louis-Benoit used to be available for me anytime I needed but he lost his focus. Of course, I didn't want him dead, that's the opposite of what I wanted. I love him with all my heart. All you had to do was blacken his eye, but you let your jealousy get in the way as if you don't understand our relationship. Now, here you are whining about whether you would have done things differently if he was free. He was right about one thing—you've been wanting to get at him since the day he arrived. And since your boy died you've never been the same," she paused, her voice softening. "You've been so sad, I wanted to give you something to make you feel better. I thought, Gaspard can let off some steam and remind Louis-Benoit of his place at the same time—kill two birds with one stone. I thought you had the sense to be prudent, but you went after him drunk and now look. Months of him getting better and walking around like a ghost, mumbling to himself and going out of his mind. A shell of himself. And he hates *me*! Both of you are ingrates."

It was quiet for a long moment and then Gaspard spoke.

"Well, no matter how it happened, he's your enemy now. I would like to kill him, for sure this time, Madame," Gaspard said. "Dispose of him, discreetly. We could say he ran off. If King Louis XV were still alive, he would approve it."

I already knew I was leaving in a few minutes, but with his words I decided to burn the house down on my way out. I'd enlist Salanave's help in getting all the living things out—most of them, anyway. There were enough candles that no one would question if it was accidental. And even if Madame escaped, I would take pleasure from her watching the Chateau burn as I galloped away. If I could trap Gaspard, somehow, I would be satisfied with his demise. The thought of it brought a smile to my face.

"No," Madame said. "If what he says is true he's under their protection for at least the time being. If any harm comes to him, it will only reflect badly on me. Leave him alone until after the investigation is closed and I'm free. How could I have been deceived by such a vile, cruel man?"

Ah yes, I was vile and cruel. She was about to see how vile when I set all her favorite clothes on fire. I'd put them in a giant pile and burn them, just like the dress that Véronique had bled for sewing for her, only for Madame to force me to burn. Well, she thought I had burned it. That had only been pretend. This fire would be real.

"He had nothing to lose by betraying you, Madame, especially if they promised him a comfortable life in return. He's no better than a Judas. Maybe we can't make him pay now, but there are others we can take care of."

I lifted my head and stopped ruminating to listen.

"That Henri fellow is still around. He's afraid to come back here for some reason but I can find him again. It seems the page likes him quite a bit. Or, of course, there's the cook."

Salanave? My hackles rose. Once Salanave heard what they were planning for her, heaven help them. She'd poison them and they'd never even taste it, her cooking was that good.

A long hesitation in her response showed just exactly the type of person Madame was as the cold started trickling down my spine.

"But then who would cook our meals? She's excellent. No, I heard he and the cook are at odds these days, anyway. He might be happy if something happened to her. Besides, it wouldn't be right to take out ill feelings toward him on innocent people who knew him. Not the Christian thing to do. We're not savages, like the revolutionaries."

"Well... of course not. But some people aren't so innocent. That female blackamoor servant who left a few weeks past?—the one who made that horrible gown for you? He always tried so hard not to look at her, there was surely a relationship. She left a note giving up her post around the same time that some things went missing. Some of the servants say she paid someone to get a little house not too far from here; I'm sure she paid someone to stay there with money from those stolen goods. At the very least, she can answer some questions. No point in getting the police, I'll bring her in myself. Even this new government doesn't take kindly to a thief. She'll be sorry she stole from you. I'll take my time bringing her in—make sure she pays for the betrayal of that ungrateful bastard."

My eye was twitching hard now as Gaspard's words hit something in my body. My fingers shook with a rage growing deep inside me. I waited out the hesitation. Waited for her to turn him off Véronique's scent. Waited. Waited...

"All right," Madame said, brightening. "She deserves at least that much for trying to embarrass me at my own ball with that horrible dress. Bring her in but don't do anything that can reflect badly on me. You were too rough with him. Be gentler with her; we're not animals."

"I'll make sure there are no visible marks."

I knew what that meant. My body jerked involuntarily from the memory of the countless kicks and punches to the ribs, gut, and back. And that had happened under Madame's protection after she complained about him leaving marks on my face.

Now, here we were again, only it was spreading to the people I cared about. My mind ran through all the ways he could harm Véronique that weren't visible. He was known to take advantage of women; she'd had to pull a knife on him before in this very house with me and Madame around. Véronique was alone now.

They continued to talk but I'd heard all I needed. I didn't have time to burn the house down. Instead, it took me but a few moments to quickly gather my things. I didn't dare speak to Salanave—I wanted her to be clueless in case Gaspard came to her asking where I'd gone. She wouldn't have to lie. I took a quick peek at her as I passed the kitchen doorway, watching her leaning into the oven to pull out bread, cheeks wet from the heat and a strand of hair falling into her face. It would have to do.

I kept moving, stopping only when another thing caught my attention. The little dancing lady figurine that Véronique loved so much sat on a small podium. Slipping inside quickly, I grabbed it to plunge into my bag. I couldn't have said why, except it reminded me so much of her ... all I had left of her.

I strapped my bags and my violin to the sandy-colored horse I'd trained and rode away from Louveciennes as fast as I could. Along the ride, I turned over what I'd heard in my head.

She hadn't gone home to Burgundy? Somehow, she managed to find someone to buy her that house she loved! I would have smiled at that—knowing what a resourceful woman she was—but there was too much happening to take even a moment of joy. Gaspard was on his way, and I had to make a plan to ensure he would never take out his hatred for me onto her.

I kicked the horse into action, and we galloped at break-neck speed out of town. Soon, we arrived at a little spot in Croissy-sur-Seine just where the jagged edges of the banks joined.

Chapter Thirteen

I slipped around the side of the house, my horse hidden in the trees closer to the river. The windows glowed bright in the dark night, and I looked into the one farthest east. It would give her good sunlight in the morning. She was sitting in an armchair, back to the window, facing a gentle fire. It being a cool evening I could imagine how pleasant it was inside that cozy room. From the way her elbows were out to the side and bobbing, I knew Véronique was sewing. My lips turned up to see that she was doing just what she'd wanted.

A dry leaf crackled under my foot, and she stopped for a moment. When her head turned up at the sound, I could see her lovely features highlighted by the fire. She wore no headwrap, her hair was free about her face in the dark, soft curls that my fingers thrilled to feel. She listened as if she had heard something but soon went back to sewing.

I wasn't there to stare at her, but it had been a while since I'd seen her, and my greedy eyes felt they were finally getting their feel of the most wonderful treat.

Then, I heard the approach of a carriage a short way down the road and went back to my hiding spot just a little back beyond the trees.

I had planned from the moment I heard Gaspard from outside the office, and felt it was sound. But one never knew with these things. My blood was pumping furiously as I saw him park a distance away, probably so she would not hear him approach.

Sorry Batard! But his nefarious purpose worked to my advantage because I didn't want her to hear me, either.

I crouched and moved up closer, quiet on my toes, as he exited the carriage. I also noted the shadow of the driver in the carriage. I had been hoping he'd come alone but, of course, someone would have to drive while he was assaulting a woman. He wasn't too drunk yet to forget that. He went to the front door and knocked. Even a few paces away I could smell the alcohol on him. Once again, it would work in my favor.

I tiptoed forward. Quickly and quietly, reaching up, deftly, to slip the noose around his neck while at the same time making a barely able to be heard "tsk-tsk" whistling sound. It was the signal to the horse to move forward quickly, and with force. The horse did as it was told and the rope that was secured to it—looped around a sturdy tree, leading to the noose on the end—jerked him back and tore Gaspard off his feet.

His legs came up off the ground and he landed hard on his back at the bottom of the little porch stairs, the rope cutting off the sound of his voice as he reached to try to loosen it. I couldn't help the sound his body made hitting the ground—like a sack of wet potatoes. I hooked him under his shoulders, pulling with all the strength in my body as he struggled, his arms moving between trying to grab me and trying to undo the noose.

He was strong enough that if he got a hold of me, it was over. I had hoped the noose was enough to keep him busy, but when he reached around to grab my arms, I gave a "tsk-tsk" with a different pitch and the horse moved sideways, hiding itself in the trees and *pulling, pulling, pulling!*

A choked sound emerged from his lips as his body was dragged over the dirt road towards the trees. I could hear Véronique's footsteps towards the door even as Gaspard's hands kept moving to his neck, trying to loosen himself.

"*Tsk-tsk...*" I whispered, fervently, before tiptoeing into the woods to avoid being seen. Gaspard's eyes bulged as the horse finally dragged him under cover of the woods as if a string had snapped him back from space. I *tsk-ed* again and his body landed deeply enough that if she were to poke her head outside, she wouldn't see him and would, hopefully, just assume the noise was from animals in the woods.

Another low whistle and the horse hid himself, too. I looked around to make sure no one had seen anything. The dusty, lonely street was silent. I ran to find Gaspard rolling, trying to get the rope from around his neck. He looked up and saw me and went to sit up, but I pounced on his chest with all my weight. The back of his head slammed against the ground as I searched his body to make sure he didn't have a knife.

It was going better than I had planned. His hands were searching for a way to remove the rope from his neck while I was searching for a weapon.

But I wasn't a fighter like he was. That moment of me searching his pants for a weapon gave him the opportunity he needed. My eyes widened, feeling his large, beefy hands around my throat, so big they almost overlapped on my neck. Suddenly, they squeezed as he throttled me, and I felt like I was in a vice. I opened my mouth to suck in air only to hear my own fruitless gasps as he shook my column once, twice...

Distantly, I heard the front door of the house open. I moved my chin down and to the side just enough to get my mouth beneath the edge of one hand. Biting down so hard I could almost feel my teeth meet, I almost took a chunk of flesh from his hand. The iron taste of a gush of blood filled my mouth.

Releasing me, he still couldn't scream or breathe. But I was able to get up, scramble back, spit out his blood and breathe. I saw her through the trees, standing on her front step and looking around for the person who had knocked. His hand grabbed my ankle with his good hand. I kicked free, crawled back over, and delivered two punches to his ribs. He curled for a moment before going back to trying to loosen the ropes.

I fell on my backside. I knew it had only been moments, but this fight felt like forever. I had hoped the lack of air would have hampered him by now, but he was still awake and alert. Now, he was sitting up and, though gasping and scratching at his own neck, soon, he would be free.

Véronique called out, "Who's there?"

I scrambled over outside of his reach and came up behind him, jerking his noose with one hand while I covered his mouth with the other.

I thought about giving one more signal. One more hard jerk and his neck would be dashed up against the tree I had looped the rope on, maybe taking off his head. It would be death, but it would be messy. I couldn't afford a mess. I wouldn't do that to Véronique for anything in the world. But how was I going to finish this when he was still so strong? Despite the smell of alcohol that seemed even stronger now, coming out of his skin. Despite his age. Despite no air, he was still strong!

I was holding his head, and he had been feeling along the ground beside him, getting his bearings. Any moment now he would lurch up and we would both go into the air. That's when I saw his hand come up and the glint of moonlight reflect off the tiny little knife.

I'd missed a knife! He looked at me with his sneaky, beady eyes just before he brought the knife up and sliced through the rope pinning him to the tree. He couldn't get leverage. If he got leverage over me, all was lost!

I scrambled up and practically stood, stamping on the hand with the knife. His fingers went stiff as the bones shattered under my boot. His face went blue in the darkness but barely a squeak came from him.

I catapulted myself on top of him. His legs scrambled to get a foothold under him. Though he'd sliced the rope holding him to the tree, the noose was still wrapped around his neck. He went to reach for me, and I grabbed the loose end of the cut rope, jerking it to shut him up.

He gurgled and I jerked. Gurgle. Jerk.

It felt like we'd been out there all night, but my brain registered, as she called out again, that it had only been seconds. Minutes, maybe. Any moment now he would get his legs under him and use his good arm to wriggle me off. He still had one hand, albeit without a chunk. And he was strong.

But what I knew for sure was that to let go would be to let this beast loose on my Véronique, and I would die before I let that happen. So I would fight like I'd never fought for anything. I had never been a strong man, but what strength I did have was in my arms. And I could wrestle.

I heard the front door close and the sound of it was a release to me. I sucked in deep breaths—once, twice—and then I began to wrestle him. Focusing on that leg that was trying to get a foothold, I reached down and grabbed it under the knee and pulled it up, quickly. The sudden stretching of his leg almost over his head, while I still held the rope, had him gasping. He tried to use his good hand to grab me and then, instead, used the arm of the bad hand to ram his elbow into my lower torso—into my scar.

Stars exploded behind my eyes and a whimper came from deep within me as the area I had thought fully healed felt like it was splitting open. I released his leg but not the rope, quickly changed positions, scrambling up him and scooting so I was behind and above his head, still holding that piece of rope attached to his noose. Gaspard's struggle for air was now more of a whistling screech as his body devolved to simple animal desperation. I had scooted backward until I felt the base of a tree behind my back and propped a foot against his neck on either side of his head. Then, I began pushing down with my feet for leverage while still pulling up on the rope. It kept my arms out of the reach of his, though he looped an arm, the hand flapping, behind my leg and tried to pop my knee backward. I screamed silently as I pulled on that rope until it nearly pulled his head out of its socket. His hands scratched and grappled at his own neck as we tussled in fits and starts in the brush of the forest.

We must have sounded like squirrels wrestling in the cool evening autumn air. Sounds of us as insignificant and harmless as the red and brown leaves blowing across the path.

And then, after five, then ten seconds of every bit of both of us tensed in the soundless struggle, suddenly, he stopped grappling his neck to grapple the air. From the way his hands flailed I knew his eyes could no longer see. From the way his legs kicked as in spasms I knew he was no longer in control of his muscles. I felt something in my forehead wanting to burst as I strained. His heels kicked the dirt as he went into some sort of fit. I double wrapped the rope around my hands, even though it was cutting through the skin, and I pulled with my hands and pushed with my feet. Pulled and pushed. I was close, so close, and I didn't have much more fight in me.

Desperately, I gave one last, mighty jerk, hearing something crack and give. And then he ceased all movement, head skewed to the side, and all of his limbs drooped and plopped against the ground. His body went fully limp.

But I didn't let go. I didn't know if it was an act. I sat there, my breath heaving from my lungs suddenly the loudest thing in the night. The pile of him lay there like a sack of wet sand. He was the man who had tormented me all my life. Ten seconds and no movement and I began to feel like maybe I was safe. Twenty seconds after that and I knew he was finally dead.

I let go of the rope and the night seemed suddenly quiet. The air was cool against the moisture on my face. Either sweat or tears—I couldn't have said which.

I sat there for a while, my shoulders dropping down as I slumped back against the tree, heaving air into my lungs. Realizing what I'd done. I'd killed a man... again. Though this one had always been inevitable, it didn't make it any less difficult.

No one would cry over his death. Even Madame would cry less about his death than about how his death would affect her. There was nothing here in this place to mourn.

Some time later, after I'd calmed my breathing and brushed the leaves off me, I walked quietly up the street a ways to the carriage, taking a gamble that the driver hadn't been informed of my duplicity. Taking a gamble that the Gaspard I knew wouldn't have informed the driver that he planned to assault someone in the carriage while he was driving.

Unfortunately, he was a witness. My head told me that dealing with him was necessary.

The distance from the trees to the carriage seemed to grow with every step. A voice in me told me the man had to be taken care of! But I didn't want to hurt him. I had nothing against him. I didn't want to! I wasn't a murderer, not really. I didn't enjoy it. I didn't like it. The second I stopped moving I would be sick. But he was a witness.

I walked up to the front of the carriage where he was reading a paper. He looked down at me.

"Bonsoir, Monsieur Zamor, I didn't know you were here. Coming back to the Chateau with us?"

I didn't want to. I didn't want to. I gave him a sick smile.

"Oui, when we're finished. But Gaspard asked me to come get you. We need your help with something," I said to him with a friendly smile.

He only knew me as Madame's confidant; he had no reason to doubt me. He secured his whip and climbed down, following me. I spoke to him casually. "I came ahead to convince her to come quietly but she ran off that way. Gaspard says three of us looking is better than two. Right down there, but we must keep it down." I pointed into the trees.

If he had been thinking he might have asked more questions, like when had I arrived? And how? Because that horse I'd trained was still hidden. As it was, my face was familiar to him, and he didn't question it. My eyes began to water as I allowed him to walk ahead of me towards the woods, and I followed. He walked, jovially, like he hadn't a care in the world. Like he didn't have a thing to fear with me behind him.

It was the only thing to do. I had nothing against that man. He was simply at the wrong place at the wrong time. But I knew I could leave no witnesses, nor could I leave any corpses. It was—

"Stop," I whispered loud enough to gain his attention. He stopped and turned around.

"Oui, Monsieur?"

I shook my head at him as much as myself. "You can't go down there."

"But you said, Monsieur Gaspard—"

"—I work for the Committee for Public Safety, you see. Gaspard has been arrested for planning to do harm to an innocent this evening. I know you and I'm certain you were unaware of what he was planning, but if you go down there, they will arrest you alongside him, and I can't guarantee you will survive till morning." I shook my head. "Don't ask more questions, I've already told you too much. Just go home. *Your* home, not the Chateau. Don't go back to the Chateau. Never say anything to anyone about this evening or you and I will both face the same fate as he, and you will never see your family again. You understand?"

His face was a sober mask of fear.

"Go home, Citizen," I whispered, urgently, since he was still standing there. "Then, go ahead and take the carriage if you like—disguise it when you get to where you're going—just don't go back to—"

He didn't let me finish the statement. Suddenly, he was moving, shuffling past me, down the road. I could tell he was trying to run, but it was just a shuffle. I could tell from the way he ran, trying to pump his arms to get up speed, he was afraid for his life. He didn't climb into the carriage but kept running down the dusty street in the middle of the road, his flat shoes kicking up dust as he worked his arms, trying to move faster than a fast walk.

That's it, keep running, I cheered him on silently.

He was scared. I hoped his fear would keep him quiet.

I was a fool, but I didn't want his blood on my hands.

It took all night for me to dispatch Gaspard so that he would never be found. As if I'd been hiding corpses all my life, I handled it with efficiency and expediency.

By the time I stepped from behind the trees the day was rising, new and fresh. I spared one last look at the house, pulled the horse from the woods, and took a slow, quiet walk up the street to the carriage. I attached my horse to the frame next to the other waiting horse.

The two of them carried me into Paris, while I wondered the whole way if I would pass the driver and his little arms pumping as he ran all the way home.

Chapter Fourteen

Sebastien didn't ask questions when I showed up at his house in the middle of the night. Upon his questioning glance, I asked, simply: "Do you know anyone who can discreetly dispose of a carriage with the shadow of a fleur-de-lys on the side? They would get a royal horse in return." I would keep the other horse for myself.

Sebastien hesitated only briefly before nodding. "Of course."

"Can I stay with you?" I followed. "I can pay rent."

And so I took a room in Sebastien's home while we awaited trial. Immediately, I hid private things under a bureau – habit from a lifetime of hiding stolen goods. It felt wonderful being able to go to club meetings freely, without having to sneak in or out.

For some strange reason, Sebastien told his boys that since I was living with them, they could call me *Uncle* Zamor. I gave him a wry look, but I was hardly in a position to object, nor was I in a mood to start any sort of argument.

My nerves seemed ready to rage at any moment. I couldn't trust what I might say so I kept my distance from the family, coming down only for uncomfortable meals. Until, finally, I began eating alone in my room so the family could get back to being a family.

One morning, Sebastien was brewing thick, hot coffee while Élise took care of the children upstairs. His face was dark with his morning hair still unshaved. Sebastien would turn into a bear if left to his own. He gave me one of his hooded glances, pouring coffee into three cups.

"How much time will it take before you go back to being yourself?" he asked simply. "I'm a patient man, but even I have my limits."

"This is myself, you just never lived with me to know," I said, grabbing my cup to go back upstairs.

"I hear Gaspard is no longer accompanying Madame du Barry through town. That he's run off," Sebastien said quickly, stopping me. "And that Grieve has gone back and arrested her, again."

I looked at him quickly.

"They say when Grieve went in to get her she was tearing the study apart. Papers all over the place, they say. But Gaspard was nowhere around. Any idea where he might be?"

"No idea." I still hadn't told Sebastien what I'd done. I'd only mentioned to him that the night I left I overheard him say to Madame that he might visit Véronique. But Sebastien was no idiot. "The last I saw him was the night I left the Chateau."

"Well, with him running loose," he said, casually, "...maybe you should check in on Véronique? Especially after what he said about going after her."

"I'm sure she's fine. She can take care of herself."

"Maybe. But I have a hard time believing you would leave her to do it alone. I know you're no longer together—you still haven't told me that story, either—but I don't think you hate her. Do you?"

"Mon Dieu, Sebastien, she's fine. Gaspard won't be bothering her, and I'm done talking about it."

He looked down and frowned into his coffee before taking a long drink. "I don't need to know what you've done, nor do I want to know. But a lot's changed while you were gone. The King's death seemed to loosen our grip on a singular purpose. Now, we have the Federalists revolts…"

"What's that?"

"The revolts against the Jacobins and the new republic throughout the countryside. They don't dare do it here in Paris, but in the country… Max is getting more unstable every day. He walks around with that small army protecting him. It's a miracle you got through to him to make your deal." He took some coffee. "It seems like everyone is working on their own now. Élise wants me to leave the club; she says she doesn't trust it any longer. But the Club is the only place to get real information, non? At least, for us sans-culottes, it's our only tie to the government. Let's go out for an evening, you, me and Valentin."

And so the three of us took an evening to go to a bar like in the old times, drinking and laughing with the bartender they called One-ear.

On October 16, 1793, Sebastien and I went to the Place de la Revolution together. We watched as Marie Antoinette marched, stoically, to the guillotine. The crowd was brutal, throwing rotten fruit and trash they brought from home specifically to do this. I watched as she made her way to the platform.

It wasn't a quick thing. Someone from the tribunal came to draw it out. He announced to the crowd: "Before you stands the woman formerly known as the queen, Citizenness Capet from Austria!"

"She doesn't look like a queen now!" came a shout. Hoots of agreement and laughter rang out.

"This evil woman shamelessly spent the money that rightfully belonged to the people of France on clothes and jewels, having made all those magnificent wigs and having a whole farm built on which to play with her friends at the Chateau of Versailles. Having stolen the most expensive necklace in the world to fund the Austrian army against us. All while France starved, our coffers left at the very brink of bankruptcy."

His words were met with vile names screamed at her, followed by a bystander turning his back on the scene, showing his rear end toward the stage and flashing her. Peals of laughter exploded around us. Laughter all around, teetering on hysteria, while bloodlust was just beneath the surface. Civility so thin that you had only to scratch lightly for these people to turn into avenging hellions.

And the representative from the tribunal must have felt it because his face grew wary and cautious, not for her, but for his own safety.

"Why doesn't he hurry up and be done with it?" I said to Sebastien.

Sebastien nodded soberly. "He'd better make it quick if he doesn't want this crowd up on that platform doing it for him."

Marie Antoinette didn't say a word. She stood there, with her head up, and took the abuse and vile comments.

I didn't hate Marie Antoinette. I agreed—she misspent the country's money and was as out of touch as her husband, but I had never hated her. To my way of thinking, it was Louis XVI who had been in charge of the country's finances. It was he who had the power to determine how much money his wife had access to. It was he who made it difficult for enslaved people to gain their freedom and continued the slave trade.

So, I didn't hate her; at least, certainly not as much as her husband or his grandfather. Of course, it might have been she supported him in everything. Perhaps she had the power over him this crowd thought she did. Or, perhaps, she just didn't care enough about the pain of others to concern herself.

She looked up and gazed above the crowd. Everyone quieted to see if she would speak. I wanted to hear her words, but I didn't want her to rile them further because the guillotine would be a kinder death than dismemberment by being torn apart.

She opened her mouth to speak, and someone threw a rock at her, hitting her in the mouth, drawing blood and rabid laughter. Hands still behind her back, she had nothing to protect her face and the blow stunned her. Blood ran down her chin and dripped onto the front of her shift.

I thought about the comment I made to Max—the comment about the cake that I suggested he consider in determining how to present a case to the people—and felt a morbid guilt at my part in this, however small. I never would have suggested it had I known it would take on a life of its own. I never imagined he would turn that story I'd read about someone else into something that would generate such hate. I felt shame at the manipulation that had come so easily to me and for not much in return. For taking part in stoking the hatred toward her. Even though I'd been angry at her plenty of times in my life, I never would have wanted this. Though, I knew, the enemies of the Queen already had plenty of excuses to put her where she was. They wanted to believe the lie and would have made up another if none was readily available.

She closed her mouth to whatever she was going to say. The crowd was happy and laughing. The Tribunal representative gestured to the executioner to get on with it.

"Sing your song, Sanson!" they called to him.

The executioner beckoned her towards him and motioned to her to press against the board that would tilt to lay her on her stomach and she briefly stopped. "Pardon, Monsieur," she said. "I did not do it on purpose." The crowd silenced when it became apparent she'd stepped on his foot.

"Do not speak on it, Your Majesty," Sanson replied. She nodded her head slightly at him and then lay down on her stomach on the board. But the crowd was stunned silent. Going about his business, it was obvious Sanson didn't even realize what he'd just said, or that he could be in trouble for it.

"She cuckolded our dear sweet King," a woman said, disgust in her voice. "Made a fool of him and of France!"

The jeering and yelling and profanity started again in earnest. And then the executioner walked to the side where the chains were. I looked up at the blade that glistened in the sun. The sound of chains unraveled, and it felt as if everything slowed down. And though I looked away, the sound of the blade made its own song coming down.

Hush... swish ...

The blade hit its cradle hard and, one second later, a thud rang out. The crowd screamed and cheered with approval as the ones closest to the platform were showered with the blood of the woman known as The Austrian, formerly known as the queen.

"I can't get used to it, no matter how many times I see it done," Sebastien said, pulling his eyes away from the scene. "If it must be done, why can't it be dignified? Why the mockery?"

I wanted to tell him the mockery was even more important than the execution. It was the mockery they came to see.

We turned and made our way out of the madness.

CHAPTER FIFTEEN

I *knew it was a dream, but it was too pleasant to leave. Véronique and I had snuck away from the house for a rendezvous. My dark horse, Lightning, drove our small carriage through town where we passed a glade of wild flowers. An array of soft colors dotted the field and the expression on her face seemed to open up directly in proportion to the amount of wildflowers she spotted.*

She slapped at me, eyes firmly on the beauty. "Stop the carriage. Hurry up!"

"What for?" I asked, pulling back slightly, enough for Lightning to slow to a stop.

There wasn't much coaxing needed between me and my horse—we knew, instinctively, what each other wanted. She and I had taken to each other years earlier when she was pretty much a baby and I was a ten-year old new to the Palace. Growing up together, we shared a difficultness of personality that was off-putting to everyone but each other.

A majestic black horse with a beautiful main of dark hair and white streak down her forehead to her nose, Lightning was still alive in my dreams. I climbed down and patted her on the nose, ready to hand her a sugar cube from my pocket. But her attention was on other things as, like Véronique, she seemed enamored with the field of flowers that she bent, her nose twitching with tickles.

Véronique was already down and running through the field.

"This is beautiful!" she called to me. "Look at all these colors!" The sun was bright in a clear blue sky, and I smiled watching how happy a stupid field of wildflowers made her. She stepped through the colors—yellow, pink, purple, red poppies the most striking of them all—and yet, somehow, she was the most beautiful, turning in a circle, face up to the sky as if adored by the sun.

I knew the feeling from when I went to Saint-Chappelle and the colors caused by the sun streaming through stained glass would rain down on me like a blessing from above.

"Hurry up and come over!"

For what? To stand in the field? I shook my head. I didn't want to look silly.

"That's your problem, Zamor. So afraid of looking foolish that you actually do—what's the point of standing there with your hands in your pockets when you can come over here and enjoy this day? Look at all this natural beauty, and the poppies. The poppies...!"

She twirled with her arms out and my lips wiggled. She called me foolish. I wasn't going to let that stand.

I looked around to make sure no one was watching. And then, without warning, I began running into the field, yelling like a fool, arms out. I passed her, hearing her giggle and feeling her skirt swirl up as I rushed by, then stood still and looked up, twirling, like she had. I twirled much better than she had, in my opinion. I twirled until I got dizzy. I twirled until the sound of my laughter matched hers and, together, we reveled in the beauty. I reveled in being with the woman who helped me to see it. I heard Lightning neigh and knew her head was tossed up to the sky as well, soaking in this day.

I laughed with joy and abandon. Freedom and... love... Love.

Mon Dieu, how I loved her...

Chapter Sixteen

October 24, 1793

Sebastien's home was on a downslope, not far from the town square and the center of activity. More than once I'd sat at his table for dinner, interrupted when the neighborhood washerman emptied his buckets too far off center of the road and the slope would carry the dirty bubbles down the road and underneath the front door of Sebastien's home, always preceded by a trickling sound. A warning of more to come.

I suspected he rather enjoyed the opportunity to let out steam. Élise would get to remind him how nice it was to have a washerman so close to home, but off he would stomp to give the washerman a piece of his mind. All the while the younger boy would be entranced by the bubbles floating up from the dirty bubbly water. He would run over, squat on chubby legs to watch the bubbles rise and if any did, clap at them as they rose before his face.

A child's peculiarity, that they only see the bubbles, never the filth.

We were finishing dinner one night when the trickling sound alerted us to the coming puddle of wash water.

"Batard!" *Bastard!* Sebastien growled, standing up to head to the door on his way to the offender. Jerking open the door he skidded to a stop at a familiar face, hand raised to knock. It was fellow Jacobin Jacques Brissot.

"What are you doing here?" Sebastien asked.

"May I come in, Sebastien?" Jacques said furtively, face pinched. "Please."

"Yes, all right, watch your feet." Sebastien looked down and the wash of soapy water was now generously swirling around their feet. They both stepped through it quickly, and Sebastien cursed, rushing to grab some rags to mop the water up as Jacques saw me and nodded, his lips pinched.

"Zamor, bonsoir. Madame, so very sorry to disturb your evening." He nodded, always the proper gentleman. But I could tell something was off.

"What's going on? What's the matter?"

Sebastien had finished closing the door, pushing the cloths under the door jamb and stepping inside, finally noticing Jacques' stiffness and worried expression.

"I'm sorry," Brissot said. "You were the closest place I knew to come. I think they're after me, at least, that's what someone told me."

"'Someone?' What are you talking about?" Sebastien pressed.

Brissot's normally well-coiffed hair was disheveled, his collar loose and cravat hanging. His face was ruddy and panicked.

Brissot was the leader of the Girondins (often called Brissotins), one of the three largest factions of Jacobins; the others being the Mountain and the Cordeliers. Sebastien was a Girondin, too. Instantly, we were all tense.

Brissot was also a co-founder of the Society of the Friends of the Blacks, the group of nobles who believed—in some part—in the abolition of slavery. Or, at the very least, the adoption of the rights of the gens du coleur. It was Brissot who had introduced me to fellow member Josephe Bologne. It was Brissot who had taken me seriously from the moment I stepped into Paris.

"Someone stuck their head through my window and just told me to run, that they're after the me."

"But *who's* after you?" I asked.

"If I had to guess, I'd say it was the Mountain, of course."

"Max Robespierre?" I asked, confused. "Why on earth would he be after you? That doesn't make s—"

"—And you came here?" Sebastien interrupted. I looked quickly at his face, now awash with fury. Another thing that didn't make sense was how quickly Sebastien absorbed what was happening enough to be angry. "My kids are here, man!"

"I'm sorry, I had to go someplace. I'm sorry, Sebastien, I didn't think. Please, help me. I think it's just Max not thinking clearly..." Brissot stopped and cocked his head like a dog. "I hear the police. Please, help me."

"Get out!" Sebastien hissed, trying to keep his voice low. His younger son began to cry.

"Please, Sebastien, you have to help me..." Jacques pleaded, the fear in his eyes fighting his rational tone.

"Here," Elise called to him, motioning him toward the small cubby in the kitchen that usually held garbage for burning. "In here, hurry!"

Sebastien's eyes swung toward her, exasperated and panicked. But her lips were firm, and he capitulated.

"Okay, then, hurry up and do as she says!"

Brissot hustled across the room and folded his wiry body into the small space as if he'd been doing such a thing all his life. No more than ten seconds later there was pounding on the door.

Élise closed the cubby and stood in a way as to hide it, motioning the boys to come stand beside her. She clutched one child to each side and plastered a look of non-concern on her face. Sebastien wasn't as good at pretending. His face was flushed, and I could see him starting to shake.

"I'll get the door," I told him. "It's fine. Breathe and get a hold of yourself." He nodded but didn't speak. I opened the door.

"Yes, what can we do for you?"

A man shouldered me out of the way. "Who owns this house?"

"Uh, I do, Monsieur," Sebastien spoke up, finding his voice and strength again. "We were just finishing dinner, how can we help you?"

"We're looking for Jacques Brissot. We lost him down this street somewhere and we're going to each house. Have you seen him?"

"Why, no, Monsieur. As I said, we were just finishing dinner."

The guard looked doubtful, swinging his gaze to Élise. "What about you, Citizenness? Have you seen anything?"

"Non, Monsieur," she said, her face flushed with false innocence. "But I'm so glad you came. I feel so much safer knowing you officers are on the street protecting us. May I offer you an evening café?"

One of the children looked about to burst and I wondered if I was going to have to launch across the room to do something to keep them from noticing the boy's face about to explode into tears. Children. Fortunately, Élise simply reached over and gently smoothed the boy's arm to keep him from losing his cool as the guard looked me up and down and then peered up the stairs.

"I sleep up there," I explained. "You're welcome to look through my room," I said.

"And ours!" Sebastien agreed, nodding. The officer looked like he would take us up on it when, suddenly, another man came into the open doorway and called to him.

"We found one of his deputies, he can't be far from him. Allons!" *Let's go!*

The guard looked us over once more and Élise gave an attempt at a smile. Then he left the way he'd come.

Sebastien's eyes closed briefly in relief. I moved quickly to the door to watch them run down the street and then shut it, motioning them to let Jacques out. Normally a well-kept, polite man, seeing him come out of that little cubby, disheveled with a mask of naked fear on his features, shook me. I didn't understand this at all. What had happened while I'd been gone?

"Merci, Madame." Jacques brushed off the dust and kitchen grime from his nice clothes. "I'm so grateful. It was the sincerest kindness. Thank you."

"You can stay here," Élise said.

"No, he can't," said Sebastien.

"But..."

"No buts! I won't argue with you, Élise! You're a good man, Jacques, but I can't let you put my family in more danger than you already have. It's a miracle they didn't take me! I wish I could help but my family is my priority."

"Of course." Brissot nodded, as he shook his jacket lapels and looked around, as if he'd lost something. Not a physical thing, but lost his bearings.

"It doesn't make sense," I said. "Why would the Mountain turn against you without the approval of Max?"

Brissot gave a sad smile. "It appears this is all *with* the approval of Max, my friend. Likely upon his orders."

"Well, you can't go home," I said. "They'll be looking for you. Maybe you should hide out under the bridges; there's lots of nooks and crannies underneath. Go to one of them, so you can hide out until morning. Then, maybe Max will have come to his senses. Or maybe then you can get down to the docks and smuggle onto a fishing boat."

"No one's going to let him on," Sebastien said.

"If he pays, they might," I said. "Maybe. Do you have a better idea? Come, Jacques, I know how to get through the dark alleyways. Let's go."

He nodded, having lost his words it seemed.

"Jacques," Sebastien caught him before we slipped out the back way. "You understand, it's just my family. You understand?"

"Not to worry, Sebastien, I'm sure he will come to his senses in the morning. I'm certain it's just a moment of being improperly influenced by the rest of the Mountain. Don't think another moment about it, mon ami, Madame." He nodded at them both and gave something as close to a smile as he could muster.

And then we were slipping through the back alleys of the townhouses as stealthily as two shadows in the night. By the time we made it to one of Paris's many small bridges, we were both breathing heavily. There was, indeed, a sunken spot beneath one edge that was pitch black and deep enough for him to hide himself behind the beams.

"All right," he said, trying to muster up good cheer. "This will certainly do for the night. I might even get a bit of sleep. Tomorrow, I'll stop back home to grab some things."

"No, Jacques, you can't do that. If it's as you say and Max sent them, they'll be waiting for you there. You need to get out of Paris. Stowaway on a boat and hide for as long as you can."

"Max has been impulsive, lately," he said. "But everyone is rational first thing in the morning, like you said. Tomorrow I'll speak with him, rationally. All of this is unnecessary."

I thought about how firm Sebastien was and wondered if my friend knew something I didn't. If so...

"No, no, no, you mustn't go back. If Sebastien is worried... you should leave Paris."

In the darkness we couldn't see much but I felt the disappointment rolling off him. "I appreciate you trying to help me, but I didn't leave home with any money or clothes. The thing is, Zamor, I don't have it in me to be a fugitive. I don't think I'd be good at it, and I can't imagine leaving Paris. I don't believe I have that type of survival instinct."

"Then you must find it, Jacques. No one knows what they can do until they must." I dug into my pocket and pulled out a few coins and tried to shove them at him. He put his hands up to deny them, but I shook him by his lapels. "Jacques, take it. You never know, you might need it to get onto a boat, or for food. Now, stay here. I'll come back in the morning with a change of clothes for you and help you find a boat or a barge. We'll get you out of Paris, all right?"

Finally, his shoulders dropped, but he took the coins.

This was a far cry from when we'd met. His Society of the Friends of the Blacks was a membership-only group, dues being more than most common people see in two or three years of working. "All right. Thank you. Thank you." He smiled at me. "Who would have imagined when we met that someday you would be saving *me.*"

"Life is like that. Ironic, and all that. After you're gone, I'm sure your Girondins and the Society will rally to clear your good name. Maybe England is the place for you, after all. But first you must do as some of the best of us have—disappear."

CHAPTER SEVENTEEN

I thought I had gotten through to him.

But by the time I snuck back out to the bridge the next morning with a shirt and a pair of pants, he was gone. A week later, we found a flyer in the street which said that Jacques Brissot and the highest members of his Girondins had been captured and were being put to death.

The day of the execution, I sat at the table sipping coffee with Élise, waiting for Sebastien to show up. Finally, when I could wait no longer, I walked to the Place de la Révolution myself to see Jacques off. I knew there would be more than one. I had no idea they had rounded up *twenty-two*. They were faces I knew and recognized. Faces from the Club, people I'd laughed with and toasted. *They were Jacobins!* They were us!

Almost as shocking as the number of them was the speed with which they were dispatched. Each fed to the beast quickly, the blade still dripping from the last when the next neck was shoved into the cradle. Over and over and over. Screaming and wailing from the crowd because this was different. These people weren't hated enemies. The Brissotins were good people. But the beast had no favorites.

Hush...

Swish...

On my return, I went straight to my room. For hours I sat on the bed, willing my eyelid to stop twitching and my muscles to stop jumping. Willing myself to forget the sounds.

Dear God, twenty-two Brissotins were dead.

I clutched my knees to my chest until, finally, I rolled over and curled up on myself like a baby with one thought on my mind as I fell asleep: It had taken less than thirty minutes to guillotine twenty-two men. The wailing rang through my head even in my sleep.

Voices woke me up in the early morning and, having finally fallen asleep, I was annoyed.

I sat up and climbed out of bed, opening my door to the sounds of voices trying hard to whisper and failing.

"...Look at you, you're a mess!" Élise said.

"...Stop fussing over me, I'm a grown man!" came Sebastien's voice.

"...You're not acting like it! Get yourself together..."

I stepped forward gingerly, far enough down the stairs to crouch down and watch, unseen, through the railings. It wasn't right to eavesdrop, especially since I was a guest, but Sebastien was a mess. Always a hairy man, he was like a walking bear, having not seen a razor for more than a day. It almost covered most of his cheeks, came over his upper lip and swallowed the bottom of his face. His forehead and nose were brief bands of skin in all that hair. Eyelids normally hidden beneath his hairy brows were so swollen they protruded like fat burned fingers, shimmering with wetness. He was beyond drunk.

"Coming into this house like this," Élise scolded him. "What if the children had been awake? You scared me to death, all day worrying about you."

Élise's words were sharp but I saw in her ruddy, shiny cheeks, and the way she swiped the back of her palm across her face, she was holding on by a thread.

"Let them see..." he stopped and staggered on his own two feet, looking stunned. "They would know their papa is a co—"

"Don't you say it, Sebastien, I forbid it! I know you're in pain, but I'm going to say what I feel and let it be said once. I'm sorry for your friends and Jacques, but I'm glad you're still here. All day, waiting around wondering if I'd see you again or if you'd thrown yourself off a bridge, I've earned the right to be honest. I'm glad you walked through that door, drunk and all. So, before you start complaining about what you are I will *tell* you what you are. You are a husband and a father, first! And if you have another day on this earth, I'm thankful. Do you hear me?" Her face was wet with strands of her hair stuck onto her cheeks from silent tears.

I knew she was only trying to save him, just like Véronique had tried to save me. I knew she didn't realize it was that kind of strength—one I only seemed to see in women—that held people, families, communities, and worlds together. Women, who could make even the most wretched believe there was hope. I had almost believed Véronique, after all. But then she would be the one standing there trying to hold me together—a shell of a man like Sebastien was now.

Sebastien swayed on his feet and then dropped to his knees in front of her, clutching about her waist with his two arms wrapped around her like a tied winter scarf. He pressed his face into her middle. "My friends, Élise. My friends... Jacques...!" Then, a muffled wail escaped him.

The sound of his pain rang out through the kitchen and the house. Even muffled, his heaving guttural sobs caused his shoulders to shake. Without holding onto her, he would have surely dropped to the floor. But she reached down with her two arms and held him back. It was as if her two arms were enough to keep him afloat on a river. She pressed her cheek to the top of his head and began to murmur words of comfort.

My own face twisted, feeling his pain. Feeling sorry for myself that I no longer had someone who would clutch me to keep me afloat. My eyes filled as I thought about what I'd had not so long ago. What I'd given up...

"Uncle Zamor, is that my papa?"

I twisted, quickly wiping my eyes, to see one of the children had come out of his bedroom. It must have been the unusual sounds from below that woke him. "Shush," I whispered, quickly putting my finger to my lips. I quietly stood to usher him back to his room, getting him back into bed. Then, I tiptoed back to my own room to try to forget what I'd just seen and to ignore what it made me feel.

That night, I dreamt that all us members of the Jacobin Club of Paris were lined up on the platform awaiting our turn. All of us happily dancing on stage to take our final bow before the roaring crowd. I woke in the morning thinking, for the first time, that perhaps we were all doomed after all.

Chapter Eighteen

"What's the matter?" Sebastien asked Élise as she stood at the stove, spooning the last bowl of soup for the littlest one with jerky movements. Her body was stiff as if in pain and when she turned to us her face was puffy with reddened eyes. She put the bowl in front of the little one and sat down, avoiding our eyes.

"Do I take that to mean you haven't read the papers or is it just that you don't care?" she said. Sebastien's face was immediately alarmed.

"What, what happened? I read the paper..."

She took a spoonful of soup, eating like it held no taste or pleasure in it. "Then you know they're sending Olympe de Gouges to the beast." At his silence and the slack relief on his face her lips grew tight. "That's what I thought. You don't care; she's just a woman after all."

"No, my love, it's not that I don't care. I just don't know her, not like the men I used to see every day."

"She's a woman and you don't care!" Élise spit out, her words ending with a bit of a sob. "She was speaking for *us*. Something you don't care to do!"

"No, I..." Sebastien broke off as the sound of trickling reached his ear. "I'll kill that batard with his damned washwater!" he said, chewing the potatoes in his stew, happy to change the subject. "How many years does it take to figure out where to empty a bucket of water. It's like he wants me to—"

Cat-like whimpering of the younger son cut his rant short, and we looked at the boy who was looking at the door. Or, rather, the gap on the ground under it. We followed the boy's gaze and watched trickles of blood seeping into the house.

"No big thing," Sebastien said, rising. But then the trickle became a gush before our eyes, like some macabre horror blossoming just for us. Someone was being murdered, for sure. We were too far away for it to be from the Place de la Révolution, so this wasn't the beast. This was a regular people murder. And yet, no screaming or noise. Nothing but that quiet, silent wash of blood. A shiver made its way up my neck as I stared.

"Don't look at it; it's nothing," Sebastien tried, making an effort to keep his voice jovial as he jumped up to find a rag to shove into the space.

But the child had been expecting bubbles to play with, only to see blood. So much blood. And then he began to cry. The older one, like me, just stared, eyes wide.

Then he asked, simply: "Are they going to kill us, Papa? I dreamt they came and killed us all. They killed all those Girondins. Aren't you a Girondin? Are they coming back to kill us like they killed Monsieur Brissot?" That sent the young one into peals of hysteria.

"Of course not," I said, because Sebastien's face had gone ashen and his voice had lost words as he tried to sop up the mess that kept coming. "Your papa's right, it's no big thing." I turned to the young one, hoping by putting my head in his line of sight he would stop looking at the door and screaming. "It's just like that time when you lost your tooth. Remember? Your papa told me how you bled all over yourself, remember? Then it stopped and you got a treat, didn't you? For being brave. That's what you need to be now. Brave. It will be fine."

The child ignored me, got up, and ran to bury his face in his mother's midsection because my words were insufficient for the horror.

"That's not what it's like at all," the older boy said, looking me in my eyes. "We're not babies. You don't have to lie. In my dream—"

"—What's all this nonsense about a dream, son?" Sebastien spoke up. "A dream is just a dream. We have thousands over a lifetime and none of them mean anything. Valentin says it will be over soon, and I believe him," he said, as if it made perfect sense, shoving another rag to stop the gap.

"What will be over soon?" I asked.

"The worst of it, Zamor, what do you think?" he asked, as if exasperated with me. Like I was his third child.

"I'm sorry, I didn't realize I was supposed to know what you meant, Sebastien."

"It's obvious, isn't it?"

"No, not really. It really isn't."

"Mon Dieu, will the two of you stop?" Élise said. "You've been snipping at each other for days, it's enough. We're all under stress, but I expect you both to remember we have children in this house. And remember this revolution doesn't just affect the two of you!"

"Of course, my love," Sebastien said. He stood up, clapping his hands together as if blood came off like that. Then, he spied the bucket of wash water across the room and plunged his hands in. "The worst is over now. It will be over quickly. Just a few more people they had already identified before the Qu—before the Widow Capet was put to death. Just a few more, no big thing."

"Merci à Dieu." *Thank God*, Élise mumbled.

"Well, it's a big thing for those people and their families, I would imagine," I grumbled over my bowl, spooning a bit of potato into my mouth.

The older boy looked at me. "But isn't there still your Citizenness du Barry? After you're done with her? It will be a big thing for her family, too, won't it? The people who love her?"

I stopped chewing, looking closer at the boy. It seemed quite a pointed barb to be innocent. I glanced over to see Élise and Sebastien quickly avoid my eyes. I was certain this was a conversation that wasn't supposed to be had in my presence because the boy looked at me like he knew exactly what he was doing. His father's eyes in a little boy's face, saying the words out loud that his parents were likely saying in private.

"We can't possibly know what the future holds for Citizenness du Barry," I said. "She's very resourceful. She might make a strong case for herself. And she's got friends and all that. Like you, young man, rallying to her defense and you don't even know her. The power of a pretty face. All I can do is tell the truth; I have no control over what happens afterwards."

Sebastien and Élise were quiet and looked down into their bowls as they continued to eat. Silent judgement. Silent indictment.

The boy looked at me dead in the eye as if he was a grown man. Since his father wasn't setting things straight, I would. "She'll have a trial to plead her case, young man. If anyone can talk themselves out of prison, it's Jeanne du Barry. I'm certain she'll maneuver her way to freedom and be back to cursing me for my ingratitude in no time. And then you can visit her and tell her all about how you championed her from afar. She would like that very much."

CHAPTER NINETEEN

The Revolutionary Tribunal

December 6, 1793

"Why did you go to England?" George Grieve all but barked the question at the Citizenness Jeanne du Barry. Sitting on the uncomfortable seat on the stand in the uncomfortably hot, stuffy room, before a roomful of people who hated her. Even though it was December, the amount of bodies in the room raised the heat. Somehow, Jeanne du Barry still looked cool and calm, barely batting an eye.

I could tell from her outfit she'd tried to dress demurely. Tried to look simple and humble. But her plainest dove gray travel dress with its little leather riding jacket was fashionable without effort. The cut and professional trim of it encased her well and managed to make her eyes look larger, her hair shinier, her skin flawless... I could feel the discomfort in the room that happens when people who had never seen her encountered her natural beauty without description.

In contrast, most of the men and women watching were working class sans-culottes, sweaty with blotchy skin and cheap clothes that wilted under duress. Pale skin with cheeks sunken in from lack of adequate food or poor drinking water. Clothes that were rank because money for water was sparse and one often had to wear an outfit several times before getting hold of wash water. Her simple elegance only highlighted how privileged she was, to be able to look so put together under all this.

Making sure to get in early, I was watching from the far back corner, behind a man with a tall torso so I wouldn't be easily seen. It wasn't that I was afraid she might see me; I just didn't want any attention to be diverted my way. I didn't want to give her any excuse to stand up, point at me and call me names. And I wanted to hear her answers to the accusations.

A few bourgeoisie and one or two nobles were there as well. The nobles made a discreet effort to position themselves so their bodies were as far away from the commoners as possible. I expected more nobles. But I expected more of *them*. I craned my neck, surprised to see so few people who knew her.

She continued her testimony.

"I left the country because of the theft of my jewels," she replied simply. "There was reason to believe the thieves were in England." The jewels had been a major point of questioning, and I knew now she was regretting her actions after the "theft" in publicly listing all the missing items. I was certain she'd done it on Gaspard's advice and, as I knew it would, it came back to haunt her. Paris was scandalized by the value of the jewels in her possession. And those had only been the ones she claimed were stolen.

"You left the country, knowing we are at war with England? Why?" Grieve asked while pacing in front of her, no doubt his effort at drumming up drama. Only the stiffness in his face told how important this was to him.

"I was given permission to leave prior to the declaration of war. I saw no reason to wait and re-file for permission. I certainly didn't want to impede the investigation."

"And were the stolen jewels your only jewels or do you have more? Perhaps hidden away?"

"Yes, I do sometimes choose to hide my valuables, likely near the greenhouse or the ice house."

"Interesting that you are at the center of two very large jewel thefts. France has never recovered the necklace the deceased former king gifted to you. The Affair of the Necklace has never been truly solved..."

"I understand a noblewoman was charged with the crimes along with two others."

"But the jewels were never found, Citizenness. Just like the jewels in this, your second theft."

"I had no idea about the first necklace. The King was going to surprise me with it as a gift, but he died. I never even laid eyes on it."

"Yes. Still, what are the odds the same woman would be at the center of two jewelry thefts, is what I'm saying."

"Unhappy circumstance, I'm sure."

"How old are you, Citizenness?'

"Forty-two."

She was fifty. She lied as easily as she breathed.

"Did you know a man who goes by the name of Citizen Rotondo?

"Yes, he told me if I gave him money, he would stop the printing of a comedy featuring me in 1792."

"You paid his extortion with France's money?"

"Well, I... I mean, it's *my* money..."

"Have you hosted émigrés?"

"No, absolutely not."

"We have evidence you hosted a priest named Fontenille."

"Fontenille? Oh, I didn't know he'd emigrated and returned."

"Did you give money to émigrés?"

"I gave them my own money to gamble on my behalf."

"France's money?"

"Well, I mean … it's *my* money."

"Knowing there's a law against communication with émigrés, why did you break it?"

"I have a passport for travel. I didn't think the laws applied to me under those circumstances…"

When Georges Grieve finished questioning her, he stood aside to allow another man to stand and pass him, then sat. I recognized the new questioner. It was a man named Fouquier-Tinville. He was the same man who'd questioned Marie Antoinette. The same man who had gotten so angry with me when I'd spoken up at the Jacobin Club years ago. The second I saw *him,* I knew it was going to be bad for *her.*

Within minutes, under the hostile gaze of him, her composure began to crack just a little. Tiny beads of sweat now glistened on her forehead. At one point she readily admitted to transferring exorbitant amounts of money to England, transactions her own bankers had no knowledge of.

"Do you remember when you received news on the passing of the man known as Citizen Capet?" It was what they were calling Louis XVI now.

"I do."

"And where were you?"

"I was in England."

"With émigrés."

"I-I don't believe so. I can't be certain. As I said—"

"—And when you returned to Paris, what color clothing did you wear on passing through town?"

"Color? I don't remember."

"Well then, it's fortunate we have several witnesses who do remember and are willing to attest to it. They say they saw you parading through town wearing mourning black for Louis Capet. Do you deny it?"

"Black is a standard part of my wardrobe. I don't recall but if someone says—"

"Don't recall what you were wearing or don't recall if you were openly mourning for the treasonous Citizen Louis Capet?"

"Don't recall what I was wearing. I would never have mourned for Louis Capet. I have no reason to; he was never particularly kind to me. He nor his wife, the Austrian. It is because of them that I was exiled, you remember. A good French woman such as myself, banished by the Austrian."

"Yes, we remember. How many years were you the lover to the royalist Duc de Brissac?"

"Pardon?"

"The Duc de Brissac. He was given the opportunity to denounce the Citizen Capet after the forming of this new government, and he refused. In fact, he was on his way to his own trial when his caravan was intercepted by a roving gang, was he not? They tore his head off and threw it through your window, oui? Why didn't you end your relationship with him when he first refused to denounce the king months prior to his death? Knowing he was an enemy to the people?"

"I-I was never involved in his work affairs, I was simply his partner."

"Being a partner to a traitor seems reasonable to you?"

It went on for some time. The longer I sat there the more I became convinced with each question... they were allowing her no quarter. Far from relying only on my testimony, they were covering every possible subject from her dress to her words to her friends to her spending, leaving no stone unturned.

When she was released to be taken back to the Conciergerie I could tell she was shaken. Fouquier-Tinville was a mad dog years ago. Today he was a mad dog with power and his ruthlessness dripped off him like sweat.

Leaving the crowded room only one thing filled my mind: *Were they actually going to do it? It wasn't possible, was it?*

Chapter Twenty

December 7, 1793

The next day I arrived to testify. As a witness, I was to wait outside the room until called. Upon approaching the bench, I was surprised to find Salanave—my old friend and cook of the Chateau de Louveciennes—siting there, primly as if going to church. She looked up, spotting me, and after a brief look at each other I sat down beside her.

What was she here to say? What had she seen? Was she going to tell them about what happened to me? Please God, don't let her tell the world what happened to me!

All those thoughts ran through my head while we each sat quietly, waiting our turn. Afraid to speak to each other

They called Salanave first. She stood stiffly and walked into the room. Only minutes later, she was done. When she exited the courtroom, her face was pinched with discomfort. She walked over and stopped in front of me, and I stood up.

There was probably much to be said, but I didn't have the emotional fortitude to get into anything with Salanave and testify against Madame on the same day. She must have felt the same because, at the same time, we both nodded curtly to each other like we were strangers, and then she turned and walked out of the courthouse, her shoes sounding on the marble floor.

Then it was only me.

The path to the stand wasn't long but it felt like a thousand steps. It felt like a lifetime. Once seated, I looked at her, once. She was giving me a stare to bore into my head. As if to say, *You'd better keep your mouth shut, Louis-Benoit. You'll be sorry, Louis-Benoit. I'll get you, Louis-Benoit.* Or, perhaps, that was in my head.

I avoided looking at her during my testimony. But I could feel her admonition in my brain. I could feel her disapproval as I proceeded to sever our relationship.

I didn't lie. I had already handed over the list of names of nobles that had left the country, with the value of funds it appeared she had given or loaned them. And then, the household purchases came into question.

"How often did the household pay for live music?"

"Quite often. Once a week, commonly."

"How many gowns did she buy?"

"There were many. She needed different clothes for the change of seasons, you understand."

"And the art?"

"A great deal of art."

Her defense attorney tried to trip me up. "And you? How much did she spend on you?"

"Quite a bit, I'm sure. I earned a small allowance for drinking money in Paris. But my clothes and food were all taken care of by the Citizenness."

"Is it fair to say she kept you in a manner befitting a nobleman?"

"Yes. I don't deny that," I admitted. "She liked me to look a manner befitting the royal court."

"Aren't there even two portraits of you hanging on the walls?"

"Yes."

"And what do you say to the hypocrisy of testifying against the woman who gave you such a lifestyle?"

"I say, I was reared under an absolute monarch. It was all I knew. And I behaved as such until the very day I first read the words of Jean-Jacques Rousseau. They changed my life. Reading his words, I became a different person. Maybe not in deed, but in mind. And ever since, I've been changing a bit more every day to become that person. A man who believes in an equal society and is proud when he looks in the mirror, not because of how much he has but because of inner substance and the desire to be of value to society. It is why I became a Jacobin. The first time I could be that, fully, was the day I left the Chateau de Louveciennes."

Madame leaned over to whisper furiously to her avocat. He straightened.

"Don't you mean to say the day you were kicked out of the Chateau?"

"If Citizenness du Barry chooses that description, then yes. The day I was able to reveal the man I had become was the very same day she ejected me from her abode because of it. It seems, while my mistress could tolerate all manners of royalists and émigrés, she could not tolerate a revolutionary under her roof. It breaks my heart. For so long, we were close, and all that."

Her lawyer sat back down and Grieves stood up again with more questions.

I told them about the lifestyle at the palace. I confirmed her relationship with Brissac. I confirmed her trips to England. Everything I said was true.

"Merci," Grieves said to me, turning to the people in the room. "A true example of a man pure of heart and unsullied by the excesses of his mistress, that he would turn his back on incredible wealth and privilege to be an honest man in our new, just society. If only we all had that fortitude."

After I was released, I had planned to leave but then slipped back in to sit in the back of the audience.

A woman from the convent Madame had been exiled to testify as to how wonderful Jeanne du Barry was. Someone who worked at the Chateau for less than a week testified as to how terrible Jeanne du Barry was. After the witnesses she was called to testify again.

She sat slightly forward in the chair, as if eager to speak, referencing a petition she had presented to the court on her behalf by the remaining staff at the Chateau. She listed off all the charitable works she had done, all the money she had given to orphanages. And she appealed to the people in the room, giving a tremulous smile.

"I implore you to remember, I'm a humble French woman. I'm one of you. Forgive my mistakes and I'll prove to you how loyal I can be to this new, wonderful government." She smiled.

"Citizenness du Barry," Fouquier-Tinville said, his face puzzled. "Are you trying to bribe or seduce the good people in this room? Because I'll have you know, you will not corrupt our new republic with the ways of the age of kings. And we don't take kindly to the attempt."

She sat back, her face going white, her smile disappearing. I winced.

Throughout my testimony I couldn't ignore the heaviness that lay over me. With every question asked and answered, the truth settled into my bones. They had no intention of releasing her. No matter what she did or said, the tribunal had decided from the start how it would end. I was besieged with a strange combination of feelings I couldn't identify.

I walked back to the house, in my room, pulling a bottle of Chartreuse from under my bed and drinking from it like water. I didn't come down for dinner. And later that evening, there was a knock at my bedroom door.

"I won't disturb you," came Sebastien's voice. "I just thought you'd want to see this." I heard the scratching of paper against wood and saw the newspaper sliding under the door. Standing up, I walked over and stood for a long moment before bending down to pick up the sheet of paper.

"CONVICTED!

Citizenness Jeanne du Barry, sentenced to death!

Lead witness, former page and closest confidant, Louis-Benoit Zamor, *condemns his benefactress!"*

The world swayed.

Yes, I had always known it was a possibility but there was a small part of me that thought—*was sure*—she'd find a way out of it. *Certain* that one of her noble friends would show up for her and save her, somehow. *Positive* that she would find a way to charm Max Robespierre himself if need be.

I had only just testified that morning, how was the trial over already?

Yes, she was as guilty as Marie Antoinette, but she was much more personable, born a sans-culottes. And she was one of the most convincing people I knew—she could sell dirt to a farmer. She was smart and knew how to hide it. She was funny and knew how to make it seem accidental. She was beautiful and knew how to use it. She was duplicitous and made it into an art. And she was French!

That last part, the fact that she was French, was something she'd told me time and again. The biggest difference between her and the dead queen was that at least *she* was French. She had thought it meant something. In the back of my head, maybe I did, too. Maybe I allowed the legend of her to cloud my judgement.

I continued to read.

"...Betrayed his mistress, guardian, and godmother."

Why was the story all about me? Why only me?

Shortly thereafter, another knock.

"The courier just left you this," Sebastien said. Another sound of paper scraping against wood. I walked over and bent down to pick up the envelope. Opening it with shaky fingers, I pulled out the papers confirming my citizenship.

I was free.

Chapter Twenty-One

The night I received my citizenship papers I almost didn't want to go to bed, worried about Jean visiting me in my dream. I already knew how he felt. I had no desire to spend all night in the Labyrinth soaked in blood.

I fell asleep anyway and was pleasantly surprised that it wasn't Jean who visited me. That relief was short-lived.

Occasionally, Louis XV popped up in my dreams, as real and alive as if he'd never died of smallpox. He would chat with me like he used to when I was eleven, as if I was his best and only friend. As if I was there for any reason other than the fact that I couldn't get away.

On that evening's nocturnal visit, I was transported back to a memory. I was eleven and he and I strolled the gardens at the Palace. He was wearing his blue silk coat with black short culotte pants and white stockings. I was in a burgundy coat with a cream-colored turban to match Madame's pink outfit that day.

We both walked, clasping our hands behind us, chins up. I always watched him to see how he moved. To see how he could walk among people and manage to remain so haughty and removed; how he could walk among them and not see them.

I mimicked him that day.

He had shared a little of his love of astronomy and astrology with me by that time. How the stars had something to do with the habits and behaviors of people. How being born under a certain alignment determined one's traits. I had thought it was fantasy those many years ago. But here I was, deep into a dream that replayed a memory I had all but forgotten, with surprising detail.

***

"I can see from the look on your face you don't believe me, but it's true." He smiled. We had paused our strolling to sit on a bench in the garden one night. Plenty of nobles were clustered in groups on the grounds as nighttime was always full of activity, candles lighting up paths and creating mysterious shadows.

The sky was besieged with sparkling dots. XV took the wooden and bronze tube from where it was pressed against his face as he'd been looking through it. "Here, look." He handed it to me.

Putting the tube up to my eye, suddenly the sky was right before me, and I jumped. He laughed. "I told you, they are stars. Where they sit is important. It's a shame you can't remember when you were born. I'd know more about you if I knew under which stars you came into life."

I pulled the tube away and handed it back. "Your Majesty, that sounds like witchcraft."

"Bah, everything sounds like witchcraft until we learn it's not. Instructors will teach you in class that some of our most intelligent minds were accused of witchcraft once. Witchcraft is evil. Astrology is just science. I showed you that book in the study? When writing about astrology, a circle is used to denote the way the sun revolves around the earth and each sign is a point on that circle. So, each sign has an opposite. Twelve signs and twelve symbols, just like there were twelve apostles to Christ. Some even say each sign symbolizes each of the

apostles. So, you see, it's connected to Christianity in a way. And each sign is ruled by an element."

"What's an element?"

"Like a natural part of life. Something not made by man. Earth. Fire. Water. Air."

I wondered what star alignment would create a man so evil as to not allow a child to go home to his parents. What element was that?

"What stars were you under, Your Majesty?"

"It's the alignment, boy, not the stars alone. It's how they sit in relation to each other. I was born on February 15, the year of our Lord, 1710."

"You're old!"

"Yes, I am. I am called an Aquarius, ruled by air, named after the Greek story of a young shepherd who was whisked away from earth and up to the heavens by Zeus, the king of the Gods."

"I thought there was only one God."

"There is. But you will find there are ignorant people who believe there are many. They are called pagans. We do not believe in paganism; we believe in God. But the story is about a boy taken away by a pagan god called Zeus to live in heaven. Like you!"

He laughed at his own wittiness.

"People born under the sign of Aquarius are very, very smart. Deep thinkers, fair and wise. But also, brave and firm in their belief of right and wrong. We love being among people and people love us. And me being ordained by God as I am means I am all that, ten times over. And your Madame was born on August 19, which makes her what's called a Leo. Hers is the fifth sign of the Zodiac. Leo stands for the mighty lion, one of which was slain by Hercules as part of his twelve labors. You see, twelve is an important number."

"What does it mean that she's a Leo?"

"It means Madame is ruled by animal fury. You can see it in her spirit! That animal magnetism that shoots from her eyes when she's passionate or angry. Or making love! It's all because she's a Leo. Leos love life and they are strong leaders! Nothing shy about a Leo. They take what they want and stand up for themselves. And they love completely. Just like the lovely Madame du Barry loves me."

He was brave and just and she was full of animal fury? I wondered what I was that I should be caught between them.

"Pull out the pocket watch I gave you." I reached into the pocket inside my coat. "Now, when you look at the face of a clock you won't only see the time of the day. You'll remember the signs of the Zodiac, won't you? You'll remember there are twelve. I have a secret." He leaned down to whisper in my ear, "At the Chateau at Louveciennes I had the gardener plant bushes around the property in a circle; one for each Zodiac sign, and then one more to symbolize you."

"Me, why?"

"Why? Because you're like our very own. You are our favorite thing, even more than some of my children. I can't say that in front of people, you see, because it's not proper—my own children are real people—but you are very dear to me. To us. What better place to express it than at the Chateau de Louveciennes? None of my children or grandchildren have ever cared about the property like it's our own special place. I've put twelve bushes in a circle, with the house at midnight. But I also planted a thirteenth bush to represent you, both ornery and a blessing to us. The number 'thirteen' represents change, you know. Our little family is precisely that. Not even Madame knows why I had the bushes planted the way I have, but you love plants, too. I know someday you'll appreciate my reasoning. Maybe, someday, you can share the information with Madame if she needs it. This story might give her comfort." He gave me a mischievous grin. "It's a mystery, where the thing *is! Maybe you'll be the one to solve it. After all, you are the Governor of Louveciennes!"*

He cackled with laughter, the title having been a joke from the moment he bestowed it upon me. I lost my interest in the Zodiac. It meant nothing to me if it could produce two people as selfish as Louis XV and Madame du Barry.

"Let's agree to keep these conversations between you and me, oui? The rest of France isn't quite ready to understand such advanced science. They will look at it as witchcraft and not see the good."

***

I couldn't have explained why I dreamt about him at that time, except that he was trying to guilt me from hell.

It wouldn't work. I hated him as much as I hated her. My one regret was that the smallpox killed him before I did. But my attempt to slip rat poison into his chocolat had been thwarted by Salanave. Probably for the best, but it would have been so satisfying if it had been me to bring him to his end.

Of course, it was a miracle it had been Salanave—who had a fondness for me—who found me and not any one of the other hundreds of people who shifted through the Palace kitchen every day. Salanave intervening had saved me from being caught, and from certain death.

Of course, he would show up now, trying to twist our memory into something pleasant. Making himself known on the very evening that his favorite's fate was sealed.

Maybe the dream of the Well-Beloved was a goodbye. I hoped so.

Chapter Twenty-Two

Place de la Révolution

Paris

December 8, 1793

We walked together—Sebastien, Valentin, and I—to the place where the guillotine rode high in the sky.

The bite of December air made my cheeks smart from the chill, but I was numb inside.

The crowd was thick, but I walked as close to the front as I could.

"How are you?" Sebastien said softly beside me.

"I'm fine, of course," I said curtly.

"We don't have to stay; we can leave if you like."

"Yes, I do," I snapped. "I'm fine."

Sebastien went quiet and moved away from me, slightly, as if unsure of me. While on the other side of me, Valentin had already finished the cup of beer he took when we first arrived and was now headed for his second.

"I'll take that," said Valentin, pushing an empty cup at a man passing by with a tray and grabbing a full cup of beer to replace it. He turned to the man on the other side of him and yelled, boisterously, "Bon santé!" The sound of it rang in my ears.

"Stop making a fool of yourself," I told him.

"Mind your fucking business, page," he said quickly, drinking the brew down like water.

Of course, I knew Valentin had his own personal history with du Barry, she having refused to help save his older brother's life and all that. But he had no personal relationship with her. Her lack of stepping in for his brother, while hurtful, hadn't caused his brother's death. Louis XV had done that. But leave it to Valentin to make everything about himself.

The sound of the carriage wheels rolling towards the spot over the cobblestone road caught the attention of the crowd. And then we saw her, along with her two accountants, in prison garb. The three of them, sitting up and out of that carriage, arms tied behind them, like three pegs, bouncing with every movement of the cart. The crowd began to hoot and cheer, vicious joy spreading quickly as if in a theatre about to see a well-received play.

"She's as bad as the Austrian," said a man behind me.

"Worse!" said his female companion. "At least the Austrian wasn't one of us. Jeanne Bécu is a French woman and should know better!"

I was close to the front near the guillotine and watched her from a distance, knowing eventually she'd be closer to me. Her head swiveled back and forth over the crowd like she was watching a sports match, stunned by the celebration. The revelry.

I'd been to enough of them by now that I knew how they went. But she hadn't. And I could feel her emotions, as if she and I were joined by a tether, ratcheting up even from a distance.

Her hair had been shorn off jaggedly, and she wore a rough, brown shift. Her face was devoid of color or paint, making it look much younger and innocent. Making her eyes that much larger and blue. Making the tears more pronounced as she began to cry, speaking frantically to her cart-mates. In turn, the men were quiet and stoic, faces frozen with shock, all while nodding at her as she spoke and cried. I recognized them as the father and son accountants who assisted her in liquidating and moving her assets to England.

"Not so pretty now, are you?" someone yelled.

"Yes, she is," came a soft-spoken, begrudging response. "Even without hair and with ugly clothes she's beautiful." It was said with reverence and sadness, quieting the nearby voices for only a moment before the laughter and cheering began again.

I'd never get used to the laughter and cheering.

Jeanne du Barry's chattering stopped with the slowing of the wagon. Her head swiveled back and forth, as she seemed to search for the sources of the laughter, finding it in most of the hundreds of onlookers. Seeing no quarter of mercy in their eyes.

She stood up, wobbling, to take in the scene before her, gaze sweeping from one end to the other—back and forth—as the laughter died down and discomfort began to settle like a blanket. Then, her lips opened and she let out a howl of despair that carried through the sky. Mouth wide, the howl ended in sobbing gasps. The crowd quieted.

Finally, the executioner called for her to be brought. Normally, the crowd would immediately go back to hooting but, this time, the normal flow had already interrupted. Things were different.

The guards led her from the cart to the platform. When they attempted to get her from one end of the platform to the end where the beast sat, her cries gave way to words ringing out in the eerily quiet space.

"You are going to hurt me, please don't hurt me! Just one more moment I beg you!"

The quiet was deafening, the crowd still in shock. Smiles died. As immune as the city had become to the sight of headless bodies, it seemed this new thing stunned them out of apathy. Normally, the crowd didn't interact with the people who were being executed in front of them. Sure, they yelled at them. Called them names. Laughed at them. Levied all manners of abuse at people who were too frozen with fear to respond. But most of France had never actually met Jeanne Du Barry. They couldn't have been prepared for this.

A shocked gasp went up as she wrestled her arms away to dash across the platform, far away from the beast. But her hands were still tied behind her and she couldn't get up speed, nor know which direction to go to escape them. Seconds later they had caught up to her and two of him were dragging her back as she screamed.

They pulled her along, each dragging her by one arm as she cried and screamed the whole way across the platform. When she resisted, her bottom dragged the ground as her feet scuttled along. Silence.

Something within me began to quake, and I was in my own world, remembering. Remembering her first embrace. Her smile for me had been the first time I thought I was safe upon arriving at the Palace. Of course, it would prove to be false. But back then, for a split second—for a single moment at ten years old—her false smile had been a balm to my soul. For a split second I had thought she might be a new mother to me. I had thought she cared. I had blossomed with hope in people, and hope in the world. Just for a second.

Madame's face shone with the desperate neediness that had always made her impossible to resist to soft-hearted men who wanted to be her protectors. Vulnerability that made many soft-hearted women want to support her. I glanced around to see the faces of the others who were enraptured, moved by Madame's emotion and fear. If it was possible, perhaps she could cause a groundswell of support and prevent her own execution. Was it possible?

But the guards on stage were unmoved, or if they were, knew how to hide it. They wouldn't be diverted from their task. They, nor the executioner who was gesturing to them to hurry up. Get it over before the crowd became too upset by what they were seeing.

And I felt no joy. Even though I knew this moment would be the beginning of my new life as a free man, I felt no joy. I felt nothing at all.

Upon the scaffolding, she was scanning the crowd, searching for a sympathetic face, and then her eyes fell on me. I felt her gaze like the lightning that lit up the trails of the Labyrinth—a brilliant strike of white lighting up the world, in her sudden gaze.

And with the strike in my head came the inevitable: The stone fox flashed in front of my face. *Go away,* it called to me. *You have time to escape!*

I couldn't imagine why the fox who only came to me in times of despair should come now, or what it thought I needed to escape? I waited for sadness and regret for the scene before me, anything beyond the basic acknowledgement that the woman on the platform before me had been the most important person in my life for over two decades. Serving her had been my primary purpose in life, after all. She had been my world. Du Barry and her Page, and all that.

I could hear the sniffling of strangers in the crowd, but I couldn't have defined what *I* felt for all the money in the world except... *I felt no joy.*

All that I'd known as a child was wrapped up in the face of the woman staring at me. All my life in France, tied to the woman in front of me. And now, at the age of fifty, she looked at me with a questioning glance, her eyes as wide and surprised as though seeking some meaning. Seeking to understand what was happening. But she knew what was happening.

The sound of rushing filled my ears like a storm.

A quick jerk of her arm prompted her to lie against the plank before her. She released her gaze and began crying out to the crowd once again.

"No, no... why do you want to hurt me? No!"

Memories flooded me: holding her train as she walked through the Palace. Her teaching me how to dance and prompting laughter when I stumbled. Another of me comforting her, hoping she would do the same for me in those times when my soul was hurt. Hoping and believing that at some point in life she would actually look at me and see a human being and not her property.

I never expected to enjoy it but nor did I expect this feeling like a block of lead filling me. If I could have found another way... *any* other way...

I knew the expression on her face. I knew what she was feeling. I knew when her head began swiveling, she was looking for me, *again.* I knew what she *wanted* from me, as she wanted from me all my life. I was there to please her, after all. I was there to comfort and soothe her. My very existence, my very being, purchased just to make her smile. She wanted, wanted, wanted... from the thing that belonged to her and her alone.

But I had never been a thing. Only a human who wanted to be free of the thing that held him captive. I had nothing left to give.

Suddenly, realization came to me. I understood, now, why she did the thing she did from the time I was ten; why she tried out so many faces on me like an actress trying on masks to see which one fit. When one can't *feel* human emotion, one must attempt to display that which he or she doesn't feel but thinks is right for the situation. I cracked the code!

And so it was, knowing I was being asked to give and needing to respond with *something,* that I did what I'd seen her do throughout my life.

I allowed my face to change, going through expressions—sadness, shock, horror, sympathy—trying to find one to fit the occasion. I tried out these masks on her because it was all I had left to give. And when my face settled on a blank, emotionless mask, in her eyes I could tell she finally saw me, for once. Finally—after a lifetime—her eyes softened on me and for the first time, for a split second, she finally saw something in me that she recognized. In her eyes, I could tell she saw me for what I was: a human being.

It struck me from within with something close to pain. Her seeing me now, after all these years and all the pain and hurt; the death of my emotion was the thing that finally brought us closeness. That my emotions had to die before I could understand her and she understand me. That look that said that, perhaps, we were the only two people who could truly understand each other.

Oh, what I wouldn't have given for that look twenty, ten, or even one year ago. It might have changed everything.

A second later her eyes lost focus on me as she remembered and started crying out, again. She was still calling out when the board in front of her was tilted so that she now lay horizontally, on her stomach. Still crying out while the only sound from the crowd was a single woman weeping. Still crying out as some man called her a dirty name and the person next to him immediately punched him in the face and told him to have some compassion. Still crying out when the executioner took the chain holding the blade into his hand.

Don't look! said the fox. *Come away with me!*

I saw her face as I saw her the first time, young and sweet and pretty. I thought of all the times when I was cornered and attacked by the children of her enemies and convinced myself that she didn't know. Telling myself that she really loved me. Cared about me. Lying to myself that she was my safety. Hoping her false smile was real. *Desperate* to believe it.

Those memories were dangerous as they began to unearth the fear and overwhelm and endless desperation. I was that child, again, screaming with an endless inner cry for her to *be my safety! Love me! Protect me! Help me!*

My eyes threatened to roll back in my head, but I forced myself to stay present. Forced myself to ignore any possible escape.

I was looking in the direction of the beast, but my eyes were frozen in the past, hearing the sound of her favorite music as I listened beside her, smelling the scent of her perfume and feeling her arm hooked in mine as we walked side by side, staring into her eyes as we lay on our stomachs in front of each other, locked in an endless gaze, the *Favorite and her Page.*

None of those things were ever done by choice. Never out of affection. Always because she commanded and I had no choice but to obey. And that fact turned these memories into twisted evidence of a relationship that was a lie.

Jeanne du Barry's scream rang through the silent air. "No! No! No!"

And the blade came down, as the bright sun glinted off the edge all while she screamed into the void below her.

Hush ... my little Cupid, I will love you like a mother.

Swish... don't you know you will always belong to me? You are mine. You are mine. You are *mine.*

Slam!

My body jerked at the jarring of the blade hitting the cradle, my eyelids fluttering as I came back to myself. A second later I heard the thud of something heavy hitting the bottom of the basket. I waited for the sound of the crowd cheering, but there was none. The very air was still, as if nature had stopped.

And then, a second later, my eyelids drifted closed, instinctively, as I knew what was coming and steeled myself. The gentle spray washed over me and coated me like a warm summer rain...

Part II
AFTER THE STORM

Gilded Orange Books

Chapter Twenty-Three

*D*ear Citizen,

You must think me a monster.

It sounds bad, what I did. I assure you, I took no pleasure in the death of Jeanne du Barry. It felt like a waste to me. She and I might have been friends in another life... if she didn't own me, and all that. She and I might have liked each other for real, if we were in the world as equals. Or, we might have hated each other freely. We'll never know.

Much later I found out that after Fouquier-Tinville had at her that day at trial, she wrote him a letter, directly, assuring him she'd never provided money to émigrés intentionally and had never cavorted with anti-revolutionaries. At least not willingly. She said her murdered lover Brissac had been a forced relationship, because in her situation that was the only relationship she could get.

I couldn't blame her for those lies. They were small, in the grander scheme of things when one's survival was at stake. Madame was a fighter, after all. She would have said anything to save herself.

In a second effort to save herself, she had also tried to bribe her jailers and the committee by instructing them where she'd buried more jewels—ones that even I didn't know about. She told them the republic could have all of them if they let her go.

Officers of the committee went to the Chateau and, according to her rough maps, dug up several packets of hidden jewels from the grounds. Some of those jewels made it back into the governmental coffers but I'm certain most of them ended up in the pockets of the officers who dug them up.

It was said that she was in good spirits until they took her from her cell and sat her down in a chair and began cutting off her hair. That was when it dawned on her that the bribery wasn't enough and everything had gone to shit.

I hate to keep repeating myself, but until the very end, part of me expected her to be saved somehow. Throughout her life she always landed on her feet. I would have resented it if she had been saved, but I wouldn't have been surprised.

In these modern times, people will tell you that I was an idiot. They say I was duped by the republicans; the nègre peasant too stupid to understand I was being used. Too feeble-minded to realize that I was a pawn.

Of course, I knew that Max and George thought they were using me. That didn't change the fact that it was the only way to get my freedom. I would have gladly accepted any other way, but Madame had made it clear it would never happen.

As strange as it sounds, after her death I began to feel indignant on behalf of Jeanne du Barry. At least with me, she was well aware of how much I resented her for keeping me trapped to her. Gaspard knew it. Everyone who worked at the Chateau, the King and Queen—they all knew it. Ours was a false love and she took great pleasure exaggerating the depth of our relationship, precisely because it annoyed me. Not because it was real. At least not on my part.

But all those others she actually helped? All those nobles whose favor she tried to earn, the ones who knew she would do anything to become a darling of the royal court? The ones who knew that she would put her own freedom on the line just to be a part of the club that is the noble class? They didn't bother to cross the channel to put a good word in for the woman who secured their freedom or called them friend. They didn't bother to walk down the street to comfort her or show their support. They were as quiet as mice and no one says a thing about them.

Someone was truly an unsuspecting pawn in all this, but it wasn't me.

I have regrets. It's natural to wonder if things could have been different. But I'm a pragmatist, not a dreamer. If I hadn't done what I had, I would have ended up sitting in that cart with her and the Vandemyers, en route to my doom. If I had ever had a choice in my life circumstance, I might have deserved a seat in that cart. By keeping me captive, she removed any ounce of guilt I might have had in how I was forced to protect myself.

In essence, she had ensnared me. She had chained herself to me to hold me to her for as long as she saw fit—obviously to be a lifetime—and thus became the appendage that I had to chew off to be set free.

Still, it didn't feel good when the end came.

All the emotions I felt at the time have simmered down now. But I have to admit, back in the time immediately after the beast fed upon her, I felt some anger towards her that she had forced me to do it when all I ever asked for was my freedom. Having a hand in the death of someone you haven't always hated, passionately, is a difficult thing. And I hadn't hated her in the beginning.

My life didn't end when Madame's did. I know that comes as a surprise to some who never truly saw me as a human being in the first place. But, Citizen, at this point in these journals you must know that the will to survive has always been strong in me. You, also, know I'm a thinking man. And you know that the link between us has always been more of what was put upon us rather than what was true.

Of course, I knew they would come for me. But I thought if I could make myself of new value, it might save me. If I could give France something as amazing as the Declaration, it might keep my neck out of the mouth of the beast. Madame was gone, and I now had to survive another hunt with new hunters... and all that.

—Zamor, 1820

Chapter Twenty-Four

December 29, 1793

I took my morning cup of coffee and opened the front door. Stepping outside in the morning before the family rose was always pleasant. Living in someone else's home, often I felt I had to socialize in times that I would prefer to isolate. The cost of living with others, and all that.

I headed down the street and purchased a paper from the vendor, walking back with it to lean against the front door while I sipped and read. Moments later, the sound of singing and revelry reached my ear, as if a sign of renewed life. It was a steady, simple rhythm, palm pounding on little drums with just a few notes over and over. Accompanying singing with gaiety. I pursed my lips to smile, eager to enjoy anyone's happiness these days. I straightened and looked up from my coffee as the noisemakers approached.

I recognized them! It was the group of troubadours who, long ago, caused me and a small group of budding revolutionaries to give chase across a bridge! They were tapping their tambourines just like this back then, trying to bilk us out of our property. Chasing them down, we'd gotten our things back and the leader had tipped his hat to us as if to say, *All in good fun*. He'd been pleased when I told him his tip was worthy of the King's presence. Genuinely pleased.

Several of us on the street glanced at them as they came, marching and singing, faces ruddy and slightly glazed as if drunk, but happy with broad smiles. But as I peered closer, my smile slowly died.

Where a normal group of dancing, singing musicians would carry banners and flowers and streamers to release into the air, these revelers carried tall spikes. And on the spikes, moving up and down as they marched and danced, were an array of fifteen or so human heads. Some were cleanly cut. Some look like they had been hacked off by an ax that had missed a time or two, the facial expression of the owner of each head showing horror. Some eyes were open and some were closed. Some had seen, and some seemed blissfully unaware when their time had come.

My stomach lurched in warning.

All of us standing along the street stopped what we were doing as we watched the approach. A paperboy was brave enough to ask, "Who are these people, Citizen?"

The leader turned to him and, as happily as if he had been asked if he was having a nice day, replied, "A group of nobles caught in a poker game. Gambling obscene amounts of money with each other while our city starves. We took care of them for the republic!"

"The republic asked you to kill them without trial or chance to defend themselves?" I said without thinking. "I didn't realize the National Guard was short of men to have turned to the town troubadours to carry out capital punishment on its behalf."

The leader turned to me and gave a sunny smile. "We serve the republic without being asked. We are *active* citizens. Patriots, you see. We see a need and we fill it." One of them began to giggle hysterically.

Active citizens. It was a term the republic had adopted to separate the tax-paying, voting men over twenty-five years old from the non-voting men who were young or didn't earn enough money to pay taxes. It had nothing to do with being allowed to slaughter at-will. Their perversion of the rule of law was criminal.

His green eyes tightened on me. "Do I know you?"

My stomach continued to churn but I didn't dare set this one off. If he didn't remember me, that was a good thing.

I shook my head and held my cup to him with a quirk of my head as if it was every day that I saw such a sight first thing in the morning. I willed my knuckles not to shake when one of the faces was swung my way and I saw the lick of light brown hair, the freckles, the wide-open blue eyes... *Henri.*

He was my friend from the Chateau who had kept the horses. For a very long time he had been my only friend until we had a falling out and he disappeared after Christmas the year before. His eyes looked at me, lifelessly, as my cup began to shake in my hand, coffee sloshing over the edge. I forced it still and my knuckles went tight when the leader of the pack, having picked up on my momentary unsteadiness, said to me, with an ebullient voice, "Viva la Révolution, Oui, Citizen?"

His eyes were sharp on me. It was a challenge and a dare. Oh, for the day I could stop lying. When I could just be a man without fear or explanation.

I fought to keep my lips from shaking. "Vive la Révolution," I replied. To do otherwise might unleash the madness upon me and all around me.

My response was convincing enough that he tipped his hat, and they continued down the road, singing their song and frightening everyone on the street in their wake. I watched the back of Henri's head bouncing up and down like a party favor and then turned and retched on the cobblestones.

The morning had soured, and I went back inside the house to see Élise trying to button up the kids' outer coats onto them.

"Bon matin, Zamor, we heard the circus. I was just letting the children out to catch some entertainment."

"No," I said. The whole family looked at me like I was crazy but didn't stop dressing.

Sebastien grabbed little hats off a shelf. "No, what do you mean? The children are missing some fun. There hasn't been a bazaar in a long time."

"That's not a bazaar they should see." Sebastien stopped when he saw my face.

"Tell us." He straightened.

"But... the children."

His shoulders dropped and darkness fell over his spirit as if it was a bird cloaking him. "The children should know. They have to know what's going on. What we have, boys, is a marauding gang of so-called revolutionaries. Carrying their spoils of war and parading them right through Paris as though they haven't a care in the world. It should be a lesson to us all to be careful."

Élise had stopped now, and the relaxed look on her face was gone. "Ridiculous!" she spit out, angry. "They make a mockery of the real work we've done! They use the changes we've made as an excuse to become savages, so they can blame Jacobins!"

I nodded, equally indignant. "They said it was a group of nobles at a card game, but I recognized Henri, my friend from the Chateau." My throat felt ragged with unshed tears. My feelings were hurt in a way I didn't expect in light of what he'd done. I was angry with him, but I didn't want *that*.

"Henri, your horse friend?" Sebastien said. "What would he have been doing with a group of nobles? He was a sans-culottes, wasn't he?"

"Gambling, apparently," I started but stopped. It was something about the way Sebastien said it; the way his eyes avoided mine and the lack of surprise on his face.

"Do you know anything about it?" I asked him.

"What would I know about it?" He joshed, but still his eyes didn't meet mine.

"Sebastien. . ." I said, wanting to cry. "...You didn't...?" His shoulders froze in some inner turmoil and my heart sank. He looked at me and I saw clearly in his eyes. "How could you? How could you have done that? Mon Dieu, Sebastien...!"

"All I did was tell some people that he might possibly be one to watch, and he was. It was a while ago; it might not have anything to do with what I said. I mean, it was only a matter of time. You remember back when you brought him into town, his eyes were everywhere even while he was pretending to be a harmless simpleton. While you were missing, he came back to our clubs, whining about you cutting him out of the action. Claiming to want to join the cause. We only tolerated him because he was with you in the first place. And when we told him he wasn't welcome he told us we would be sorry, right before he disappeared. Do you think he wasn't talking about you? So yes, plenty Jacobins had to wonder about you and questioned your good sense for being with him."

"He was a sans-culottes! We are all sans-culottes! We should be trusting each other!" The disgust I felt must have showed on my face.

"No, you're not a sans-culottes, Zamor, you're a noble servant pretending to be a sans-culotte, as he was. You worked years to earn our trust; you could ill-afford to have your loyalty questioned worrying about him. And believe me, he wasn't worrying about you while he was ingratiating himself to Gaspard, spying for the nobles."

"That's a lie."

"Now I'm a liar? Do you even know what's happening in this country? Do you think the nobles are sitting still while the government decides they now have to pay taxes and no longer get the privileges they've always had? They have no problem throwing their money away on parties and property but ask them to give one livre back to France in taxes, like us commoners have been doing for centuries, and they revolt! And your friend Henri was working with them. Now," he put his hands up in supplication, "I can see you hate me right now. I see it in your face. But save some of that recrimination for yourself."

I couldn't stop shaking my head, willing myself not to cry.

"It wasn't a matter of *if* he would turn on you, he already had! And it wasn't a matter of *if* he would get himself killed but how long it would take. Don't look at me like that, you're no better than me."

"After what I just saw—" I huffed.

"—Where is Gaspard, Zamor?"

The question caught me off-guard and stopped me short.

"What was that merde you told me? That he was going to send someone to question Véronique about stolen goods and you just said, 'Well, I guess I'll leave since I'm no longer wanted', and that's it? You, who killed a man for even *suggesting* he might blackmail you? And you expected me to believe that you would hear Gaspard threaten the woman you love with your own ears and not do something about it?"

I looked around and saw the kids had disappeared, but Élise stood there with not a lick of surprise on her face. He told her.

"I ask again, where is Gaspard, Zamor?"

"Mind your business, Sebastien!"

"This is my business, you stupid idiot! This is all our business. You are like family to me, and I'd do it a thousand times over. Mon Dieu, man, he put Gaspard on Véronique's tail. All I did was put out a word for caution. Why didn't *you* take care of him?"

"I thought Gaspard had tortured him. Maybe he did, and he felt so guilty he couldn't look me in the face. But now I'll never know what happened because of your mouth. You might as well have put a target on his forehead!

You know all it takes is one person speaking against someone to rouse suspicion these days!"

Sebastien's face took on a puzzled expression, his voice low and gentle.

"Oh, now you're going to lecture me about the dangers of reporting someone? I thought we were pretending not to know the power of our words. What happened to 'I can't control what happens afterwards'?"

My words about Madame used against me hit me like a slap in the face and for the first time, I wanted to hit Sebastien. He continued to press his point.

"Well, your friend very clearly put a target on *Véronique's* head, serving her up to the one man who hated you more than life. Yet you stand here almost in tears over him. You've lost your judgement. How could I do it? Easily. Very, very easily, friend."

We glared at each other and my fist clenched. His words ran through me and even though they made sense, the pain hurt more than the logic of them. We were still glaring when pounding on the door reverberated through the house. We both looked at the door. No one pounded on doors like that except for the police.

"Sebastien," Élise said, worried now.

"It's okay," Sebastien said. "Everyone, stay calm." He walked past me and opened the door, which was immediately pushed open as revolutionary guards made their way inside. One of them stepped into the room and looked over the three of us. His eyes swung my way.

"Are you Louis-Benoit Zamor?" He asked me. His cheeks were ruddy.

"I am," I said.

"We come on orders from the Committee of Public Safety."

"I'm the secretary of the Committee of Public Safety," I said, chin up.

"Not anymore. Do you live here?"

"I rent a room." I gestured toward Sebastien. "He's my landlord."

"Can you prove it?" he asked Sebastien.

Sebastien's face had gone white, but he caught on quickly. I saw his mind click with the memory that every week, faithfully, I gave him a little coin and demanded he record it. He went immediately to his shelf where he kept his money log and opened it to the pages recording payment. "I record his payments here."

The log seemed to satisfy the man in charge. "Where does he stay?"

"Upstairs to the right."

Two guards headed up the stairs.

"What am I accused of?" I called up to them.

"Counter-revolutionary activity, of course."

"That's ridiculous!" I said, but I could hear the three guards plowing through my room, pulling papers out of the desk drawer and tearing pamphlets off my walls, going through my satchel, being clumsy with my violin case.

"I expect you'll pay for any walls you destroy," Sebastien blustered, playing the part of a landowner concerned for his property.

"You should have thought about that when you decided to rent space to this man."

"What type of counter-revolutionary activity?" I asked. "I demand to know."

The guards came down the stairs, shaking their heads. "You don't make demands."

The one in charge turned to me. "But if you must know, you're accused of being an accomplice to the crimes of Citizenness du Barry."

"I testified *against* the Citizenness; without me you wouldn't have had a case."

"Whatever you've done, you can explain it to the committee at trial."

They pulled me out of the room. I caught eyes with Sebastien, helpless but sober. There was nothing he could do for me now. We both knew almost all of the people who were pulled before the tribunal these days found their blood running in the street the next.

I thought I'd have more time.

As our carriage moved through the Paris streets, I looked at them as if the sight was my last.

CHAPTER TWENTY-FIVE

They took me to the Conciergerie prison. Even with the cold, the putrid smell of body odor and piss and shit hit me before my eyes had even adjusted to the dank. My hands were tied behind my back, and I followed one guard downstairs into the depths of a place not fit for animals, with holes dug out of stone walls with iron grates for doors. Somewhere water dripped and the mildew was almost stronger than the overwhelming smell of human waste. Even though it was daytime, it was dark in this place. Torches lit the way.

As I passed each cell I glanced in. One cell held a man who sat on the edge of his bed, wracked with sobs. The next man was simply lying there, looking at the ceiling. The next, a tall man was seated up on his bed, leaning his head against the wall. It was the movement of his fingers next to his neck as if he held an instrument that earned him a second look from me and then I burst out.

"Josephe!"

He looked up, his eyes glazed, handsome face dirty, but it was him. He seemed to have to force his eyes to focus on me to see me.

"Is that you, Page?"

I wanted to laugh but if I did so I knew I'd cry.

"Get on, will you!" A kick from behind and I staggered forward a few cells down where I was deposited and my hole shut with a clang of metal. I kicked the bed, and a furry thing jumped out, looking at me like it would fight me for the right to the mattress. I kicked again and it ran off, but it couldn't get far. I knew it remained with me in that cell, waiting for its moment.

I sat down and listened to the noises of prison. I looked around and tried to adjust myself to this new place. Tried to figure out how I'd ended up here when everything I had done had been for my freedom.

"Page," I heard Josephe call, though his voice was weak. "What are you doing here? I thought you were a Jacobin."

"Jacobin!" Someone in another cell picked up on the word and hawked a glob of spit onto the ground, loud enough for us all to hear. "Fucking Jacobins destroyed this country!"

"Shut up!" somebody yelled. "It's not the revolutionaries that's the problem, it's Robespierre!"

"Shut up, unless you want to die!"

I waited for it all to die down; no need getting caught up in the nonsense. And when all had fallen silent again, I answered my friend.

"It seems like very few of us truly want things to get better," I said. "They say I'm an accomplice to counter-revolutionary activity."

Josephe countered with, "They say I stole my troops' money. That I spent it on food, wine, and women instead of buying shoes for my soldiers."

"What? That's madness. You're already a decorated leader; anyone should know you would never do anything like that. You're an honorable man."

"It's my word against another and the other has white skin. It doesn't matter what I say. No matter how many battles I fight and win for the republic, I will always be a black man and always seen as something other than a man. I was a fool. I was such a fool."

"No, not a fool," I said. "Loyal. There's no shame in that."

"Will the Comtesse get you out, do you think, after she stops being angry at you for being a Jacobin?"

"The Comtesse is dead. I was a witness against her at trial, and she was executed."

He fell quiet for a moment and then responded. "If she wasn't moved to give you your freedom in all these years she didn't deserve your loyalty. We all have to make choices at a time like this."

Gratitude caused water to spring to my eyes, but this wasn't the place to show weakness.

Josephe continued, "I had a comfortable life before the government asked me to run the regiment. But this revolution was about bigger things. At least it was at first. The Citizenness formerly known as the Queen was my friend, once. My fondness for her did not change what I felt was right. I was approached and asked to help her escape, but my conscience wouldn't allow it. And now she's dead. We all make choices, Page. We just have to be able to live with them."

The next day they let us out to walk around a small courtyard and Josephe and I found each other again. He explained more about what had happened to him and the man who had accused him of stealing money.

"I was proud of what I was doing, leading a regiment of Black men. But in the end, my title, my lineage... none of it meant anything against the words of one bitter White man," he said. It was cold and our breath came out in puffs of smoke, but it was still better than being downstairs in the dungeon. "Do you think if I had the money I wouldn't have used it for my troops? I asked for it and they never gave it. But, somehow, they reason I misspent funds they can't prove I ever received. Even still, we fought and won on behalf of the republic. Only for me to be called back and sent to this place. And all I can think about in my cell is how much I want... I wish... I just want to play my music. That's all I want."

We were walking in a never-ending circle around the courtyard, all of us strolling along like it was a spring day.

"What happened to your love? The woman you stayed for," Josephe asked me. A streak of pain went through me. I shrugged.

"It just didn't work out."

"That's too bad. We thought you would see us off, Thomas and I. We were surprised when you didn't come to say goodbye, if you wouldn't leave with us."

"I wanted to, but I was ill."

We were interrupted by a guard standing up on a stone bench in the center of the courtyard.

"This happens every day," Josephe said to me. "They call out the names of the ones to go to the guillotine the next day." That explained the sudden tenseness that struck all the men simultaneously. Slowly, methodically, the guard began the list. As I looked around, some men wept, some were stoic, some angry and punching their knuckles bloody into the stone walls. Throughout, Josephe was quiet and still. His eyelids drifted shut and his hand came up to clasp an imaginary violin, the other drawing an imaginary bow across its strings.

It was as if he was taking the sting away from whatever that guard would say. The music in his head providing beauty to whatever trauma might be served up.

I wished I had his talent to compose music out of thin air. I only had the memory of playing *his* tunes, and never had I done so under this pressure.

Eventually, the guard stopped speaking and I realized he hadn't said our names. They ushered us back into the building. Though he'd been miles away in his head, as we walked back Josephe seemed to deflate. He caught me looking at him and said simply, "It takes a lot out of you, happening every day. I'm just so tired."

I was tired and I had only just got there.

The next day they put another mattress and man in my cell. He was a thief who liked to expose himself in public. Even now he looked across at me from the other side of the cell as if it was all he could do to keep from stripping himself bare to show me his goods.

"Louis-Benoit Zamor," called a guard. The man shuffled over to unlock my cell. "Time for trial."

Trial! Finally, a chance to defend myself.

I was ushered into a room already filled with spectators and the committee with its tribunal. Though I recognized many members, unfortunately, I also recognized the lead questioner. I felt him before I saw him. *Fouquier-Tinville.*

The room was full and noisy with high windows. I looked around and also saw Sebastien and Valentin sitting in the galley. Sebastien was risking himself by being here and being seen to support me, I knew. I was still angry over Henri but it meant something that Sebastien was there. He looked concerned and nervous.

My questioner opened the discussion with a report on my history of having been a palace page and my closeness to the royal family. But he wasn't an attorney or an actor who knew how to drum up suspense to make a compelling case. He was a man who couldn't tolerate a Black man who had questioned him once. Now he was frothing at the mouth to get me killed for no real reason.

My heart pounded from fear of the unknown. I looked around to try to get a bead on someone, anyone, to find out where I stood. So many people I didn't recognize. A lot of them were not even paying attention to me at all.

"As close as you were to the Citizenness du Barry, you understand we find it hard to believe you were unaware of her activity. I understand you were in her rooms every morning, every night, and all the hours in between. Closer than a lover, they say. Tell us about the hidden valuables."

"What hidden valuables?" I asked.

"Citizenness du Barry herself described the many hidden jewels and items of value throughout the grounds of the Chateau de Louveciennes. She made us a very explicit list of everything she'd buried. May I remind the members of the tribunal of the wealth of valuables buried on the grounds of the Chateau de Louveciennes." He then proceeded to systematically list jewelry. "And you were her most trusted servant. As a member of the Committee of Public Safety, why did it take her being on the verge of death for us to learn about the hidden valuables. She attempted to use that very list to bargain for her life, like the corrupt aristocrat she was. Are you going to tell us you didn't know?"

Yes, I knew she'd buried things on the grounds but how was I supposed to know exactly where? The only thing I knew about for sure was the thing I wanted to forget—the head of her murdered lover Brissac.

The questioner was doing the very thing I always feared; he was yoking me to her in the minds of the tribunal. He was suggesting to them that we were a package deal. Partners in crime.

"I was unaware of the jewels."

"You lie to us now, Page?"

My lips went dry, and I knew my fear was doing me no favors. I had to fall back on what I did have, what I had honed—wit, a smart tongue and arrogance. The arrogance of a king. I knew how to recreate that. And as long as I was alive, I could pretend, even now.

I let my voice ring out firmly, more forcefully, a hint of noble disdain in my tone. "I ask you, as much of an immoral deviant as you think I am, if I knew of these jewels would I not have taken them for myself?" Everyone knew about my reputation at the Palace, and no one would think it out of character for me to steal anything that wasn't nailed down.

"Perhaps you wanted to provide just this excuse should you get caught."

I shrugged. "I'd rather have a fortune in my hand than an alibi for a crime. A crime I haven't committed, by the way. It was the Comtesse who used her money to make a home for herself in England, not me. I have barely enough to pay for a roof over my head. Had I known there were jewels underfoot I'd have taken at least a bauble or two to feed myself."

He frowned. There were grumblings. It occurred to me there were very few people interested in punishing me. Could it be that the one standing in front of me was the only one?

"You lived in that house. You expect us to believe you didn't help her?

"Why would I?" Once again, I leaned into my reputation as a selfish sycophant. "Why would I help the ruling class that has held me to a lowly servant all my life? I loathed Jeanne du Barry. I detested the royal court. The only thing I have been passionate about is my duties as a member of this republic. My country asked for my help, and I gave it and would do it again."

His face twisted and he pounded on the table in front of him with frustration. "What about all that you knew about Citizen Louis Capet? You suspected he would attempt to escape. Why? How did you know?"

So it was about that conversation years back, deceased King Louis XVI, now called the citizen Louis Capet, and his betrayal. This man was still upset that I'd dared question his judgement or, more likely, that he'd been proven so wrong. The embarrassment was eating at him, and he wanted to take the pound of flesh from me.

"Am I to be blamed for the actions of Louis Capet, now? You blame a lowly servant for the actions of a king? You, my fellow Jacobin, in our meetings you told me time and again how wrong I was to suggest the former king might not be as true to the republic as he appeared. *I* warned my club members with all the passion I could muster—based on a lifetime living in the shadow of kings—that I believed Louis Capet was not true to his word. It was *you* who told me how wrong I was. It was *you* who shut down my words as the ravings of a foolish servant. It was *you* who—"

"Enough! In your effort to toss the spotlight off yourself you prove how much alike you are to your deceased Madame. You will also do anything and give up anyone to save your own hide." He turned to the tribunal. "I remind you, gentlemen, of all the pamphlets and stories written about this man, if he can be called such. He conveniently joined the Committee of Public Safety when it was obvious his benefactress would be tried and convicted. He gave her up in his selfish attempt to save his own skin just like she gave up those jewels to save hers. At least we can say she was a French woman. Here he sits, a foreigner on French soil. If a Frenchwoman lost her head, he deserves at least as much."

My lips trembled with sudden fury and hurt. I didn't think anything he could say would hurt me, but to call me a foreigner made me feel as lost as I'd felt all those years ago, pinned to the floor of a ballroom and forced to perform. Like I was less than human. Not a part of this country. Just something to be bought, sold, played with by the real people and tossed out when done.

They took me back to my cell.

"How did it go, Page?" Josephe asked me after I was back and deposited in my cell. The rodent in the corner eyed me, only its fur and the reflection from candlelight on its eyes showing me how closely it watched me. My cell mate was a heap on his bed, deadweight. The echo of Josephe's voice was calming in the quiet night.

"I don't know," I said, my voice craggy in contrast, heavy with latent fear. "My mouth gets me into trouble."

"Ah, so our own voices raised in desperate defense convict us as overly passionate and enthusiastic traitors. Can't keep your mouth shut and can't yell. What else is there? Did you remind them what you've done for this republic?"

"I tried."

He was quiet for a while and then he said: "When they arrested me, they told me it was Thomas who reported me—that *he* claimed I had stolen from the regiment."

That explained a lot. His sadness and depression–his general malaise. I grew angry.

"And what do you believe?"

He hesitated again and sighed. "Thomas is my friend from years back. If he did what they said..."

"If..."

"*If* he did what they said it would break me. I know it seems strange. I felt badly turning against Citizenness Capet, but she and her husband took more than they had a right to. I truly feel there was justice in the two of them being tried for their crimes. And no matter what they say about us being friends, one can never truly be a friend with a monarch because one can never be on common, equal ground. I never forgot I was there to serve her. But Thomas and I were equals; even though I teased him like I was his better, we both knew the truth. I valued Thomas and our friendship was real."

"Josephe, if he did what they said it would be a bitter surprise because the man I know was one of integrity. More than you or I put together. Lying is what some people will do if the lie serves them, Josephe. Whoever spoke against you to put you where you are would have no qualms about setting the two of you against each other. That avocat of law that questions me, he said the Qu—Citizenness Capet—defiled her own child. That he dare to say such filth out loud and claim the child said it tells you all you need to know. It is what the worst among us do to destroy our spirits and keep us from fighting. If we are to survive, we must remember what we *know*, not what we hear. I don't believe Thomas would ever do that to you. If Thomas had any issues with you, he would stand up to you and call you a thief to your face, not run behind your back to report you to a man he barely even knows. Not the man I know. Not the man *we* know."

"I don't want to believe it, I trusted him with my life, but this revolution has changed people, Zamor." His voice cracked now and I knew he was struggling for composure.

"If you don't want to then don't until you have a true reason to believe it other than rumor. Remember the man you knew. Mon Dieu, look at the case against me. They are trying to convince me that I did the opposite of what actually happened. It's what they do, Josephe," I repeated. "And in my case, they might succeed. For all it matters. I might lose myself to the beast, yet."

My words sent my cellmate into peals of laughter causing my lips to quirk upwards with the ridiculousness of it all. I leaned my head back against the wall and couldn't help but let out a little chuckle myself. Laugh or go insane.

The next day they came for me in my cell, and they didn't even call out for me.

"Come on," the guard said, swinging open the door. I was jostled out by two guards. "Hey, Page," my cellmate said. I hadn't even known he knew who I was. I looked back and he had stripped his pants down to his ankles to flash me with his sad, shriveled privates. "A proper goodbye, Governor!" he called, swinging his jewels and smiling.

"Put your clothes on, deviant!" the guard called. My head swam in a fog as I realized this was it. I passed Josephe's cell and, unlike the other times I passed his cell when he was lethargic and sitting on his bed playing imaginary music, this time he was standing upright, hands clutching the bars, eyes fevered.

"Zamor," he said to me in a fierce growl, his expression eager and scared, as if suddenly he had a lot to say and no time to say it. His look must have matched mine. "And *you* are one of my closest friends, too. Remember the *mus*-ic," he said. "Listen to the music and let it take you to a better place. Close your eyes and imagine being on the stage at Versailles, in the Opera Hall, playing beside me. Listen to the music and let it save you. Someday we will play together in heaven, mon ami." *My friend.*

I nodded to him, my mouth suddenly too dry to speak. I clutched his hands over the bars of the cell. *Yes, yes, I heard. Yes, I will do that!* I said those words with my eyes until a push got me moving again.

They pushed me along, up the stairs, and I steeled myself for what was next.

I wasn't fooling myself about whether or not I deserved to die, but where I went wrong in my choices, that was what plagued me. Finally, we came to the gate outside and I looked for the cart. The ugly, lumbering cart with benches on both sides. I would sit in the spot where Madame had just a short time before and end up with my head in the same basket. It was almost enough to make me laugh, like the man in the dungeon. Laugh at the ridiculousness of life.

But the cart didn't come. Instead, the guard faced me, then took up my shackled wrists and unlocked my handcuffs. He led me to the outer gate with a push.

"You're free to go."

"What?" I blinked away the water in my eyes, the cold winter air seeping through my thin shift. He unlocked the gate and pushed me, again. I stumbled ahead outside of the gate, taking a few steps in isolation. I turned and watched him close the gate behind me, watched their backs as they walked away from me, back into the prison. I looked around and took a few more steps, my eyes squinting from the light of day. Then, I noticed three figures across the way. Holding my palm up to shield me from the glare, I recognized Sebastien, Valentin, and George Grieve.

Grieve. The man with the sandy-colored hair and strange eyes whose sole purpose was to indict Jeanne du Barry.

He looked small now; lost and devoid of fearfulness or anything to be afraid of. It was as if with Madame's death, his purpose had exorcised itself from his thin frame. He had no more use. Until, maybe, today.

I walked up to them, eyes on the one I trusted the least. I didn't ask Grieve why he'd gone after Madame. I didn't ask him why he'd freed me. And I didn't thank him for his part in my release. For all I knew, he was the one who had me imprisoned in the first place.

He turned and walked away and left me with Sebastien and Valentin. Where he went after that, I didn't know and didn't care.

Chapter Twenty-Six

But I couldn't leave things as they were. I had woefully few friends and I couldn't spare even one. Two days later, I went to pay a visit to Robespierre.

This Max Robespierre was different than the first one I'd met. That first one had held calm energy and the conviction of someone who believes he's right. Someone who believed in justice. The man behind the desk now was skittish, his eyes skipping to the door, to the window, to the fireplace... rarely settling on one thing for long. His shoulders were hunched as if in defense.

Two men stood by—one by the door and one by the window—equally as nervous and on the look-out, for what I did not know.

"Citizen Robespierre, thank you for seeing me," I said, stepping inside to stand before his desk.

He looked up and then dropped his gaze to the papers before him on the desk just as quickly, jotting and signing as we spoke. "I've given you your freedom and your citizenship. What do you want now from this republic?"

My eyes blinked in surprise. It was a spiteful thing to say when I'd already given all to the republic. But I wasn't there to argue with the man who single-handedly turned over a government.

"I truly appreciate all the republic has done for me. Though I must admit, I don't understand what I did to lose my position on the Committee and land in prison."

He smirked a little. "You don't understand? Let me explain it, then. You were there enjoying the spoils of our society as much as any noble. Just because you weren't noble-born doesn't mean you weren't as guilty as Citizenness du Barry in taking advantage of the people of France. Now, you did very well to bring her to us. It was the right thing for our society. But when one looks at how you did it..." He looked up from his papers, disgust curling his features. "When one considers what you did to the person who fed and clothed you—the one person who truly loved you for all of your life—turning on her as if she were a stranger on the street...? It's obvious you are a soulless human being. Bereft of human compassion. I heard about the execution. The woman like a mother to you screaming and crying out for mercy and you standing there like a statue. Unmoved. Some might say, inhuman. If I could charge you for being a horrible person, I would. If I could take *Jacobin* from the moniker of your name, I would do that, too. You're no friend of mine and no longer fit material for the Committee."

Blood rushed into my cheeks hot and fast as I absorbed the insults. I once almost admired him. I once thought he was a rational human being. I hoped all the rumors I'd heard about him were lies but now I knew they weren't. He used to be a man but now he was a twisted thing who dared sit in judgement of me.

"I'm sorry to hear you say that, Max..."

"Citizen Robespierre to you."

"*Citizen* Robespierre. I find it a bit unfair of you to castigate me after holding my freedom like a carrot, pressuring me to turn her in. I mean, you could have easily just given me my citizenship if the thought of sending her to the beast was morally repugnant to you."

"Oh, but then you wouldn't have had so much fun. And it was hard earning it, wasn't it?" His mouth twisted and his eyes darkened with anger as he looked me over. "How much wine did you drink, Page? How much tender meat did you gorge yourself on? How many items of the finest silk are still in your closet, shoes of the best hand-stitched leather on your feet...?"

"I don't know, Citizen, I never tallied those things but perhaps you can tell me yours since I just saw on a tray right outside your door a fine plate of veal and cheeses and a bottle of red wine waiting to be consumed. My mouth was watering just waiting to be received. I thought to myself, how lucky I was, about to enjoy the modest repast of a fellow, humble Jacobin. But I've been here and not been offered anything so I see the feast is just for you."

It just slipped out. But his eyes cut up to me, quickly, his lips pinched.

"You dare compare yourself to me?"

"Of course not. I would never claim us to be equals, Citizen. Nor friends. It breaks my heart to have fallen out of your favor by doing what you asked. But considering how you treat your friends, perhaps it is best that I'm not one."

He took a beat and dropped his quill down into the ink, then glared up at me. "What is the reason for your visit, Zamor? If you think I'll let you speak before the assembly, it will be over my cold, dead body. I have little patience for your passive barbs so get to it, and quickly."

I had almost forgotten I'd come for a favor. It was surely a dead cause, now. I straightened my lapels.

"Very well, merci. There is a man in the Conciergerie who shouldn't be there. Josephe Bologne, the—"

"—Citizen Bologne, the former Chevalier de Saint-Georges. Yes, I know of it. He was one of the Austrian's lovers."

"That is merely a story, all untrue."

"He's been accused of having stolen money from the National Guard because, like you, he has a penchant for expensive things. I've been told that while traveling with his regiment he would often be seen in town playing music and living the life of a playboy with his republic's money. Now, this republic needs many things, but it does not need a traveling band of musicians or a man whose sole exercise is bedding half the women in France and beyond."

"With respect, Citizen Bologne had inherited money and property from his deceased father that supported him. He would never steal the money meant to put shoes on his soldiers' feet. He served honorably, defending the republic against foreign adversaries and helped to thwart the traitor DeMouriez, who would have smuggled the widow Capet to freedom."

"You rattle off his accomplishments like a proud mother."

"Just a proud Frenchman, Citizen."

"I grow weary of this. People constantly coming here to plead cases but usually it's their own. You barely made it out of the Conciergerie yourself and yet you're here putting yourself at risk for his sake. Why?"

I sighed and told the truth. "It's simple, really. He is the best representative of us. He is a man who was born to a slave woman with every right to hate the country that put her in chains. Instead, once here he embraced his education and became all that France endeavors to be. A master fencer, master composer, master swordsman, master horseman… have you ever heard him *play*? I tell you, Citizen, he is the finest musician in all of France. I strip my bias and tell you, frankly, one day France will be very sorry for abusing this man. If he is not freed, they will look back and they will say that France destroyed the most talented man this country has ever produced simply on the word of a man who hates people with dark skin."

"Interesting. Knowing the little I do about you I would have thought that being the most talented man in France was a distinction you saved for yourself."

"No, Citizen. I am only a page."

Robespierre's face twisted a bit in what I believed might have been a smile. "This revolution has been as productive as expected but, also, just as painful as I feared. I didn't plan for it to work out like this, but here we are. I will protect this new republic no matter what it takes." He shuffled his papers. "There has been no firm evidence against the Citizen Bologne and not enough people to care about him for a trial to take place. You have saved your friend's life. You are all out of favors, Page. Pray, hope you need no more."

Chapter Twenty-Seven

I didn't plan to need more. I planned to thrive in my new life.

And I had developed an appreciation for fresh air. An uneasiness had settled over Sebastien's household, so I left the house when I could. Walking through Paris I almost felt at peace, realizing I could come and go as I wanted. Freedom was still new to me and I enjoyed it in small sips like fine wine.

It was during one of those small sips—strolling through the city center with my hands in my pockets, eyes on the ground—that I heard the rattle of a horse's reins up ahead. I glanced up and stopped in my tracks. Up the road, only two or three body lengths ahead, I saw her. It was Véronique!

She sat atop a small two-seat buggy being pulled by one horse which she slowed.

I kicked into action, stepping quickly to hide myself in the shadow of a building. Self-preservation.

But you can be together, now! Said the little voice from inside me.

My heart beat faster at the notion, my breath hitched in my chest.

She climbed down carefully, making sure her skirt didn't impede her descent. It was a plain blue dress. Nothing like the fancy gowns she was capable of stitching with her bare hands. The memory of her wearing her own gown in preparation to hand over to Jeanne du Barry, flowed through my head. That memory of the brilliant fabric against her warm brown skin, her swirl that allowed the soft silk to billow and float down again, the way her dark brown tightly coiled hair lay against the column of her neck...

My eyelids fluttered back to the present as she secured the horse to the post.

Go to her!

My mouth went dry with possibility.

Her hair was restrained in a sunny yellow wrap. Véronique of Burgundy. Véronique of the East! That's what I used to call her in front of people. *My* Véronique, is what I used to whisper into her skin as I trailed kisses the length of her and back again.

All this in mere seconds. I was frozen in indecision as she finished securing the horse and then shook herself to, as if trying to gather courage. Then, tilting her chin up, slightly, she walked around the horse post and up to the doorway of a fabric shop storefront.

She would need the courage. Women weren't allowed to run their own businesses, still. And there was a restricted guild of tailors, who were the only ones legally authorized to sell their dressmaking services. And yet, there she was. Lies would have to be told and she would need to be convincing.

But, by now, I didn't doubt she could do it. My Véronique could do anything.

A passerby opened the door for her and she walked inside, neck firm. I watched while my fingers shook.

What if it wasn't too late for us?

I was free now, to live my life as I wanted! But, I had blood on my hands. I'd never told her I was a murderer and never would have, before. But things were different now. Especially after all the horrible things I'd said to her, I would have to admit to everything. I would have to lay myself bare. And maybe I'd consider it if ... if I thought she could...

My teeth worked on my lower lip as I saw the store owner step away and then return with a bolt of fabric. A look of quick and fleeting pleasure floated across her features such that I could see even from the road. But it was gone almost as quickly as it'd come. If you blinked you would have missed it, because the little worried frown was back. Probably due to the cost.

Reality set in. I'd said horrible things, hurt her terribly. Even if she could forgive that, I knew she could never accept the things I'd done.

I could have stood there all day watching her but the longer I was there the greater the chance she would catch me. Hands in my pocket, I continued up the street until coming to a small shop that sold little expensive things some of us still bought. I slipped inside the non-descript building and let my eyes grow accustomed to the darkness caused by mostly-shuttered windows. No need to invite eyes on luxury in this day and age.

I walked over to the shelves that held my favorite tins of caviar. A consolation prize ... and all that. Nothing near to the value of what I had lost.

Two women walked behind me as they chatted.

"...It will be the talk of the season," one of them said.

"I don't have a clue what I'll wear. All the business I gave to my dressmaker and you know he moved to England."

"Everybody's moved to England, why on earth are we still here?"

They were browsing the shelves for little pots of hand lotion and didn't even notice me.

"France is my home. Besides, it's the noisy ones they notice. So long as we keep to ourselves and do what they ask, we're fine. The sans culottes are too busy killing themselves, the idiots. And our noblemen know how to form armies, too. This whole mess blow over, eventually. And, truly, the parties are all the more exciting when you have to go in disguise."

So, that was what they were doing now? Living their lives, but doing it quietly.

I had things I wanted to say, of course. But I had only just saw the love of my life and I still felt the shakes, even as I took several tins from the shelf.

"Pardonez-moi, Mesdames," I said to them in my softest, most respectful voice. They looked up only because my voice, with its noble clip, made me noticeable. I overheard you express concern about a dress for a party. I happen to know the woman who used to dress Madame Jeanne du Barry is taking clients...

"What?" they looked back and forth at each other. Eagerness won. "I happen to know the man who was her tailor, you lie."

"No, that was her official tailor and dressmaker. As you know, women are not allowed to have the title. But at the Chateau du Barry, Madame and many of her guests employed the services of a woman, very quietly. I worked at the Chateau, you see. I've seen her work. It is exceptional. I couldn't tell you for sure if she still takes customers but it might be worth checking. Her name is Véronique Clair. She lives in a little town not too far from here called Croissy-sur-Seine. I know she would appreciate discreetness."

"Madame always cut a fine figure," said one woman. The other looked at me.

"And who are you, Monsieur?"

"I'm..." I hesitated. It wouldn't do for word to get back to her. "No one important. Just another house servant."

I wanted to help her even if I couldn't have her. To me, she would always be the woman who could make her way where there was, seemingly, no way. But she deserved something good to come to her, easily, for once. She had the courage to live her life by following her own moon. And ... I wanted her to be happy. One of us should get what we wanted.

Chapter Twenty-Eight

We tore bits of a baguette and passed it around the table. We'd eat half and Élise would wrap the rest for breakfast, so we were careful not to take too much.

I'd been out of prison for about two months, but things were still tense between Sebastien and I. He was always in a bad mood to match mine that wanted to pop out at any moment.

"Did you hear?" Élise asked her husband. "The Hébertists went to trial this morning and are scheduled to die tonight. They say it's because of all of the wild parties, but rumors have it they were plotting against Max."

Since the very beginning, the Hébertists had been the primary group of slithering snakes that most wanted to do the greatest damage to the country. Held at bay in the beginning, they rose in popularity after Louis Capet tried to abandon his kingdom. After that, they published their own radical paper. Most recently, they created a form of religion called the Cult of Reason, designed to fill the void in a country that had been de-Christianized. But Cult celebrations were light on religion and heavy on debauchery and drunkenness. Rumor had it, orgies abounded.

"How many?" I asked.

"Twenty or so, it seems."

At once! It was to be another blood bath. I had no care for Hébertists. Still...

"That's not appropriate table talk," Sebastien groused, dipping his bread into his soup and hovering over his bowl like a dog protecting a bone. I looked up, surprised at the bite in his tone.

"We've spoken about things like this before at dinner," she said, defensive.

"We shouldn't have," he said, looking up at her with reproach. "We have children at this table."

My eyes widened. Of the two of them, Élise was not the one to be criticized for lack of parenting skills. The kids began looking back and forth between their parents and her face flushed. I sipped a spoonful of soup and changed the subject.

"Well, I have good news. I spoke with Danton…"

"…Can we talk about anything other than this damned government?" Sebastien said.

"What else would we have to talk about, Sebastien?" I asked him. "It's the only thing we have in common. No need to snap at us; we didn't make the rules."

He dug back into his food as if he couldn't find an answer. I proceeded and spoke to Élise, as she was rational.

"Danton has gotten permission from the National Assembly to allow people of African blood from Saint-Domingue to speak before the Assembly. They're going to make the case against slavery."

"That's wonderful." She smiled. "Isn't that good news, Sebastien?"

He grunted.

"Of course, I wanted to speak," I went on, taking another sip. "But Max told me I'd speak to the Assembly over his cold, dead body and all that, so… Georges Danton had kind words for me. He complimented me on my speech last year at the Jacobin Club. He said, 'I listened to that fantastic speech you gave at the club!' He even clapped his hands, overcome by the memory of my words."

"As he should have been." She smiled again. "Your speech was magnificent. I'll be honest, I never expected it. And for you to speak for women the way you did…"

"Oh, aren't you the hero of women," Sebastien said, sipping his café. "Do I need to remind you, Élise, that he hated Olympe de Gouges?"

"I didn't hate her; I hated the play she wrote about me. What is your problem, Sebastien?" I asked him.

He shrugged. "I'm just sick and tired of your steady focus on yourself, my friend." He stood and tossed his napkin on the table. "I'll be out for a little while," he announced. His footsteps sounded through the house as he left through the kitchen, shutting the door harder than he needed to.

"Don't pay him any mind," she said. "These last few months have been hard on him. He's taking it out on us all. Go on, tell me what Danton said."

I smiled. "He called me an unexpected champion of the people and told me I should be speaking at the Assembly. Of course, I told him that Max won't have it. I even told him my thoughts about writing a book."

"But Max has shut most of the presses and is censoring the others. It's almost as bad as when Louis Capet was on the throne."

"Yes, that's what Georges said. I suppose my book will have to wait a little longer. But then he brought up a conversation he and I had some time ago when I mentioned to him that he should have someone from Saint-Domingue who understands the immorality of slavery speak to the Assembly. It never even occurred to him to have someone of African blood represent Saint-Domingue. If I can't speak at the Assembly, I'm glad someone who truly knows about slavery can. He told me that there are émigré slave owners threatening to join with English to fight against the new republic all so they can keep owning slaves."

"That's treason!"

"Oui." I drawled the word, leaning toward her conspiratorially. "They said they'd rather have their slaves than be faithful to France. They say losing their free labor would leave them bankrupt. And if that's not enough, they're encouraging other nobles still here on the mainland to oppose the government, too."

She shook her head, tearing off a piece of bread as she said thoughtfully, "It's sick all on its own but, honestly, I can't see the republic standing for threats of treason. Not as determined as Max is to root out all opposition."

And she was right.

A short while later, the representatives from Sainte-Domingue spoke before the National Assembly. The revolt had proven the enslaved people of Saint-Domingue were fierce warriors. Best to have them on the side of France if the émigrés were trying to start another war.

Danton gave a full-throated endorsement of the abolition of slavery and the National Assembly voted to abolish it. On February 4, 1794, slavery in France and all its colonies was finally deemed illegal.

Finally! *My brethren were free!*

***

Shortly thereafter, Max Robespierre had had enough of the Cordeliers and Georges Danton in particular. Against the will of most common supporters, on April 4, 1794, Georges Danton and his top followers were rounded up, tried, and convicted that same day.

And with a *hush*… and a *swish*… fifteen times, Max Robespierre was fully in power.

Chapter Twenty-Nine

I was a boat without direction. Any leader I might have followed was gone. I couldn't write. I was lost.

Danton's death had shocked many of us. We just never thought Max would do it to a *close* friend.

Almost immediately after having Danton killed, Max organized a celebration of a new religion he'd created called the *Cult of the Supreme Being*. Then, he passed the *Law of 22 Prairial* that decreed that anyone accused of counter-revolutionary activity could be convicted without trial or evidence. Since I knew how he felt about me, I couldn't help but think he was waiting for me to breathe his way so he could smite me.

Reading the newspaper at the dinner table, I groused out loud. "We're acting like we have no power, Sebastien. When did we turn into mice? You, me and Valentin should go over to Max's office and—"

"—Shut up."

"What?"

"Shut up, I said. You, me and Valentin will do nothing but live our lives and let the government do what it will. Keep our heads down and try not to be noticed. Just like we went to that hellish celebration and smiled for two hours, pretending to be happy, while crying inside. We'll do it and shut up about it because we have to. Because we want to live. Have you even noticed that Valentin has been kicked out of the Mountain? Valentin! If

Max can do that to his greatest supporter, what do you imagine he will do to us?" he asked, as if disgusted with me.

"It's easy for you," he continued. "You have no family to worry about. But you won't put mine at risk by spouting off. You say anything in this house even remotely counter-revolutionary and I'll turn you in myself. That's a promise. So shut the fuck up."

Me, Élise, and the children stared at him as he dug into his bowl of stew, staring into the bowl, a frown on his forehead.

Gone was the Jacobin I knew. Sebastien was a shell of his former self. But I wouldn't push him, not today.

I shifted my eyes back to the paper and read some of the next article out loud for the table. The story was regaling the brilliance of France's medical advances and this new thing called internal surgery. My eyelid began to twitch. I hadn't yet dispelled of the last of my enemies; making him pay seemed a reasonable use of my time and energy.

"I'll find him," I said, chewing the delicious stew with bits of chicken, vegetables, and potatoes. "He thinks I forgot what he did, but I'll get that bastard who cut me. Thinks he can just get away with it, well... he'll be sorry. I'll make him pay."

"Mon Dieu, do it then and stop whining," Sebastien drawled, his angry eyes raising to find me. It was as if my very voice infuriated him. "And when you're caught and sent to prison, there will be no trial. Max will just send you to the beast and I won't be there begging for your life. Go ahead, Citizen Strong Man. Go make *everyone* pay."

His rudeness drew Élise's eyes to him.

"He's been complaining about that man since he got here," he told her. "The world has moved on and I'm tired of hearing it."

"Well, I'm tired of *you*," came the wittiest reply I could think of at the moment, so off-kilter at Sebastien's obvious anger toward me. "I *am* going to do something about it."

"When?"

I stood up from the table, indignant. My face was hot.

"Where is he going, Maman?" The little one asked as I stalked to the door.

"Says he's going to get justice, son," Sebastien told his son, derision in his voice.

I moved the sticky, brown blood-soaked blanket from under the door so I could open it. A puddle of blood gushed inside onto the floor. Sebastien got up and gave me a dirty look. The second I stepped outside, turning to finish a thought, he slammed the door in my face.

He was one to talk. I'd been doing things all my life. I could take care of one butcher.

It was dinnertime, but with all the activity I was sure there would be a government official or two still at work. Sebastien had goaded me, but he was right. It was time for me to do more than complain about the man who had cut me open. I didn't want to go to prison, so I would do it the right way. The government needed to know that there were wayward men out in the world cutting on people without permission.

The rain drizzled, compelling me to pull my hood up as I walked the sparsely populated streets to City Hall at the Hôtel de Ville in the rain. It was quiet in the late afternoon rain, and when I rounded a corner to the building I was surprised to see groups of guards and police gathered around. I kept walking, noticing how the people spoke in serious tones, pointing every which way. I entered the building and dropped the hood from my head once inside.

Though candles were lit in sconces on the wall, the emptiness of the building told me that maybe no one was working after all. A scuffling sound caught my attention from the second floor. I climbed the stairs and, seeing a light from under a door that was slightly ajar, I walked down the hall and pushed the door open. The room was not much of anything, dwarfed by a desk with a single lit candle in a holder on top. The candlelight cast shadows that almost obscured the figure in the chair behind the desk, back to the door. I stepped inside.

He was shuffling around in a bag. Happy to have caught him before leaving for home, I waited patiently. From behind, he appeared disheveled—clothes torn and hair messy in tufts on his head—as if he'd been in a fight. His movements told me he hadn't heard me arrive, his hand slipped into his bag and pulled out a handful of sheafs of money, putting them onto the desk. The movement drew my eyes to notice a revolver that already sat on the desk before him. I cleared my voice.

"Go away," he said, then turned to look.

"Max?" I said, surprised.

"What are you doing here? Who's with you?" He looked around me, craning to see behind me.

"No one." I reached back and closed the door so he could focus and stop looking so nervous. "What are you doing here, why aren't you at your office? Why are you here so late? Where are your guards?"

He continued to fumble in his bag. "Get out and then close the door behind you."

"I came to file a report. A complaint. There's a doctor cutting people up..."

"Do I look like I want to hear about your problems?" he hissed, spittle spraying from his mouth as he glared at me. The foam caught on the edge of his lip like he was a foaming mad dog. His eyes, bloodshot; a vein popped out on his forehead. "Mon Dieu, as sure as the sun rises in the morning Louis-Benoit Zamor will have something to complain about! Get out of here!"

I hardly thought anything I'd done tonight was enough to generate this level of distress. On a normal day, I would have left to keep from annoying him. Max was a dangerous man these days. But curiosity and the lack of guards made me imprudent. "What's going on, then? What's happened?"

He was rifling through his bills and slapped his hand against the desk in annoyance, obviously unhappy with what he had. He held his head in both of his hands for a moment, thinking. As was I.

Money. A gun. No guards. Desperation. And all those officers crowded in the streets. It clicked into place.

"Are they after you, Max?"

His eyes shot up to me. He stood up, shuffling the things from the desk back into the bag, sloppily, with one sweep of his arm. Bills and papers fell onto the floor as he headed towards the door, his mind already onto what was next.

It was happening again. He wasn't the first leader I knew who turned tail and ran when things got tough. The last one had been caught by Max himself.

I thought of that celebration he'd planned for the Supreme Being. I thought of Brissot and all his followers being marched to their deaths. Danton and his followers. Olympe de Gouges. The many, countless names and faces since he put the law into place that allowed people to be cut down on no more than a whisper or innuendo. People cut down by lies from people annoyed at small slights and petty grievances, all because of him. And, yes, I thought of me, and how as soon as he no longer needed me, he threw me in jail, just to show me he could. He made a move to leave.

"No, no..." I said, stepping into his path in front of the door. He stopped, his face confused.

"What are you doing? Get out of the way!" he said. His bag was under his arm as if he didn't dare take the time to put it over his shoulder. He stepped forward and I blocked him, again. "Get out of my way, Zamor. Are you mad?"

If I was wrong, I'd be food for the beast by morning. No trial and not a moment's hesitation. But I was feeling the fury of something I hadn't felt for a while: anger at the hypocrisy. The unequal treatment. It was the very reason we'd started the revolution. Anger at what he was doing now made me reckless.

"I have something to say," I said in a clipped tone. "We had something wonderful with this revolution, and you perverted it. If those police out there are coming for you, then I'm going to help them put you behind bars where you belong."

"Get out of my way," he almost yelled but caught himself and lowered his voice to barely above a whisper. "Don't make a mistake you can't come back from, page."

I wasn't a large man by any means. He was taller than me, as most were. But I was about the same size as he was. Likely, I had better arm strength. He wasn't going anywhere.

"All those people you stood as judge and jury over," I said. "Why should you get to leave without justice?"

"I'm not going to stand here and listen to nonsense from you. We wouldn't have equality today if people like me didn't do the ugly things that other people don't have the stomach for. Changing a country isn't pretty, page. It's bloody. *Somebody* has to be brave enough to do the hard things to make it happen. I will accept the blame if it frees my beloved country, but that's all. I don't deserve to be crucified for doing the hard thing. The *right* thing."

"We had something wonderful and look what you've done. You killed a lot of good people. You said I had to pay for my crimes, why not you? Max, the Incorruptible, what about justice for you? You're a murderer. Maybe they'll give you a day in court, unlike what you've been giving to others."

"Says the murderer of women."

"*You* had Jeanne du Barry put to death because you wanted to and used me to do it. And now you judge me?"

"I *will* judge you! You are the embodiment of all the debauchery and immorality of the age of kings. She had to die—we couldn't take the Austrian and not take the Favorite—but seeing you as witness against her made me physically ill. You were so eager on that stand, frothing at the mouth to see her dead. Look at you now, not an ounce of regret. Not an ounce of shame. Walking around Paris a free man with your head up as if proud..."

If I didn't know better, I wouldn't have believed this was the same man who had pressured me for years. But he was revealing the truth. It wasn't the testimony that irked him; it was the fact that it was *me*. That I showed no visible remorse. That I wasn't riddled with guilt. His disdain for me was palpable.

"Perhaps you aren't the only one who believes wrongs need to be righted. Or maybe you're laying your own guilt on me."

"I used to think you were a victim until you began playing with me. Dangling the evidence I wanted in my face and denying it, even as you knew it would be used for the good of the country. You're *worse* than du Barry. She, at least, was clearly devoted to her adopted noble class. And at least she was French. You played your hand only when and how it suited you. Who do you think you are?"

"I'm everything this country made me."

"All your talk about abolition and freeing your brethren. I look at you, this boy who calls himself a man, who hid behind a woman's skirt and then cut her down without a second thought, and I'm disgusted. *Both* of you should have been put to death, Du Barry and Du Barry's Page; *together*, just as you lived! Together, just as you sinned! Only my foolish promise and honest nature saved you. You have no idea how close you came to death, page. No idea. Forget the executioner; I wanted to shove your neck into that cradle myself. I may still do it when all this mess is done. Now, get out of my way."

It was the arrogance of power that led a man to think he could threaten the life of another and then just walk away.

He moved toward the door again, but I blocked him. Unexpectedly, his arm struck out and a fist hit me in a sensitive spot just below my rib. I almost buckled but gave him a hard shove and he looked at me, sizing up where he would lash out next. Then my gaze caught on a glint just beyond him. He glanced over to see what I was looking at. We both went perfectly still for a long moment and then, both of us lurched toward the thing on the desk. I was quicker, grabbing up the thing he'd forgotten when shoving the money into his bag. I held the gun up in my hand, pointing it at him. He took a step back towards the desk.

"What are you going to do with that? Have you ever held a gun? Do you even know how to use it? A child playing with men's toys. Put it down before you hurt yourself. I saved you, page. I kept my word even though it nearly killed me. I don't lie, unlike you."

"I've had about enough of your mouth," I said, my voice clipped and the gun shaking in my hand in front of me. I willed my hand to still.

"Make no mistake, you are blessed to be standing here today. The Supreme Being has saved you, champion of the people," he sneered.

"Isn't that what they called you after that speech you gave at the Club? Louis-Benoit Zamor, Champion of the People. Ça ira! Nonsense!"

Ça ira, the words of the revolutionaries. *It's all good*. How dare he mock me with them?

I heard sounds in the distance but he seemed to hear nothing as he ranted.

"You might have been of use. The slave trade is an abomination, and the one useful thing Danton did was bring it before the Assembly with a rational argument against it. But you, page, you are not one of *those honorable people*. Your plight has never been the plight of the enslaved, your plight is that of your own and those like you. Your plight is that of the weak and wretched."

"Shut up, shut up!" My eyelid began to twitch. Perspiration trickled over my forehead, dropping into the other eye, causing it to blink, madly. The gun jiggled in my hand from a combination of fury and helplessness.

"You speak for the cowards and slugs and filthy things of the world," he continued. "When I think of Jeanne du Barry and how that beautiful woman loved you, it makes me shudder with disgust. And when I think of all the people of African blood who toil and suffer and experience horrific pain, and then think of *you,* it makes me want to lose my lunch! How dare such a thing as you outlive that woman?"

"Shut up, shut up—" I said.

"—You're a travesty. You're a pathetic embarrassment—"

"—All those people," I reminded him. "Twenty-two Girondins in one day. One day—!"

"—It's a miracle she trusted you for all those years—"

"—Georges Danton was your friend!"

"I feel shame on behalf of all people of African blood that a thing like you stands here claiming to be one of them. The world is a sorry place when they suffer unfairly and you're here walking free. You might possibly be the one man anyone would least want to *ever* speak for them…"

"Shut up!" My head was pounding. "Shut your mouth!"

"Wherever your parents are, merci à Dieu they're not here to see the thing their child has become. Now, get out of my way."

His words were meant to provoke and distract me as he had been inching forward, slowly. Now, he pushed forward suddenly, slamming into my chest. I used one arm to push him back and he stumbled onto the desk behind him. His face contorted with anger and determination, and he came forward at me again.

I would do whatever it took to stop him from running. A flesh wound would stop him in his tracks and bring the police. They could deal with him from there. That was the plan.

But he decided to rush me again with the gun ending up between us.

"Get back!" I pushed him away as he lurched toward me again. I raised my hand and, finally, the tremors stopped. I aimed surely and steadily and pulling the finger on the trigger. The sound of the shot rang out and my eyelids blinked as my arm jerked up with the force of the bullet leaving the muzzle.

He stumbled backward, still on his feet; both of us stared at each other with eyes wide in surprise. Yes, I had aimed the gun at his arm to shock him into stopping his escape. That was the plan. But I'd always been a bad shot. His eyes widened even further as a blossom of red opened up along his lower jaw. I had shot him in the face!

My eyelid began twitching so fast I could barely see out of the eye.

"I heard a gunshot!" came a shout from outside. "…The Hôtel de Ville, hurry!"

When Max moved to open his lips a mouthful of blood fell from his parted lips. Pressing them closed, he clapped his hand against his face over the wound and began a close-mouthed squeal, opening his lips just enough to keep from choking. I looked at the gun, then tossed it back onto the desk as the reality of what had happened dawned on me. Max was squealing, both hands on his face, both covered in blood, and I was standing there, guilty. I would go to the guillotine this time, for sure.

My eyes darted quickly and I spied the open window.

Boots stamped loudly inside the building now, on the floor below, and then lumbering up the stairs.

I looked at Max. And then, I ran toward the window as the stampede of approaching boots came closer. Max was squealing still, which seemed all he *could* do. I lifted a leg over the sill.

We were on the second floor. I would have liked to have taken my time, but the boots were very close, now. Max was squealing, holding his face with one hand, eyes wide and bloodshot. At last glance he was pointing a bloody index finger in my direction, furiously. But by the time the police burst through the door, I had already dropped to the bushes below, wincing as branches snagged and pierced my clothes and skin, breaking off and bending. It was an uncomfortable landing but it broke my fall. Rolling off, I hit the ground with an *umpfhh* coming from me as my shoulder and side took the jarring impact. Grunting, I rolled underneath the thickest bush, with its wide shadow cover in the darkness of the night. The open window above allowed me to hear what was next.

"You're not going to get an easy way out of this. You're under arrest!"

Then, the horrible sound of his squealing and the police yelling. I heard so many boots pounding above it seemed impossible so many people could be in that little room. The sound of their voices raised in anger and indignation mingled with his indecipherable screams. Eventually, the ruckus moved out of the room, and soon after I could hear only a hum of the crowd.

My pounding heart filled my ears, and I clutched myself in a hug. I pulled my knees to my chest and lay like that for a long time when the crowd spilled out the front door. I didn't dare raise my head to see; I only knew it was them from the inhuman sound of Max trying, unsuccessfully, to speak.

The master avocat and orator was unable to utter a single word.

***

I didn't have much time to consider how I felt about Max beyond utter disappointment and waste. He had proven himself to be a lying hypocrite, after all. We chose the wrong leader. He almost single-handedly undid all the progress we had made with his thirst for blood; perverting the very values that spawned the revolution, itself. And, he'd almost turned me into a murderer again, and that was unforgiveable. I spent a night I should have been sleeping seething with anger and nursing the cuts and bruises on my skin from the hasty get-away.

The next day, July 27, 1794, Max went to the beast along with twenty-one of his most fervent supporters for crimes against the republic, without trial, as established under his very own Law of 22 Prairial. His face had been wrapped to keep the bottom half of it from falling off. I was told, when it was his turn, a guard came up and ripped the bandage off with joy. Max screamed, wildly, like a wounded animal in a trap. The beast didn't care if he had a jaw or not; it took him anyway.

Over the following days, another one hundred or so of Max's closest followers were hunted down and, similarly, fed to the beast.

I didn't ask Valentin what sort of falling out he'd had with Max that had, somehow, protected him from the same fate. We weren't friends, after all.

Though I was surprised he would dare to show up at the executions. After Max's execution I made an effort to go to that of the other members of the Mountain just to stand beside Valentin, anyway. He had helped free me from prison, and I knew his heart was dying. As wordless tears fell down his face I wondered if he was crying for Max and his friends, or crying because, like Sebastien, he hadn't been considered important enough to warrant being rounded up after all.

Hush...

Swish...

The Reign was over.

Chapter Thirty

*A*utumn 1794

Without the fear of my blood running through the streets, the end of the Reign meant I was finally, truly free. But my plans were no longer viable. There was no place for me in the new government. The printers were all still shut down. And, worst of all, my friendship with Sebastien was hanging on by a thread—until the day that thread snapped.

I came back from a long walk to find Sebastien and Élise standing in the front room looking caught in the midst of discussion. They both stopped talking upon seeing me.

"Gossiping about the children again?" I joked wryly. "They deserve better."

"What's this?" Sebastien said, waving some papers. "I found these in your room."

My smile died as I saw the flapping papers. "Why were you in my room?"

"I own this house."

"I pay rent. I'm a legal tenant. You have no right to go into my room." I knew what those papers were. "You had to go digging for those, Sebastien."

He put them on the table. "Well, the boys were playing where they shouldn't have been..."

"It sounds like this is a parenting issue that you can't keep your children out of my room. Teach them respect for other people's property, and all that."

"…They rolled their little ball under the chest of drawers. I had to lift it and move it, and I found *that* hidden underneath."

I looked at the two boys who were in the kitchen appearing shame-faced. Little shits.

"What's it got to do with you?" I asked.

"Those papers prove that I've allowed an evil man to live under my roof."

"Oh, here we go. Don't be so dramatic—"

"—A man who would hide the traveling papers—"

"—This history, Sebastien—"

"—Of a woman so she couldn't leave France if she wanted to—"

"—And why would she want to leave France? Let me think. Oh, yes, could it have been because she was trying to escape justice? It doesn't even matter; they were expired even then. She was unlikely to be able to use them, anyway."

"That's why she was tearing apart the office when they went to arrest her the second time, isn't it? She was trying to find those papers. She was trying to leave and all along, you'd taken them."

"I'd say by the time she was tearing the office apart it was already too late, don't you think? Besides, what if I did? Turnabout is fair play. I asked to leave for years, why should she get to?"

"That was just plain cruel."

Anger slipped through me like hot syrup. "Now you're her defender?"

"She most certainly didn't deserve to be trapped and cornered like an animal."

"No, only I deserved that, isn't that right?"

"If you want to know the truth, I have my doubts about what she might have deserved all along. I only ever heard your side of the story, after all."

"Sebastien," Élise tried to interrupt.

"Careful, Sebastien. Listen to your wife," I said, my voice low and soft, my throat constricting further with every second as the anger tried to choke it closed. "Watch what you say to me."

"What, watch what I say to you?" His expression showed incredulity. "I'm not afraid of you, little man. I can break you like a stick. I'll say what I want. I was at the Chateau, remember, so worried about you I went out there to save you. I met the woman. I never said anything because you always get a little crazy when anyone says anything nice about her..."

"Both of you, stop it!" Élise said. "Before you say things you can't take back."

"It needs to be said, Élise!" Sebastien snapped at her. "Jeanne du Barry was a perfectly lovely woman to me. It made me wonder if she was ever as bad as you said. What did she do that was so terrible, Page? She fed you, clothed you, gave you a home and all of the finest things," he counted off on his fingers. "So what, you got a beating. Any man who's been in a bar fight might have gotten worse. She even saved your life, and you hated her for that! You might have been grateful!"

The top of my head felt like it was coming off. "What the fuck did you just say to me?" I choked out.

"Boys, go upstairs," Élise told the children. The younger one immediately ran upstairs.

"I said it! She gave you a *safe* life. People have it worse than you, Zamor. You've never lived like a true enslaved person. Hell, you've never lived like a sans-culotte or even an indentured servant! You've lived like a nobleman, complaining all the way. You're a spoiled child! Yes, maybe that asshole Gaspard deserved what he got but did she, really? And now this." He gestured toward the papers, shaking his head. "This makes me see you differently. This is plain wrong."

He said it so smugly, cloaked in self-righteousness... Bitterness blossomed in my mouth. The sound of wind rushed through my head and I could barely hear my own voice over the sound of the living rage. "And you're suddenly the authority on right and wrong, Sebastien?"

"He didn't mean it like that," Élise tried, stepping forward to give a weak smile, hands up in supplication, trying to speak for her stupid husband.

"No, I think he did, Élise." I stepped around her to glare at him, full-on. "I think he meant exactly what he said. Sebastien, *everybody's* friend, and all that. Sebastien, who—when push came to shove, you didn't care a lick for your Girondin brothers, did you? Sent Jacques out into the night alone and scared, like he was nothing more than trash on the street."

The tips of his ears went red. "You're not going to make me feel badly about that. I did what I thought was best with Jacques. I couldn't save him. But I did save *you*." He pointed towards me. "Like she saved you, *I* saved you."

"She set Gaspard on me time and time again! Over and over letting him punch me like a man when I was just a little boy no bigger than yours over there. Turning her head while her enemies took their hatred for her out on me. And you stand there, knowing all this, and have the gall to tell me she's a lovely woman? All these years listening to my stories and five minutes in her presence over a year ago and you're defending her. You never even knew her."

"No, I know *you*, and I'm starting to think you were just a jealous, spurned man all along..."

"How could I be spurned when all I wanted was to get away? She was the one keeping *me* captive; if anyone was spurned it was her!" I hopped a little in my zeal. "None of her plans had anything to do with me being allowed to leave, ever. It turns out I was smarter than her. She set me up to take the fall or die alongside her. *Well, Sebastien, I didn't want to go!* Do you hear me, I didn't want to die! Yes, I took those papers so she couldn't find a way to leave before the trial. Why should she get to sneak out? The royals and nobles, always screwing everything up and then when things go bad, they have the audacity to crawl out like slithering snakes so they don't have to deal with the shithole they made. I wasn't going to let it happen! So, yes, I outsmarted her and I'm not sorry for it. Making that deal was the only thing that saved me. She didn't save me! *You* didn't save me. The asshole Valentin, who hates me, and the pervert Grieve... *they* saved me. No matter how I feel about them, at least they weren't blinded by how *lovely* she was. You simply came along for the ride."

"If it weren't for me, they wouldn't even have known you were in trouble. I was there for you, just as I've always been."

"Oh, you're everywhere, aren't you? Pointing out who needs help, but not lifting a finger to actually get involved. All those years ago when I first saw you, sitting in bars fishing for men, like Matthew fishing for souls. Like me. Men foolish enough to put themselves on the line. I wonder now, what have you ever done besides finding other people to go onto the front lines before you? How many people did you recruit for the cause, Sebastien, only to find themselves abandoned, standing on the platform of death with you nowhere in sight? How many of your apprentices did the beast feed upon?"

"Shut your mouth. All of this has been hard on everyone—"

"Has it really?" I screwed my face as though thinking hard. "I don't think so, friend. I think, somehow, you've escaped unscathed. Somehow, we've all lost something except for good old Sebastien. Somehow, you've managed to escape without a hair out of place. You knew that as long as there were people like me and Jacques and Valentin around no one would ever look at Sebastien, isn't that right? Just like *she* did, blaming me for her own jewelry theft because it was convenient. Is that why you defend her, because you're so much alike? The fact that I'm here, in your house, that keeps you safe, doesn't it?"

"Why don't you get out, then?" he yelled. "No one's keeping you here! I'm to be your Madame now, is that right? Your scapegoat for misery?"

I looked at him, incredulity twisting my face. "Why do you think? I'm here so your family can eat! They were practically starving when we met—your poor wife slipping you her food in secret so you don't have to feel bad. Surviving on stone soup. At least with my money from rent she has a chance to get a little meat every now and again. I thought I'd help a friend."

"Bah!" he said, pushing his arms down like it was bunk, but now he couldn't meet my eyes. "I never asked for anything from you."

"You didn't have to. I stepped in to fill a need for a friend. Since I've been here you've been eating well, haven't you? Been eating meat and chicken? Potatoes? Real bread? Fish? Able to afford fresh vegetables? You haven't seemed to mind one bit when you know I'm not above stealing to keep myself in stitches. I saw a need and I filled it because that's what I've been reared to do—save stupid, weak people like you!"

He shook his head, not looking at me. "You sanctimonious piece of shit. I'm the one who took the risk of housing you when everyone knows death follows you like it's tied around your neck."

That sent a lick of pain through me and my eyelids fluttered as he noticed he'd found his mark. He continued, meanly.

"The gall to stand here talking about my wife when you've had one woman killed and gone and left another—"

"—Sebastien!" Élise interrupted him sharply.

I sucked my teeth in annoyance. "And you, all upset over one woman when you killed Henri and God knows how many others. There's too much blood on your hands for you to stand in judgement of me, Sebastien. Listen to your wife." I nodded furiously. "You've had no problem taking the little money in your pockets from your family's mouths and spending it in bars and cafés, drinking wine and brandy with me. Claiming it was for the cause. Turns out, this horrible *page* cares more about their welfare than you do!"

"At least I have a family! What do you have? You don't even deserve a family. I'm glad Véronique left you, you're not fit to be around!"

"Don't you speak on Véronique!" I had had it! "You bring her up again and I swear, Sebastien, death will come here today. I'll kill you with my bare hands if you don't shut up. Or maybe I'll tell your wife about all the pretty barkeeps you managed to flatter when you were out being a revolutionary."

Élise choked on a cry she held in.

It slipped out of me. I hadn't meant to say it but when I was angry there was no telling what would come out of my mouth. Immediately, I felt bad. It should have been between me and him, but now I'd gone and hurt Élise, just because he mentioned Véronique.

Sebastien went red and his face looked about to explode, but his voice went low and dangerous.

"You get the fuck out of my house."

We both heaved in our anger over the magnitude of our words. Our breaths struggled with the heaviness of what we were saying and what was happening. But what was there left to do?

"Gladly!" I said.

I ran upstairs and began shoving papers and clothes into my bags, grabbing my violin in its case on the way out. I descended loudly, banging my way down the stairs, searching for Sebastien—to call him some names—only to find him nowhere in sight. Élise was standing there, her arms folded across her body as though protecting her insides. I watched to make sure she wouldn't hit me, before reaching over and grabbing the papers off the table.

"I didn't mean to say what I said. You know I'm right, Élise," I said to her, shoving the papers in my bag. "He's out of his mind."

"Shut up. You shut your mouth right now, Zamor," she hissed at me. I was confused. Certainly, she saw how wrong her husband was. That this was all his fault?

"He had no right to say those things to me!" I reminded her.

"He had every right! After everything he's done for you. Everything *we've* done for you. We took you into our home and this is how you repay us?"

"Fine, defend him like you always do. Like a good wife," I sneered. "Do your bit then. Curse me so your husband can feel like a man, but he wasn't worrying about your feelings when he was out living it up in bars like an unmarried man with me, Élise, that's all I'm saying."

"I *will* hit you if you don't leave."

"Fine. Goodbye, Élise. I'm sorry it ended this way," I said curtly, backing out of the front door and closing it only to turn towards the street to be confronted by the older boy standing there outside. He was glaring at me, fists bunched by his sides like he was preparing to do something.

"You can't talk to my papa like that, Uncle Zamor. I won't have it."

Standing there with his father's furrowed brow and deep-set eyes. Any day now he would pop into manhood and sprout hair from every bit of skin on his body, become a baby bear, just like his papa. But at that moment, he was still just a baby-faced boy. Not this, now...

"Stay out of adult business, child, and move out of my way."

His fists clenched. "You can't talk to my papa like—"

"—I can do anything I damn well please and before you step up to me you should know I will knock you flat. You have two parents who love you and keep you a safe little boy. You are very fortunate. Go back inside to your mother. You don't want to be out here in the world picking fights. If you knew how the rest of the world treats children, you would understand. You're fortunate you don't have to know." A small mean part of me wanted to tell him that, quiet as it was kept, his papa was a killer just like me. But I wasn't ready to kill his love for his father that day. "Go back inside. Because I'm not your uncle. I'm a man with very few morals and no longer a reason to care about you, what with your father proving himself to be an asshole. Now, un-bunch your fists and go inside before I lose my temper."

He let that ruminate for a moment, then his hands relaxed. He gave me a dubious look and then stepped out of my way, walking to his door to open it. He went inside, looking at me the whole way until the door came between us.

I walked to the corner of the alley to collect my sandy-colored horse. He carried me away from Sebastien's house and through town. I ended up near the bridge I had hidden with Jacques Brissot, tethering the horse to a post in a nearby alley, out of sight. Then, I tucked myself into that corner underneath the bridge so I wouldn't be disturbed.

The fury that had driven me since the beginning of our argument finally died under that bridge. As darkness fell and my heart slowed from a gallop to an even trot, I found a comfortable position by moving my backside in between two stones.

I took a deep breath and the smell of not-so-clean water, dank and musty, filled my nose.

What was I doing? The mess of the Reign had kept us all frozen with fear but now it was over. More importantly, I had my freedom, which was all I ever wanted. The press was shut down to people like me and I couldn't write, but I had my freedom. I could start from scratch.

All those years ago, as a child, it was simple. When I climbed onto Lightning's back I had only one purpose. Childish, immature, and illogical–but I was determined to get that one single thing. Free. What was my one single thing, now?

I fell asleep with that question in my brain and woke up with the answer dancing on my soul.

When the rays of the sun began crawling up the rocks on the banks, inching toward my feet, I roused myself from my spot. I stretched my cramped muscles as I climbed down from under the bridge. Taking a return route to where my horse was tied, we traveled a short way to a man I knew who fenced stolen goods into money. A short while later, after having sold a good portion of my baubles and trinkets, I led my horse on the road away from Paris.

I was a person before I became Louis-Benoit Zamor. It was time for me to find out who I was by going back home to Chittagong, India.

But first, I had to make a brief trip to Croissy-sur-Seine.

Chapter Thirty-One

To my dismay, Véronique's house was empty. Through the window, I could see a sweater on a chair and a teacup on a small table. The house was still being lived in and that meant she was well.

I was disappointed I couldn't see Véronique before I left the country. Walking back to my horse I climbed atop and sat there as he cantered impatiently. The young, always so anxious.

The horse was right, of course. I was supposed to be invisible. I wasn't planning to speak with her. I couldn't have said what kept me atop that horse on that road for greater than twenty minutes, except—maybe—hope.

Deciding I'd tempted fate enough, I took her prolonged absence as a sign to leave her alone. Instead, I rode to the center of town and visited a little bar some ways up the road. To my surprise the bartender was a black man.

A drunkard stumbled up to the bar asking for more drink to which the bartend came around and sat the man down, speaking gently. He then poured the man a cup of coffee. The man broke down in tears looking into the hot drink.

"I can't find work, Edouard. There is no work anywhere. I think every day I should throw myself in the river."

The Black man, Edouard, spoke gently. "If you do that, what will happen to Béatrice? Her heart would be broken, she loves you so. Here, drink this coffee and get your head right. Stay here and drink as much coffee as you want until you're ready. And then go home and talk to your wife, oui?" The drunkard looked at him, and the coffee, then did as he was told, drinking the hot coffee like it was medicine. I watched the bartender as he returned to his place behind the bar.

"Kind of you," I said of his interaction with the man. The bartender was tall with a handsome face and strong shoulders. He was a man that others, including myself, envied. But his kindness was even more impressive.

"It's nothing. People around here are having a difficult time. But we help each other where we can. We all have dark moments, non?"

I nodded. And watched while he worked. He was sure of foot and handy. He was confident and smart and had an easy smile.

"Hey there," I said to him as he poured me wine. "You are a free man?"

"I am. I was born just north of here. You?"

"Newly free," I said.

"Then you get this, on the house." He poured and slid me a small glass of brandy. "Are you headed to the gathering town, then?"

"Gathering town?"

"Oui, the town where many of the newly free decide to settle."

"Actually, I was planning to leave France for a bit. I'm going to keep riding until I reach a port so I can board a boat."

"I see. Well, there is a gathering town on the way to the port at Le Havre. Perhaps you should go through on your way out of the country. It might convince you to stay."

"I doubt that, but thank you, Monsieur," I said and meant it. Then I got a kernel of an idea that grew quickly in just the time it took to drink my drink. "I have a friend who moved into town not long ago. She lives on the street overlooking the river just where the jagged edges of the Seine meet. If ever you're looking for a little extra money in your pocket, I believe she could use some handy work done around the house. Just to help out."

"Certainly," he said. "I look in on some of the older widows in town time and again. I'll check in on your friend, see if she needs anything."

"Good." I didn't correct him from his assumption that she was an older widow. Let him think she was helpless and he would surely pay her a visit–that was the type he was. "Thank you. Don't mention I sent you, she would only be angry at me for the suggestion that she couldn't do everything herself."

Chapter Thirty-Two

*D*ear Citizen,

It's difficult to admit that I began to feel the loose strands of fear gathering up in me as I traveled toward the port. I couldn't have said if it was fear of what was behind or before me. But as I traveled, I began to feel a bit like a lost soul, meandering all about with no direction and no clear goal. It was in that frame of mind that I found myself headed into a place I couldn't even imagine existed.

—Zamor, 1820

***

I heard the gathering town before I saw it. My horse must have heard it before me because I allowed him to choose the path at a fork in the road, and he cantered directly towards an enclave.

The town was generous for what it was. There were people bustling about what looked like a market with stands filled with skimpy supply. The items being sold were not the prettiest but there was some produce someone had managed to grow. Mostly the least desirable vegetables—onions and potatoes and carrots—things many people didn't like (and nobles wouldn't eat). But there was a man with a bucket calling out that he had fish. Fish! It couldn't have been much more than one or two from the size of that bucket, but too costly for most people who looked into it longingly before passing by.

I happened to like potatoes, so my eyes lingered.

Women gathered in a small line where, at the head, another woman had what appeared to be torn pieces of baguette. Bread was so expensive these days, the seller had rightly assumed she'd actually sell something if she cut down her product into manageable, affordable bits. Some of the women looked at me, eyes taking note of the stranger.

I'd been through small towns before. What made this one unique was that every single person I saw had black skin. Every single one. It was thrilling!

I slowed my horse to a stop and then climbed off, leading him by the reins to a pole next to a trough of water set up for the purpose of tying up horses. I did so while feeling eyes on me. I knew, instinctively, there were more people looking at me than I could see.

A boy who looked to be about fifteen was seated on a stool outside a building with a pile of papers beside him. I walked over to him.

"Young man, what is this place called?"

He looked at me, confused. "France."

I bit back a smile. "Yes, yes... clever child."

"New in town?" I turned toward the voice and found a black man of average height.

"Bonjour," I said. "I'm just a traveler passing through. Headed to the port at Le Havre."

"The port? You're planning to leave France?"

"If I can, yes."

"Of course you can, you won't have any trouble getting out of France, trust me. Not you. You're not far. Make sure they don't mistake you for one of the enslaved, or you'll never get to where you're going."

"But slavery is still abolished now. It's illegal."

"For those who are caught, maybe. Just be careful. If someone looks like they're sizing you up, they probably are. Many of us here know the look only too well."

That explained it. Port towns where black people came either freely or in captivity, where people engaged in trade of all kinds, but also where dock work was.

My own childhood home of Chittagong had been a port town; my parents the descendants of people who had come in captivity to India. Same story, different place.

"Are all the people here formerly enslaved?"

"No, some have always been free. Some are born on the French mainland, but some come from other places."

I was having a hard time imagining living in a community where I didn't have to think about all those things that come with being a different skin color.

"My name is Louis-Benoit, I'm from Paris."

"Louis-Benoit Zamor?" The boy on the stool spoke up, his eyes lit up now. "You were in the papers, weren't you?"

The man said to me, "He can read. A few people here can. He has a skill like that, and he uses it to read gossip from Paris.

"You were du Barry's Page, weren't you? The one who sent the king's mistress to her death."

"Hush," the man said.

"Were you lovers?" asked a woman I hadn't even noticed. I looked around and saw a few people had gathered to listen, now comfortable to ask what was on their minds now that the ice was broken.

"No," I said, face heating. "I was with her from a child. I don't much care to talk about it, though."

"Who ever wants to talk about their lives?" the woman asked with a smile. "But you come into a new town you must be prepared to explain yourself, oui. The most beautiful woman in all of France, they called her. Was she?"

I thought about that. "That's what they said. I've seen more beautiful."

"Well, you are right to leave. With the new government pretending like they detest what Robespierre did and allowed to be done, they will place the blame somewhere. They'll be turning on you, soon enough, for forcing their hand in killing that one."

"I didn't force anything, I..." I stopped because they were right. They had come after me in their regret. The boy informed them.

"They already put him in the Conciergerie!" he said, quickly. "They say you were helping her steal France's money all along. Living the high life and helping her plot against the new republic."

"Were you?" the woman asked.

"I was a servant. I had all the power of a page, which was none."

"The French. When she was alive, they talked about her like she was dirt but after they put her to death it's *you* who must run and leave your home. At least you have the brains of your ancestors that you know well enough to leave Paris."

"Yes, well, I don't like to talk about it much," I said again. The people around me fell into silence, perhaps sensing the subject was done for me.

"I'll show you around," the man said. "Maybe you want to stay a bit. There's a man who might have room if you don't mind the floor. If you stay longer, you can probably find people to help you build a small place."

"I'm really only passing through," I said, following him. But the truth was, I didn't mind maybe staying a night or two on someone's floor.

As we sauntered town the dirt path, everyone went about their business as if we weren't there. I wondered what it might be like to live in such a place. The horse could use a break and whatever food I could find for him. My rations were low, though I'd stashed some dried beef in different spots on my body. Who knew how long the journey to India would take? And I had a nice purse, also hidden on various parts of my body. I could afford a decent meal for me and my horse. I would sell him at the Port, but for now we were a team, and I was responsible for him.

I walked beside the man as he pointed people and things out while we walked. Beyond the center road, there were small houses on the roads extended from it, each with plenty space between. At one point I noticed a woman sitting in front of a house on her knees, packing the soil of what appeared to be a small garden in front of the house. He saw me looking at her.

"I'd recommend you leave that one alone. She's pretty but dangerous. We call her the *murderess*."

I wanted to tell him I might just be more dangerous than she when the woman sat back on her haunches and twisted her arms up to get the kinks from her back. When she lifted, I saw the faint line that went around the neck column and my hackles rose. Could it be... was it possible...? It was unlikely. But...

I took a step, and then two towards her.

"Whoever you are had better back up if you don't want a knife in the gut," she said without turning. The man stepped back. Quickly, I leaned in and spoke.

"Bonjour..." I called out. "...*Jour*... like a whisper."

She froze and then, slowly, turned, and revealed the grown-up face of a person I hadn't seen since we were children. It was the little girl who had helped me learn French all those years ago. The little girl who I'd last seen being knocked into stillness while her slaver clasped an iron brace around her neck. She was a grown woman now, with few lines to show for it. She stood up, slowly, and looked me over. Her face settled into calm pleasure.

"Mon Dieu, you've grown up into a fine man, haven't you? Still small but handsome in your way. What a pleasure to see you and know you are well."

"The pleasure is mine, Mademoiselle. Nothing else could have made me happier this day than laying eyes on an old friend."

It was true. I wanted to burst from happiness. I wanted to grab her in a hug, but I took my cues from her curious, careful nonchalance. She sidled forward as if this was no big thing to her. My lips were wiggling from trying not to grin.

She finally gave a sly grin and a wink for my eyes only, and then looked at the man beside me who had grown stiff with discomfort. "See, Nicholas, someone knows how to be a gentleman. Instead of just spreading rumors and gossip about a woman. Go run and tell the others that this one is a friend. Do you have a name, now? My name is Sara. What shall I call you, friend?"

Though we'd stayed with each other for a while in childhood, at the time we'd had no use for names after I told her I'd forgotten mine. But today was different.

"You may call me Zamor. Louis-Benoit Zamor."

Her eyes widened. "You ended up at the Palace and became the scandalous lover of Jeanne du Barry?" She burst into laughter. "Oh my, if I had known my schooling was enough to get you a seat beside the King and a spot in his lover's bed, I would have come back for my due payment."

"No, I... we weren't lovers. Why do people keep asking me that?"

"That's not what France says. No matter." She hooked an arm through mine, leading me towards the front door of the little house. Then she leaned in to whisper so only I could hear: "Don't ever tell anyone you *weren't* lovers, chèr. At least if you were lovers that whole sordid mess would make *sense*. Otherwise, the relationship sounds strange and unnatural. Come in and rest your feet. Goodbye, Nicholas."

That was a funny thought, that anything about that relationship could be natural. She shuffled me ahead of her into the house.

"Sit, sit. And tell me all about our years apart while I make us a nice cup of tea. And you can meet my sister."

"Your sister?" I sat at a little table and twisted towards her where she put tea to boil on the small stove top. "You found her!"

"I certainly did. Did you doubt it?"

"Well, I *hoped* you'd manage but I can't imagine how you did. The odds. Where did you even start?"

"Fate brought us back to each other."

At that moment, footsteps caught my attention and a woman a bit younger than me entered the kitchen doorway from the front room. Her face was similar to my friend only there was not a line on her skin to show any sign of aging. Her hair was braided and secured to her head. Her stomach was big with child.

"We have a guest?" the young woman asked. "Who's this man? Is he coming to stay with us? He has a nice face, can he stay? Do you..." her eyes lit upon my violin case. "Do you play music? Sissie, he plays music. Music, music!" She clapped happily, her face awash in sweet joy.

It made sense now, how protective she had been all those years ago. The sense of responsibility she had towards her sister since her parents' death. The overarching need to find and save her.

Sara spoke without turning, filling little cups with tea. "Settle down, Sissie, he has only just gotten here. Mind your manners."

"But Sara, I like music, you know I do. Play something, Monsieur strange man, play something!"

Her older sister looked at me and shook her head imperceptibly.

"Maybe later," I told her sister. Her happy face went dark like a thundercloud.

"I want to hear it now! Now, now, now..." She stamped her feet and her eyes welled with tears. She burst into an open-mouthed wail, the strength of it reaching the rafters.

Sara slapped her hand on the table sharply, stopping everything.

"You will not misbehave when we have guests. He will play later. After we've had our tea. You will sit and be polite, won't you?"

The young woman's wailing stopped, though her lips quivered. She nodded solemnly, making the sign of the cross over her chest and putting up her hand as a sign of her oath.

"Good girl, now sit so I can give you your tea, love. You like tea, don't you?"

The woman wiped the moisture from her eyes as her smile emerged as if it couldn't contain herself. "With cream." She eagerly put her hands out for her little cup of tea. Then all three of us were sitting, sipping tea. Sara told her sister that I was the man she had met as a child.

"The one you taught French? You said he was little. This is a grown man!"

"I was little, back then." I shrugged. "Am still, depending on who I'm standing next to." Sara smiled.

"Sissie said you tried to help her when the bad man put the thing around her neck. She said you were so upset for her."

"Yes, well... it was a difficult time." We went back to drinking our tea quietly as unpleasant memories settled in.

Later, I pulled out my violin and played a song. The young woman's face was still as she watched, as if in a trance, while the music filled the small space. When I finished, she clapped vigorously, unabashedly, eyes closed as she shook her head with appreciation.

"Magnifique!"

"Merci, Madamoiselle." I smiled and bent my head in acknowledgement.

"He called me 'Mademoiselle', Sissie." She giggled.

"Oui, he's very polite. Now, why don't you enjoy that book of yours in the bedroom so my friend and I can speak?"

She bounced out of the room like an obedient little girl, the smile on her face from making her older sister happy. Sara sat down on the floor next to me in front of the fire.

"What happened after we were separated?" I asked. "How did you get free? How did you find her?" It seemed impossible.

"When you arrived in town today, did they tell you to stay away from me? That I'm dangerous?"

"Oui, they did." I saw no reason to lie.

"Good. I am. After we were separated, I was passed through many hands and had several owners. Eventually, I ended up with a man who took me to a chateau deep in the woods. I was to be the sole servant for this man, his wife, and his son. He was cruel. Whenever I wasn't within his sight, he kept that thing around my neck and chained me. His wife and son were no better.

Occasionally, he would drive me into town for shopping. On one of those times, I saw my sister across the square with another man." Sara's eyes had gone off as if in another time and place. "All of a sudden, after so many years, there she was. Much taller but still, she looked the same. Her face hasn't changed." she smiled.

"She looks like you," I said.

"Oui, I was thankful I could still recognize her. I can't tell you the emotion I felt seeing her that day. I had almost lost hope. Then, all of a sudden, she was standing across the square through no effort of mine. She was supposed to be paying attention to him, but you see how she is. She wasn't paying him any mind."

"Ah, to be in a world like that," I said with a smile. I had the world of my stone fox, but that was never a happy place.

"At that time, I hadn't even figured out how to get away from the man who owned me, let alone how to find her. But, suddenly, there she was. I knew, while I couldn't get away from him, maybe I could get him to want her, too. I begged him to buy her from the other man. He asked me what was in it for him. I swore to him I would never try to get away or give him a moment's trouble. I promised the two of us would work hard and he could get her for next to nothing, since she was simple."

"But the other man..."

"He was anxious to be rid of her and sold her right on the spot because of how she is. Seeing recognition for me slowly dawn on her face... it was like nothing I'd ever experienced. The years fell away, and we were children again. It was like being home."

"I'm so happy for you, Sara," I said.

"It's strange hearing you say my name," she said, giving me a wry smile. "You used to just call me Teacher. Teacher this, teacher that..."

"I didn't remember that," I said. I truly hadn't remembered calling her anything. She went on.

"Once we were together in that house, she did what I said, and I knew how to keep her attention. The man who owned me was satisfied for a time. They came to trust me and to relax. But, of course, I didn't plan to stay there. So, one day, while they were asleep my sister and I snuck into the son's bedroom, shoved a towel down his throat and my sister held him while I cut his throat."

My throat hitched a bit at the matter-of-fact statement.

"Then, we did the same to the man. Halfway through the wife woke up. When she saw the blood, she panicked but I told her what to say to the police. That prowlers had come in and killed the men for money. You remember how it was for a time, thieves roaming the streets willing to kill for any reason? It was an easy story to believe."

She said it like it was nothing. I thought back to the first time I killed anyone. That man in the parlor at the Chateau who'd threatened me might have deserved a dagger to the chest, but my body reaction felt like I would die, too.

"But you didn't kill them all?" I asked, picturing the woman waking up to that.

"If the whole family was killed with only his *servants* missing, they would have come after us, for sure. We needed a witness who could place the blame elsewhere so we would be free. I told her I would let her live if she did this. That we only wanted our freedom and would go away and never return. But that if she didn't, I vowed I would track her down and give her a much worse death. She did what we asked and then died naturally, six months later. They said she died of a broken heart."

She said that wistfully as if the notion of it was romantic. I imagined the woman died of delayed shock or fear that Sara would be back—nothing romantic about it.

"I don't have freedom papers, but in a place like this, no one cared. And then slavery was abolished and it wasn't a concern. It's decent here. I like having my own home. It was a pile of nothing when I got here but I think I made it nice. I take a lover when I want. The only rule I have is that the townspeople leave my sister alone."

The woman's swollen belly popped into my mind. Of course, someone had taken advantage of the girl. I couldn't imagine how, with her older sister watching over her. I didn't think it was a pleasant story. "The baby's father?"

"Dead."

I nodded. I understood. "Good."

"You can stay if you like," she said, the subject changing so quickly it caught me off guard.

"I was only planning to pass through."

"You might like it here. Stay for just a little while, then. It will be nice to have a friend. Someone who knows me."

I was thinking the same. "I have a little money I can pay for my stay."

She nodded. Then said, "You don't have to pay. You're a friend. If you don't mind sleeping on the floor in the front room and helping out, you can stay. My sister and I share the bedroom. And sometimes I have a guest. If someone comes, I need you to leave."

I shrugged. "Okay."

"Good. You'll stay. Wash up for dinner." She smiled.

CHAPTER THIRTY-THREE

I took care of manual labor around the house. Most times we chatted like old friends. The sister came to trust me, and she was almost like a little sister to me as well. I played her music and told her fables and child's stories that made her clap with glee.

Since my life-threatening beating, I sometimes lost track of where I was or what I was doing. And I still had dreams. So much so that one night, when I had one of the bad dreams with myself covered in blood, I woke up screaming. My screaming woke up the younger sister who screamed out from the other room in fear. It took Sara fifteen minutes to calm her. Then, she came to me where I lay on stuffed pillows on the floor of the main room.

Immediately, I began apologizing, wiping the sweat off my forehead with my sleeves. She sat down beside me, hushed me, and pulled my sweaty head into her lap. Then, she began making comforting sounds to me as if I was a baby that needed a lullaby. At that moment I remembered she used to do this for me all those years ago when I cried after a beating. She rocked me until the sweat was no longer pouring from my head and I was myself again.

"I'm sorry for waking you both," I whispered.

"Don't be. You're human, as we all are. Is Véronique the woman you love? You called for her. Does she know about the cut across your body?"

I froze. I'd thought I'd taken care to only wash myself in private so no one would see. Not careful enough, it seemed.

"There, there, don't be that way," Sara said when I didn't respond. "I'm a friend. We live in the same house, you couldn't keep it hidden forever."

"It's a curse. I could never have let her see it, it's hideous. To see the curse of it."

"Curse? Ah, it must have felt horrible? But I don't look at it and see a curse, chèr, I see proof of your strength. That you lived is a miracle, non?"

I didn't think of any part of me in those terms.

"This woman," she continued. "You gave her a chance to love you?"

"She wouldn't have loved not having babies," I mumbled. I don't know what got into me, but being held and stroked like her child opened me up unexpectedly.

"There's more to life than creating children. You are smart and funny and brave—any woman would be happy to be with you. Perhaps with time you'll change your mind."

"I'll never ask her to give up a family for me. Never."

She sighed. "You men. Determined to make all the decisions when women are very capable of making our own. At the very least, she deserved the truth, don't you think?"

"No." I said it firmly, as though I wasn't behaving like a child. "Let's not speak of this again. I'm sorry I woke you, but no more about her."

We left it at that and went about living as though we'd never had that late night conversation. And as we shared the space in quiet companionship, I developed feelings for her. Nothing like what I felt for Véronique, but feelings all the same, simply because she didn't judge me. She was a calming presence for me. She liked me. She had been kind to me.

And she had her dark moments, too. Moments when she would suddenly become sad or angry as if a cloud descended upon her. Or she would lose focus on what was going on in the middle of an activity or conversation. Once, we were eating soup at the table when her gaze drifted over my shoulder and out the window. I looked behind me to the empty grassy space behind the house. I turned back to look at her face, still focused outside.

"Teacher," I said sharply, softening my tone when she pulled her eyes from nothingness to my face. "Sara, what were you looking at?"

She looked at me as if she didn't know whether to say. Then, "It's one of the ones I ended."

"Pardon?"

"You know, one of the ones whose lives I took. They stay, don't they? They make themselves at home and show themselves at odd times." She pulled her cup up to her lips. "You don't believe me."

"No, I didn't say that."

"Haven't you been listening in town. They call me the murderess. How do you think I got that title?"

"I think you did what you had to do, just like we all do. Half those people in town who talk about you would do the same."

"Half *have* done the same," she said wryly. "But it's different when men do it. Men kill and they are the hero to everyone's story. Women do it and we are evil and dangerous."

"It's not fair or right," I admitted.

"I don't need you to tell me that. I don't need you to approve my words; I know what I know. But I appreciate your show of support. The ones I ended are angry with me, but they wouldn't be dead if they didn't deserve it. They did it to themselves."

"How many do you see?"

"Four or five, regularly, the others drift in. Seven total. You?"

"Me?" I joshed as if I found the question ridiculous, but from under hooded lids I could see she wasn't put off by my deflection. My chin came up. "I don't know. Three directly. Another one, indirectly."

"And you see yours when you sleep." She nodded, knowingly. "I'd rather see them out by the tree than spend all my sleeping time running from them. Letting them steal my peaceful time. When I'm awake, all they can do is glare at me. They only bother me if I let them, and I don't. They're not worth my time."

"But you still see them."

"You say that as though they're a part of my imagination. As if seeing them is some sign of a guilty conscience. I have no guilt. They're real. It's nothing to do with whether I choose to see them or not. I choose not to allow them to matter."

She wasn't the effusive sort, but I could see on her face she was sincere. She had found peace here in this place, and with herself.

Maybe this was where I should be.

The tiny crush of feelings I had for her began to grow. And when I caught a glimpse of her from behind sometimes she looked a bit like Véronique and I felt my body stir. I had thought that was over for me, but it seemed my body wasn't completely broken after all. Just ugly. It occurred to me, maybe this was where I should settle. Why did I need answers about a past I couldn't even remember when I could have a future right here?

I helped around the house. I chopped wood for the fire and cleared out the brush. We walked in town together sometimes and people would sneak glances at us while we didn't care a bit, chattering with each other about everything. She was the friend I never knew I needed.

But there were days when she would ask me to leave in the morning and I did, without complaint, because that was our deal.

The first time, I offered to take the sister with me. Sara looked at me hard but only nodded in ascent. I passed the test, returning with her sister happier than when she'd left. And safe. I'd earned Sara's trust.

A few weeks later, we had café and then Sara told me she needed me to leave until noon.

I have to admit, by that time I had come to care for her. Being sent away began to irk me because of what I suspected.

I walked into the town square with the sister to pick through the best of the worst pieces of sad vegetables for soup when a woman came over and teased my choice for a carrot. I laughed at her.

"You see a better one here, please show it to me."

"That's why we grow ours; you won't find a good one here."

A woman *tsked* at her from across the square and she looked up.

"You know he's claimed by the murderess. Leave him be, we want no trouble."

The woman gave me a regretful look and a small wave goodbye.

The fact that I'd been claimed was news to me. I began to feel some sense of having earned permission to make demands of our relationship, to claim her back. Every day I stayed I grew more attached to both of them. I liked my spot as the man of that house. It wasn't my house, but I did live there.

So, in the coming weeks I began to deeply resent being sent away during the day. Sara wouldn't tell me why I had to leave or what was happening. I took to hiding to see who would come to the house when the sister and I left, struggling to keep her sister quiet as we hid out in the trees for me to watch as a man knocked on her door and was allowed in with a smile. A welcoming smile.

Chapter Thirty-Four

Rules are made for a reason.

I knew that, and yet, one day, I returned an hour after Sara sent me away with the instruction not to come back until after noon. The sister hadn't joined me this time, was no doubt enjoying the woods around the house, so I hadn't had her chatter to distract me. I returned to the house, jealous and angry. I walked through the front door and allowed it to slam behind me, signaling my arrival. The bedroom door opened, and Sara emerged, her face showing her surprise.

"What's the matter, what's wrong?" she asked.

"Nothing's wrong. I finished my errands so I'm back," I said, pulling my bag off and sitting down at a chair at the rickety table, leaning back in it arrogantly. "I thought I'd have lunch."

She looked at me for a long moment. "Get up and leave until after noon as I told you," Sara said, no give in her voice.

"No. That's ridiculous."

Her face went blank for a moment and then she turned and walked back into her bedroom. Moments later, that man came out, looking at me sideways. "Bonjour, Monsieur," he said in a voice that wished me the opposite.

"Bonjour," I said in a sing-song voice as he walked out the door. "Don't come back."

He frowned as he shut the door behind him.

Sara turned and walked slowly towards me, arms folded across her chest. "Who do you think you are?"

"I'm the man of this house," I said, beginning to count off on my fingers. "I work, I clean, I keep you safe. I deserve some respect." I sipped from the water glass on the table like I didn't have a care and then felt the wind whoosh by my face as she knocked the glass across the room where it clattered, spilling water on the floor.

"You are nothing in this house but a guest." Her face was transformed by fury, her pretty features twisted with anger. I let my chair legs land on the floor as her anger pricked mine.

"*I'm* the man taking care of things around here, I told you! *I'm* the one doing all the heavy lifting, being there for whatever, whenever you need me and all that. I'll be damned if I'm sent out of the house like a child while you do whatever it is you do with whoever it is you do it with."

"Is that right?"

I pointed in the direction of the town center. "They're in town saying you claimed me. How are you going to claim *me*? That all the women are supposed to stay away from me, but you can do whatever you please?"

"I told you how it was when you got here."

"Well, I won't be claimed, Teacher. So, get this straight..." I stood up. "I won't leave this place for anyone else ever again. I'm not a servant anymore! And I won't leave here to allow you to sneak another man in. You understand? I've had enough disrespect, and all that. You will respect me!"

I sniffed and turned my back. I'd made my point. Seconds later, I felt fingers in my short, coily hair and a quick jerk later, my head was snatched back, and I felt the sudden, quick, sweet sharpness of the point of a blade at my neck.

"This is *my* home," she said softly and firmly into my ear. "You don't tell me what to do, ever, not unless you want to be haunting me from outside by the tree like the others. If I tell you to leave this house and not come back until after noon, that's what you'll do. That's what you'll do!"

It was as if she'd loosened a part of herself that I hadn't met. I heard in her voice she was liable of anything; felt it in the strength of her grip. With each breath, my throat bobbled precariously, head so far back I was looking at the ceiling. A tiny swallow caused a nick and warm liquid dribbled down the front of my neck. It was only then that I realized I'd entirely misjudged the situation.

"Please, Sissie, don't kill him!" came the voice of her sister from a distance. She had been outside following the rules and staying clear of the house until noon, as I should have done. She'd no doubt heard our scuffle. "Please don't kill him! He plays music so pretty!"

My legs started to wobble. It seemed my body knew I was in mortal danger, even if my brain hadn't caught up. She wasn't a woman to make idle threats. She was the *murderess,* and I'd been foolish.

I was breathing heavily through my nose, losing my bravado while trying not to move a muscle more because of the straight edge cutting into my neck. It took five more seconds for her to pull the blade away and release my head. I immediately sprung away from her and dashed across the room to jerk open the door and stride outside, breathing deeply of fresh air, wiping the blood from my neck with my sleeve. It was barely a drop or two, but my quivering limbs didn't care.

I decided to take a walk. Eventually, as the quick pulse slowed in me, I realized how stupid I'd been. Stupid and rude. I went back later that evening. The house was quiet. I began gathering my clothes, strewn in odd places around the house, and put them into my bag. I felt her slip into the room from her bedroom quietly. There was none of the feeling of anger floating from her.

"You don't have to leave," she said. "I'm sorry I put the knife to you and frightened you. But you have to know the rules."

"I wasn't frightened," I bluffed. But, looking at her soft features, I knew *she knew* I had been. "Well, I deserved it, and all that. You were right. I had feelings and I don't know why. I have no claims here."

"I didn't claim you like you think. I only dropped a hint here or there in town that you were *with* me—as a friend—so they'd know to treat you right. It was never to claim you for mine. I wouldn't have minded if you found a woman friend. I think of you as a little brother. Like you think of my sister."

I winced. She wasn't interested in me at all. And why should she be? I was still the little boy to her. I nodded. "Well, I'm sorry. I was out of line. I can't explain it."

"I can. You're newly free. And, perhaps, you wanted something of your own. But it's not going to be me or mine. It's the folly of men that they naturally think they are owed rights to women. I had thought you were smarter but I see there's still something to be taught. You'll have to find and make your our own. If you understand that you're welcome to stay."

I shrugged. "I understand, but I can't say I won't have an outburst again. I can be... temperamental. The two of us... we're likely to kill each other."

She nodded slightly.

"I will always be thankful to you," I told her. "You showed me kindness. Twice. You showed me how to survive. I've never felt so worthless as when I wasn't able to protect you all those years ago."

"When we were children? You were even younger than me."

"But I'm not now. I guess I was hoping to have a chance to be what you need now, but... you don't really need me. And uselessness and powerlessness don't sit well on me. They bring out my ugly bits."

She smiled. "I appreciate your honesty." I returned the smile, feeling lighter now that we were better. My bag was packed, and I walked over to kiss her two cheeks.

"Besides, I've been putting off doing what I need to do and it's time for me to move on. Le Havre isn't far from here. I'm going to walk. You keep my horse. If you decide to sell him, make sure you get a good price. He's worth more than ten of me..."

***

I walked to Le Havre on foot. I showed my papers to board a ship, but they barely glanced at them. Looking around, it struck me that this was the first time I was crossing a border as a free man. I took in all the sights and smells and banter of people boarding. And then, I found a corner to try to melt into, pulling my hood over my head to make myself unnoticeable.

It was going to be a long journey, I knew. But I could use the time to think.

Of course, in the middle of the night, two men tried to rob me, thinking I was asleep. A small, quiet man alone was an easy target. But I had trained myself to sleep lightly, knowing the time would come when someone would make a move. And knowing that if I was going to make the first time the last, I would have to make it clear I wasn't to be bothered.

I was feigning sleep when the first leaned over to reach for the bag on the other side of me. I quickly drew my own razor, sat up and sliced him along the back of his ankle. His howl rang out loudly and jerked all the others from their sleep. I pulled my razor away, folded it, hid it, and sat back into the position of one who had slumped off into sleep. But I watched as one of the shipmen yelled.

"Who's that waking everybody up? What's wrong?" he yelled at the man who had slumped into his friend's arms. They both glanced at me, their faces doubtful now. It was the way of the world. You never knew what danger was before you.

"Nothing," he croaked on what sounded like a cry. Better to be thought of as a weakling than to be thought of as a danger on a boat on which people were trapped. "I tripped over all these loose tools laying around."

"Yeah, well, keep it down or I'll throw you overboard."

They slunk away, slipping me suspicious looks as they went. I settled into my corner, satisfied. My sleepless nights were over. And I slept like a baby.

Part III
HOME AGAIN

Gilded Orange Books

Chapter Thirty-Five

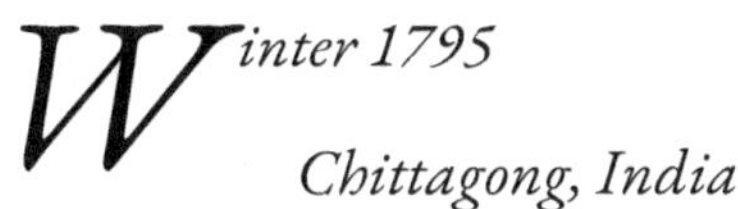

Winter 1795

Chittagong, India

Once in Chittagong, I walked through the door of a small merchant on a street that seemed vaguely familiar to me. The woman behind the counter asked me what business I had.

What business? No point but to be plain about it.

"Bonjour, Madame. I was born here in Chittagong and lived here until I was taken by slavers some time back. I've come to find my people," I told her.

"Slavers... *humph*. We all know about them. Look outside. Even though the British have taken over and it's illegal for them to import slaves, they still manage to trade. Everyone knows what's going on, but the Brits certainly won't stop it. The dark people they enslave and the light people they force to work making clothes for little pay. They've taken over our country."

"Import slaves? They brought Africans into India for slavery."

"They used to. Like I said, it's supposed to be illegal now. But you said you were taken a long time ago. Was it before the East India Company? How long ago?" she asked.

"Twenty-five years or so."

"A long time!" She squinted at me. "Are you the child who was taken from the market right here in town?"

My heart leapt. "You know of me?"

"Everyone in this town knows. At least, those of us other than the white people, we don't discuss those things with them. But we know what happened back in the 60s. The other two are accounted for so you must be the first of the *three*. Three children stolen after near many generations of safety in Chittagong. Everyone had thought the slavery times were over until they took the three. After that, most of the townspeople with dark skin took their children and fled. And then, there was the great famine..."

My heartbeat increased in my chest.

"My parents, do you know where I can find them?" I asked, almost afraid to hope.

She looked me over as if scanning to see if I was to be trusted or not, as if people showed up every day claiming to be lost sons of Chittagong. Finally, she nodded. "Everybody knows where to find the parents of the first stolen boy from Chittagong."

"How do you know I was the first?"

"Like I said, because of the other two, of course. We know they were taken afterwards, and what happened with them."

A half hour later I stood over two gravestones and looked down at the place where my parents lay.

I had run out of tears long ago, but I had plenty pain at that moment. I didn't recognize the language or the names. I felt cold looking down at them.

"They couldn't live forever, waiting for you. We use them as a cautionary tale: never get too comfortable around white-skinned people," the woman said from behind me. She had a tone that said she blamed me for not getting back fast enough. That somehow, I had caused their deaths.

"No, none of us can live forever." I turned away so she wouldn't see my face. "But I came back," I said, more for myself than her. "Can you give me a moment, please?"

"What for?" she asked but at my glare she stepped away.

What for? Maybe it wasn't a bad question. Was I going to speak to them? Was I going to speak to God? Was I going to cry? None of that. I couldn't even remember them.

I stood there for a moment more, my hands fidgeting in my pockets. I should have something to say to them. Shouldn't I? Shouldn't I have felt *something*?

It had taken a ship ride, many wagons and a season just to get to Chittagong and now there was no reason for me to stay. I thanked the woman and then left to wander, perhaps to see if there was a place for me to decide what was next. I took a small room in an Inn and then struck out on foot, finding a small drinking spot. I was sitting at a bar when a group of men came in behind me. I heard their boots first, loud and aggressive in the small space.

It wasn't until that moment that I realized I was in danger in this place. I felt them behind me and knew they were staring at my back. The tan-skinned barkeep began to fidget and looked at me nervously. I put the glass of spirit down and spoke as though I didn't know they were behind me.

"Can I get a hot tea, sire," I said to him in English. It seemed the language was spoken in most ports where French was not as well known. "My bones, broken long ago, ache. There must be water in the sky as I feel it settling in my joints."

"That, I understand well," he said. "Anything else I can get you?"

"A draft of laudanum to take the pain away would be welcome."

He smiled nervously. Footsteps behind me moving again told me the group of men was no longer paying me any mind. A few moments later and they were gone. The barkeep brought me my tea.

I took a sip. "Is it like that all the time, then? They scope the streets like vultures looking for fresh meat?"

He nodded. "We used to think it was a temporary madness, but it seems to hold on. I don't think it will end any time soon. I see from your clothes you aren't from here, and I hear the French in your voice. But you're young enough and seemingly healthy enough they will always be watching for someone like you. Why are you here in Chittagong?"

"I was born here," I said. "It was a foolish, childish thought I had that maybe I could come home. That my home would still be here."

"Not foolish," he said. "But unfortunate. This town has fallen back to what it does best–it trades. It just so happens now the most profitable commodity is human beings. If you have someplace else to go, you should. But you say you were born here? Do you remember no one from childhood?"

"I understand they all left after I was kidnapped. My parents are buried here, but the rest of them fled after three of us were taken, so I'm told."

"Ah, you're from one of the communities of dark-skinned people that fled, you say?"

***

The conversation didn't get on much farther after that, and I left. The next morning, I was in my room preparing to leave for good when a knock sounded on my door. Not knowing anyone in this place, I was hesitant to even answer the door lest I open it to a group of slavers ready to pluck me up for a second time. But a voice spoke to me through the worn barrier.

"Monsieur, I'm told you are asking around in town looking for your people. I can help."

I hesitated a moment but then opened the door to find a dark-skinned young man of about twenty-two with a serious, earnest face, facial skin that had never seen hair, and eyes that looked like they could break out moisture at a moment's notice. He should have been at home at his mother's lap with sensitivity like that written on his face. I peered around him to make sure he was alone.

"I am Moti. It's just me," he said. "I'm a guide. Many of our people return looking for family and I try to get hold of them before the slavers do. The others leave for an education or just to find a new home. I understand you were taken as a child. The first of the three, I hear. I can take you to your people if you would like, but we'd have to be quick and quiet. More quiet than you've been." He smiled.

"Do you speak French, too?" I said, suspicious.

"Oui, I speak it well enough to understand most." He switched tongues to my language like he'd been doing it all his life, with only a slight accent.

"You speak it well."

"Thank you. It comes from living near a trading town and extensive travel. I know four languages and many dialects right here at home."

"You can take me to my people? What do you want in return?"

"No, Monsieur—"

"Tell me up front what you want. I've had a difficult time already and I'm not in the mood for nonsense." My nerves had frayed overnight as the reality of my dead parents had set in. I had spent the night tossing and turning trying to remember their faces and woke up cursing myself for the ungrateful excuse of a son I was, living my life in a palace while my parents died in grief and poverty longing for me. I was sad and angry and on edge. I couldn't deal with one more betrayal and I was ready to take my ire out on him. "Choose your answer carefully, son. I'm small but I'm bitter and I'm not in the mood for another joker."

"Monsieur, I don't want anything from you. You are Chittagong-born, and you have returned. We of the communities of African blood are small and few, but we take care of each other. It is my moral obligation to take you to your people... if you would like to go."

I looked at him, dumbfounded for a long moment. He said pretty words, but I still wasn't sure I believed him. His eyes were so wide and open and sensitive I might have been looking at Jean Amilcar all grown up. I blinked away the sudden association and the pain that streaked through me at the thought of the little boy who'd never had a chance to grow up. The man standing before me wasn't Jean and he wasn't offering the world, just offering to take me to my people.

"Surely, you want *something* in return? Don't put me in a position to find what I seek but then not be able to give you what you require. Tell me what you expect in return."

"It would dishonor me and our people if I were to take anything from you in payment for connecting you with our community," he said. I heard a *but* in his voice. "But if you want to buy me a drink, I wouldn't turn it down. Liquor is expensive here."

Hope flared, once again. I was suddenly desperate for any connection to my parents. So it was that a few minutes later, after settling my bill and buying him the drink he requested, he and I climbed into the wagon of a cart and a driver led our horse-drawn wagon to begin a trek deep into India to reach my people. We started out in the back of a cart.

Jostling along, I tried not to remember my childhood cart rides through the country. He looked at my clothes and closed shoes and gestured toward my bags. I carried a burlap bag with my three changes of clothing, my leather satchel with my writings and quill with ink, and my violin case.

"Are any of your clothes lighter, sir? It gets very hot in the jungle."

We were rolling over rough ground, but his words caught my attention, his baby face earnest.

"You didn't say anything about the jungle before."

"My apologies, I should have explained. Very few communities of African people live in the cities today."

"Why not? No markets? There were markets when I left. No mosque? What about the men who fished at the port? Surely they want to work."

"They want to be free, also. Very few will risk being taken for work as a fisherman or tradesman in the busy areas. Don't worry about the clothes, I will get you lighter ones the next time I'm in town and bring them to you."

"I can pay."

"That will be fine."

A few minutes later I asked: "How long is it, then?"

"Quite a distance, sir." He reached beside him in the cart and pulled out a wine cask, pushing it toward me. "Water. You'll want to take sips only when thirsty, Monsieur. You'll need most of it for the last part."

Along the way, Moti chattered like a child about how he'd been educated—one of the few in the community with a formal education—about how his family had been worried about him until they'd learned that he planned to be a convoy for their community, after which they had praised him for doing the work of Allah.

He chattered so much in the wagon through each town that I fell asleep sometimes.

"Our ancestors were varied. Some came as servants or through indentured servitude. Some were soldiers and tradespeople. Some were nobility or high military leaders. People with black skin from every country in Africa, in every way you can imagine. At one point, India and the countries of Africa respected each other and traded freely, you see."

"What happened?" I asked.

He smirked. "Europeans decided rather than trade with us, they'd just trade *us*. They changed the rules of the game without telling Black people." He glanced at me wryly. "After France and England finished fighting over us England left their East India company to rule us. Now, no matter, we have a rich history of building this country, we are mostly taken as laborers. The East India Company is our government now whether we want it or not. All of our former African empires are gone. Now, it's indentured servitude and the sickness of whatever kind of slavery they force Black people into. I've heard rumors but none of us really know what they're doing to the people of African blood they take away from us. Maybe you can share that. All we know is that the desire for slavery and all that comes with it is like mold on bread—one day only a spot and the next, taken over the whole piece. The colonists brought it, but our country has learned the mold is valuable and has given in to it as well."

The road went from rocky to worn grooves over earth and then to grass. I had fallen asleep at one point and when I woke up found that our horse and carriage was trudging through a forested area with no road at all.

"Where the hell are we?" I snapped at Moti, whose head jerked up from his chest, him having fallen asleep also. He looked around, alarmed, and realized my panic was just due to me and not due to any circumstance like an overturned carriage or mortal danger.

"Ah Monsieur, we're just part-way into the forest. The community is in hiding; you can't reach it by road."

I looked around. "I know they said the community moved, I didn't realize they were *hiding*." I don't know why I didn't. It made perfect sense.

"It traumatized the community, the way you and the others were taken, Monsieur. They had thought that was over. So, after it happened, the members with dark skin decided to go to where most people are afraid to go, to protect the children and themselves."

As our carriage rumbled through the grass and trees, I realized that it was only a matter of time before the horses wouldn't be able to penetrate as the forests grew denser. An hour later, the carriage slowed and the driver yelled down to Moti. The young man turned to me.

"It is growing dark. The driver will allow us to sleep in the cart with him until morning, and then the rest is on foot, Monsieur."

I spent that night cuddled up against two other grown men under a blanket that we had sat on the whole ride there. The temperature dropped lower than expected considering the heat of the day. I had a hard time sleeping out in the open, the stars above us and strange sounds around us, and soon gave up trying.

At first light, we climbed out of the cart and, after relieving ourselves, Moti and I trudged along on foot. Unaccustomed to serious walking on uneven ground, forty-five minutes in, I was drenched in sweat and huffing like an old man. The trees were now so thick, we sometimes had to push vines out of our way and the insects landed on every inch of my skin that wasn't covered. My sack of clothes felt like a bag of lead and my violin case like it was studded with bricks, but I panted my tiredness out with loud breaths and kept moving. Kept moving. Took sips of water when I felt like my lungs had been emptied like an Irishman's bagpipes, asking myself what in the hell I was doing.

All said, the journey from Chittagong was about eighteen hours. When we reached an area in the woods that looked like we were in the middle of nowhere, suddenly, in the late twilight darkness before us, torches lit up and it seemed a village sprouted to life before us with small huts surrounding an area of cleared ground and the sound of donkeys and chickens nearby.

A man stepped forward. He was dressed in a long, white shift that seemed to be made of gauze that settled over equally light pants, with sandals on his feet. He looked me over.

Water dripped down my face and I could barely stand upright, but I squinted through the salty sweat to stare at him back.

He then spoke to Moti in a foreign tongue, though my ear strained to recognize it. Moti responded and more people were now coming out to see the disturbance. I heard Moti say in English—*"The first taken"*—and, suddenly, all focus was on me.

The man looked at me intently, then his face split into a smile. He yelled something out and faces began to light up in smiles, until everyone began cheering.

Sweat dripping into my eyes made all of them barely discernible and I couldn't understand a damn word they were saying, but I didn't have to know the language to understand I was being welcomed like a long lost son. A smile spread across my face.

CHAPTER THIRTY-SIX

Moti promised to stay a few days to help me gain my bearings. He looked thrilled and got many slaps on the back and hugs from the others for this rescue mission. As the man who'd stepped up to me first led me into the clearing, I lost sight of Moti, still caught in the storm of excitement.

Many voices and nods and affectionate slaps on the arm and back from the crowd came as I seemed the returning hero. After they each had had a turn to greet me, they melted away, almost as if by design, and I found I was alone with a few people speaking to me in a language I didn't understand. Finally, one said hello in French.

"Bonjour..." I said eagerly, my head swiveling to find the source that had spoken.

"Do you speak English?" came another voice.

I nodded. "Yes, English, too." Relief washed over me. I would be able to communicate. The ones who didn't speak either language gestured with their hands, and I began to as well. It would take us some time to figure out how to speak to each other.

They set me up in my very own hut and that night I tried to sleep, again, but I was dirty and tired, and the sounds were all so new. Someone had left a small lit candle on a crate that filled the space with shadows along with a bowl with water and a cloth which I used to try to wipe off some grime. Then I slept in fits and starts.

The next day, I didn't know how to greet them, so I nodded and bowed. They did the same in response to my awkward, confused lead. Moti was in the clearing as if waiting for me.

"You'll be wanting to see the community now that it's light out. I'll show you around. This way." He led me away from the group and to a small stream.

"This is the drinking water. It's not meant for bathing, but some people sneak and do it because it's cleaner. There's a larger watering hole a bit away," he said. I wanted to wade into the water, too, feeling so grimy. I hadn't had a bath since I left the Chateau. "Off that way is where to relieve yourself. They like to keep things organized."

"Are all of the communities like this?" I asked.

"Every community of African people is different; rules, traditions, religions, how they keep the peace—it varies by community. But we are friendly towards each other when we have occasion to meet."

"When would that be?"

"Like when I go around asking if anyone has heard any news of a lost member. I try to know who comes and goes in case one of our lost returns and ends up in a different community."

"Do they pay you to do that?"

He laughed as we trudged through the woods. "With what, Monsieur, we don't use money. At least not those of us in the woods. The communities closer to the cities might, for when they go into town. But most avoid town, even if they are not far. Slavers."

It felt strange, to live in constant fear of slavers. It was one thing I hadn't worried about on mainland France.

"You ended up in the French colonies?" he asked.

"The mainland."

"I see. Word will spread and the French speakers will want to speak with you. But today is for celebration. We will eat and all the children will come to pay their respects."

"In France, we only do that when people are dead."

"Well, you were dead, of a sort, Monsieur. Dead to the community because they had lost you. You were the first of three boys taken. They want to pay respect."

Later, I put on fresh clothes in my hut. When I came out, I was led a little further into the enclave where a fire was burning and something delicious and charred was roasting over it. The blistering of the skin of a wild boar made my mouth water.

"A few here do not eat meat but most of them eat what they can find. And for celebrations, like today, meat is welcome," Moti said. "We will sit in a circle by the fire and eat together."

The plates were thick, awkward pottery but served their purpose. A man stood up and with wild and reckless swipes of a machete, hacked off pieces of the roasting meat to laughter and conversation as chunks were passed around. Then, a pot of rice appeared, and we held out our plates for scoops of it, which we ate with our fingers and using pieces of meat to shove into our mouths.

Moti leaned over to me. "They do have eating utensils if you'd like. But this is tradition."

"It's okay, I'm fine," I said, licking the juices from my hand.

Moti translated for those who knew no French or English at all. Eventually, the man who'd stepped up yesterday sat down beside me. "You were in France, I hear," he said. I nodded.

Again, he wore a long, cotton tunic-like shirt. The women all wore the same type of clothing, with colorful coverings over their hair. Some had hair that escaped the covering, hanging in braids with beads of ribbons running through them and much jewelry.

I had long since shed my silks, laces and layers and layers of underclothes. I wore a simple wool shirt and rough-hewn pants with some shoes that, though worn-looking, were leather and had conformed to my feet. Despite the heat and sweat I was glad to have them because any other shoe would not have survived the walk.

"We were told others from other communities were boarded onto ships headed to the colonies for labor," the man said.

A woman across the fire heard us and spoke up, loudly. "I hear French people are eating each other in the streets. They say they come to the town square with knives and forks ready to feast. Is that true?" She spoke English.

She was frank, her gaze openly commanding.

"That's the medicine woman," Moti whispered. "She is one of the town leaders."

I squinted at her. "Who told you the French were eating each other?" She pointed to Moti, who flushed.

"That is indeed what I heard," my chubby-faced friend said defensively. "The papers say French people are beset with madness that spreads. That there's bloodlust like with rabid dogs. But I can't say what papers are real and what are just telling stories. You come from there, you tell us, is it true?"

I immediately felt the need to deny it, but truthfully, was it that far off the mark? The months during the worst of the Terror were bad, but not that bad.

"No, of course not."

"It seems a strange story to tell if it's not true," she challenged.

"Don't people do that everywhere? Tell a story a bit wilder than it truly is?" Her eyes seemed to peer into my brain, and I offered, grudgingly,

"...Certainly, at times knives were carried to the streets but there was no eating of people."

"Uhmhum," she said, her face showing she didn't believe me at all.

"And what of you?" the main man asked me. "Tell us what happened when you were taken. Tell us about your life."

Many faces previously disinterested turned my way.

"I can't remember much of the actual kidnapping," I admitted. On seeing confusion on faces, I clarified, "I don't remember much of being taken."

"How could you forget such a thing?" the medicine woman asked.

"Go ahead," said the man. "Tell us what you remember. Moti says you are called Zamor? I've heard it told that they do that to the enslaved—take your names from you and give you a new one. They say many people refused their new names. Did they beat you to force you to answer to a new name?"

I flushed as their gazes fell on me. If I told them that I willingly lost my name—had given it up—not for a beating nor threat of one—they would think me a traitor or a coward. Neither was a good thing. I shrugged. "I was young. My name fell away. I didn't get a new one until years later in France."

I described my life as best I could while leaving out anything I didn't want to have to explain, which was most of it. I told them I lived with a couple who called me their son. That I'd been educated and baptized in a Christian church. That I taught myself to play a musical instrument.

They listened, politely, those who understood English nodding at my story. But the more I skipped over uncomfortable bits the more I felt them shift from me. They could tell I was leaving things out and didn't want to share. By the end of the meal the warmth that had been there at the beginning had cooled considerably. I felt their awareness of my lies of omission.

The children began to disappear first, bored of my uninteresting stories. They ran off in groups like children do. Then the adults drifted away, one at a time, to tend to their affairs until it was just me and the man who'd stepped up first.

"We don't often get visitors," the man said. "Now you come here after traveling over water from very far away to find us. After several years of hearing your tale bandied about, to see you in person and to know that you want to be here–it is special. No matter how uncomfortable you may be about sharing with us."

"I don't mean to offend. Where I come from we don't share so easily."

He leaned toward me and said under his breath, "But you come from *here*. You have only forgotten. It's not your fault. We had hoped the *Three Stolen* might have ended up together but that didn't happen."

"The *Three Stolen*? You say that like it's a name."

"It is. I told you, you are a legend. The *Three Stolen* is the reason we ended up here, deep in the woods. Three of you in one month, gone. Parents were panicked. Seemingly overnight we traveled as deeply as possible into the jungle where no one else would want to go. We rebuilt. And yes, we have lost some of the easiness of living near a growing town, but we have our children. It's worth it."

I looked at his profile, his forehead with many horizontal lines that told me he was a worrying sort. His beard was kinky curly with strands of silver.

"Are you the leader here?"

"We have no leader, not in the way you mean. But I'm an elder. People look to me for guidance. Me and the medicine woman."

"I appreciate the kind reception."

"I misspoke, I called you a visitor. You probably don't remember me. I'm wrinkled now, but I recognized you right away. You and I played together as children. When you left, I had no front teeth."

Something flashed quickly in my head. The memory was sharp like a jagged piece of glass shoved into my brain. It was a flash of an image of a little boy grinning to a group of us playing stones in the street. He was preening, very proud that he was more grown up than we were. I was jealous. Because I hadn't lost my baby teeth, then. I remembered running home and asking my mother to pull my front teeth out to speed my growing up.

My throat choked immediately. I had thought all memories were lost. But now, this thought of the toothless child brought with it a memory of my mother. I couldn't see her face, it was a blur, but her words came to me:

"...Ah, child, your big teeth will never have anything to do with how grown up you are. Maturity comes with wisdom and age."

"Can it also come with missing front teeth? You spank me for free, surely you can knock my teeth out for my sake?"

I tried to hold onto that memory but, just as quickly as it came it flittered away, a flame doused by a bucket of water—only to be replaced with a less pleasant one. I remembered losing my front teeth before they were ready to let go on the road from the back hand. I remembered the acrid taste of blood as he derided me for my smart mouth.

"That was your fault. For your stupid backtalk. Keep your mouth shut from now on."

It hurt and I wondered why I had ever asked my parents to be hit.

"D-do you know how old am I?" I asked the man beside me softly. I didn't want anyone else to hear my shameful question.

He looked at me, surprised. "You and I are the same age. We are thirty-three years old. I'm one month older than you." He told me a date and looked at me as if it should mean something. "Don't you remember? How could you forget your own birthday?"

How could I forget my own birthday? I forgot my own name. There were days when I forgot I was human. Days when I forgot that I wasn't dirt on the ground upon which everyone walked. But there was no telling that to someone who'd never known that type of disruption.

A few minutes later he clasped my shoulder and then took his leave. I didn't mind. I was tired of the questions. I found gazing at the dying fire comforting. My comfort was broken soon enough when a voice spoke beside me.

"Finally, we can speak," came the gravelly voice. "My brother was the third taken."

I squinted to look up. Firelight lit the man's face from below as if he was a haunted wraith come to life. He sat down beside me without invitation, folding his lanky body down beside me.

"My brother was four and sickly," he continued. "You remember him? Very cute, but sickly. Always with the nose running. Always hurting himself and stubbing his toe. He was clumsy and weak, but my parents loved him most. He was their favorite. My father went looking right away and when he caught up with the slavers, they killed my brother and threw his body off into a ditch onto the side of the road."

"That's horrible. I'm very sorry."

"It was probably because he was so sick and weakly. My mother couldn't get over the fact that they could have just let him go. They didn't have to kill him. If they didn't want him, they could have just left him. They didn't have to wring his neck like a chicken. But he was sickly and would have died anyway."

I looked at his stoic face. He showed no ounce of sadness. Perhaps the passage of time had numbed him.

"And did your parents find some comfort in bringing his body home?"

He shrugged. "Two days after my father came back with my brother's dead body my mother drowned herself in the watering hole where we bathe. A week later, my father fell while climbing and hit his head and died."

"Mon Dieu, I'm so sorry," I said. "That's horrible, I'm so very sorry. So, what about the other? Who was the *Second Lost*?"

He looked at me, baffled. "The *Second Lost* was *me*."

Him? My mind started scoping the story he'd just told me as he looked as confused as if I'd been the storyteller. I felt a shuffling beside me on the other side and looked over to find the medicine woman. But I still had more questions. She sat down and looked pointedly at the man. His face soured, but he stood up, without a word, and walked away.

"Hello, Madame..." I started. "That man said he was the *Second Lost*. I don't understand, what happ—"

"—Shubho Shondba," she said, placing a hand on my arm and patting me as if trying to impart something.

"I'm sorry, I don't understand you. Perhaps we can find someone to translate."

She stared at me. "Shubho Shondba."

It was like she wasn't hearing me or wasn't listening. But her eyes were on me so intently.

"Shubho Shondba!" she said again. Then she spoke in broken English. "You were seven when you left us, old enough to know your name, your age and your language. Your mind is broken," she declared.

We stared at each other for a long moment. Though it wasn't terribly hot, a bead of sweat made its way over my brow to plop off my face. I wiped at it and told her, "With respect, it would be easier for me if you didn't try to force me to remember a language I lost as a child. Madame."

"Do you normally wet so much?"

"What?" I wiped the sweat off my forehead and glanced down, noticing the front of my shirt pooled with moisture.

"What is that on your neck?" she asked, grabbing me by the collar of my shirt and pulling me closer to look.

Before I had a chance to respond she was up and calling out to others.

I didn't know why I was so hot. She leaned over and put a hand on my forehead. And then the world swam around me, and I was out.

Chapter Thirty-Seven

I swam in and out of consciousness. Each time there were different people looking over me and speaking to me in a language I didn't understand. One time, Moti came into view from the blackness, looking into my eyes with his deep ones.

"Zamor," he said. "Do not panic. You have the fever; Denghe fever."

"What the h-hell is Denghe fever?" I asked in French, trying to get up and failing to even raise my head.

"From a mosquito. It will run its course, God willing, but you must rest."

***

Rest? I was constantly sleeping but never rested. Every time I woke up there was someone putting a wet washcloth on my forehead or feeding me sips of water. I was never alone but never lost the need to run screaming into the night the second I woke up. My body didn't obey. I just managed to move enough for someone to tell me, *"There, there, Zamor, lie still. You must rest."*

When I wasn't struggling to wake up, I was struggling to grab hold of the thoughts that came like snacks to me, the meat of them just out of my grasp. People floated in and out of my mind. Nightmares came often and sudden.

I was standing in the Pavilion and everyone was there. Both kings, the Queen and Madame. Sebastien, Salanave and Henri. Josephe and Thomas and Véronique... all of them. But it was storming outside, and a crack of thunder shook the little building. Then, it grew quiet, so quiet it was like the atmosphere was devoid of sound. And then, faintly, I heard the sickeningly familiar *hush... swish*! And suddenly Sebastien dropped down dead onto the ground next to me.

"Sebastien!" I called out to him, but his open eyes were already cloudy with death. I looked around at the others who stood as if in a trance when I heard it again. The familiar sound came again, louder this time.

Hush... swish!

Henri dropped as if he'd suddenly lost all his bones. But when I ran to him, the sound came faster and louder the next time and the next person who fell was too far away for me to get to quickly. The sound sped up, taking them all, one at a time. Taking LaFayette, Salanave, Brissot, Josephe, Véronique...! Taking them all one by one as I screamed. Taking them all as I asked for forgiveness until I was the only one standing in the midst of the pile of dead bodies and a pool of blood. And still, I combed over them all searching for my parents. Searching... still searching... And then, little Jean was standing before me, an eight-year-old with soiled royal silks and a dark ring from throttling around his neck. Then, the thunder cracked in my eardrums and my eyelids flew open...

"...Zamor."

My lids flickered and blinked fast but the image in front of me didn't waver. I gasped in air like I'd been jogging but the image didn't leave.

"He's back," Moti said to the room. He smiled. "You were sick for a week, but the fever has broken. You survived. You are like the forest creatures; you're slight but you refuse to die. And good thing. It would be a shame for the legendary *First Lost* to survive kidnapping and slavery only to come home and be killed by a mosquito. Welcome back."

Thunder rumbled and lightning cracked the night sky. I could hear the thick rain that caused the air inside the little structure to be heavy with warm humidity. Moti left with the promise to be back soon, and the medicine woman came into my hut with a bowl of water. She sat down beside me and used a washcloth to mop my forehead.

"This is my community," she said, as if she needed to announce her place there. "I heal the sick and *I* decide who comes and goes. We're happy you're awake again so we can sleep. Ever since you fell ill you spend all your sleeping time screaming and fighting the air with your arms. You frightened the children."

"Oh. I'm very sorry."

"You cried and yelled. You cursed yourself and others and you begged. Once you sat straight up with your eyes wide open and looked up like you were looking at something horrible... Let out a sound that sounded like an animal to slaughter, but you were still in fever and dropped back down onto the bed like you suddenly lost all your bones. You scared some of the others and they refuse to tend to you again."

I blinked the sweat that still rolled down my forehead into my eyes and sat up gingerly, feeling like I'd been lifting heavy logs until my muscles failed. She continued.

"You kept yelling at someone to 'die, die, die!' No one will say it aloud because you are one of our own and one of the *Three Lost*, but the whole community is wondering if you are a murderer of men."

A gust of rain pushed through the windows and felt good on my heated skin, but she still stared at me, undistracted by the wetness on her face and clothes. She looked at me like she could see into my soul.

I didn't like to lie, and I could hardly deny what I was when I'd been confessing all my sins in delirium. But something told me that to say the words out loud would get me expelled. It was the way she waited, perched as if ready to call on people to take me away. I lied.

"What?" I laughed weakly, trying to pull up the charm born of necessity. "Of course not. It was just nightmares. Do I look like a person who could harm anyone?" I pulled myself up on my elbows. The blanket fell from my naked chest, and I pulled it up quickly to cover myself. "I-I came a long way to find you all and I won't cause any harm. I'm no saint, but I'm far from evil. A murderer?" I laughed like I was baffled and shocked by the thought.

She leaned toward me, wiping my head and the back of my neck, dipping the cloth back into the water. My eyes filled at the feeling of the coolness against my neck. I felt like a weakling, wanting to break down so badly it took everything in me to keep still, looking away from her.

The fever did something to me. It cracked my resolve. I felt like I could break at any moment, and I wasn't at all sure I wanted it to be in front of this woman when it happened. I kept clutching the blanket to me as she tried to move the washcloth down my back. I squirmed to see if I was wearing anything beneath the blanket and she picked up on my discomfort.

"I changed your clothes and your bedding while you were in fever. I saw the broken places and the marks. The scars. No one will hear from me about your private business. Always keep your shirt on so no one will see that horrible thing across your body."

I flushed with embarrassment. I hadn't asked her to undress me in the first place. "Yes, of course. I'd like to be alone, please."

She didn't press further, just took the bowl, stood up, gave me one last suspicious glance, and left. I waited until she was well and truly gone before I lost the ability to hold my reserve.

I pulled my knees into my chest, clutching them as I shook, allowing the blanket and my thighs to absorb the sound of my heaving sobs. I couldn't stop. Lord, I couldn't stop the anguish wracking my body. It came out of me like the fever had, erupting from my pores with the fervor of my passion.

I rocked on my bed, back and forth, allowing the sound of the pounding rain to drown my cries. The noise of the storm gave me the chance to make all the noise I'd never been able to make. I cried and begged like a man possessed. I was possessed with a need to get the blood off my hands.

The next day I ventured out to the bathing water and found a group of young men already there. I heard lots of whispers and ducked behind a tree to look because whenever there were whispers there was someone being whispered about. The men were huddled in a group in one area. They were talking amongst themselves, but they were sneaking glances to the other side of the water. I squinted and saw they were looking at another lone figure further away, swishing his arms around in the water, alone. It was the *Second Lost*. I could tell from the way they snuck glances at him that he was the subject of their whispering. The looks on their faces said they were both horrified and fascinated by the man. But one of them had a look of pity on his face. It was a look I did everything in my power never to see on the face of someone looking at me.

My fellow abductee pretended not to hear or notice. I understood his loneliness and separation.

Clearing my throat to announce myself, I emerged from behind the tree. The group looked up at me, caught staring, shame-faced. I nodded at them but once reaching the water, walked on the stones at the shallow end over to the other man. From where he crouched, he looked up at me, eyes suspicious like he couldn't tell if I might hit him when I reached him.

"It's a nice day for the water," I called out. His shoulders relaxed just a little. "Care if I join you?"

His face was so immediately relieved it almost made me want to cry. He smiled a little.

"I thought you wanted to come over and mock me directly," he said with his gravelly voice. "They always manage to come to the water just after I do and stand over there to laugh at me."

I had reached him by then, his face both indignant and hurt.

"They just don't understand," I told him. "They're young. They've never been out of this community and don't know what it's like to be taken. They don't know how hard it is."

His eyes lit bright then. "That's right! They don't know. They hurt you, didn't they? I saw. When you were sick with fever the medicine woman sent me in to change your bedding and I saw some damage along your middle and your spine was twisted wrong. Bones looked broken and set wrong. They did that do you?"

She had said she was the only one who saw me. Now, something about the way he made his admission—almost with his lips wiggling trying not to smile—didn't sit right with me. It annoyed me, how instantly salacious he had become, considering I had come over here in good will to make him feel better. That he should ask me as if wanting a bit of gossip put a bad taste in my mouth. Because I hesitated to confirm or deny, my silence was enough for him.

His face lit up like he was happy. "You *do* understand. What did they do to you?"

"I don't want to talk about it."

He nodded vigorously. "That's all right. It's enough to know you understand how I feel. They look at me like I'm a monster. All I want is to be treated like everyone else."

"I am curious, you spoke so much about your brother," I said. He wanted to get all the juicy details about me, let him have a turn. "You talked as if he was the only one taken. You didn't speak about yourself at all."

His eyes darkened and brow furrowed quickly. "I tried to protect my brother."

"Very brave of you."

"My papa said it was my duty as the older brother. But I was a child, too."

"How old were you?"

"Fifteen."

Fifteen?

"Did you see them kill your brother, then?"

"No." His eyes skittered away from me. "If I had seen, don't you think I would have stopped them? I don't care what anybody tells you, it wasn't my fault. They didn't even care that I came back."

"I'm a bit surprised the slavers let you go."

"Why? They came for little children, not for me."

"Why'd they take you, then?"

His head swiveled to me, eyes sharp. "Why are you asking me so many questions? Do you want to blame me, too?"

His face was now so clouded I was sorry I pressed the point. "I didn't mean anything. I was just wondering about the story. I'm sorry for your brother and your parents. Being stolen couldn't possibly have been your fault. I'm sure you coming home made an impossible situation a little better. I'm certain your parents were happy at least one of their children su—"

"—She told me I should have been the one they killed. She asked me why I hadn't died instead. Right before she walked into this very water." His eyes were glazed now. "I know she didn't mean it, but she hurt me. I felt bad already. She didn't have to say those words to me. She didn't have to tell me my only value was to protect the son she loved. She walked all the way out over to there…" He turned and pointed to an area deep in the middle of the lake. "Then she must have changed her mind because she started flapping her arms. Kept going under and coming back up. She started gasping and I watched her. I know she wanted me to go get help, but I didn't. I stood here and watched. She wasn't a good swimmer. I watched. She shouldn't have hurt my feelings. She shouldn't have said those things."

Coldness had been seeping over me as he told his story and he was still turned, his arm pointing, his gaze stuck in the past as he matter-of-factly described watching his mother drown.

I cleared my throat and thought about how to leave. The sound of my voice jogged him back to the present and his face cleared as he turned toward me again.

"I'm glad you're here, Zamor. Everyone here thinks I'm strange. No one wants to speak to me or spend time with me, but now you're here and you understand how it feels to be a victim of evil. We can explain to them, together."

I could think of nothing I'd want to do less than that.

"Don't let it hurt your feelings, they don't mean to. They will never understand what they haven't lived. You can't think about that. You can only think on yourself, and being happy. We're home. That's a blessing."

He looked doubtful but nodded. "You're very confident. I would like to learn from you."

"I'm not confident. I'm pragmatic." He looked confused. "I accept things as they are. There are some things you simply can't change. Other people, usually. The only time I'm hurt is when I think a person is going to change. Now, I don't expect people to be anything other than what they are. And then they don't disappoint me."

"That's strange. I expect people to be better than they are."

"And you are constantly disappointed, are you not?"

He didn't say anything but his eyes flashed with hurt. I could see his feelings right on his face.

"I'm glad you're here. We will be friends," he said.

I wasn't so much interested in being his friend. I'd had enough of murdering friends. I no longer wanted friends, but I didn't mind it if he thought we were. No one should feel alone.

Chapter Thirty-Eight

The *Second Lost* would come around every once in a while, sometimes to sit beside me. Sometimes he showed up when I was out learning to fish or planting. I took his presence for what it was–he was comforting himself somehow with my existence. Having lost so much I couldn't begrudge him whatever made him feel better.

But then there came a time about a month after I arrived when I noticed he wasn't shadowing me so much anymore. And then one night over a communal dinner I looked up and noticed him frowning at me from across the fire. Coming from a man who barely looked at me, even when he spoke to me, the look was jarring.

Moti noticed this on one of his visits. His normally happy face frowned with worry.

"Moti, it has been weeks. How have you been?"

"Fine, thank you. Yes, I arrived here earlier today but you must have been planting."

"I've become a farmer, Moti. Imagine that. Carrots and potatoes and all that. I quite enjoy it."

"Very good, Monsieur Zamor. I need to tell you something." He sat down beside me. I looked up and *Second Lost* glared at me and stood to stomp away. Moti continued. "As I said, I came by earlier and brought some things with me from town. As you know, much literature from all over the world comes through the ports. I was keeping an eye out for news on France and came across this, written in English about France. I brought it earlier and some of the people here in the community saw it and told some of the others."

Moti handed me a printed document. It was an illustrated drawing. It was a drawing of a chubby Louis XV sitting on his throne eating a giant chicken leg with grease smeared over his cheeks, Madame beside him smiling and leaning over to slap me on my bare ass, all of this done with a backdrop of the palace and a carpet of money underneath us. To make sure our identities were clear, each of us was labeled with our name. I could date it as having been published back when I was about eleven. It was referred to in an article on the lost monarchy. It was an insulting drawing meant to show us as slovenly, debauched, greedy slobs surrounded by luxury. Thankfully, it wasn't one of the obscene ones.

"This—this is a rag cartoon. Many of them came out over the years."

"Yes, that is you with the King and Queen of France?"

"She wasn't the Queen but, yes, that's meant to be me, though the likeness is poor. Don't pay any mind to it. All of France seemed obsessed with stories of my intimate activity, all exaggerations if not outright lies."

"No, it's not that. There are trash pamphlets all over the world these days. It's that it appears you lived in the house of a king. We were all surprised but, I believe, the *Second Lost* expressed he felt very... insulted. He said he felt a fool having thought the two of you were the same when you were out living a life of wealth and indulgence—like a king. You did leave out some details when you told us where you'd been."

At one time I might have responded with a sarcastic reply, but I didn't want to insult Moti or anyone. When I felt attacked it was my instinct to strike back but I couldn't afford to do that here. In their place I might have felt equally betrayed. They'd taken me in, and I'd only told half-truths.

"I didn't mean to mislead anyone," I said. "What should I do, do you think?"

"Most of the others don't care if you were rich or poor and won't begrudge you either way. But it will help if they understand a little more of what happened to you and why you are here. What you want with them. They need to know they can trust you."

If these people kicked me out, where would I go? I had no one left. If they turned me away, what was left?

Over the next couple of hours, the *Second Lost* continued to give me dirty looks whenever we passed until, finally, I took the opportunity at the evening meal to speak.

"I would like to say a few words, if someone wouldn't mind translating to the others?" I said after clearing my throat to gain attention. Everyone quieted. They still treated me like I was an oddity; that made it easy when I wanted to speak. My childhood friend nodded and I proceeded, Moti's voiced translation following mine like a soft echo.

"I-I... ah... realize I didn't adequately explain my purpose for coming here. As you know, I traveled to Chittagong looking for my parents but when I found they were gone and the opportunity to visit this community came I could not pass it up. I want to apologize if I presented myself in a way that was misleading. I wasn't enslaved like the others in the colonies, like some of you thought I was. Except for the time I spent with a small group of children when I was first taken, some of the years after were spent in the home of a king."

"What is a king?" someone asked.

"Like an emperor," someone else replied. I nodded.

"Yes, like that. I was a servant but ate well and was clothed nicely. I lived in a home with a lot of money. Never at a loss for comfort when it came to things. I'm not going to pretend those things don't matter because they matter very much when you don't have them. I'm happy to give all that I brought with me if it helps the community."

"You were happy where you lived?" asked a voice.

"No. I mean, France is a beautiful country. I escaped heavy physical labor, but I didn't escape pain or cruelty. I was dealt it and I gave it back in return. Many people hated me. Many of them mocked me. I'm not proud of some things I've done. Some of them I felt I had to do to gain my freedom and the fact remains that had I not done them I wouldn't be standing here today. I'm certain I would have never made it back home." I took a breath and laid myself bare. "You have every right to ask me to leave, but I'd like to stay for a while. I just mean to say, a person doesn't stop longing for the people that love them. I'll contribute in whatever way is needed. I refuse to be a burden. I-I need to be here. For a short while. I need the comfort of my people. Please."

Moti had been translating quietly and now several people nodded their heads. My fellow abductee looked disgusted, tossing his water from his cup onto the ground. He spit when he spoke. "You come here only after you have lost everything. We have no need for you to come bearing arms full of nothing. Pity you didn't think of this community or others when you had everything. I only ask that the next innocent soul to be kidnapped from this community, if they have the good fortune to live in the home of a king, they will be so good as to bring some of that wealth back to the people they claim to love." His face twisted in anger, and he spit onto the ground before he walked away.

I wanted to shout at him, *When I had the advantages of a kingdom I couldn't leave!* In the back of my mind I wondered what wealth would even mean for a community such as this, separated from the world in which to spend it. I wanted to follow him to explain, but the chatter around me stopped and Moti stepped up to take my arm, a smile on his face.

"The community wants you to stay, Zamor."

The medicine woman stood and gave me a look from my head to my toes. "I knew there was more to your story. And even more than that, I'm sure. Finally, a little truth."

She walked away and Moti smiled. "It's understandable you had no control over where you ended up and when you could come home, you did. You may stay for as long as you want."

"But, the *Second Lost...*"

"Don't worry about him. He is prone to explosive anger. It's not you he is angry with. His family is gone and there have been rumors about him ever since. It's nothing to do with you; you came when you could. It means a great deal that you cared enough to return. These communities lose so many young people every year—thinking there is something better in the broader world. That you came back means more than you know. The community doesn't want your property. All that you are is enough, Zamor."

All that I was was enough? I'd never heard those words before.

***

For three days *Second Lost* avoided me. When he saw me coming his way he walked in the other direction. I didn't really want to be his friend, but I didn't want him to feel bad either. I could ill afford any enemies.

But even I had my limits. I decided if he didn't want to be cordial I wasn't going to waste any time on it either. It took another week for him to bound up to me where I was crouched over, putting seeds into the soil to grow some vegetables. His demeanor took me by surprise because he came with a smile on his face.

"Zamor, how are you?"

I looked around, confused, but no one else was around. "I'm fine."

"Good. Good. Wonderful. It is a beautiful day, isn't it? What's that you're planting, friend?"

The smile on his face stretched as if fake. He looked like he would break into a sweat trying to keep it plastered there. I was familiar with masks. I had no desire to see his.

"You were very angry with me and now you approach me like we're the best of friends. I don't understand."

"Yes." He wrung his hands, the smile slipping. "Yes. I was angry with you, it's true. You lied to me."

"I didn't lie." I wiped the sweat from my brow with my sleeve.

"You did, indeed."

We could argue all day about lies of omission, but I felt for as little we knew each other he hardly qualified for deserving all my truth.

"I never lied to you. I might not have told you all the details of where I'd been, but I never lied. You believed what you wanted to believe. That's not my fault."

His smile faltered and I saw a flash of anger. "You are right, friend. Perhaps I only thought I understood when I saw your deformed body. I thought you were a victim like me, but I was mistaken. It is like you said, I expect people to be better than they actually are." He smiled.

Now, a flash of anger streaked through me. But if there was one thing I knew, it was how to control my anger. I was here for myself, and this man wasn't going to throw me off my plan.

"Yes," I said with an answering smile. "A victim for all of, how long were you gone? Three days? Yes, it is like I said, I expect people to be exactly what they are. I'm going to finish planting, if you don't mind."

"I can help if you want."

"No, thank you."

"It's unfair of me to blame you," he said. "You can't help where you ended up. Anyone would have behaved the same way you did, if in your shoes."

"That drawing wasn't real. You don't know anything about my behavior."

"Well, we can still be friends."

I kept putting seeds into the soil. He'd called me deformed and a liar.

"We can still be friends," he repeated.

"Fine," I said. "Please allow me to finish planting."

Anything to get him to leave.

Though we didn't stay around each other in the following days, he tried to inch his way back, bit by bit. He smiled at me; a smile that would disappear the second I looked away, only to pop up again if I looked back quickly.

I wasn't a fool. I could tell he was putting on a show. But I didn't care enough to spend much time worrying about it. I had more important things to think about.

Though I'd never thought of myself as particularly handy, I spent every second learning how to build. The work was hard, and I was perspiring at the end of every day, but it was good, cleansing work. I was permitted to do it without a lot of talk. No one asked me more about my life in France and I didn't volunteer. Often, the other community members avoided me, and I was certain they were whispering about me, too. I didn't care.

I worked. I spent my days building and my evenings walking in the area around the community. I breathed fresh air. I drank clean water. I didn't pay attention when I was looked at strangely. I became the guest that no one quite knew what to do with. They allowed me to stay, and I tried my best to heal when I hadn't even realized I needed healing.

In my mind I thought to only stay for a year, but something happened.

After about eight months Moti came into camp one day with a thin, gaunt man following him. The man looked like he hadn't eaten a good meal in a year. I was helping build a fire for the evening meal when I saw him as I squinted from the smoke. He stared in my direction, and I was about to make a comment about rudeness when Moti stepped forward and motioned the man closer. Moti looked at me, expectantly, but before he could say anything the man next to him stepped forward and looked at me intently.

"Zamor," he said softly, unsurely.

"Yes, that is my name." I'd been saying it over and over since I got here, by now used to people wanting to see the *First Lost*, the legendary man who'd left and returned home. I poked at the burning twigs to keep them going.

"Zamor," he said, louder this time.

"Yes." I looked up at him, mildly annoyed. "What is *your* name, Monsieur?" I asked in English. He responded in kind.

"My name is *Papa*. I am your father."

My hands stopped working and I looked at the man. He was skin and bones and his hair was longer than any gentleman's hair should be.

"That's nonsense, my father is dead. That's what they told me in—"

He blinked and something in the twitch of the movement, in the way his eyelids flickered a little and his head jerked back just a bit... something in the move was a long-forgotten, familiar movement. I looked at his face, lined and wrinkled, but suddenly relaxing and collapsing in on itself in silence and then I saw it. Then I saw in his cheeks and his wobbling chin. I saw in his hairline and his jawline. I saw a face I hadn't seen in so, so many years. Like a portrait fuzzy around the edges.

I stood, unsteadily on my feet, dropping the twigs. "Papa?"

And then he was coming across to me and his arms were around me, clutching me, saying my name over and over. Beyond him I could see Moti smiling, tears running down his cheeks.

As for me, while my brain tried to catch up to the tableau, I felt myself go into stillness and knew I would soon be out of my body, hovering over this scene–separating myself from the emotion I sensed was just on the edge of breaking through.

I knew I had come all this way for this but when presented with it, fear almost overtook everything. After all this time, all these years, it couldn't be this simple. I couldn't have my father standing there with me, could I?

He pulled back and took my upper arms in a hard shake, smiling with his eyes floating in pools of water. "It's me, son. I know you are in shock; you always looked like that when you were shocked or frightened. But this is real. You hear me, Zamor. Oh, my son, my son…" His face crumpled again, and he pulled me in his arms, rocking me to and fro with his face buried in my neck as he sobbed.

I wanted to disappear but decided to trust that maybe, just this once, feeling was going to be okay after all.

I put my arms up and held him back.

CHAPTER THIRTY-NINE

The community rallied around the man just as you would think for a long, lost son. After our embrace, he was immediately swept away. He tried to keep me in his sight, but I allowed myself to melt into silence. Waiting for something and searching for more. Trying to see myself in him.

"Where have you been?" someone asked him.

"All over. In the United States, mostly."

I bristled upon hearing that. I'd wanted to visit the new country myself. The fact that he'd been there reminded me that he was free when I was not. My eyes hardened on him and, as if he could feel it, his smiled died on looking at me.

"Please..." I heard him say to the people milling about. "I must spend time with my son."

He was talking about me. My feet moved me away and carried me into the woods on a fast clip to get away from the whole lot of them. To get away from him, mostly. I was afraid of what he'd say, somehow certain it would make me hate him. Perhaps not a rational explanation for wanting to avoid the man but it was the truth.

I had more than enough reason not to trust him already, what with Louis XV's words about him selling me and his admission to enjoying his traveling. Faked his death, apparently, and used it as an excuse to gallivant all over the world while his wife rotted in the ground and I suffered. I didn't want to think these thoughts, but I did.

I returned by supper for our outdoor meal. The fire was warm and I took my plate and seat around it. In a foul mood, I was poor company. But since I so rarely spoke to anyone already, I thought I'd do as the others and sit by the communal fire to eat my rice and vegetables. There would be meat the next day, I was sure, but there wasn't time for a proper celebration this evening.

I was surprised when my father sat down beside me, crowding me. Instinctively, I moved away from him. I may as well rung a bell at the attention that suddenly came my way.

"Why did you do that, boy?" came the medicine woman's fast reproach from where she sat across the fire. "Why did you just disrespect your father like that?" Everyone grew quiet at the bite in her tone. But she didn't frighten me.

"I like my space when I eat."

"This man gave up everything for you," she said. "You're just like your stubborn mother. He gave that woman everything she wanted, and she always wanted more. Greedy. And look at you sitting there, *Greedy*'s son in the flesh."

That made my skin a bit hot.

"Leave it," my father said, I don't know to which of us. It didn't matter, because, of course, I couldn't leave anything alone.

"Stubborn, was she? Well, it seems like the wrong parent went looking for me. Perhaps if it had been *Greedy*, as you call her, her greediness for her child would have been put to good use. I might have actually made it back home instead of having to find *my own way back* as a grown man. Greediness seems a valuable trait under the circumstances."

There was silence for a long moment and a quick glance from under hooded lids caught the hurt that flashed across my supposed father's face. Then, it caught the fury on the woman's.

"You ungrateful excuse of a man, you deserve a beating for how you just spoke. Someone hand me a stick, I'll beat it out of him myself. Beat that woman from your spirit so your *father's* goodness has a chance to live in your ungrateful body." She spit out some words that I didn't recognize and looked like she was serious about waiting for that stick to beat sense into me.

"Stop," came my father's soft voice with a hand raised in signal to her. "It's all right. He is angry and he has a right to be. He was an innocent child and anyone can clearly see how this all has hurt him. You may be right, son. Your mother was a person who always did what she set out to do. She would have found you if she could have, I'm sure."

My irritation died under his quick capitulation. Hurting him meant nothing if he was simply going to take it.

He stood up with his plate and walked away from the fire.

I felt small as they all stared at me, trying to chew my food with a tense jaw while everyone watched. Finally, I stood, too, and walked away. I didn't go back to the hut for a long while, hoping to put some distance between my words and our close proximity in our home. But eventually I wanted to go to bed.

Peeling off my clothes, as quietly as possible, I began sponging my body with a cloth. He lay on a pallet with his back turned to me still, as if asleep. But the second I finished wiping myself down and lay on my pallet, pulling a covering over me, he spoke.

"When they took you, she insisted I go find you that very day. She wanted me to go along with the other man, the father of the *Second* and the *Third Lost.*"

"My life would have been different if you had cared as much as he did," I said curtly. I didn't want to talk. I felt anger rising in me again. His quietness annoyed me, and I spoke with spite. "Was the money so good even the plea of my mother didn't move you? Or, maybe you'd already gotten the money and didn't see the need to pretend."

He was silent a long time.

"I didn't go after you right away because I was afraid to leave her. She was dying, you see. Very weak, some days she didn't even know where she was. Don't you remember how she had gotten so weak she could no longer hold you? Every time you tried to climb onto her lap she almost dropped you, so she kept pushing you away. Don't you remember how she kept pushing you away? She was in pain, and we didn't know what to do. She was sick inside and the medicine man at the time—he didn't know how to save her. I was afraid if I left for a day or two, she would die alone and in pain and afraid. I told myself two days wouldn't matter. And exactly two days after you were taken, she died. I stayed long enough to bury her and made sure they made a spot for me beside her and then I packed a few things and went searching for you on the third. It was selfish of me, and I don't blame your anger. But, you see, I loved your mother and she was dying."

A quick flash of being pushed away streaked through my head. I certainly remembered that. It was being pushed away that had made it so easy for me to believe what Louis XV had told me–that they no longer wanted me.

"She was a strong woman," he continued. "Watching her lose that strength was torture, but she was my wife. I loved her. I loved you, too. So, I promised her before she took her last breath I would never stop looking for you, and I never did."

"What do you mean you never stopped? You said you were in the United States, you must have settled someplace. Are you saying you've been looking all this time?"

"That's exactly what I'm saying. You're my only son. My only child. What is my life without you?"

I didn't answer and we didn't talk anymore that night. I didn't understand. None of it was making sense.

The next morning as we were wiping off to dress, the town leader came to the doorway. His eyes looked us over, curiosity heavy. "Now that there are two of you, if you are both going to stay you will have to build a new hut so we can leave this one for visitors. You'll start today."

My father nodded and they both looked at me. I nodded, also, and my father hid a quick smile.

"So, we will get to know each other now," he said when we were alone again.

I shrugged. "Might as well. We're both here, and all that."

"All right," he said, pulling on his shirt. He didn't look at me as he spoke. "I'll go and start looking for a good place for us to stay. We should make sure to face the sun in the back so we can grow. Hurry up and prepare and meet me out there." He walked out of the space.

I waited a few minutes. I couldn't say why, other than that I didn't want him to think I was doing anything because he told me to. He wasn't the boss of me.

Some half hour later, I sauntered out into the filtered sunlight. Children ran around chasing each other as if they'd been up for hours. I took my time walking through the compound, nodding at people I passed. I relieved myself in the spot for that activity, and then calmly walked around to the outskirts, seeing him sitting in an area that was verging on the deep woods. He sat on a fallen log and held a small knife in one hand and a good-sized log in the other. He was using the knife to carve away at the end of the log. He glanced up as if he felt me and then nodded toward the wood.

"The other huts have straight flat ends. I thought we could curve ours a little, to make the final look more special. What do you think?"

I looked at the log dubiously. "I think that's a lot more work and will take more time."

"You have someplace you need to be, son?"

He was still looking down as he carved the rounded end. I thought about resisting—I couldn't have said why.

"All right," I said.

He started to rise. "You take this knife, I'll get an—"

"—No need," I stopped him, pulling my knife out of my waistband. At his surprised expression, I added, "I came here on a ship with all sorts. Had to have a way to protect myself in case of trouble."

He nodded, sitting back down. Then, he gestured for me to take a seat on the log beside him. I hesitated and he simply dropped his gaze.

I walked over and sat down beside him next to the pile of logs. Pulling one over, I began to carve as he was and, soon, we were both working with only the sound of the forest birds keeping us company.

It was nice, not speaking. Most people were uncomfortable with silence, but he seemed to be fine with it for as long as I was. Minutes passed. The songs of the birds changed. We sat in silence and in the silence, a tiny seed of trust for him implanted itself.

In the following days I stopped moving away whenever he showed up. I watched him when he wasn't looking, trying to recognize him... trying to remember. I watched him, trying to see the type of person he was and trying to find the liar in him. I looked and looked and looked... but I never found the villain.

Being that I was the difficult one, I knew it was up to me to start any conversations. We had developed camaraderie in silence, so every spoken word was important. I started by chatting about how cool it could be at night and how I was still struggling to get used to the silence that was so different than the city of Paris. He was always willing to speak to me; always in good spirits, even as we skipped around serious subjects like strangers meeting and struggling to be polite. Until one day when I delved a little deeper.

"The medicine woman didn't like my mother, and she doesn't like me," I acknowledged as we pounded nails into the wood that would be our walls. It was a prompt for information I hoped he would pick up on.

"Don't pay her any mind. We all grew up together. She and your mother never got along. She felt your mother was too bold."

I thought about that, and it made me think of Véronique and her little town in Burgundy. How her father had waited too long and was too picky to find her a mate. It worked out for me, of course, because she took the unconventional approach, traveling across the country to the Chateau du Barry. But it had been difficult for her in a society that expected women to marry. I didn't know about the expectations of this community, but it made me happy to know that bit about my mother.

I went to gather wood planks from the pile I had chopped and brought them back, dropping them on the ground beside the makeshift building.

"You still have the arm strength," he said to me as I began hammering nails into the planks set on a frame.

I wiped the sweat from my forehead with the back of my arm. "God didn't bless me with looks or height, he at least owed me some strength. So, you say you've been to the Americas?"

"Unfortunately. You?"

"No, not me. But I'm curious about it, a country founded solely on the idea that people can live without a king. Maybe I'll go some day. Why'd you go?"

He nailed a plank. "Do you imagine I was on a White man's holiday? I told you, I never stopped looking. It took me many places."

I looked at him quickly and his face, averted from me, didn't look like it had a lie in it. I'd been watching and watching and I hadn't seen a lie in him yet, and I was good at identifying liars. I had come to the conclusion that he wasn't a liar at all. That he was my father and, unlike the man who partially reared me, lies didn't come easily to him.

"I was told you and my maman... the King said that you... that I was..."

"You don't have to say, I know from what you've already said. He told you we sold you. Slavers lie. I've seen it many times when I was on plantations in the Americas, when I was enslaved. Usually, the masters didn't bother to lie and just sold children from their mothers right in front of their faces. But sometimes, when the White men wanted a slave not to be angry or sad—because grief slowed down the work—they would lie and tell the parent their child had run away when they had sold or killed the child. They tell whatever lie suits them. You were our only child. You don't have children so you may not understand: For some of us, there is no reason for money without a child to spend it on. Your mother and I would have gladly given our lives to have you back safe. There is no amount of money that could have convinced us to part with you. Not even a king's riches."

Shame flooded me. I nodded though he wasn't looking.

"I'm sorry," he continued. "We never taught you that people could do evil things. We should have prepared you better for the world. But we thought it was safe to let you be a child. We let you believe the world was a good, decent place. Chittagong *was* a good and decent place for a long time."

"Don't blame yourself," I said. "Nothing you could have told me would have prepared me. I wouldn't have believed you if you had."

"You can tell me about your life if you'd like. What it was like for you. If it brings you solace?"

It was a kind offer. I knew anything I told him would hurt him and, now, hurting him was something I cared about. It wouldn't change anything; it would only add to his suffering. He'd been torturing himself for years, and I didn't want to add to it.

And that's how we spoke to each other for almost six months. Slowly but surely we began talking normally. Eventually, we even began to laugh. My father thought my sharp tongue was a sign of intelligence. He smiled broadly whenever I said something that would've gotten me a slap from Gaspard.

We were at dinner one evening, chatting comfortably around the fire. I had made a flippant comment about the *Second Lost* peering at us across the square and I had quickly made a comment about giving the watcher something to frown about if he kept giving me dirty looks. It slipped out under my breath.

"Perhaps grace has a place, Zamor. Use that tongue of yours to offer words of peace to him. No one can speak as well as you."

His easy acceptance of my bad habits made me laugh at him. "It's funny how you think my weaknesses are strengths, and all that."

He looked confused. "Your smart brain and quick wit? They *are* strengths. Why on earth would you ever think otherwise?"

Why on earth, indeed. I looked at him, frowning. It had occurred to me that one day he would change his mind about me. One day he would turn on me. When he realized who I was. I decided to broach the subject, tentatively, to test the waters.

"Some people call me sneaky, conniving—evil, even. But you take me at my word and believe what I say is true. Is that a smart thing to do with someone you've barely just met?"

"That question is beneath you. Even as a little child, you were the smartest person I knew. If you've had to lie out in the world that's because you were taught to. Forced to, maybe, to survive. But you are not a liar inside. You're my son, I know who you are."

"I *was* seven when I left, a lot has happened since then. I've changed."

"I knew you *before* the rest of the world ever met you. You were a child who would rather take a punishment than spend the time coming up with a story to save you from a whipping. Your mother used to say, 'I wish he'd, for once, let me catch him in a lie. Then I could talk to him like a child instead of deal with him as if he's a grown man in a child's body, haggling over the terms of his own punishment.'"

I laughed as he smiled into his vegetables, warmth blossoming in me. I put some of that evening's roasted goat in my mouth and drifted into silence.

"Do you remember your mama?" he asked.

"I remember what I trained myself to remember, but most of it's gone. For years I remembered that song she used to hum to me, but I've lost it now."

"The song she used to hum to put you to sleep?"

"Yes, it got me through plenty times... well, I lost it, anyway."

He frowned. "I can't think of it now." He looked so troubled about that I wished I hadn't brought it up. "The two of you were so close... I used to tell her, let me have him sometimes. Stop hogging my boy or he will never learn to love me as he loves you."

"Huhm," I said, "I don't remember." I continued eating and he fell silent. "But I lost lots of time. I was hit in the head. Most of the journey I can't remember. I felt like it was a couple months when, by the time I got to the Palace, it had been years. And sometimes I escape my mind. I don't know how to explain it. But it loses me time. I don't know why I can't remember her, if we were as close as you say. I mean, I remember telling myself that I was loved back home. But I don't remember the love itself, you understand? Just the words I told myself."

"Even now?"

"Even now, your face is somewhat familiar to me, as is your voice, but memories of actually living with you–they don't come." I pushed the food around on my plate. "The medicine woman says my head is broken. I don't know. It might be."

We ate in silence for a long moment.

"Maybe God is protecting you," he said. "Sometimes memories can be dangerous."

Chapter Forty

I reached over and deposited a wriggling worm into my father's cupped hands. We were downstream where the fish were plentiful.

"I don't know why he keeps giving me these worms that look like they're starving to death, how are we supposed to catch anything?" I groused about the man who'd given us the fish food.

"Ah, but we never have a problem bringing home fish," he said, squinting into the sun. "Patience. Everything in life can be resolved with patience. Time is the great healer."

I fell quiet. It seemed my father's favorite thing to say; I was too impatient. But it was the strangest thing. I kept quiet and listened without argument. I'd found that even though his way was different from mine, he was often right.

An hour later under the darkening sky, we carried our bundles of fish wrapped and tied in sacks to take back to camp. When we walked up and my father held up a bundle, a cheer went up. My lips wiggled in a smile.

Papa was immediately taken to conversation with people who hadn't seen him for hours and were starved for his company. I took my fish over to the cook who had his son quickly clean it before threading the six healthy fish onto sticks for the spits. Seconds later, the skin began to crackle, and the air was rent with the smell of the roasting fish.

"Is this all?" I asked the cook. "No one else brought any meat or fish?"

He glanced at me, poking the flesh with a large knife to see if it was done. "Not today. Tomorrow, I'm sure."

It annoyed me. Yes, it was six fish but there were at least forty people in the community. We'd all barely get a taste.

I watched my father where he held a small audience enthralled with whatever stories about our day of errands might amuse them. He was a natural socializer, my father. I looked at the fish that dripped white into the fire.

"It's done. I'll take this one," I said, reaching for the one closest. I noticed three or four people around the fire looking at me. "Well, at least give me quarter to share with my papa. We caught the damn things, after all."

He pulled the fish off the fire, laid it down, and cut off less than a quarter of it. My lips went tight, but I took the portion on my plate and then portioned that onto a plate for my papa. Rice and vegetables followed.

Walking over to him I handed his plate down to him where he sat.

"Ah, thank you, son," he said. Then, he stood up, walked across the communal space, and handed it to another man. "My son Zamor made this for you." *Lies.*

The recipient smiled across at me while I sat down, uncomfortably soaking in the unwarranted gratitude. Papa then went over to the fire and waited his turn as the crowd of the others got their food before he did. Some time later, he sat back down beside me with a new plate.

"I made that first one specially for you," I groused, eating my rice and vegetables petulantly.

"I know, and I appreciate it. He appreciates it just as much, look how happy he is."

"I gave you a particularly nice portion of fish. Now, *he* has it. I didn't make it for him."

"Thank you, son," he said.

"For what? You don't have any fish. Look at your plate, there's hardly anything left. And *no fish*..."

He smiled at me. "Tomorrow we'll go fishing again."

"And will you give it away again? Because I'm not going to bother myself to fish if you're just going to give it away to people who don't feel like spending hours to catch it."

"But you have nothing to say about the vegetables you eat that aren't from your garden, or the rice that you haven't harvested. There will be fish tomorrow and, yes, I might give it away again. But that's not a bad thing, Zamor."

"It's a stupid thing," I mumbled under my breath.

"Say that again to your father and you will get a knock on the head," he said. I looked at him quickly to see if he was joking and saw no humor in him. His voice softened.

"You're used to looking out only for yourself but that's not how you get along in a community like this. You have to show people you want to be a part of things."

"Nonsense, the world is every man for himself." I jabbed fish into my mouth, looking around to make sure no one planned to reach over and take it from me. Then, I took the last chunk and plopped it onto his plate. I lowered my voice. "Why is it me who still has to prove myself? Why don't they show *me* they want me to be here?"

He leaned over and looked me in my eye. "If they didn't want you to be here, Zamor, you *wouldn't* be."

"But they like you. You're just a much nicer person. You give them your food. They will take advantage of you. I don't know how to be like you," I admitted.

Sure, I had to do things I didn't like in my time, but I would earn it back somehow. If I had to suffer, someone one else damned sure was, too. I didn't give of myself for no reason, not like him.

"I learned something from when I was in the Americas. I watched the way they help each other. Even strangers, like me. More than once, even though if they were caught it would be severe punishment. More than once I would have been beaten or worse if there hadn't been someone to step in and help me or hide me or protect me in some way. I didn't understand, at first. I was like you are now... I expected they wanted something from me so I resisted. But the longer I was there the more I saw what was unlike anything I'd seen before. They looked out for each other. And while I was there, they looked out for me. For no other reason than they felt it was the right thing."

"It's a country of saints, then?"

"No, there were some who wouldn't lift a hand to help someone, but there were more who would. But the slaves in the Americas felt that damage to one is damage to all. To see one person punished hurt the spirit of all the others who had to see it. And to see even one person escape... it was a balm to the soul. You must understand – those people were stripped of everything. Many had grandparents who came, speaking a different language, and it was taken. With different religions and traditions. All were stripped. Stripped to their very souls and treated no better than animals. And in that dark place they found God within. They don't sing with their voices, they sing with their very souls. They hide messages in the words. They dance battle plans with their steps and sew maps in the design of quilts—codes hidden in plain sight! And they are always, always planning for escape. There are many revolts the masters want to keep secret but we know of them. Everyone is always planning for the day when they are free.

"They didn't have to know me to want freedom *for* me, even if they didn't have it for themselves. It came to a point where I began to want to help because it was a balm to *my* soul."

His words sent a shiver through me. I felt equal parts fear and admiration, but reached for optimism. "I had thought to visit the United States one day," I admitted. "I thought it might be special to be in a land built on equality. Surely, *most* Black people are free there? I have my freedom papers."

He gave me a quick, sideways glance. "Freedom papers are only as valuable as the people who find you deem them to be. I met several slaves who were free at one time, and made unfree simply by virtue of being taken by slavers. It is a sickness. The White people have convinced themselves we are animals and that God put them in charge. A sickness that has spread so that even those rare White people who show any compassion at all are set upon by the sick—punished for daring to suggest we are human. They make laws on the side of the slavers. If you go, stay as far north as you can. I heard rumor that it was safer up there. But, better to stay away from the place entirely. Freedom in the United States is only for people with White skin. The only people who truly understand how sick the slave owners are are the enslaved with Black skin."

"You don't think the people here understand?"

"The people here have never experienced what it's like out there. God willing, they never will. It makes them... less compassionate than they should be. Especially when they hear that a slave is fed and clothed. They remember our ancestor's servitude; safer and limited. It came with freedoms. It came with permissions to keep the names and the traditions. It came with the ability to buy ourselves out of it. To the people here, that is what they believe when they hear about slavery now, that it seems a comfortable life. They don't know slavery as it is now. They don't know that slaves in the field live torturous lives. They don't know that the ones in the house are tortured in other ways. They don't know what they do to women and babies, or how they punish the men..." He shook his head as if to shake himself out of the memory, continuing.

"I was the lucky one that I didn't have anyone there that I loved that they could torture in front of me. Because when I decided to escape there was nothing keeping me. Because your mother was already gone and you, blessedly, weren't there. Even though I went looking for you, I prayed I would never find you in any of those places. Because if I did, and anyone knew you were my son, they would have me forever. Finding you would give them something to threaten to take from me if I ever tried to leave again."

That brought to mind Salanave's words from long ago: *"Stop giving Gaspard things to take from you."*

"It's a blessing to forget some things," he said. "Sometimes, I wish I could forget more."

He seemed to shake himself and bumped my arm with his. "I don't do nice things because I'm a saint or stupid, son. Most of the people I knew in this place have moved or died long ago. Aside from three people, you and I are strangers to this community. They don't know the horrors of the world and wouldn't believe how bad it is if you told them. So, they will have no problem putting us back out into it if we don't earn our place. You understand?"

I did now.

The next day, I grabbed the first French language paper Moti brought from the stack. According to the newspapers, a man named Napoleon Bonaparte who had overtaken the Directory government in a coup d'état—*overthrow of government*—had now crowned himself Emperor. It was 1804.

I was happy not to be in France to see the start of a new monarchy under a different name. I wondered if the people of France had second thoughts about putting Louis XVI to death after all. I read the quote from the new Emperor, and it jarred me to my core:

"I have dethroned no one. I found the crown in the gutter. I picked it up and the people put it on my head." —Napoleon Bonaparte

Chapter Forty-One

I listened to Papa whether I liked what he said or not. For some reason, I wanted his approval. I craved it. I didn't care about the others in the community but I cared about him. So, the next time I had a chance, I put his advice to use.

Papa was about to take a small bowl of onions into the hut when someone's child ran over our garden to get God-knows-where, happily trampled over my lettuce, crushing it. I looked up and saw his father, not too far away, working in his own garden. The man was looking up and had seen his child kill my hard-earned produce and said nothing. I knew what my father said but lifetime habits didn't go away overnight. Of course, words happened.

"By all means, just sit there on your hands while your rotten little child destr—"

"Your boy has healthy energy!" my father, having seen the whole thing, cut off my rant. To me, he whispered: "It's only lettuce."

The other father raised a hand in acknowledgement and smiled at my father. Then he yelled something to the child who walked back, shame-faced and stood in front of me.

"I'm sorry, Monsieur Zamor," the child said in English.

I looked around. I was still angry, and the apology caught me off guard. "It's…" Be kind. *Be kind!* "It's all right," I said reluctantly. "Don't let it happen again."

The child ran away. His father was looking at me expectantly, and I nodded. He smiled and went back to his gardening.

"Well," I said to my father. "I don't know exactly what you did or why it worked."

"I stayed calm, Zamor. I spoke to the father with respect so he would speak with his child, just like I'm speaking with mine."

"I'm not a child!"

"And all is well, isn't it? The lettuce is still edible?"

"If I want lettuce that tastes like feet."

"You have your mother's temperament."

"I know. She *was* the smart one in the family."

Papa laughed out loud, and I smiled. He reached down and picked off a wilted leaf, speaking without lifting his head.

"I know you might want to go soon."

"What?"

"I know you are more familiar with populated areas, and you might miss a faster life like you used to have." He stood and faced me, without looking me in my eyes. "I see how eagerly you read the papers to find out what is happening in France. I would understand if you feel the need to leave."

I didn't know how to respond to that. I shrugged. "Or you could come to France?"

He gave a sad smile. "I'm afraid I no longer trust places where people with white skin have control over everything."

I wanted to remind him that people with white skin were in control here in India, too. I took too long to respond, and a look of pain washed over his face before he turned toward the house.

"Don't stay out in the sun too long, son, you give yourself head pain."

I watched him walk into the hut and wondered why I felt unsettled. We had come so far since meeting, and I admired him. I looked up to him. But

I couldn't release something within me that stayed removed from him. Just a small part I couldn't give.

We chopped up vegetables harvested from our garden for our meals and, later, after wiping down, I lay onto my pallet for bed. I looked over at him on his pallet, his thin arms holding the blanket to him.

It came to me... the reason why I felt removed from him, even now. He didn't really know me. He should know who I was. A lie of omission was fine for strangers, but he was my father.

Maybe I wanted to shock him. Maybe I wanted to get this part out of the way so if it wanted to cut me loose, he could. It would save us both the time.

I looked at him steadily, my teeth chewing the inside of my cheek. I couldn't have said why I was nervous, but there was nothing to be done about it.

"Papa," I said. He grunted. "You should know I'm a murderer," I said flatly.

He didn't move.

"I've killed more than one person. I should have told you sooner so you could have asked for another place to sleep. But I'm telling you now. I'm sure they could find a place for you." There. It was a practical consideration—that's why I was telling him. At least, that was how I hoped he'd take it.

"I see. Do you plan to kill me?"

"Of course not. What kind of question is that? Why would I kill you?"

"You just told me you've murdered many people, what's one more?"

"I'm not a *murderer* like you say it. I've killed. I had reasons for killing people. I didn't want to. I never wanted to. I *had* to."

"That's what every murderer says."

I felt a lick of anger.

"Tell me how you did it," he said, turning his head to look at me over his shoulder. I blanched. I didn't like that he wanted to know details.

"No."

"Why not?"

"It's none of your business."

"You brought it up, son."

"Don't call me that."

"I can't call you that anymore, or just now that I'm questioning you in a way you don't like? What should I call you, then?" He said a name that was a distant memory.

"Don't call me that, either. Just Zamor is fine. I never gave you permission to call me son. I'm a grown man, it feels strange. Just call me Zamor, like I asked. I didn't start anything, I just thought you should know for your sleeping comfort."

"It was for my benefit, then, that you tell me something that ensures I will never have an easy night of sleep ever again from worrying about you killing me."

"I'm only telling you because it might show up in a paper and I don't want you to be surprised."

"I can't read, son."

"Stop calling me that. Look, of course, you're safe. I did what I had to do."

"Are you proud of it, then?"

"Proud? What kind of question is that?"

"A question you ask of someone who, willingly and opening, speaks about murdering people. One can only assume, Zamor, that you want some sort of response from me. Pride? Admiration?"

"No, that's not it at all. No." I was disgusted. I was getting annoyed and frustrated. "I told you because you deserve to know who I am—get it out on the table now, and all that."

"Well then, if you won't tell he how or why, at least tell me if you plan to kill me?"

Anger flared and I raised my head. "Stop asking me that! Why would you ask me that?"

"Because, Zamor, you've willingly told me you've murdered many people. Why wouldn't you want to murder the man you feel betrayed you the most? Now that I know you're capable of doing it. So, I ask how do you feel about having blood on your hands? I want to know how you feel about taking the lives of those people, however many there are. Are you my son or are you a monster?"

Anger flared in me, and I sat up and glared at him. "How dare you ask me that? I'll remind you, I've been on my own since I was seven. Don't you judge me..."

He sat up in response, but he had angered me now so I stopped whatever he might have said with the beginning of a rant.

"What about *my* blood?" I said. "My blood is on plenty hands—*including yours!*—and no one's crying over me. No one's ever lost sleep over me. Now, I'm supposed to give up my life to live with you here in the woods? You?"

My father didn't respond but stood and walked over to sit down beside me. I was too far gone at this point to stop.

"I don't care why you stayed. All I know—all I remember—was being carted around this hellish country, picked over like a rotten piece of fruit, wondering *where is my papa?* I remember that! You care about the type of man I am, you should have cared back then! Back when it seemed everyone in the world was trying to show me how much of nothing I was. The most powerful man in the world told me in every way he could that I was nothing, and no one—not even God—saved me. And you sit here..."

"Zamor," he said, trying to interrupt me, but it was too late. I slashed my hand, giving him the universal sign to shut his mouth.

"Three were taken. But the other two had a father that looked for them. And I had a mother who, even dying, had enough common sense to know what was most pressing. Even dying, she understood what might be waiting for me and made the choice for you. Mon Dieu, she told you to go after me, even on her deathbed! You left me to fend for myself. You left me to fight all of them, over and over and over... you chose her over me... " I felt something coming up in me that I never expected or planned. "Now, I'm not even allowed to hate you because you were helping my mother. What kind of monster would I be? So, now, I don't need your sadness or your pity. I just need you to tell me, who can I blame for what I am? Who can I hate? Who serves justice for me? Or is everything just my fault? Just mine?" My eyes filled, despite me trying hard to keep emotion at bay. The last question came as a whisper. "When do *I* get some grace? At least the same grace you show everyone else?"

His face was pained and his mouth opened and closed, wordlessly.

"Papa," I whispered, shaking my head and dropping my eyes to the ground. "I'm not a good man. I've shamed you and Mama."

"No. No! No, don't you ever say...!" He was quiet for a long moment. Then, I felt his hand as he reached over to cup my head and pull it toward his chest, holding it firmly, his other hand rubbing it gently as if I were still a child.

"I asked you what I did because when I look at you, I don't see a murderer, I see my son. If you were proud of killing, or enjoyed it, it would be difficult for me to see my son in a cold-hearted murderer. I am proud that what you have done hurts you, even if you had to do it. That is the son I raised."

I'd never been held this way, firmly and with purpose. At least, not by a grown man. It stripped me down in a way I didn't expect. I tried to pull away, the vulnerability was frightening, but he held me. In the warmth of his arms, tears fell down my cheeks.

"Bah, I've seen evil," he said, his voice clogged with emotion. "I look into your eyes and that's not what I see. This life has been crueler than I ever imagined it could be. And still, in all the horror, I'm holding my son in my arms again. Whatever you think you are—whatever they told you—you are the greatest thing your mother and I ever made! Still. *You are the best of us.* I know you must have felt alone and scared, but you taught yourself how to survive. You brought yourself back home. Do you know how amazing that is? You are a blessing to this soul of mine. There hasn't been a moment since the day you were born that I haven't woken up and fallen asleep thinking of my boy. My *brilliant* boy. And it's no different now that you've told me your truth. I love you, son. I'm so thankful for you. Please forgive me for not being the father you needed." He kissed the top of my head as I dissolved into sobs against his chest.

They were the words I'd wanted to hear all my life. I felt his love as pure and complete as I'd ever felt anything. I allowed him to hold me in his grasp as I cried, my shoulders shaking with every breath, as if I was still only seven years old, shaking off a lifetime of pain with this man who was a stranger not so long ago.

He held me, rocking me back and forth, well into the night.

By morning, I felt healed.

Chapter Forty-Two

*D*ear Citizen,

We didn't have the discussion, but I decided I wasn't going to leave Papa ever again. Our conversation brought us closer than I'd ever thought possible.

Over the next several years, it was almost like he was trying to raise me again. There's no other way to put it. Though counter to my nature, miracle upon miracles, I was compelled to follow his lead. I trusted him and I admired him. I realized how rare it was to have a parent as kind and patient. He'd been through difficult times, but it hadn't broken his spirit. And sometimes, when I was quiet and went off to be alone, he would give me a little time, but then he would find me. It was as if he was making up for the time when he didn't find me. As though he was reminding me I was no longer alone.

Words cannot adequately describe how it felt to be embraced by my father. I wished with everything in me that I remembered him—and Maman—from the before times. But I accepted this relationship as it was, a new thing.

And like that, the years passed, almost without me even noticing. I took pleasure in farming and fishing and hunting. I watched the people of the community fall in love with my father as I did the same. Though I was getting older, I truly felt young again. Young and cherished and loved.

I wasn't one to be held easily. I didn't like to be touched, usually. But I didn't mind Papa doing it. Tears sprung to my eyes almost every time he did but, thankfully, he didn't ask why or make any noise about it...

—Zamor, 1820

***

Sixteen years later

India, 1812

We were almost like an older and younger brother. Papa filled out from the steady supply of food. Unlike in the beginning when we both came to this place physically exhausted, we were healthy. Inside, we were jubilant. I liked the man he was, and he liked me.

The community loved Papa. He was a calming presence. While he didn't laugh a lot, he was easy to smile and did so often. Soon, people were coming to him for advice as the father of the *First Lost* and the honorary father of the community.

Sometimes *Second Lost* tried to speak with me and other times he glared at everyone with some inner anger that consumed him. I tried to keep conversations with him short and quick. On and on it had gone for years, so that one day he would smile at me and another I'd catch him frowning. Or worse, the smile dropped the second he thought I looked away only to come back when he found my eyes on him again.

"Why are you following me?" I asked one afternoon. I was in the woods with a bow and arrow searching for something with legs to eat for dinner and heard the rustle of feet over leaves and grass behind me. The second I spoke, it stopped. By the time I turned, he wore a smile, his head cocked to the side in supplication.

"Friend, I only came to say hello. We so rarely speak anymore."

I turned back around, frowning. I didn't see a goat anywhere. He probably scared them away with his loud walking.

"You can talk to me at the compound, no need to follow me out into the woods," I said, turning back. "You've scared away any game."

"So very sorry. We will have fish, then."

"Will we? Who's going to catch it? You?" I heard the bite in my tone and told myself to keep it down. Grace. *Grace.*

"You know I leave that to those of you who are good at it. You are very good at it, aren't you? Did you hunt much in France?"

"Not at all, we had people who did that."

"People whose job it was to hunt and kill and deliver the butchered meat for you to eat? My, how special you were. I can't imagine how wonderful such a life must have been." His eyes were sharp though his smile didn't waver.

"But of course you can," I said. "I come out here and hunt and kill and deliver the meat to the community for you to eat at least twice a week. You never go hungry. What a wonderful life you have. Now, if you don't mind, I—"

"—Are we still friends, Zamor? I've kept your secret all these years. Surely, that's earned your friendship? We barely speak. Sometimes I think you hate me." I feel about you like I feel about everyone in the community, no less."

"But we are the lost three. No one else has a bond like we do."

"Yes, well, that was a long time ago. We are all in a happy place today, right," I said, walking by him to pat him on the shoulders as I passed. He was slightly taller than me and I glanced up into his face to see his smile dying like he was coming upon something unpleasant and horrifying. It was precisely why I avoided him. "Come, smile, enjoy this lovely day."

I kept walking and waited to hear his steps over the grass behind me. I kept walking all the way back to the housing area and then turned to see I had lost him, somehow.

On the way to our hut, past the playing children and the people chatting about their day, I spied my papa outside another hut across the way. We'd been in this place for many years now and, with his decent looks and positive demeanor, he had gotten much attention from widows and unmarried women. But only one woman caught his attention.

I smiled as I saw him with the woman he was sweet on. She usually wore a head scarf but when it blew in the breeze you could see she had braided her silver black hair in a crown around her head. Adorned with jewelry and always wearing vivid, vibrant colors, I could see why papa was drawn to her. Even now, they were laughing and playing with each other as he helped to paint her hut a bright purple color. He laughed like a schoolboy, and she chased him with the threat of a paint-filled brush.

I chuckled.

He had come to me before allowing himself to fall in love. While taking a walk, he broached the subject, gingerly, as if I had any right to speak on any relationship he had.

"Do you mind, Zamor? If I spend time with her? You know no woman will ever compare to your mother, but... I like her. And I miss a woman's touch. And these days I finally feel happiness again and it feels good to share it."

It had seemed important for him to get my permission, so I gave it. "Of course, don't be silly, papa. You should spend all the time with her you want. I don't mind."

His face lit up and, immediately, as if he didn't deserve happiness without me having some too, he changed the focus to me.

"You're a strong, healthy man, still vibrant at fifty. Why don't you find a woman, son?"

It wasn't a new subject, but it didn't come up often over the years. My obvious discomfort kept him from prying too much. But still.

I had a stirring, occasionally. I didn't know how far it could get me, but it didn't matter because of the scar. My father never asked about it, but he had seen me changing a time or two. He knew why I couldn't marry; I didn't know why he kept bringing it up. But bring it up, he did.

"I'm certain one of the widows would be happy to be with you if you don't have the patience for children. You're a bit old for that now. All the women who have no husbands find you attractive. Some of them really like how you play that little instrument; they even forgive the fact that you don't know what to do with drums or how to dance."

I'd tried both with stunning failure.

"Besides..." he said, hesitantly. "...Plenty women would feel blessed not to have to put up with their husband's touch, if that is your concern. You've learned the language well enough now, so that doesn't matter." Another thing he had taught me. "Isn't it time to stop being sad over one woman, Zamor?"

"And how long has it been since Maman died?" I asked pointedly. He was indignant.

"I was busy. I wasn't walking around just living."

"Well, I like just living," I groused. "I have nothing to offer, and I don't like to fall short of expectation."

"Have you tried? Maybe you can."

I blushed. "I didn't say I couldn't. I won't. There's not a woman on earth I dislike enough to subject to me trying."

"When a woman cares for you, it is not a burden. You do know there is more than one way to pleasure a woman? I can teach you..."

I knew all the tricks there were. But he wasn't going to rest until I put an end to this by telling the truth. "I just don't want to, Papa."

"Okay, maybe you don't want love. You can be with a person for companionship, even if you don't love them. Even if you don't touch them intimately."

"Why would I want to be with someone I don't love or want to touch?"

"Why are you certain you won't fall in love again if you try? Sometimes the touch comes first."

"My heart has already been claimed. The best I will ever do is tolerate someone. I will never love like that again and I don't want to. Losing it was painful. I'd rather be alone."

He looked at me sadly. "That is because you still have not truly felt what loneliness is. I hope you never do. Maybe, someday, when you stop punishing yourself you will see you deserve love. What was she like, this woman you loved? "

A thought of Véronique flitted through my mind and my eyelids fluttered from the shock of it. Her scent wafted through my memory along with a flash of the first time I saw her struggling with those wet sheets and a clothesline on a windy day.

"Determined," I said, putting an end to the conversation.

Seeing papa chase the woman around the little purple house made me smile. It was nice to see that love. It was nice to be in this place.

That evening, I pulled out my violin. No one in the community understood or appreciated the sound coming from what they called "the screaming strings" on its own, but when I encouraged the drum player to start first, and then added some music to match, the place came alive.

I had never planned to be here so long. It was 1812 and it had been sixteen years now. I still gravitated towards the French-language papers to find out what was happening in France. Over the years I read about the bastard Napoleon, re-instating slavery in Saint-Domingue and selling French colonized territory to the United States in what they called the Louisiana Purchase. Ironic that two territory thieves should trade amongst themselves as if the land was ever truly theirs to buy or sell. The same as they did to people.

Jefferson, the slaveholder who didn't believe in slavery, and had visited the Chateau all those years ago, was now the American president. Yet another leader who said one thing and did the opposite. Another leader who was a contradiction and a lie both at the same time.

I held the paper with its sketch of a likeness of the Emperor, Napoleon, in profile. It rustled in my hands as I gripped it, thinking about all that was happening in France.

"How does it make you feel, Monsieur Zamor?" Moti asked, having watched me read. Moti had grown plumper over the years. He had a wife and two children now. They were mixed blood with the lighter-skinned Indian woman. They had their own challenges in this society, so he still lived in a community of African descent, his people having included her into it. But he'd lived many years and been educated abroad, the recipient of a wealthy sponsor who had sought out children in the communities to educate. Moti had received his education but then returned home to share as much as he could with his people and help people like me get back home.

"Does it make you miss France when you read about it?"

"I fear I wouldn't recognize it today. I have no concept of what an empire is, I only know a kingdom or a republic."

"Well, you seem very happy here with your papa." We both looked across to where my papa and his gray-haired lady friend were giggling like teenagers. "Your papa is well-loved. The man I see today is nothing like the man who showed up in my community all those years ago, broken after spending a lifetime looking for his son. I'll never forget when he showed up, half-starved, having traveled to us hidden in the trees. Stowing away in the underbelly of ships. He came feeling a failure. He said he'd failed his wife and his son. And now this community has a leader and hope. That's what you provided when you arrived, and it is what he symbolizes."

"I think papa wants to marry again."

"What?" Moti broke into a broad grin. "What a blessing!"

I'd seen some marriage ceremonies. A lot of dancing and food. Special clothes.

"What if we were to start preparing, to surprise them?" Moti looked thoughtful and excited. "A surprise wedding? She'll want to look her best so we need to warn her."

"Maybe let her friends know and they can find a way to make her look her best without telling her. And I can do the same with Papa?"

He smiled slowly. "I like the way you think. I'll tell the leader to start planning. It will be a beautiful wedding!"

Chapter Forty-Three

One morning after a walk I went directly to the far end of the garden where some vegetables were making themselves known.

It was new to me, this feeling of being thrilled when something I put into the ground grew. I'd enjoyed the botanical gardens at the Palace but never worked on them. I liked gardening when I was in the little town near Port Le Havre, but it wasn't my garden. I didn't feel invested in Sara's garden like I felt now, with mine. It was a sense of protection and pride of ownership that caused me to smile every time I saw a perfectly formed carrot or onion or pepper.

A strange sound hit the air but was gone so quickly I thought I imagined it. I looked down at the tomatoes, lovely and green. Not yet ready for harvest, but soon.

Walking to the back door of our house, immediately something felt wrong. My eyes adjusted to the comparative shadow of the room and when my vision overcame the shock of light to dark, I could see the *Second Lost* sitting on the floor on the edge of my pallet. He wore a hangdog expression, his elbows propped up and leaning on his knees. Then, I heard a soft woman's cry, interrupted by *Second Lost*'s gravelly voice. He looked up at me without his usual false smile.

"I'm sorry," he said. "It's not fair. When they came, they weren't supposed to take you or me. Only him. My parents loved me until he came. Those White men offered me money to make it easy for him to be taken.

But they must have seen me standing beside you and they thought you were him. And after they took you, when I tracked them down at the Port, they complained that you were too old. Seven! They wanted a four- or five-year-old. But I told them, they took the wrong one! So then, they came back for him, but they took me, too. I asked them, 'what about my money'? and they laughed. They said they'd make a lot off of him and a little off of me. They double-crossed me!"

Any words going through my head died as I watched his lips move, as if he were putting me in a trance. His voice with neither inflection nor emotion, strangely numbing to me as the words impressed themselves on my brain. He continued and somewhere I heard, with my mind's eye, the gentle crying.

"And then my father caught up to us and the only thing he cared about was getting my brother back. 'Papa!' I yelled, lifting my arms out to him where I sat in the cart. He looked at me, like he was dead in his eyes, and he told them, 'That one can take care of himself, he's almost a grown man,' he said. That he wouldn't make a fuss if they just gave my brother back. I was only fifteen. I still needed my papa to save me, too! But he was going to leave me. My heart was broken. My brother kept crying. The slavers kept arguing with my papa and told him the little one was to go to France, they said. A king wanted a cute little one to give to his mistress to play with. The king would pay good money to give that child a life we could never even dream of. They argued over that boy like he was the sun and the moon. They didn't care about me at all. They were busy arguing over him. I looked down at my brother. He looked up at me, cheeks wet and his eyes so wide, like he was confused about it all. I just reached down and did what I'd seen my mother do to the chickens. They were still arguing over him when I tossed his body over the edge. They didn't even notice until the sound his body made when it hit the ground. 'He fell and hit his head!'

I yelled. They were already running to him. You should have seen my papa holding my brother, rocking him in his arms. You should have seen how angry the slavers were. They pushed me off the cart. One of them told the other they couldn't trust I wouldn't destroy all their property in the night. That they would have to make due with the first one, after all. The first one would go to France. They left us there in the dirt. And after my father finished crying, he took us back home. You should have heard the wail my mother made when he brought her my brother's body.

"I don't know why my father lied to my mother to make her hate me. She wouldn't have done what she did if he hadn't told her lies and made her hate me. He slipped on that rock, I didn't push him. Yes, he said horrible things to me, but still... So, then they died and I was all alone. I'm still alone! But you... the *First Lost*... you were taken and lived with a king... smiling in drawings. At first, I was angry—I didn't think you'd really have such a special life. I thought they'd send you to labor like everyone else. But they put your name in papers! Put jewels on you. You came back here well-fed and healthy. And then your father came, and you got your family back. I was all right with it. But now, they were going to get married and you'd have a mother and father just like all those years never happened. You'd have everything back! But I want it to be just you and me again. No one knows what I went through! No one but you. With him gone, I won't be alone. *You're* my family because you have to be. The *First* and the *Second* is how it should be. Now, it's you and me again. I'm sorry. He was a nice man."

The crying was garbled and low, guttural and deep. Maybe I lost time again in my head because suddenly the crying didn't seem so far away. Suddenly, what I had thought was my father's clothing draped on a chair was the cloaked back of a woman hunched over.

The dread had been rising in me as I watched the *Second*'s expressionless face and listened to his voice enchanting me like a metronome. That's when I finally noticed his hands. Both hands were dripping with blood.

My own blood seemed to drain suddenly and with it the coldness of marble in wintertime washed in as I looked around the room for real this time and saw my papa's legs on the floor on the other side of the blanket covered pallet. I rushed over to him. My papa's lady friend was crying, holding his head in her hands. There was so much blood for a moment I couldn't see my father at all. For a moment all I saw was red. Then I saw the gash across his throat before I ever saw his face. His eyes were open but dull. He was already gone.

"I had no choice," *Second Lost* went on like he was talking about a dust mote. "I was going to do *her*, but I figured I didn't need to if I did him. He's the one that brought you together. Without him there's no family and you're free. You and I can be together again. No one knows how we suffered. No one knows what it was like. No one knows how they speak to you."

Sounds were coming from my throat, which was clutching for air as if it had been the one cut.

"No one understands how tricky they are and how they lie. Only you and I know. It's not fair that I have no family. I'm sorry. He was a nice man."

My knees wobbled but I didn't fall. My eyelid began twitching on its own so fast I could barely see out of that eye. I heard the lightning strike threatening to take me away—I knew my stone fox was coming to claim me—but I wasn't ready to leave my body this time. Not now. Not now!

But people underestimated me all the time. It was understandable. Most of the time I looked as quiet and still and small as he looked sitting on the bed, probably thinking he was finished with his work for the day. Spent of the adrenalin and energy it took to murder an old man. But I wasn't spent or depleted, and I was enraged. More than that, I was insane. I was panicked. I was frenzied as my eyes lost focus and all rational thought left me.

A quick glance around the room and I saw a fork on a table. Sunlight through the window glinted off of its tines like a beacon. No match for a sharp knife on most days, but this wasn't most days. And I'd just seen the body of my only remaining family lying prone, drowned in his own blood at the hands of this man.

It was Henri all over again. I now knew Sebastien was right about Henri because it had happened again. Someone I thought was a friend had gone after someone I loved more. Had intentionally tried to take someone I loved away from me. *Had* taken someone I loved away from me.

I sprinted to the fork, fast, and gained even more speed headed his way. I let out a yell and strode across the room to the man sitting on my pallet, fast. He was still in the process of talking in his monotone, emotionless voice, still with his bloody hands hanging down and the knife in one of them. He still held it. Had he been paying attention—had he known who I was—he might have been holding that knife up ready to defend himself.

Only when he saw me coming at him did he lift himself from his fog. He looked at me and seemed to only see me coming his way. He began to smile, as if I was coming to embrace him.

Had I been rational I might have held compassion for him. His smile... vulnerable and hopeful. Something inside me crumpled at the sight of that desperate smile but the other thing in me–the animal who suddenly found himself in front of a man who had orphaned him—didn't even register.

I came at him so fast I'm sure he didn't realize what was happening until he was on the floor underneath me, swiping uselessly—aimlessly—at me with that knife. He swiped but I jabbed with my overhand fist. I jabbed. I jabbed...

The knife used against me, defensively, caused cuts here and there but I didn't feel anything. I had fever and bloodlust in me now.

I jabbed. I jabbed.

I felt moisture dripping from my face, dripping from my eyes like sweat but dripping into my mouth and tasting like metal–mixing with saliva as I drooled like a rabid animal over my catch. I clutched one hand over the other fist.

I jabbed. I jabbed.

Over all, I wanted the guttural screaming and animalistic grunts to stop. The sound filled my ears! It wasn't until hands came from somewhere to pull me up off him—many, many hands—did I realize the screaming was from me. Because when I could no longer feel the satisfaction of those tines plunging into him, the scream became a howl of disappointment and grief. Sucking in air like I had never breathed before.

In all my life, only one other time had I *wanted,* with every element of my being, to inflict harm on another person. And that time I wasn't able release a primal yell. I released it now for all the screams I'd swallowed throughout my life and for all to come.

As they dragged me away, the white lightning of my nightmares struck, and I let myself go to the Labyrinth. Suddenly, all was silent and still as I stared into the eyes of the cold marble fox before me, both of us in stark silent communication—frozen in time under the brilliant white of a storming sky.

CHAPTER FORTY-FOUR

*D*ear Citizen,

Of course, in hindsight, I should have seen it coming, but in the process of enjoying my life, my instinct had turned rusty. I had been too happy to feel my hairs standing on end.

Pity. A wedding would have been nice...

—Zamor, 1820

A wash of cold water brought me back to my senses. I blinked the water out of my eyes, noticing the pool in which I stood. How many buckets had they poured over me to leave me standing ankle-deep in murky reddish-brown water? Seconds later, another cascade came down and my shoulders hunched up to my ears at the onslaught.

"He's awake now," the medicine woman's voice brought my attention up.

There were five men surrounding me, but she stood the closest, standing directly before me. Defiantly. She looked at me plainly. "Enough water to wake you? Like I said, you scare the children."

"Is my papa dead?" I asked her, shivering in the cool night air. Hoping it was a bad dream.

"You know he is. There's been much bloodshed today. In a community where there is *never* bloodshed you caused so much it will never be forgotten. No one will ever feel safe again. We might have to leave this place if we can't scrub the horror from our memories. Because of you. All because of you."

"No," I denied. But I had a hard time raising my eyes to look at them. "Because of *him*. He murdered my papa."

"Yes, it is bad what he did. But you know his head was broken. You are different."

I brushed a forearm under my nose to wipe away the water dripping off its end.

"How? Didn't you tell me my head was broken, too?"

"Only because you lost your memories. Not because you were like him. He was fine until you came. You brought the horror here with you."

"Fine? You all treat him like an outcast," I mumbled. "I didn't do that to him. I didn't make him feel alone and desperate. You don't blame yourself, yet you blame me?"

"He was different, and he didn't fit in, but he was safe and under control until you came along. He was broken but he couldn't help it. *You* could help it. He wasn't right in the head, and you knew it and still rubbed your happiness in his face."

"You feel compassion for him but none for me," I said, looking down. I didn't need to see her face to know it was true.

"He was one of us."

White, hot anger welled in me.

"*I'm* one of you!" I yelled, my fists bunching and hopping a bit. The men took a step closer to me as if they expected to have to wrestle me to the ground.

"You used to be, when you were a little boy before you left. You came back a stranger. But not like the *Second Lost*. He was like a child."

"He told me himself he sold his brother, killed him and watched his mother die from grief and didn't lift a hand to help her. Probably killed his father, too. Does it even matter to you? He sold his own brother for money."

"Like I said, his head has always been broken. But you, you're not broken like that. You've always been a sneaky stranger. We took you in and fed you and you turned on us, just like you turned on that nice White woman who fed and clothed you like her very own child. Put jewels on your head and fancy clothes on your body and look what you did to her."

"You don't know what's happening in the world or what it's like..."

"Slavery has been around since the very beginning, it's nothing new. We don't complain about it."

"You don't know it like it is today."

"You had a lady keeping you safe. And you killed her."

It was the bottom line to her, it seemed. No point in continuing to argue that point, she wouldn't understand any better than Sebastien had.

I was still looking at my feet. "Like I said, *she wasn't nice*," I mumbled.

"I hoped that the longer you stayed you would eventually show yourself to be decent, for your father's sake. Your papa was the only connection we felt to you."

I felt a slice of hurt. I'd been there for years. I thought some of the people liked me.

"We saw his love for you and trusted his judgment. But what you've done here is a crime to this community and an insult to the father who loved you so much. You shame his memory. You bring shame upon his name."

Water welled in my eyes as I seethed. Another bucket of cold water came at me from behind that seemed directly trying to douse the wave of hot anger that had risen in me. I blinked as the coldness washed over my face, looking down at rinse water that was now pink. I wondered how many buckets had washed over me before I came to, to wash the blood from my body.

"Get him over here," she instructed one of the men with a full bucket with a gesture of her finger. Cold water hit me from the side, and I flinched. "Do you think it's easy living in a community away from the world? If I let a murderer run loose, our community has no hope. I'm responsible for the health of these people. You must be punished to restore order. You can agree to take your punishment–labor and shunning for as many years as we decide–or you must go."

"Shunning? What does that mean?"

"You will work and clean and be obedient. You will not speak unless spoken to." Endless toiling and never treated with any respect. I'd had enough of that. "If you refuse, you must leave. You can try another community like this, but I will go to each of them myself, if I must, and let them know what horror you unleashed here today. After I finish telling them they will never let you in."

I looked at her serious face, delivering this news as if it was nothing. My lips went numb. "Why? Why would you do that to me? What have I done to make you hate me?"

"Stop your whining. You are half a century old, you are the only one responsible for your actions. I blame your mother's evil blood. In the end, it overtook everything good from your father. She was a witch all along to birth something like you."

We stared at each other for a long moment. I wasn't going to let her see how she hurt me.

"With Papa gone I have no more reason to stay," I said curtly.

"Fine. Moti isn't coming until the day after next. You will go to your hut and stay there. Men will guard it to make sure you don't leave except to relieve yourself. When Moti comes to drop off supplies you will leave with him."

Chin up, Zamor, chin up! "Will you prepare my papa's body for the ride into town? I want to bury him with my mother in Chittagong. She's all alone there and his name is on a headstone already."

She hesitated, as if surprised. "His betrothed would like him buried here, I'm sure."

"I feel badly for her; she's a nice woman and my father loved her. But they didn't get a chance to marry. I'm sure she'll understand. He had only one wife and she needs him more. She's all alone in Chittagong."

"You don't even remember her, what do you know of what she needs in death? She deserved to be alone, that evil woman. We loved your papa very much. We will honor him with a burial and keep him with us as a true son of this community."

"You might have honored him by preventing that man from slitting his throat like a roast pig. But you did nothing, so he is mine now. I will take my father to his wife."

"A true son should be with his community—"

"*I* am a true son of this community!" I yelled, finally glaring at her and the men who stood around looking at me like they were afraid. "I am one of yours! I came here looking for my people and my home. You loved me more when I was gone, when I was simply a legend and not a man. Well, I'm tired of people taking from me what's mine! You'll prepare my father's body and say whatever goodbyes you need to say. But he will be going with me when I leave this place or heaven help you all."

The man had stopped throwing water on me, and I stood there, dripping and heaving breath.

She stepped closer to me and looked into my face, her dark eyes delving into mine. I saw something in them I didn't expect—just a tiny spark of fear.

"You threaten us? This community that has welcomed you? Yes, used to be one of us. We will remember that child. We mourn for the *First Lost*; the boy whose name you don't even answer to. I understand now. First, I thought you brought home the sickness of wherever you've been. We don't attack each other with the brutality you displayed. We don't mutilate each other with eating tools. We don't eat each other. We don't slaughter each other and dance in the street in celebration over bodies we've slayed and spread entrails over like decorations. That's the devil's work and only a devil finds that to be normal. *Second Lost* was broken from grief. He was only trying to stop his pain. But you–I saw your face when you were on top of him and I believe it was a relief to you, like you've been wanting to do it all along to someone... *anyone.*"

"That's not true." Was it? Was it true?

"When I saw that scar across your belly all those years ago, I almost turned you away. I thought, what type of person can survive a cut like that? But now I know for sure. The devil cut you open and tossed out the boy we knew and climbed inside himself, sewing you back up from the inside. You can't remember because the boy you were is no longer there. It is the devil I'm looking at."

I laughed mirthlessly, looking to the others to see if they were listening to her nonsense. The more I laughed, the more concerned they looked. She continued to indict me with her words and her eyes.

"You are no victim. You are the devil come to take his due. Come to curse the people that boy loved, just for fun. Either that or you're cursed *by* the devil, either way is bad enough. But there's nothing for you to take here, this is a place of good people. You are a Frenchman."

"I was born here. I belong here. You can't take that from me..."

"You feel nothing for this place. Your home is where you are most comfortable, and it seems you fit right in with those White people you came from. You think I don't see, you can't get to those papers that Moti brings fast enough—anxious to find out what's going on in the white country. You never stopped dreaming of the city of murderers. That's where you belong. As for this place, you will find no peace here because you're no longer welcome. Go, you devil, and go back to your playground. And..." she swallowed hard, her eyes, for once, filling with water. "...take your father to Chittagong, if you must—we want nothing here to draw you back. Tonight and tomorrow, we mourn the father who was killed today and his child who died when he was stolen at seven years old, all those years ago. You will stay in your hut. After you leave, you will be a cautionary tale to our children on the dangers of leaving our community. You will be of some use, no matter the pain you have caused."

When she walked away, they led me back to my hut and then stood guard outside. Once again, I was confined.

They'd washed the blood from the floors and walls while I'd been washed outside. I sat on my bed and stared at the spot on the floor where he'd died. In the dead of night, I blew out my candle and lay down on my pallet, looking over at his empty one. I didn't know why they left it except to torture me.

The next day, the sound of drums woke me, joined by singing. I'd only ever heard happy songs here in this community. Now, the singing sounded more like wailing. I stood up and used a cloth, dipping it into the washbowl to wipe my face. Then, I stepped over to the door, quietly. Maybe they wouldn't be there.

Two men stood the second I poked my head out. One of them shook their head at me. "I'm sorry, Monsieur Zamor. We can't allow you to leave."

I looked at him for a long time, until shame covered his face. But he didn't move, and I didn't have it in me to tackle two of them. I went back inside my hut and sat down on my pallet. My eyes burned from wanting to cry. How dare they refuse me this? How could they?

I stood and walked over to the corner where my clothes were folded next to my back and violin case. I picked up the case, opened it, and pulled out my violin. Moments later, the sound of the singing from the community was joined by the scream of the strings of my violin, playing my feelings for my father. I heard the voices wobble, unsurely, when they heard the instrument.

"Don't stop!" yelled the medicine woman. "He will not stop this most important ceremony. Drown him out!"

The voices picked up again, but not nearly as loudly as I knew she wanted. It didn't matter. I played for me, and I played for my father. It was music I knew Josephe would have appreciated, the notes long and slow and lingering. They wouldn't forget my father. And, yes, I wanted to make sure they wouldn't forget me, either.

They stopped singing after a while, but I continued to play. I played until my fingers were tired. I played until my vision started to blur. And, when all was silent outside the hut, I stopped, sat down, and put my instrument away.

Late afternoon, a young woman came to the doorway, looked at me with fear in her eyes, slid a bowl of food across the floor, and was gone just as quickly as she'd come. No telling what the medicine woman had told them about me. I wasn't going to eat but I knew how long the trip back to town was and needed my strength. I half crawled, half walked to hook a finger on the edge of the bowl, dragging it back towards me. I ate the rice and dried fish, wondering who was going to do the fishing now that me and my father were gone.

Early evening, I sat on the pallet with my knees drawn up and my back to the wall. It occurred to me that the medicine woman might be so desperate to keep my father's body she might do something stupid. I went to my bag and got my knife, clutching it as nightfall came.

I was starting to nod off when there was a knock on my door. I looked up to see my father's lady friend in the doorway.

"May I come in?" she asked.

Did she want to curse me for taking his body? To rail at me for disrespecting the community? To glare at me in revulsion and disgust?

"Aren't you afraid to be in here with me alone?"

She answered by walking in. Coming over, she sat down on my father's empty pallet beside me. Glancing, pointedly, at my hand holding the knife. I lay it on the floor beside me and her furrowed brow cleared.

"I never married. In all these years I couldn't find a man I could tolerate. And then, in my senior years, your father arrives and in the short time we've had together the love we felt was worth all those years alone. When your papa and I walked into this place yesterday that man was waiting inside. He took him from behind so quickly—without giving him even a moment to understand what was happening. For a split second I wanted to take that knife and do the same to him. I understand what came over you. I understand what you did."

She reached out and took one of my stiff hands in hers. I allowed it to relax.

"I know you are taking him away. Don't let them make you feel badly about it. Your papa would want to be with your mother in death. I take no offense to that. His love for her doesn't take away from his love for me. But she is the mother of his child, and he should lay with her. You are right to take him. I only ask one thing," she said, reaching up to pull the scarf from her head. She let it drape softly over my hands. I looked into her face with her curly silver hair in its crown, kinky silver curls framing her face and eyes freely sprouting tears. "Bury this with him so he has a bit of me, also. You know I loved him very much."

"And he loved you," I said softly. "Thank you for bringing him love again, Mademoiselle. He spent so many years suffering."

She looked deeply into my eyes.

"You brought him to life *first*. The medicine woman is wrong to cast you out and I'm not the only one who feels so. I will stand with you. If you plead your case and promise you will never hurt another person, I believe you will find support. You didn't kill him, after all."

I looked at her. "What? He's not dead?"

"Why, no. She didn't tell you?"

I gave her a small, sad smile. "No, I suppose it wasn't important enough for her to tell me while she was busy calling me the devil. Thank you for your offer, it's very kind of you. I'd never ask you to support a promise I can't keep. I've learned through living, we can never truly tell what we might do in the worst of times. I may be evil, but I try not to tell too many unnecessary lies. It's time for me to go. He was the only reason I've been here as long as I have."

"You're not evil." She took my head in her two hands and kissed my forehead. "You're a survivor. You will be angry with yourself for what happened here, but I encourage you to remember your father and how he loved you. The ceremony was nice, but it wasn't until I heard your strings that I truly felt your father's spirit."

When she left, I lay my back against the wall and allowed myself to drift to a world with an ice-cold marble fox spouting frigid water. It was a safer place for me.

CHAPTER FORTY-FIVE

Moti lied. All that I was *was not* enough.

The next morning, I gave myself one last wipe down in our shared hut, looking around the small space to remember it. I went out back and gestured toward the garden. The men looked at each other and nodded me permission to go gather. I took tomatoes and pulled up some carrots–items I could eat raw along the way. It was our garden and it seemed fitting that I take something from it.

They put together a wooden box as a casket for my father and when Moti came he was surprised to find the box on a platform of branches tied together and me waiting to pull it through the dense woods.

"What's happening, Zamor? What is this?"

I could see the questions in his eyes, but I wasn't going to be the one to tell him. At my silence, he walked passed me and spoke quickly with the man who had been my childhood friend—the one without the front teeth. Moti's face went numb and sober as if he had some responsibility for what had happened.

The community stood in the communal square, watching. When I turned, a woman called out to me: "Safe travels *First Lost*. We will miss you."

The medicine woman's face swiveled, her eyes searching for the owner of the voice

"Stop it! He's the devil, I told you."

I flushed, looking over the crowd. I'd been there for sixteen years. My gaze was halted when my eyes landed on a figure sitting on the ground at the far end of the square. *Second Lost* was sitting there, his head wrapped with several scarves that were stained seeped in blood. The rest of his face and neck wore many open wounds, some that looked to be closed with thread. With his one unwrapped eye, he watched. He didn't seem broken to me. My lip curled with disgust. Too bad I hadn't killed him.

The pallet made a constant dragging sound as we walked away and ventured through the rough brush. The gray-haired woman who had been missing ran into view up to us, a bag over her shoulder. "I want to go, too. Moti, will you take me to your community or one of the others? I don't want to have to see the man who murdered the love of my life. I can't live here anymore."

I, too, felt some kind of way about the fact that the man who killed my father was allowed to stay but the people who loved my father had to leave. It didn't seem fair that me, my father, and my mother wouldn't be a part of the community, and he would. It seemed strange that my parents and me would be, perpetually, without a place. But at least my parents would have each other.

Ropes were attached to each side of the wooden platform on which the casket sat, and I clutched both over my shoulders, dragging the wooden box behind me. Stumbling a bit on the grass, I was forced to get my bearings time and again as we navigated through the woods and brush.

"Let me carry it for a bit," Moti asked a time or two but I turned him down, shaking my head no vigorously. Moti didn't speak for a long time but then he told me he was sorry about my father and sorry for everything.

"Stop apologizing for things that aren't your fault, Moti," I snapped. "You will get no points for being a martyr. I did what I did and there was no way for you to predict it or stop it. I don't care about your feelings, and

I never have so you can stop looking at me with that face. This won't stop me. I'll move on with my life. Let me walk in silence."

I said it as cruelly as I could to erase the compassion from his face. He didn't press. I had turned back into the silent, strange man who didn't speak.

I walked ahead, hearing them whispering to each other behind me.

"I'm not the devil," I called to them without turning to look at them. They went quiet behind me.

Dragging my father's body through the woods was heavy but my arm strength was still my best trait. It allowed me to drag my papa to where Moti's cart was hidden in the woods for the return to town. It wasn't a burden at all. I felt I was doing what he would have wanted so as sweat poured over my brow and my legs buckled, I didn't complain.

Eventually, we lifted the box and pallet together onto the cart attached to a horse with the same driver who'd brought me there years ago. The three of us then climbed onto the back, sitting in the cramped leftover space. We took a brief break along the way to drink water and share the tomato and carrots along with some bread she had brought with her.

It was a long trip and with every passing second, bitterness began to seep into me. Bitterness and doubt. It wasn't the first time I'd been called cursed. The medicine woman was blinded by her hatred for me, but what if a small bit of what she was saying was true? How many instances of horror had to happen around me before I began to question myself? Was it me after all?

Hours later, reaching Chittagong, Moti took us straight to the undertaker. The man took possession of my father's body with the promise to bury it the next day for a price.

"You don't have to stay," I told them.

"Of course we'll stay," said Moti. "I have friends in town, they will take us in."

"Not me," I said. "I'll stay at the same inn I was at when I arrived."

So, we separated for the night and the next day we went to my mother's grave. A hole had been dug just beside it and the headstone re-centered. His casket already sat in the hole. The woman my father loved stepped forward, wiped her tears on a scarf, and dropped it down upon the box. Then, us three men took turns with the shovel. A man of religion came forward just long enough to say his name and ask for his entrance to heaven.

"They will take both of you in my community," Moti said.

"No," I said.

"Well, if you don't want to be in mine there are others."

"The medicine woman said…"

"It doesn't matter what she said. She hasn't been out of her community for years, no one knows her and they all know me. They will never listen to anything she says over what I say. I'll take you to another one."

I shook my head. "No, India is no longer a place I want to be, Moti."

He looked at me soberly and nodded. "We can stay with you for a bit."

It was like he was perpetually looking for the good. The breeze played over my face as I considered my words.

"How many things do I have to destroy to prove to you I'm not worthy of your concern? I don't care about you. Why don't you understand that? I care about me and me, alone. *I'm* the only important thing left."

He smiled, sadly. "…Whatever you say, Zamor."

"I say it."

"I've never met anyone like you. I will miss you. I hope we see each other again, one day."

"I know we never will," I said. I'd done all I could to remove him from feeling he had anything to do with what had happened. I knew the weight of responsibility for terror, and I didn't want him carrying any of it. "I think the mystery of the three lost boys is good and dead, don't you? Two are dead to the world and the third is truly dead to the community. The legend can be put to rest. But... but," I hesitated due to the fact that this was the last. I looked down and shuffled my feet. "I'll forever be grateful to you for bringing me back to my father. You'll never know what that's meant to me."

He nodded and we were without words for a moment until he grabbed me into his arms. "I will never forget you or your father. You have both changed my life. Goodbye, Louis-Benoit Zamor." He moved to climb onto the cart, waiting for our goodbyes before moving the horse.

My father's betrothed stepped forward and touched my face. "I'm happy that the child he loved so much loved him back, also. Ask God for forgiveness. If your heart is pure, He will accept it."

They walked to the cart and climbed onto the back. The cart moved away slowly, and I stayed to watch as it carried them all away. I raised an arm to say goodbye. I wasn't the only one starting a new life.

And then it was just my parents and me. I walked over the plot that held them and folded myself down onto the ground atop them. I looked around and, noticing no one looking in this relatively private place, I leaned forward and pressed my palms to the earth, rubbing them against the soil of my father's grave and the grass of my mother's.

"Maman. Papa. I can't remember a lot, but I remember I love you. I loved you so much my mind broke itself trying to forget you. But I'm here. Your son. And I've tried to be as decent a person as I can. Under the circumstances. I hope I have not shamed you too much. I know I probably have but it hasn't been on purpose. I hope when you think of me you see me as I was before I became twisted. I hope you forgive me for the things I've done. Mostly, I hope you can both find peace, together. I'm here. Your son. Zamor. Your son..." I said the name they gave me. It sounded foreign to my lips. It felt like a lie, but I would tell it this last time out of respect for them, to give them peace.

I pressed my hands to the earth and closed my eyes. After a long spell, I stood and went back to the Inn. I had paid for a room for another night and was, blessedly, happy to be able to pay for the Innkeeper to bring pails of water and a large pail for a bath.

The next day, I got a hold of a French newspaper in town and had a cup of tea at a coffeehouse, reading.

It was now 1815. The papers said that Louis XVI and Marie Antoinette's bodies were to be exhumed from the Madeleine Cemetery and moved to the burial place of kings, the Cathedrale at St. Denis. The article made reference to the fact with the caveat:

"...With the 1814 abdication and exile of Napoleon Bonaparte and the restoration of the royal house of Bourbon, it was decided to move the King and Queen to their rightful resting place among the monarchs."

That my father and mother were laid to rest around the same time that Louis XVI and Marie Antoinette were being moved to do the same seemed a sign from God. I thought about traveling to the United States now that my father was gone and didn't have to worry about me. If I stayed north like he said, surely I'd be safe?

At the sound of a carriage close by the window I glanced up. My body jolted at the sight. Not three feet from me, on the other side of the glass, was a cart driven by one White man and one slightly darker-skinned Indian man. They sat behind the horse of a wagon full of little Black children. Even if I didn't know what was happening, their faces told the tale. Eyes frozen and haunted, faces stricken, barely dressed, seemingly numb.

My heart beat hard in my chest. My hand began to shake on its own and I practically dropped the cup on the table. *Mon Dieu, this can't be. This can't be! What do I do? What can I do? Don't show me this. Not this!*

It was me in that cart! It was me left there, still being driven in a caravan with men trying to sell me like a bruised apple. It was me, in stunned silence. It was me wondering when the nightmare would end, and I could go back home. I looked down at my teacup with the spoon beside it glistening with sugar harvested from the torture and labor of children like the ones in the cart. My vision blurred before me.

Dear God, is this still happening? Not this... What do I do? What do I do?

"It happens every day," came the voice of the café owner from where he'd come up beside me, making me jump. I searched his eyes desperately. Please, don't let it be true. But his words confirmed the worst. "It happens too many times to count. Would you like more tea, Monsieur?"

I looked at him for only a moment, but when I turned back, the cart was moving away, carrying those children off to God-knows-where. The sound of old, wooden wheels lumbering over the dirt road lingering in my head. I'd been foolish and too far removed from the horror of my childhood to remember. I covered my mouth with a shaky hand and then tried to shake myself awake.

"No," I said. I wouldn't be going to the United States to become trapped in a new world of even more brutality than this. "No more tea. Do you know when the next ship to Europe sets sail?"

***

After boarding it took three days before I felt comfortable sleeping on the boat after I had done just enough to keep people from thinking I was an easy mark. On the third day I fell asleep, my back against the side, under a cold, dark blue sky.

And in that sleep I felt a small form burrowing itself against my side, leaning into me. I didn't have to look down.

***

"Hello, little Jean," I said.

"Bonsoir, Monsieur Zamor. Are we going home?"

"We? Where have you been all these years and why aren't you resting in peace like you should be?"

"You didn't need me before. But now your papa is gone and you do." He snuggled against me even tighter. "Where you go, I go..." he said, his voice dropping off in the drowsiness of sleep. "Monsieur Zamor... is family... oui?"

Oui. I reached down with one arm and looped him closer to me. To keep him warm on the journey.

Part IV
ALL ROADS LEAD TO PARIS

Gilded Orange Books

Chapter Forty-Six

France, 1815

The little town not far from the Port at Le Havre was busy and thriving as I walked through. I had bought a horse at the port upon arriving in France and he clapped behind me as I walked through the middle of town, taking in the sights.

Years before, the market had been sparse and small. Today was different. There were several outdoor vendors selling fresh fruit, fish, vegetables, and flowers. I couldn't help the pleasure that rippled through me at seeing the place. A young Black man was selling papers on a corner and as I headed over to him a voice called out to me.

"Monsieur, could it possibly be you? Louis-Benoit Zamor from years back, passing through once again."

I turned and saw Nicholas. My face broke into a grin at his gray hair and padded midsection. "Once again, you greet me. Do you just stay in the city center waiting to accost strangers?"

We clasped each other in a brief hug and then kissed on either cheek.

"There is nothing else to do in this town, still. But at least now we have a little theatre."

"You've got more than that," I said, looking around. "There are so many people. I almost thought I'd come upon the wrong place."

"Yes, we've grown. Though there were difficult years at the turn of the century, the town has grown nonetheless."

We chatted about nothing for a few minutes longer and then he told me what I really wanted to know. "You should go see her. She's still in the same house."

I walked, leading my horse, back to the house of my childhood teacher friend, Sara. Securing the horse to a tree, I walked up and knocked on the door. Almost twenty years later and she didn't have a single strand of gray. Her face settled into a look of pleasant satisfaction.

"Well, well, if it isn't my student all grown up and come home."

I smiled, warming to my core at her dry humor.

"You didn't think you'd gotten rid of me forever, did you?"

"Ah, well." She rolled her eyes as if thinking, and then winked at me with a smile. "I'm very pleased I didn't."

"And who is this," came a man's voice, with him popping into view behind her a second later. I recognized his face. He was the man I'd interrupted at her place so many years ago.

"Zamor, this is Philippe, my lover. You recognize each other, correct? Come, come!"

I blushed. The man behind her smiled and allowed me to step inside. Soon, the three of us were sitting at the table sipping tea.

"My sweet sister didn't survive childbirth," she said. Though she said the words casually, a look of pain streaked across her face. "I'd always known she wouldn't."

I reached across the table to take her fingers lightly. "I'm so sorry, Sara."

"I almost wish she had at least found love–something to make the pain worth it. But I was with her through it all and I had a chance to tell her how much I loved her before she left. And it isn't all sad news. Her child is magnifique. Not a bit of his rapist father in him at all."

"He truly must be splendid," I agreed. I couldn't help but look at the man beside her, recognizing him. "I don't mean to seem improper, but I feel I must address the uncomfortable history between us. I behaved quite badly those years ago, thinking you were moving in on my conquest," I said to the man. "I admit, I still didn't understand your relationship when I left. Were you together?"

"Why are you asking him?" Sara said, wryly. "I'll tell you myself. No, we weren't."

"*Almost,*" he corrected, earning a sniff of disagreement from her. "We liked each other very much but it wasn't love until much later."

"I know what you're asking," Sara said. "We were just enjoying ourselves back then. I didn't want to have to explain it to my sister. So, he came only during certain times of the day when I knew she could go outside and be safe for an hour or two."

"So, I truly caused some difficulty for you when I arrived."

"Well, it was quite helpful when you took her into town, she was always so bored at home. And you were handy around the house. It only became difficult because of your crush on me."

I laughed a bit and tried not to spit out my tea. Philippe looked at me with pity.

"I wouldn't call it a crush," I said.

"Don't bother to deny it, I told Philippe years ago about the tantrum you threw that last time you saw him here. How you felt he was moving in on me and disrespecting you. Said you 'weren't having it'."

"I wouldn't say—" I tried.

"—You're not the first man to feel proprietary about me. This one goes through that once every six months and I have to take him down a bit and remind him that I decide what I do, no one else. And then we're back to normal."

"She's fortunate I love her," Philippe said. "I put up with a great deal, but she is more than worth it. Being with Sara is like being a boat on tumultuous water. But I can't imagine life without her."

"Yes," she smiled. "He does love me, very much."

I looked at him. "You had to feel a little bit of jealousy that I was living here."

"Well, like I said, we were not so serious then, we just enjoyed each other. And she assured me you weren't together in that way. I believed her," he said. "And it isn't as if I had a choice or say in the matter. Then."

"Zamor, I wanted you to stay," she explained. "…Because I have always felt somewhat protective of you. I had already told my sister all about the sweet little boy I was trapped in the woods with. I wanted her to know that there are men who are just good people. Men we can feel safe with. That women and men could be friends."

"Good people? Me?" I blushed.

"Oh, I watched you at first. Remember? I even let you spend time with her to test you, and you were always kind and sweet with her. Unlike most men she knew."

I felt a little bad about everything that happened. "Did you have to have another talk with her after I made such a fool of myself?"

"I did. I told her you accidentally fell in love with me, and it made you stupid. Almost got you killed."

I smiled into my tea. "I wouldn't say I was in love…"

"You're right, it truly was only a crush. We both know you were really in love with the woman whose name you kept calling out in your sleep. What was it? V—"

"—Well, I hope I didn't disappoint her too much by leaving so abruptly," I interrupted. "I liked her."

"She liked you, too. '*Don't kill him, Sissie!*'" she pantomimed her sister. "She just had the sweetest heart," she told her man. "Now, we've finished our tea. You must meet her baby boy."

Chapter Forty-Seven

Sara's sister's baby boy was a grown man a full head or two taller than me with shoulders as wide. He was so handsome, while he walked through the town center, a trail of young women tried and failed to pretend not to be following him. They had to keep up the ruse so when his eyes landed on one of them, he would think it was by accident. They'd done the same with handsome men at royal court. Same game, different place.

Us three adults—me, Sara, and Philippe—watched from afar, amused. Sara bit into a pear she picked up from a fruit stand without buying as we strolled. "He's being considered for mayor."

"What? Is handsomeness now the main qualification for public office?" I asked.

"When hasn't it been the main qualification for everything? But he's also brilliant, of course. It's the most amazing thing. As soon as he had his growth spurt, all of a sudden all the townspeople, who for years were calling me 'murderess' to my face, started calling me Citizenness and Madamemoiselle! It was like a magic wand made me respectable because I was raising that child. Their minds couldn't connect anything bad to him, so I was re-made into a respectable woman."

"Is that all it takes? To be around a respectable person to be considered respectable? I'm going to have to find one of those people for myself instead of constantly associating with reprobates, murderers, and murderesses."

We all laughed.

"And then you'll have to become one yourself and I fear that's beyond your ability," she teased me. I was feeling comfortable in a way I never expected. I was feeling good and welcome and warm.

"Come and meet Luc."

Luc was even more handsome up close. If I were younger, I would be envious of him myself, but he was a generation behind and a world apart from me. He took my little hand in his large one and smiled down at me without an ounce of guile or deception.

"Bonjour, Monsieur Zamor! I've heard wonderful things about you. Including that you were good and kind to my mother. It's a pleasure to meet you."

"Ah, well." I looked up, slightly distressed by the fact I had to look up so far. I felt like a little boy looking up at his papa. "Your mother was easy to be kind to. She was a lovely person. She and your aunt were generous to a fault. I'm so sorry she wasn't able to see the man you've grown into."

"Merci, Monsieur."

Luc had built himself a house next door to his aunt with his own two hands. Partly, he said, because he enjoyed being around her. Partly, because he never forgot how people treated his aunt when he was a child. He explained that evening as we sat around the table at his house, eating stew and drinking red wine.

"This town has mostly good people but there were one or two who used their children to plague me when I was small," he said, filling our glasses with red wine. It was me, his aunt and her Philippe, the young woman Luc was smitten with, and a third older woman who I realized had been invited purely for my sake.

Sara, Luc and Philippe were trying to set me up. The woman, seeing me for the first time, hadn't run. Nor had she looked particularly excited at my appearance, but she was polite enough to eat her meal beside me.

"More wine, Mademoiselle," I offered her. She nodded and I poured.

Luc continued regaling us with stories of his childhood. "One of the children caught me coming back from lessons and told me my father was a rapist, my mother was a simpleton, and the woman who raised me was a murderess and, thus, his parents told him I was cursed for life." It seemed I wasn't the only one cursed.

"That was a gutsy child," I said, smearing butter on my bread.

Sara said, "I wasn't half as annoyed with the child as I was with his parents. Who would spread that kind of gossip to a little boy?"

"So, I told the boy," Luc said. "All those things were true. Did he want to be friends, anyway? He said yes and we've been best friends ever since."

"Brilliant!" I said. "Disarm them with charm."

"It was either that or beat him to within an inch of his life and my Aunt Sara told me I should only resort to violence if absolutely necessary."

"Very good advice," I said. The stew was tasty, but the wine was better. I hadn't had French wine in twenty years and had forgotten how much I loved it. I loved Chartreuse more, but very deep red wine was a close second. I topped my glass and saw the eyes of the woman next to me as she watched me enjoy it, disapprovingly. I was enjoying it too much to care.

Sara explained that the little town filled with Black people, half of whom were former slaves, had its share of difficulties. A good portion of White French nobles had been slave owners, some who had lost quite a bit of money during the brief abolition. And some of them felt resentful of what they'd lost in the form of people. Some of them knew there were towns like this where Black people lived for safety and peace. Occasionally, they came to the community to stir up trouble where they could. Or for more nefarious purposes.

"I read the papers when I was in India. That Napoleon reinstated slavery in 1804. I felt so low in spirit. It's unconscionable."

"France will never have peace as long as people with black skin are in chains," Philippe said. "I bought my freedom just before slavery was abolished and immediately came here to the mainland. Not many slaves even have the chance to buy their freedom. Once I had mine, I knew I was coming here. Now, those people in Saint-Domingue who were free during the revolution are enslaved once again."

"Truly a sin," Sara said, her face clouded with memory. "They say now that the trade is becoming illegal it will be better."

"They just force people to mate," Philippe said, his face twisted with disgust. "Or the owners make their own slaves, forcing themselves on slave women."

"Please, let's not talk about it," said the woman next to me. I looked over and she was having a hard time keeping the tears from spilling over the rims of her eyes.

"Oh, my dear..." Sara got up quickly and came around to hold onto the woman's shoulders, speaking to her gently while she gained her composure, wiping the tears from her eyes with a napkin.

They explained that when Napoleon revoked the abolition of slavery in 1804, the town had gone into malaise. Some slaver owners went back at it, but transport was more difficult now as the trade itself was falling out of favor.

"A good number of people were here preparing for family members to come over from the former colonies," Sara said. "Then, to find them suddenly re-enslaved again. To have gone through everything, fought that bloody revolt and fought for France! To have tasted freedom, only to have that man snatch it away again."

"Batard!" her man declared. *Bastard!* The table got quiet. The woman beside me sniffed and Luc's young lady friend dropped her gaze as he reached over for her hand. The women beside me spoke for the first time.

"They play with our lives like we are pieces on a board game. Like we are nothing," she said. I reached into my vest and pulled out a handkerchief, handing it to her.

"It won't be like that forever," Luc said, jaw firm with certainty. "What we have today is nothing like before. The population of Black people in France grew with the abolition. Re-instated or not, our people will be free someday. France is better because of the work and participation of Black people. This country will admit to that. And now there are more of us on the mainland who can affect change that will reach across the water to make a real difference."

His words excited me. Mon Dieu, he sounded like a true Jacobin!

"Will you start a movement, then?" I asked him.

"Ah, Luc," Sara interrupted, wagging a finger at me. "Don't let his harmless visage fool you. This man helped transform this country from a monarchy to a republic. I feel Zamor is about to try to tempt you to re-start the revolution."

The young man smiled but kept his eyes on me. And later, after we drank wine and finished our meal, we sat by his fire and he told me his dreams about leading his town and driving the effort towards abolition again. Listening to him, seeing the fire in his eyes and in his soul, brought joy to me I hadn't felt in a long time.

Later, I walked next door to take my place on the floor in the front room, having been offered to sleep at Sara's house. She handed me blankets as I made up my little bed on the floor.

"Do you see how splendid he is? My sister would be proud, don't you think? I did a good job, didn't I?" I stopped and looked up at her; her hands wringing and her face soft and seemingly eager to hear my opinion.

"Of course. Of course." I stood up and took her hands in mine as a tear escaped her eye. "You did a magnificent job, Sara. You were the best possible person to raise that boy. No one could have done it better."

She sniffed, wiping away the tear. "Good of you to say. I had my doubts, you see. Here I was alone, having lost the only person I had left on the earth and this little baby. The murderess with an innocent life in her hands! For a bit, I thought he might be better off with someone else. But then, they wouldn't have been able to tell him about her—" Her face crumbled a bit, but it firmed up quickly.

I understood her. She didn't feel she was good enough to raise a baby. Felt she was a bad person and undeserving of the purity of new life. I understood all those feelings. I nodded and squeezed her fingers again.

"I wish I had known how you felt about yourself," I told her. "I would have reminded you that when I was small and alone and vulnerable, you cared for me and protected me. I would have reminded you that you are one of the best people I knew. If I had a child, I would gladly place it in your care a thousand times over. You hear me, Sara?"

She nodded quickly and firmly and wiped away another tear.

"And you hear me, Zamor, there's a place for you here. We are not as large or as fancy as Paris, but this is a good place to live. And you are welcome. We'll be happy to have you as part of our strange family."

Live in this little town without a name?

She was right, I had been planning to return to Paris. But, suddenly, the thought of living in this place was even more attractive. I had friends here. I could build a home. I could be comfortable here. Could I?

Yes, I could.

CHAPTER FORTY-EIGHT

Though all the young women in town had their eyes on Luc, it turned out he had his eyes only on one woman. His young lady friend soon became more.

Luc's betrothed had linked arms with me, the old man, and we were walking through the city center, discussing the design choices in the home I hadn't yet built. She fairly bounced up and down with excitement as she explained how she and Luc would help me find furniture and set up a garden.

"You know how to grow things, Monsieur Zamor?" she asked. Her skin was warm brown under the sun, her eyes dark with lashes so black and thick they looked like little curtains. The fashion for women these days no longer required the massive hoops under the skirts and the waistline was high, just under the bosom. She wore soft blue that highlighted her tone and felt as fresh as the blue sky that day in the midst of summer. She was perpetually happy and optimistic, just like Luc. It must have been youth.

"I do know how to grow things, Mademoiselle."

"Très bon! We shall have so much fun trading vegetables in the spring! We're very fortunate to have so many fine growers in town. Many across France still have such difficulty affording food, especially in the cities."

She and Luc had been the ones to decide my house should be built next to his, close to Sara, but not *too* close. After over a year of living on Sara's floor, the walls were up in my new home.

When they proposed the idea, I had been stunned into silence, feeling touched that they were so happy to live so close to me, knowing that they didn't know any better. But with me on one side and Sara on the other, the young couple would always be safe—that was for sure.

Sara's little brood had taken me under their wing after she told them all I had decided to stay. Her partner declared happiness that he finally had a new male friend and treated me to an outfit befitting the time. Luc was thrilled that I could tell him more about his mother, though I was sure I'd already told him everything I knew about that sweet girl. And his fiancée was just happy to have an old person to listen to her plans for her future.

The sun was bright as we walked through the square. Luc and Sara had gone off to speak to some townspeople about me joining the community, so his fiancé was keeping me company with plans for all of us to meet up on the other side of the square in a few minutes.

The young woman squeezed my arm. "My papa is in Sainte-Domingue," she said, suddenly serious. "He helped buy my freedom when I was very little and then worked to get all of our siblings free. The people who owned us weren't attached to us like some of them get—you know, the ones who feel they own your soul?—they weren't like that. They truly only saw us as expendable labor. Either way is bad, but at least if they only see your monetary worth there's possibility you can barter for your freedom. Papa begged and stole for years to have enough money to trade for us and once free, sent us here one-by-one. But he didn't have time to get himself out before..." Her face wobbled. "I haven't seen papa in fifteen years. I don't know if I'll ever see him again now that he's enslaved again. You remind me a bit of him, Monsieur."

I didn't know what part of me it was that was appealing to any of the people in this town, but my heart melted at her words. I gave her arm a squeeze.

"That is the greatest compliment, Mademoiselle. I am certain I would have liked your father. And I know he would be proud of the fine person you are."

We had reached the corner where we were to meet behind a vendor stand and upon turning it, came upon a scene. At the sound of our steps, Sara whirled to look at us, Luc beside her doing the same. Both of their faces were frozen in shock and panic. Then, I noticed they were standing over something. I looked down to see a White man lying prone on the ground. He wore a silk woven green vest and brown pants of high quality. His shoes were leather. His hair was blond. And his head was lying in a pool of blood. Oh, no.

The young woman set off to scream but I clutched her arm, quickly pulling her attention. "Now, now…" I put my finger to her lips. "Hush, hush. Do not panic, my dear." I let go of her to quickly step over to the other two. Luc's eyes darted back and forth, up and down.

Sara told me, simply, "He came at me."

"Why? Who is this man?"

"Someone I knew long ago. His father owned me for about a week. I escaped, of course. I hit him with a skillet. That man is his son. He was a little boy the last time I saw him. I can't imagine how he could recognize me after all this time."

Because you look the same, I thought to myself. Almost like the clock had stopped for her.

"It's amazing, after all this time, we would end up in the same place. He was going on about how I was part of his inheritance and he was taking me back. And then he tried to drag me and hit me in the face with a closed fist. So, I picked up that pan and hit him."

I looked over and saw the offending skillet on the table, blood dripping off the edge and slowly down the side of the table. "I only hit him once," she said, as if it mattered. The man was lying just as dead as if he had been hit twenty times.

Luc was two heads taller than me with shoulders as broad as two men, but his eyes were sober and his face was flushed with fear.

"What's going on?" Philippe came upon the scene, looked it over, and in a split second seemed to understand the gravity. He shrugged out of his coat and began unbuttoning his shirt.

"What are you doing?" I asked him.

"I don't want to ruin my clothes, they are expensive. Someone hand me that shovel over there. We'll find someplace to bury him." He pulled his shirt off and for a moment his back faced me. A mass of old slash marks covered it.

"Don't you even want to know what happened?" I asked.

"I see what happened. This man is dead. And since Sara and Luc are standing over him, I know he deserves to be. He wouldn't be the first White man to come here for no good and he won't be the last."

"I'll confess," Luc said.

"No!" Sara said. "Don't be silly, Luc, I'm the murderess, everyone knows. I'm justified in protecting myself!"

"In what world, ma tante? Slavery is legal and you were never freed. They could take you."

His fiancée had come out of shock and ran over to whisper to him fervently. "They could take you, too, as the child of a slave, even if she's dead. It doesn't matter the reason. Whichever of you confesses, they'll put you away. Or, worse... they'll send you to the colonies."

"I'm not letting them take my aunt. My maman is already gone, they can take me. I'll find my way back, somehow."

"You won't! I forbid it, Luc, do you hear me?" Sara said firmly, her face finally fierce with emotion that hadn't been there just moments before. A dead man was nothing compared to her feeling for her nephew. "It can't be you. I've killed many men in my time, it's justice that I be punished for at least one of them—even if they deserved it, every single one. I'm strong. I can handle myself. You've never been in chains a day in your life, and you won't start today."

People were wandering back now and some of them stood by, whispering. Discussing what they were seeing. I didn't know what to make of it or this place. Some were surprised, but others didn't seem to be. In fact, it looked like, as people surveyed the scene, they were strategizing. I was too busy figuring out what to do to worry about them.

"What about these people?" I asked them.

"They won't say anything." Philippe had found a shovel and was now looking around for a good digging spot.

Luc's fiancée looked back and forth between me and Sara, eyes frantic. "They'll put him away," she pled with us, as if we didn't know. "He won't get a trial. He won't get to plead his case as the son of a slave. They'll take you both! They'll work him until he dies. He'll *never* come back. Even if it's self-defense they send people away and work them to death. He..."

The sound of a horses' hooves sounded clearly in the square, loud because the townspeople no longer allowed horses into this space that was so filled with vendors and people walking around. We all noticed the sound.

I stepped over quickly and looked around the corner at the White man on a horse. My eyes drifted closed with dread and the group on the other side saw my face. Luc's fiancée's eyes went even wider, if possible, filling with tears. I hushed them all and whispered to them: "Cover him with something. Hide him!" Two men threw a tablecloth over the body and Philippe stepped over to place himself between Sara and everything in the world.

"Step aside," Luc said, stepping forward. "I'll pay the consequences. I'll go to trial and explain."

"Are you mad!" Sara hissed at him. "*I'm* the murderess. I'm an old woman, they'll punish me and then they'll let me go. They'll never let you go. You're too strong, all they see is a laborer and they'll use you up. This is my fault. I'll go…"

Stay out of it, Zamor! my inner voice screamed. *You finally have a home!*

An overwhelming sense of sadness came over me because for a moment, I did consider staying out of it. *Why can't I have this dream, unexpected though it is, to live in a place like this, where they actually want me? When would it be my turn to be happy? When could I live in peace? I could be happy here, I know it. And I want it. Dear God, I want it.*

The man had climbed off his horse and was calling out to the crowd of people that had quieted down, uncomfortable, with this stranger looking them up and down. He called out.

"I dropped my friend off earlier and he said he was coming to this town to… shop. But he never returned at our meeting place. I want to know where he is."

His words were coded, of course. If he dropped their friend off to "shop" in this place he was searching for human cargo. Slavery was illegal on the mainland, but Port Le Havre wasn't far. If someone could be kidnapped and smuggled to the port, they were all but lost to the trade. No matter that it was illegal, there was always a market for the most depraved.

I looked back behind me at my little makeshift family: Sara and Philippe and Luc's young love, almost beside herself, clutching onto him as if she could hold him there by will. Luc's face was firm, his eyes scared.

Sara brushed herself off. "No more talk, it's time. I've made my peace with it. I've gotten away with it in the past, just not this time. It's time."

On the other side of the wall, the stranger called out: "You heard what I said. I want to know where my friend is, and I want to know now!"

Stay out of it, Zamor! My soul was screaming.

I looked at the three of them. Sara was good to the core, no matter what she'd done. I thought about what the world would lose if it lost *any* of them.

"You've suffered enough," Luc said, beyond caring who saw. He stepped forward to round the corner to take responsibility, ready to confess. As if he was a man determined to do right to counter the wrongs done by people like Sara and me.

Curse the principled people—they put us all in danger! Just rounding twenty and he was braver than I'd ever been. More substance in his young body than I'd managed in all my years. Just like his aunt.

There was a small crowd on both sides of the curtain now, and the one behind the curtain looked like a veritable army. They stood, sober and serious, ready to deal with what was to come. Luc was leading them, stepping forward, and—

I stepped around the corner first.

"Bonjour!" I called out to the stranger, drawing all eyes my way. I heard Luc's steps stop and I proceeded to walk further into the square to draw the eyes of the stranger away from what was going on behind me. "I heard you calling out, Monsieur. Did you say you dropped a friend off earlier?"

The man looked me over. "Yes, I'm looking for him. He's a White man; he shouldn't be hard to miss here. Where is he?"

"Is your friend maybe..." I put my hand up just a little taller than myself. "...About this tall? Wearing a green vest and dark brown pants with an overcoat?"

He was paying more attention now. "Yes. You've seen him?"

"I've done more than that. I took him over to the port at Le Havre."

"What?"

I was going to have to gamble on this one. Based on my basest expectations of human beings. "The gentleman said he'd found what he was looking for. I transported him and…" I leaned in, conspiratorially, "…and a young woman, up to the Port at Le Havre. He said he wanted to make quick work of selling his goods, if you understand, Monsieur. I took him because I happen to have a cart with a horse."

He straightened. I might have gotten it wrong. I didn't think so, but one never knew. It was worth the gamble.

"Merde, I was supposed to pick him up," he said. I breathed in relief.

"Oui, he found what he needed relatively early and paid me a few coins to take him to finish his business sooner. The girl was making a bit of a fuss, you understand."

"And you helped him? Why?"

"Why, Monsieur, never let it be said I will keep a man from making an honest livre," I said.

He stepped back from me and called out, "Did anyone see what this man has said?"

A woman stepped forward. "I saw this man," she pointed at me with a nod. "He and another man took a girl and rode away." She gave me a look that confirmed she knew it was a lie. Then she put on a performance. "You're all dirt. How dare you come here and take our girls? Don't think we'll let this stand. I told your friend and this man here, I'm going to contact the police and let them know what the two of you did. Coming into our town committing crimes! The next time you come here I promise the police will be waiting for you. Batard!"

She was good. Too good. He blanched, thinking about his own crime.

"Blah, blah, Madame," I shooed off her words like she was the biggest nuisance. "Just point me to the good fruit you keep hidden and I'll be on my way. I've been searching all day for something worth eating."

The stranger turned in a circle, looking around. He was met with glares and expressions daring him to accuse anyone further. His eyes landed on me again. "Why didn't he come back here with you?"

"I offered to bring him right back. He said something about staying to gamble with his new money. He said he'd find his way back home. It's none of my business, Monsieur. But I hope he doesn't stay at the Port too long; there aren't the best sorts of people there."

I couldn't tell if he believed me or if he was slowly coming to realize he was outnumbered and, perhaps, his own role as accomplice to a crime put him in a precarious position.

"If you're lying, I'll come back here and we'll have an unpleasant conversation."

"Here? I don't live here, Monsieur, I'm just traveling through and stopped to see what the place is about. To pick up some fruit along the way. Very backwards and quaint, non? These farm communities don't hold my interest for long."

If he'd been paying attention he'd have noticed this didn't look like a farm community at all. Most of the people in this town were bourgeois, but he didn't notice their dress or the relative comfort of the town. He only noticed the people were Black and for that reason, not anything to be envied. His bluster died down. "Very convenient that I won't be able to find you."

"Oh no, Monsieur. You can find me with no problem. You might have heard of me? My name is Louis-Benoît Zamor, I'm just on my way back home to Paris. Please, do come see me there. I so enjoy speaking to noble-born about the old time in the age of kings, though I imagine you're too young to remember. When nobles were in their proper place at the head of society and the commoners were in theirs. I can tell you come from noble blood just by looking at you, you understand.

"But... you don't care about... why he was here? You're not loyal to these people, being that you're all...?"

"All...?" I cocked my head like I didn't understand him, then I laughed and shook my head in affectionate humor at his naivete. "Oh, Monsieur, I'm a noble servant. What do you imagine I could possibly have in common with these people? Please, I encourage you to look me up in Paris if you can't find your friend. We can share a nice brandy, or go back to the Port and look for him together."

I smiled one of my most placating, false smiles.

It made sense, as far as he was concerned. In the age of kings, there were hierarchies within hierarchies. None of that equality nonsense for nobles or slave owners. Even the servants of the nobles were heads above any common slave.

My stomach turned at my own ruse and the bitterness of insulting these people pricked at me. Why should I have to lie? Why did we have to live like this? Why couldn't we just be left alone?

"All right," he said. "I live in Paris as well; it should be easy to find you," he said. These jackals and slave owners, feeling they had a right to people. Feeling they had a right to everything.

A little bit of cold anger made its way into my voice accidentally. "That's wonderful news. You and your friend should look me up and we'll have a nice laugh about this. I shall be so happy to see you in Paris. We'll share a café. Or, like I said, a very good brandy and all that."

He looked at my face, and then he turned and walked to his horse. He mounted it and didn't give another look in my direction as his horse cantered away. It was the noble way, not to grace commoners with too much eye contact. I followed him a short bit.

"The Port at Le Havre!" I called, reminding him with a smile on my lips and resentment curling my tongue.

***

By that evening I had packed my things and loaded them onto the horse.

Sara stomped over to me, still angry.

"What have you done, Zamor? Why did you do that? Do you think we care if he comes back here with two men or ten? Do you really think we haven't had trouble with men like him before? Entitled nobles who think they have a right to us. We handle it, together. We would have handled them!"

"Who knows how many would come or how angry they would be? And it was the least I could do."

"I don't understand..."

I looked down to avoid her gaze but spoke to her the thoughts that came unbidden. "Sara, I was never meant to stay here. The medicine woman at the town in my birth home, she said death follows me. What if she's right and I'm cursed? I'm out of place here, just like I was out of place in India. I knew the second I heard that man's voice that it was a sign. My past has caught up with me." I tightened my bundle on the horse's back. "I couldn't live with myself if I brought death to this place."

"Little brother, death is inevitable. People die. Animals die. Plants die. Hopes and dreams, they all die, don't they? And it happens whether Zamor comes into town or not. But wherever death lives, life lives, too. It's all connected. That's why I'm not afraid when I get visitors by my tree because everything—the earth, the sky, the living, the dead—is all connected. Death has no power. Only fear of it has power. You have lived a lifetime of being told you are nothing and punished when you dare to be something other than what they call you. You are not cursed, you are simply living your life swimming against the tide."

"But I have friends in Paris—relationships to mend. And I want to write that book."

Of course, I could write a book anywhere. I could visit Paris anytime. These were excuses. I wanted to stay in the little house they built for me. I wanted to be surrounded by the warmth of this place. Yet, something in me was pulling me away. I couldn't explain it, but it was real.

She nodded, her lips pressed together. Then, "Well then, you must leave, no matter how much I want you to stay."

"I'm grateful to you and your family."

"Nonsense. You are my family, too. Write your book and send me a copy."

I smiled.

Luc walked over and stood next to Sara, his face serious and haunted. "Monsieur Zamor, would you like me to come to Paris with you, in case they decide to try something?"

A quick glance of worry streaked across Sara's face and tightened her lips. No, I would never to that do a friend.

I gave him an exaggerated look as if he was being ridiculous. "Sara, I thought you told this young man all about me. Apparently, you forgot to tell him that of the two of us, *I'm* the dangerous one. You need to be here, son, in case any troublemakers do something foolish. You and your aunt can protect each other, oui? Don't worry about me, I live for my enemies who think they'll make quick work of me. They never even see me c—"

Sara stopped my bragging with two fingers on my lips and then pulled me forward to press her forehead on mine. We held them there together as my eyes closed, briefly.

"You have a home in my heart, always, Louis-Benoit Zamor. If the day ever comes that you miss being in a place where you're loved and accepted as you are, come back."

"Safe travels, friend," Philippe called from where he stood in front of the house. I nodded to him, squeezed Sara's hand, and climbed atop my horse.

A few minutes later I was on the road to my destiny. On the road to Paris.

Chapter Forty-Nine

Homecoming, 1815

Twenty years after leaving France, I walked the stretch along the Pont Neuf bridge with a new spirit and a new sense of myself. I stopped, leaned over the edge, and looked down into the water below.

What was it Véronique had said about water? At the time, I gave her grief for giving too much credit to the old Seine river, but now I stared down into it. It twisted its way through France like a snake searching and seeking for answers in towns, big and small. It was the same river that wound behind the Chateau and swirled behind Véronique's little house.

Véronique. How I missed her. The passage of time took away the rawness of emotion, but it also put our time together in sharp contrast to the rest of my life. I hadn't known the time with her would be the best of my days. I hadn't imagined my feelings for her could grow over the years even while I was trying so hard not to think of her. Perhaps returning to Paris brought all those feelings to the forefront.

I walked the streets and took brief respite in Sainte-Chappelle. No longer being used for storage, I was able to climb the stairs to the upper level to look up at that beautiful ceiling. Paying my respects and re-baptizing myself under the colors of the sun shining through the stained glass. Finally, I walked the streets looking for a room for rent.

I went into the first door with a sign. It was a small room in an apartment building.

"I know who you are," the landlady said, almost the moment I walked in. "Here." She reached over and took a pamphlet from a drawer. It was written in the style of writing gossip as if truth. I'd seen printings of its type before I left France, before the Reign and when the King and Queen were still alive. Distasteful, disgusting things about the happenings in Versailles.

But this pamphlet had a black figure that I assumed was supposed to be me. The character was little more than an animal, and the suggestion was that I was a disloyal, rabid dog who had turned on Madame. A figure of a White woman reaching out in kindness and my character slicing at her arms with a knife.

"The whole country knows who you are," she repeated.

"Well, by all means, if this is who I am perhaps it's not wise to offend me." I tossed the pamphlet back onto the counter.

"Jeanne du Barry was a good Frenchwoman. She was one of our own. We loved her here."

I glanced at her pinched face, her arms crossed over her chest and mouth bunched like she wanted to pull me to the floor and wrestle me. Around me I caught the looks of the other two people in the small space, all tense in light of the subject.

"Shame," I said. "So many of you loved the Comtesse so much not one of you stood up and declared that to the Revolutionary Tribunal when it would have mattered. I'm sure she would have appreciated this devotion to her good name before her head was separated from her body. As it was, there was so little support for her that even the word of a lowly Black servant was enough to send her to the beast, without objection. Shame a *good* Frenchwoman—like *yourself*—couldn't have been bothered to raise her voice in defense of the good Madame du Barry." The woman shifted but her face now held some embarrassment and a tinge of shame. "So, do you have a room I can rent or not?"

Nothing she was willing to rent to me, of course, so I headed down the road.

It was curious to me, how she had defended Jeanne du Barry so quickly, without hesitation. It seemed my former benefactress had gone through some sort of cleansing of reputation while I was gone.

I found a small room on the Rue Perdu.

"I own this building with my husband. Pay for the first two months up front," said the landlady. "There's a room upstairs. Communal toilet on the floor. No noise, no parties."

I was fifty-three—felt like I was one hundred—and she thought I would be having parties. "No parties?" I played with her a bit more as I laid my coins on the counter. "I was planning to have one of those orgies like on those pamphlets still floating around about me."

She quirked a lip. "I don't have time for reading trash, Monsieur. No parties and don't be late on rent and we'll get along fine."

I liked her. I tipped my head at her. "In that case, my name is Louis-Benoit Zamor. It's a pleasure to meet you."

"The same, Monsieur."

I wondered how long her friendliness would last.

I took my bag and headed up the stairs. The room was small, but it was decent. That done, I set about the important work of reconnecting and tying up loose ends.

I went looking for Sebastien first. I moved through the Paris streets like I'd never left and was surprised at how comfortable I felt. I felt like the man I'd always wanted to be. At his door, I knocked stridently and while knowing it had been twenty years, I hadn't prepared myself for what the passage of time would look like. It looked like wrinkles like a roadmap across the face of my best friend's wife, Élise.

"Oui?" she asked, hesitating only a second; a wave of sadness passed over her features but then it melted into her sweet smile. "Zamor? Is it really you?"

"My dear Élise, it is so good to see you." I kissed her on both cheeks. "I decided it was time to punish Paris with my presence, once again."

"Well, with the two of you together again this city is truly in for trouble. Come in, come in. Not a week has gone by he doesn't complain to me that you will never come home again. I reminded him that you always liked to build anticipation of your coming. Sit! Pour yourself some brandy, you know where it is."

I did, indeed. I walked over to the cabinet where they kept the small glasses and reached for a decanter of the heady, deep liquor he'd always liked. The house was still tidy and smelled like wood. I poured three small glasses, feeling like I'd stepped through time–feeling the excitement of happiness that only came with a few people in the world.

"So, the prodigal son returns." Sebastien's voice was the same so it was a shock when I turned to see my friend, a little wider, a little rounder, with a shock of white hair where his jet black mane used to be.

"What have you done with my friend, old man?" I asked, feigning horror. "I asked to see Sebastien, not Père Noel."

His face cracked into a smile, and he laughed as he barreled across the room to encircle me with his arms.

"You sorry sack, if I didn't love you, I would tell you that you apparently have not looked into a mirror because you have shrunk to half your size and I can barely see you for all the silver in your hair blinding me!"

"Stop teasing him," she said, as Sebastien dropped me to my feet. He did seem taller so maybe he wasn't teasing and I had shrunk. I passed around the glasses. "Santé." I raised my glass and they followed. We drank quickly and I topped us off.

"Look at him, pouring my liquor freely like it's his own. Arrogant bastard hasn't changed a bit. Sit, sit!"

"Well, I wouldn't want to disappoint you."

Sebastien sat opposite me at the little table. "Tell us all about where you've been. Leave nothing out. Did you find your parents?"

Of course he must have suspected that was where I would end up.

"Maman was gone but a young man managed to find my father. He'd been looking for me all these years. We spent our time getting to know each other again. Seventeen years with my papa was a gift." Sadness streaked through me quickly but not quickly enough to hide it.

"He died of… natural causes?" Sebastien asked. He was as sharp as always. Sharp like V—

"Someone took him away from me."

"Ah." He nodded, his eyes still on me. "Did you take care of it, then?"

"Almost. I'm not proud of the attempt. He was sick about the head. I didn't intend it and don't remember it, but afterward—it was treated as if I'd tried to beat a bunny rabbit to death."

"Well, a murdering bunny rabbit…"

"The community couldn't understand what I'd done no matter the reason. The violence. Said it was the *French* in me that I could be so brutal. Maybe they were right. Who knows, maybe it's just to me that violence comes so easily," I said. The wooden chair creaked under my shifting. "So, then it was time for me to go and here I am." I shrugged a little, eyes wide with excitement of what was to come. "Here to fill your lives with joy, again."

"But what about what you were told as a child? Did your parents sell you?" I told them what I had learned about my home and how I was taken.

He frowned. "All along you might have been sent home, regardless of why you were taken. This is all because of the selfishness of the *Well-Beloved*," Sebastien said, looking pained and angered for me. "He could have let you go. The most powerful man in all of Europe and he holds onto a small child, for what?"

"I was no better, Sebastien. I let myself believe the lies. It was easier and less painful. But all that time my parents were holding onto me, and I let them go as easily as if their love and our family had never been."

"Don't say that," Élise said. "You were a scared child with no understanding of what was happening in the world. How were you to know?"

"That sorry son of a bitch bastard," Sebastien said, storm clouds on his face. "I didn't need another reason to hate the royals, but you just gave me one. Good riddance to them all."

"Calm down, Sebastien," she said. "Your heart."

"What's wrong with your heart?" I asked him. He looked at me, shame-faced.

"Nothing. What's wrong with your leg? Why are you limping?"

"Not a thing," I lied. We stared at each other, closed-mouthed, until the ridiculousness settled on us and we laughed. "We're all fine. Let's drink to that." I topped off our glasses with more of his brandy. I'd buy him another bottle.

"But all is not sadness," I said. "I passed through a town populated by Black people. I have to say, it was quite wonderful. I almost stayed there. I was only planning to be away for a short time, but while I was in India I read that France had crowned an *emperor*, of all things. My goodness, Sebastien, how did you allow *that* to happen?" I knew putting it on him would irk him to no end, which was why I did it.

He flushed deeply, his pale face now full of color. "Merde. He snuck up on us. Everyone was so happy to be done with the Terror and the Directory they just wanted to forget what had happened. He helped them to. Closed down most of the newspapers, shut down all the remaining Jacobin Clubs and any other political clubs he could find and crowned *himself*. The balls on that man. He wouldn't have gotten away with that in the beginning of the revolution but by the time he came along all of our leaders were dead. He just waltzed right on in.

"And who was there to paint him in all his anti-royal royalty? David! Best friend of Marat, you remember? Painter of the portrait of the Tennis Court Oath?" He shook his head in disbelief. "Well, he painted a glorious portrait of the new emperor. You wouldn't even know he used to be one of the most radical of the Jacobins."

"Well," I remembered David and the worst bits of the time. "You can't blame him for being afraid. All of us behaved in ways we aren't proud of simply to stay alive."

His ears went red and he shivered as if shaking off the horror. He pitched forward to whisper to me. "For a time afterwards, those of us left went underground, meeting in these new secret societies. I went to a couple meetings but then... I was tired. I was too tired to start over again. Too tired to continue the fight."

"I understand," I told him.

"The stories, Zamor, of what had happened in the provinces and the countryside during the revolution, were chilling. I can't reconcile what we started with what it became. Did we do it? Did we unleash that hell on our own country?"

"We caused changed and there is no change without turmoil and resistance. None of us wanted it. Well, some did, but they were the exception until Max came into power. Every society has a few maniacs—we were foolish to put our trust in one of them." I shuddered remembering this very room and the flood of blood under the door. I glanced over and there was no towel waiting to be kicked back into place.

"Oui," Sebastien nodded. "We had good ideas and some of them survived! We had good motives! And you, all the work you did for abolition—"

"—Meant nothing," I said. "All my talk and nothing I did contributed to the freedom of Black people. The enslaved people of Saint-Domingue–the Haitians–they freed *themselves*. I'm not sure Jacobinism had anything to do with that, as much as I'd like to believe it did. I'm not sure I had anything to do with it."

"You'll never know how many people you softened to the idea of abolition before the decision came to the Assembly. Let the other ones pound their chests for attention—the real work is done in inches by people like us. Like you. Inches... until suddenly we jump ahead a foot. We jumped a foot, my friend. Now it's back to inches until the time is right. The fire hasn't died, it's just slowed to something more manageable, and thankfully so. Until it flames again."

"At least we can walk down the street again without seeing a dead body at every step," Élise said. "I feel bad most of the kids' childhood was horrible. But now look at them, grown up and left. The oldest is in the National Guard and our youngest went to America. I know things are wrong there, too, with slavery. I tell him to remember his Uncle Zamor when people pressure him about how to feel about slavery."

"Uncle Zamor," I repeated of myself with a wry smile. "Why would you make those kids call me that? Zamor, cautionary tale to all. A walking lesson, coming and going."

"I didn't mean it like that," she said, blushing.

"I know, Élise. I know. Do either of you know anything about Josephe Bologne?"

"I heard he went to Saint Domingue, but I don't know what happened afterwards. Your friend Thomas didn't fare well—he was captured while fighting in Napoleon's army and the Emperor returned to France without him. Left him to rot in an Italian prison. When I saw him again, at Café Procope, I was shocked. You wouldn't have recognized him. They say he was poisoned while he was held there. And once the he got free, Bonaparte denied his pension over and over again. He died some ten years back. Left a wife and kids. I'm sorry."

Disappointment filled me. "I knew Thomas died, but nothing about how it happened. All I heard as I traveled was the news of his reputation as a leader. That news made it all the way across the globe."

"They called him the Black Devil," Sebastien grinned in admiration. "He cut such a fierce figure on the battlefield no one wanted to see him coming. He was a credit to our army and our country." Sebastien tilted his glass and the three of us took a sip in honor of my fallen friend. Then he looked at me like he had something on his mind. "Have you seen Véronique?"

It was like a pail of cold water in my face. I'm sure I flinched.

"Why would I have seen Véronique? Of course not. That was a lifetime ago."

"Then, you've found love again?"

"How can I find something I'm not looking for?"

Sebastien and Elise looked at each other.

"I just thought..." he said, uncertainly. "We make decisions that the passage of time allows us to re-evaluate. Have you re-evaluated, Zamor?"

They both looked at me like they were anxious for me to denounce my past decisions. "Do I regret the decisions I made? Not even a bit. They were the right decisions then and now. Leave it be. We can't undo what we've done, and I don't want to."

His wife stood and rubbed Sebastien's arm, smiling at me. "I will leave you two to catch up. Don't be too late, Sebastien. We still have the room upstairs, Zamor; stay as long as you want."

"Thank you, my dear, but I've taken a room on Rue Perdu." I stood and kissed her quickly on both cheeks and sat back down into new, unfamiliar discomfort. Sebastien's elbows rested on the table, and he fiddled with his glass, eyes down.

I was suddenly as awkward as he was. There were giant unspoken things between us that I'd tried to forget.

"About what happened before you left," Sebastien started, a hand going behind his neck to rub away the discomfort. "I don't want you to think… I truly didn't want…" He looked up from underneath his heavy, snow-white eyebrows. "I don't apologize for what I did with Henri because I'd do it again to protect the people I care about. I only apologize that what I did caused you pain. And for what I said about you and… the Comtesse…"

I shook my head. "We don't need to go over it again." I put my glass down and took him by the neck and shook him a little. "*Sebastien*, you were right about Henri," I told him. "Not that he deserved to die, but that he intentionally set out to hurt me. I didn't want to admit it at the time, but I clearly see it in hindsight." The relief in his eyes was palpable and told me he'd been carrying the burden for all these years.

He nodded. "I went through a bad period, upset with everyone because I was too much of a coward to help Jacques and too much of a coward to even see him off. Every time I thought of it, I resented you for being brave enough to. I idolized that man. And he stood in this room asking for help and I was too afraid to do anything for him."

"You have a family."

"And I had a friend. Him being cut down hurt me in ways I didn't even imagine. I took it out on you." He leaned over and clasped my arm.

"As for Madame," I shrugged. "I am partly responsible for her death, I know that. I knew what was likely to happen. It felt like it was her or me. I had *one* chance. I took no pleasure from it, Sebastien, truly. I didn't want to have a hand in it, but I couldn't see any other way. Your compassion toward her..."

"...I didn't know her. I shouldn't have said what I did..."

"...It was the compassion towards her that burned because it felt like judgement. Still, I don't ever want a friend of mine to think they can't tell me I'm wrong when I am. I took those traveling papers because by that time I was sick of people not having to pay for the harm they cause."

"I was wrong to shame you. There's two of us in this room who have done things they're not proud of, and I have no right to judge how anyone deals with pain." We sat like that for a long moment, in lieu of the hug we wanted to give. Then his face wrinkled into a smile.

"It's good to have you home, my friend. Paris has missed you, and so have I."

Chapter Fifty

Just like the hallways in noble homes were where life happens, it was the hidden spaces of Paris where city life and politics flourished.

I stepped down the stairs off the Paris street into a lower basement inlet of an abandoned building. The stairway was so narrow, no more than one set of shoulders could get through between the building and the stone on the other side. This kept the door hidden from view from the street, and even standing before it, it was almost lost in shadow.

I knocked with a particular cadence, as instructed by Sebastien. There was silence for a long time. The biting wind cut into my cheeks. I looked up and around. The place truly seemed abandoned. I tried the knock again and put my hands into my pocket. It might have been the flight of a fly or the flutter of ivy that moved and brought my gaze up to the area beside the door. What I'd thought to be glass covering rusted metal suddenly cleared a tiny slot, big enough for me to barely see one eyeball squinted to gaze out at me.

"What do you want?" came the harsh whisper.

"I'm a friend of Valentin Carne."

The eyeball stared at me for a long moment, and the slot shut. More silence. Then, suddenly, a different eyeball was looking at me, this one blue with too many tiny red veins. I recognized it. It wasn't getting much sleep, obviously.

The slot shut again, and the decrepit-looking door opened, soundlessly, as if it was well-oiled and well-used. And then, standing in front of me, Valentin looked me over.

His long hair was still pulled back in a low-hanging ribbon-bound tail down his back. His face had grooves worn in and his eyes were blood-shot, body devoid of fat, hands shaking slightly.

"I should have known it was you, get in here. You always have to make a scene," he said gruffly, standing aside and motioning me to get in, fast. I stepped in quickly into a small hallway blocked by another door. The foyer was barely large enough for one person, let alone two. I looked behind me to watch him lock the outer door.

"Did anyone follow you?" he asked.

"No, no one," I whispered back.

"Was there anyone else on the street?"

"No. I know how to be careful, Valentin, I wasn't followed." He was so close I was getting uncomfortable. I could smell his sweat and felt the heat of his body.

"That signal hasn't been used in ten years. You almost got yourself shot right through the door, you know."

"Well, that's the signal Sebastien gave me. I only just got back in town. How was I to know?"

"And the second thing you do is come here to see me? Why?" He was taller than me and it was uncomfortable twisting to look up at him in the tiny space.

"Don't flatter yourself, Valentin, I couldn't care less about you. I'm here to further the cause for equality. Or do I have to jump through hoops with you like the first time? Are we going to go through all that again? After all we've been through?"

"After all we've been through you should know better than to show up where you weren't invited."

"Well, I can leave then, if that's how you want it." We stood there in the tight space, musty with each other's sweat, and I started to get annoyed. "So, can I come in, Valentin, or are you going to stand here sniffing my hair all day?"

He seemed torn with indecision. Then, finally, he raised one hand and moved it around me. It was so dark in the space I couldn't even see the door handle, but I heard it rattle when he pounded on it in a completely different rhythm from the one I'd used earlier. The mechanisms of a door with a numbered lock sounded and suddenly the blockage gave way and opened onto a large, dark space illuminated by torches on wall sconces and candles on tables. It was a comfortable sunny day outside. Being lower than the ground, it should have been cooler inside but in this place, crammed with candles and at least thirty bodies, it was hot.

"Everyone, this is Louis-Benoit Zamor. We call him the *page*. He's back in town. He was with us in the before times."

"The Du Barry Page?" Someone called. As I stepped in, many eyes raked me over and sized me up.

"Hello, gentlemen," I said.

"And ladies. Times have changed, page," said a lady's voice. As my eyes acclimated, I did indeed see women in the room.

"Pardon. Ladies and gentlemen. I'm pleased to meet you all."

"Valentin, do you vouch for this man?" A man with a wreath of brown hair on a balding scalp gestured toward me. He was dressed in today's bourgeois style of understated dress. I had noticed first at the small town near Le Havre, but most especially in Paris—it wasn't as easy to tell the poor from the rich these days. In this room there was a mix of dress, but mostly it looked to be clothes of common professionals.

"I vouch for him," Valentin said, coming into the room and walking over to a sideboard where he poured a draft of wine into a juice glass and came back to hand it to me. He looked at me as he spoke, his eyes telling me the seriousness. "I vouched for him when he became a Jacobin and I have no reason to believe anything's changed."

"Nothing's changed," I said, taking the glass and speaking to the group. "I still believe in the strength of a strong republic."

"And where have you been, page?" Asked the brown-haired man. "How many years has it been since you left? What's the difference between you and every other émigré that escaped the blade?"

"I'm not an émigré because I was never a noble. I had no wealth to transfer to another country, nor crime to escape. I was just a servant without home or vocation. They let me walk out of France on a red carpet. But if you're asking about my allegiance, if you know anything about me you know I paid my dues."

"Did you pay or did Du Barry?" someone called out to me.

"I paid with a lifetime of forced servitude up to the very day I revealed my allegiance to the republic to Du Barry. I'll remind you, it was the revolutionary tribunal that decided to end her life, not me." More silence, and then everyone seemed to turn away, back to their conversations and drinks. No longer interested in me. Except for the brown-haired man who continued the conversation.

"Convenient that they did your dirty work," said the brown-haired man with a smirk. I was starting to dislike him.

"What do you care?" I asked him. "I'm confused, I thought this was a room of revolutionaries; an extension of the Jacobins."

"Extension?" He snorted in laughter. "No, this," he gestured with his finger of the hand holding a glass of amber liquid, "this is an *improvement.*

The Jacobins you remember were a fledgling group of toddlers trying to find their legs and woefully failing. A mess."

I looked quickly to Valentin, expecting to hear rebuttal, only to see him drop his eyes.

What? Valentin cowed by this man? What was happening here?

"Well," I said. "Our 'mess', as you call it, ushered in a new republic."

"And look at how well that worked out."

"It was a good start."

"Come on," Valentin said. "Let's not stand here talking, there's a table right there." He walked ahead of me and when I would have allowed him to pass first, the brown-haired man made an exaggerated bow and gestured me proceed.

"Your Majesty," he said, resulting in snickers. I really didn't like this man, I decided. But I moved ahead, ears prickling with discomfort. As I sat, I looked at Valentin and tried to determine what was different about him. He gestured for me to stay there while he went to the sidebar, again, where a steaming, spitting plate atop a burning oven kept a pan scalding hot. He picked up the handle with a piece of cloth and began to pour steaming black liquid into cups.

It came to me what was different about Valentin. He was quiet, now. Valentin had never been a quiet man.

Bringing back three cups of hot coffee on a tray, he sat the cups before us and propped the tray under the table against the stand. He looked tired and old, I thought. A shell of his former self. I looked away and found brown-hair's eyes on me, sizing me up just the same. I put my cup to my lips, holding his stare. I'd been stared down by a mass-murderer; this man didn't scare me. The café tasted like burnt ashes.

"Zamor, this is Roland," Valentin said. "Zamor," he repeated, and I pulled my eyes away from brown-hair to look at Valentin who had leaned into us, a lock of unwashed, lifeless hair falling into his eyes. Firm glare. "Roland. His name is Roland. He's our leader."

I looked back at Roland who sipped his coffee.

"Leader of what?" I couldn't help myself.

Valentin's jaw tightened. "Our club, Zamor, what do you think?"

"No, I mean, what is it called? We were Jacobins. What is this group?"

Roland smirked like I'd said something equally funny and idiotic. "Jacobins." He snorted again. "He says it so proudly. Jacobins are a relic from a forgotten time. Useless and pathetic," the man said. It was as if he knew humbling Valentin in front of me was setting me off. His eyes were flint and picked up glints from the candle in front of us. His scruffy chin was at odds with the well-kempt remainder of him. "Feckless and aimless leadership."

"So, if you think so little of them, why is he here?" I gestured toward Valentin. "Why did you let me through the door?"

"Everyone can improve themselves. This club will do the difficult work, but we can always use helpers and volunteers to do the light things. Small errands. Getting us café…"

He said that last part on a drawl, pulling up his cup to his lips slowly. My anger flared. He was making a fool of us.

"And what is the difficult work that is so advanced us Jacobins can't handle it? Napoleon is back, is it to do with him? Will he be challenged?"

"With Napoleon gone, Louis XVIII has crawled back onto the throne. The age of kings should be over. If the Jacobins had done their job, it would have been. But because you didn't, we have to finish it and we will. We'll wipe out the House of Bourbon this time. And then, we will truly have a new republic."

What? I looked back and forth between the two of them.

"That's your plan? To kill everyone in the House of Bourbon? That's the entire purpose of this club?"

I could see from the tightening of his face he was not pleased that I was not impressed. "One dies and another takes the throne, and we're once again under a monarch. If there are no more left, then no one can inherit through blood. It's obvious."

"You're a fool," I said. "There will always be a descendent of the royal bloodline for as long as France is a country. The tree has branches, you know. They might not even want to rule. The problem isn't the people; it's always been the government."

"You Jacobins were too soft to do what it takes..."

He was spouting nonsense. I looked at Valentin. "This can't be what you want to tie yourself to."

"He does," Roland answered for a quiet Valentin who dropped his gaze to the table, again. "Because he understands what's right. He understands how he and you and all of the Jacobins failed France. We won't fail. We aren't afraid to kill."

It was idiotic to my ears to hear anyone claim the Jacobins were afraid to kill when we had birthed the country's mass murderer Max Robespierre. Max was unpleasant, glaring proof that Jacobins had no disinclination to kill. But for the rest of us, death had never been the point.

"The Jacobins had a goal," I said. "We started with a plan from the beginning–to create a fair and equal republic. We had a cause. We had a purpose. If it hadn't been for the slithering snakes the republic would have thrived. If it hadn't been for Max's obsession with killing any and every-thing, the country wouldn't have turned against us... If we had kept focus on the institution and not gotten side-tracked targeting people we—"

"—Max's only mistake was in not killing the right people," Roland sneered. "And not nearly enough. He should have started with the weak-lings and cowards, like you. Instead, he killed people like Du Barry on *your* word. The most beautiful woman the world has ever seen. A lovely alabaster-skinned Frenchwoman taken down by a repulsive, short little renegade slave. It was the beginning of the end for Max when he legitimized you as if you could ever be equal to any White man or woman."

My head reared back. My fists clenched on their own. My eyes blinked with surprise.

I don't know what I had been thinking. Why would things be any different now than when I'd left? Was it possible things had gone backwards?

I put my cup down.

"Zamor, calm down," Valentin said. I stood up.

"Valentin, if you want to be here that's your right. Feckless? You want to know what's feckless? Thinking that mass murder is a solution. Calling it a policy or a plan. These people don't want to progress, Valentin, they want to go backwards. I'll have no part of it."

"Come now, page," Roland said, leaning back in his chair. "Like I said, we'll do the hard work. You can get our coffee. You're good at that, aren't you?"

I pushed the chair out of the way and strode toward the exit, fully aware of all the eyes on me and uncaring. Walking through the space I pulled open the first door and then the second, happy to be out in fresh air. At the top of the stairs, I looked around to make sure no one was watching and was halfway down the street when I felt someone behind me. I reached into my waistband to pull my knife before turning.

"It's me," Valentin said, hands up. "It's me. Calm down. Come back inside."

"You must be mad."

"Fine, you don't like him. But some of what he's saying has some merit, doesn't it?"

"No, Valentin. No. It has no merit. And, frankly, I'm surprised by you. When did you lose your voice? When did you lose your principle? We had a reason and a cause. Yes, things got out of hand towards the end, precisely because we lost focus on what was important. But at least we started with cause. We weren't a group of murderers..."

"But we failed. We got Bonaparte. Bonaparte!" He laughed but there was no mirth in his eyes. "And now a Bourbon, *again*. The revolution never ended, it just changed. It won't end until we get the republic we dreamt of, and that will never happen if we don't do something drastic."

"What's happened to you? We've never been friends, but I like to think we at least understood each other. I don't understand this."

He looked away from me, the gentle breeze blowing his graying strands across his face.

"How did you do it?"

"Do what?"

"Move on? You seemed so invested in France. And then, all of a sudden, one day you were gone. We placed bets on how soon you'd be back, certain that with your extravagant tastes and off-putting personality, you'd be back in a month. But you moved on. How?"

I would have made a sarcastic comment but his face moved like it could collapse at any moment. His blood-shot eyes were soft like he really cared about my answer.

"I-I went to find my family," I admitted. "I had a family before I came to France, you know. And I was finally free to leave."

"Did you find them? Was it worth it?"

I nodded. "Oui. They're gone now, but yes. I'm grateful for that time I had with my father. But you can move on, too. Find a reason beyond this—"

"A reason? This is all I have, Zamor. My parents disowned me years ago and my brother is dead. I have no money and no good name. Back before Max died, there was a noblewoman—a childhood friend. It was easy to fall again. Most nobles don't even speak to me anymore but she was interested in me and the new republic. I believed her and set up a time for her to meet Max. I didn't tell him who she was because I knew she was putting herself at risk of exposure even meeting with him. I didn't realize she was a royalist spy. When Max arrived at the location to meet the mystery woman there were two men waiting to try to murder him. Fortunately, despite me telling him he didn't need protection, his guards had tailed him none-the-less. Good thing, too. They saved him."

"That's why he kicked you out of the Mountain."

"Not immediately. He was furious with me so, of course, he asked me who she was. I hadn't given him her name." He hesitated and the dread flowed through me. "I could have made up any name I wanted. I knew it. He knew it. I could have given up any number of enemies."

He looked off to the distance and his eyes went glassy with unshed water. Of course, he'd given her up.

"But why, Valentin?"

"Why?" He looked at me with incredulity, seething. "*Because he asked me and I couldn't lie to Max*! *He* asked me. I loved her but I loved him *more*. I knew in my soul he was testing me. If I had lied what did that love mean? I told him the truth because Maximilien Robespierre was everything to me! He could have told me to take a gun to my own head in the middle of the street and I'd have done it!"

Water fell down his cheeks as he grimaced against the pain that seemed as strong as if it had happened yesterday. His shook his head.

"And after all the years of loyalty, I knew he would forgive me if I gave him this one thing. With an apology. And once I did both, he told me I was forgiven but he could no longer trust me. He told me he was sending her to the beast to teach me a lesson, and he kicked me out of the Mountain. He said I was no longer useful to him. And then, I had nothing."

He sniffed and ran a forearm underneath his nose and across his face, trying to pull himself together. "But you..." He gave a mirthless little laugh. "You just packed up and moved on like it wasn't anything at all. Like none of it meant anything. That's how easy we were to forget."

"No," I said softly. "I didn't forget, I knew all along what I was doing it for. It was only ever about freedom and equality for me, never about Max. I'm a pragmatist, Valentin, I don't put my faith in one person to be my savior." I clapped a shoulder on his hand, and he looked at it, surprised. "Move on. Find something you want. Do something better than being the errand boy for a gang of murderers. Find your purpose again, Valentin. It's more than this."

For a moment he looked like he might have actually been absorbing my words. Then, he shrugged off my hand and his face cleared of emotion. "You do what you need to do, page. Maybe worry about all the portraits hanging throughout the city mocking you. I'll take care of me like I always have. You had your chance to be part of a new movement. We'll change France without you."

Chapter Fifty-One

I was feeling extremely nostalgic for my other friends.

Someone told me where to find Marie-Louise Dumas, the wife of Thomas-Alexandre. She and the kids were living in Villers-Cotterêt, a village about an eight-hour ride northeast of Paris.

I knocked on the door and a ragged woman opened it. Her eyes were red, and her skin seemed prematurely wrinkled as her hair was dark. Not an old woman but a weathered one.

"Yes, what do you need, Monsieur?"

I took my hat off. "Bonjour, Madame. I'm a friend of your deceased husband, the General. My name is Zamor. Louis-Benoit Zamor."

Her face relaxed and softened. "Zamor. Yes, I know who you are. You are the *page*. Thomas spoke of the conversations with you, and Josephe. He said the three of you had a fine time together, the two noble swordsmen and the clever page with the tongue as sharp as a blade like three fast lifelong friends."

"I *was* the page, now I'm simply a citizen. I've been out of the country for several years and only just got back in town. I'm very sorry for your loss. He was a good man."

"He liked you very much, Thomas did. You are the same age and he said it was a good year for Black men to be born."

"We both know any year he was born he'd have considered a good year. Inflated ego, that fellow."

She laughed at that. "He said you made him laugh and that you are a romantic even though you didn't seem to know it. I can see he was right. Please, come in. Meet the children."

The inside of the house was sparse and sad. Wind whistled through the cracks in the wood planks of the wall, and I realized it must be very cold in the winter. The kids she spoke of were not kids so much. The older daughter, Marie Alexandrine, was about nineteen with curly hair and enough African blood still that her skin was very light tan. The other, Alexandre, was a young boy of about thirteen, who even though young looked like he would one day sprout up to his father's height.

I gave Marie Louise the bottle of red wine I'd brought with me from Paris which made her eyes light up. Wine seemed to have that effect on people. She smiled slightly.

"Ah, you bring the quality wine. I remember drinking quality wine long ago, I haven't had a good red wine since the day Thomas was... well, no matter. I'll open it and you must stay to eat with us. It's not much, just soup."

"That is very kind of you, Madame, but I don't want to impose."

"Nonsense, you're a friend of Thomas, it's no imposition. He would expect nothing less."

As she finished stirring a pot in the small kitchen the kids sat around the table and discussed their lives with me. The girl was working as a washer woman and the boy was apprenticing for the Duke of Orleans, who had been a friend of his father, and I knew a friend of the Chevalier. They were young but old enough to bring in money and it seemed they needed to. I asked Marie-Louse about Josephe.

"The Chevalier and his doomed legion of Blacks," she said, spooning soup into bowls. "They were always on good terms, despite Thomas taking over after Josephe was accused of stealing the money. Thomas said he still had a job to do. After Josephe got out of prison he found Thomas. Apparently, he'd been told Thomas was the one who caused him to go to prison. It upset Thomas so much he almost quit the legion himself, but he felt he had to do his duty. Thomas would never have done such a thing, and he made it clear to Josephe. He was a little hurt that Josephe believed it even for a moment."

"I told Josephe that Thomas wouldn't have done such a thing. A lesser man might have, but not Thomas. I'm not surprised I was proven right."

"He was heartbroken that they tried to do that to them both. It was like they wanted them to be at odds with each other. I'm glad they had the chance to clear the air. Josephe told Thomas he was going back to Saint-Dominque to help—I think he needed the break from Paris. Thomas understood. They were friends long before the legion and they became friends again."

She turned to her pot and one of her hands shook as she turned back and realized there was not enough of the soup for her family and me. From the way her back stiffened and she stopped it was obvious she didn't want me to see her using water to stretch the meager meal.

"Ah, Madame," I blustered as if simple-minded. "I failed to tell you I ate in the ride along the way—packed myself bread for the ride. Any more to eat and I will burst. If you'd so oblige, I'll just have a bit of that wine. If you will have some with me."

The relief on her face was palpable. She poured each of us a bit of wine into small glasses and handed out the bowls of soup to her children, leaving none for herself, and sat. "I will join you, certainly."

"Bon santé." *Good health.* I lifted my glass, and she joined me with a slight smile.

"Bon santé."

We each took a sip, and the taste of the deep old juice was delicious. She closed her eyes briefly, as if savoring the taste.

"How did you know papa, Monsieur?" Marie Alexandrine asked. She had a perceptive gaze and boldness like her father.

"Why, I almost joined the Legion of the Blacks with your father and the Chevalier de St. Georges." She looked at me, openly doubtful. "I know I don't look like it now but when I was young, I was in much better shape. Stronger. They invited me to join them. Unfortunately, I could not."

"Why?"

"Mind your manners, daughter," Marie Louise said. Some of the lines in her face had softened considerably with the half glass of wine. I reached over and poured her a bit more and she didn't stop me. "People have their reasons."

"What reason could there be not to join the fight for the republic?"

"Hush!"

"No, it's all right," I said. I liked her frankness. "I was fighting for the republic in my own way."

"Monsieur Zamor was a Jacobin, even when it was dangerous for him. He used his words and his mind to spread news of the revolution. But I have to admit, Thomas was disappointed you didn't join them. He said he could have used someone with your cunning. But it is probably best you didn't, knowing how quickly the republic disbanded it. Knowing what they did to Josephe. Though perhaps you might have seen what was happening and averted it. As it was, he was blindsided when they accused him of stealing that money. As if he would use money meant for the shoes on his men's feet in battle for his own selfish purposes. Anyone who knew him knew he could never do anything so dishonorable."

"Josephe and I were imprisoned for a short time together at the Conciergerie. I was released first, and unexpectedly. Do you know if he is still in Saint-Domingue?"

"I'm sorry, Zamor, I didn't realize you didn't know. Josephe died even before Thomas. He came back from Saint-Domingue and tried to get his post in the National Guard again. He hadn't done anything to lose it, after all. They wouldn't accept him. He was banned from military service for life. He came to visit and told Thomas all about it just before Thomas went to Italy and he died while Thomas was in prison. They say he died of gangrene, but I know he died of grief and heartache. A lifetime of loyalty to France, for what? The same with Thomas. All of his hard work, winning battle after battle, only to pave the way for the bastard that destroyed him. My Thomas was a natural leader. He was the best of France. Everyone knew it."

She reached for the bottle and topped off her glass. "You ask, my sweet daughter, what reason there could be for not joining the republic's army? Giving everything to the republic to have it turn against you is a reason. Napoleon Bonaparte is a reason. His hatred of your father put us in this position. He hated him for being better than him. It wasn't enough he left him in Italy rotting underground in that cell–he had to take his pension. My Thomas, coming home in ill health and being broken a little more every day knowing he couldn't support his family. Grief killed my Thomas, just like Josephe. And now we're alone and Alexandre here barely remembers his father. All he remembers is the misery that bastard Napoleon has left us in."

The boy got up and left the table. We heard the door open and shut as he left the house.

"I'm sorry to bring up sadness," I said.

"It's not you. He's at a strange age. Being a boy, he misses his papa in a different way. My Marie misses him too." She reached over and took her daughter's hand. "But at least she's old enough to remember him. He will need to harden, my boy."

Sadness hung like a pall over the table. The women looked at me as if desperate for something other than painful memories.

"I'll never forget the day I met your father," I told his daughter. I stood up from the table and took a stiff, straight stance, pantomiming my hand on my sword—my other hand up to straighten the imaginary hat on my head—and walked in military stride across the room. My back protested—I would suffer for it later.

"Ah! What a glorious day!" I bellowed, loudly and unabashedly in the ringing, jovial voice of the man as I remembered from the first time I'd seen him. His daughter's face lit up as I transformed into the man they loved. "They tell me to do the best job, to be the bravest, the strongest, the smartest and I say…" I adopted a look of confusion, "what else would I be?" That made them laugh out loud, Marie Louise's eyes shining extra brightly with unshed tears.

I imitated Thomas for a few more minutes and then stepped out to find the boy. He was sitting a bit away from the house underneath a tree. He had gathered a small pile of stones beside him and was striking the trunk of the tree with them, his face a study in suppressed anger.

"Young man, I'm sorry if I upset you," I said. His father's eyes looked back at me. I aimed to sit on the ground beside him. Getting down was a long, awkward trip for my cramped body. By the time I was down he was looking at me like I was something strange.

"What happened to you, Monsieur? Are you sick or crippled?"

I gave a wry smile. "A little of both, I suppose. We all have our ailments, boy. The polite thing is not to point them out."

I had lost his interest by that time, and he was back to tossing stones. "Maman cries. She's cried all my life. She says Napoleon has destroyed us. She says he hated Papa because he was a Black man and Napoleon couldn't stand to be bested by a Black man."

"Ah, she may be right but don't say that out in public. The emperor has only been gone for a month, and you just never know if a defeated leader might gain power again; they seem to keep rising over and over. And they never forget their enemies. Best to keep the hatred deep, deep inside until you find a safe way to release it."

"I don't have hatred. I barely remember my papa and that disappoints Maman. He is no one to me. I don't care."

His face was angry but desperate. Trying to find his place in the world in adolescence—the most difficult time. The boy was contradicting himself with his own words and actions. Confused about his own feelings.

I understood that place. I'd worked it out by bedding every willing woman I could find at the Palace at his age.

"I know you imagine your mother exaggerates but your father truly was as splendid as she says. He was a true hero. Your father and his friend Josephe were strong, powerful and smart. And your papa was the only Black general I've ever met. I'm certain the only Black general France had ever had at the time. Some of my fondest memories were the few times when the three of us would sit and talk about their experiences in battle and fencing and my life in the royal court. My stories weren't as exciting, of course, but it was nice having them to speak to. We didn't know each other for long but we had a deep bond."

"If he was so much a hero why doesn't anyone know who he is? We have nothing. Maman works her fingers to the bone and we barely have enough to eat. What does it matter what he did if no one knows? If no one cares?"

"Why, that is where you come in, Alexandre. That is your job, to tell your father's story."

"What do you mean?"

"Once there was a man, some say he was the true father of King Louis XIV. Some say it was his older brother, the true heir to the throne. All anyone knows for sure is that someone very important decided that no one should know who this man was. He was hidden. Imprisoned with a black velvet mask covering his face so no one could see him.

"Sometimes, if he would leave his cell where other people might see him, they would have guards to keep him from revealing his face to others. No one ever saw his face. No one ever knew for sure who he was. He was imprisoned and moved to many places; the Bastille, even the same island in Naples where your father would eventually be held. But your father got out. This man never did."

"And then what?" the boy asked.

"Then, nothing. This man died in prison after thirty-four years of being hidden away. Can you imagine? Thirty-four years of no one seeing your face or saying your name?"

"Didn't anyone miss him?"

"Miss who?" I asked. "Who was he? A man without a name or a face can't be missed. You can't tell a story about a man with no identity. But your papa had an identity. He was a strong man. A good man. Men like your father are rare while men like Bonaparte—men who are not so good—will erase the memories of the men who make them feel small, if they can. You, the son of the brave General, you have the power to make sure he is never erased. You understand? You and your sister are his voice. *You* tell the story of the man who made you. In my eyes, he is truly blessed to have you and your sister to carry on his legacy. But first, you have to stay alive. If you must make yourself small and unnoticeable until you are strong enough to defend yourself, do that. Make yourself the tiniest thing in the room—the fool sitting in a corner eating candies and speaking nonsense—and when you are ready, then you step into who you really are. The son of one of the most fearsome generals this country, and the world, has ever known."

I didn't know if it was the best advice, but it was all I had to offer. We were quiet for a moment, and I could see the thoughts running through his brain. I remembered the way my mind worked at that age and imagined he was finding something, anything, to grasp onto.

"Where did you come from, Monsieur? Who will carry your legacy?"

That made a genuine smile come to my face. "I'm not a good man, Alexandre. I'm more like Bonaparte than I will ever be like your father. Perhaps you can dig up a few people in Louveciennes who will remember me as decent. But probably not."

"If Louveciennes was your home, will you go back and restore your good name?"

The child was hilarious, and he didn't even know it.

"I never had a good name to start; there's nothing to restore. Besides, I don't have much luck going back to things, son. I've yet to determine if coming back to Paris was the right thing."

I left them a short time later with a promise to come back and visit on occasion. I pressed a few coins into Marie Louise's hand before I took my horse and little carriage down the road. The following day I headed off to find the cook.

Chapter Fifty-Two

She was bent over a bush pruning when I walked up on her. Just as the others, Salanave had aged. Her hands moved gently and gingerly as she meticulously clipped errant pieces off one cluster of beautifully full peony bushes.

The blossoms were varying shades of pink from the palest to a shockingly vibrant shade of purplish red just like the blossoms at Versailles. Sometimes it was hard for everyone to let go.

The house was small and simple but the flowers made it look like someplace a person would want to be. From the open windows, I caught smells of stewed, smoky meats, roasting vegetables and red wine.

Where she sat on the ground, her gray dress pooled beneath her and a pair of glasses was perched on her nose. When she looked up it was through the lenses that magnified her eyes.

"Bonjour, Salanave," I said, sing-song like it'd only been a minute since we'd last seen each other.

She looked at me for a long moment, laying the gardeners' shears down, and let out a little puff of air. "So, you forgive me, then?" Salanave was always blunt, but I was confused.

"Forgive you for what?"

"For not being your maman?"

I shrugged. "It was an unfair expectation; no one could possibly have been. You did your best, under the circumstances."

Her shoulders dropped as if they'd been holding something up for a long time. She gestured with her finger wordlessly to a little shovel and I brought it over, stifling a groan to pull myself down to the ground beside her.

"Hand me the tarragon, please."

I reached over and pulled from a little pile of seedlings on the ground and for the next few minutes we said nothing as I dug holes for her to put seedlings into.

"Salanave," I said after a few minutes of shoveling in the hot sun. "What about that one plant? You know the one…" I snapped my fingers trying to remember. "The one that—"

"—The one that took the edge off the day?" She actually smiled at that. "Relaxed me so I could sleep? See over there?"

I looked to where she pointed to a thriving patch of illicit plants which made me laugh.

"Don't you think you should try to hide that a bit."

"Did you recognize what it was before I pointed it out?" she asked. She had a point. "Nobody's caring about what an old woman puts in her garden. Come, pinch off a piece and we'll add it to dinner."

She pulled herself to her feet with effort, face wincing as if her joints hurt. "Come in, then." She clapped her dirty hands against her skirt. "Let's get caught up."

She had made beef bourguignon and added the special plant along with a couple sprigs of rosemary. She put bowls of the fragrant stew on the table.

"You cook enough food for a household."

"Habit. I'll take the leftovers up the road to the church," she said, pulling crusty baguettes from the oven and sat them onto the table beside a pot of sweet cream butter. The smell of the warm bread wafted to me, and I was transported to the Chateau.

"It's still alive?"

She looked confused and then gave me a look. I was talking about the levain she had used all through her time at the Palace and Chateau. The levain with its little feeders that caused the bread to rise and flavored it so well. The levain she'd been passed down through the generations.

"Of course it's still alive. I taught you how to make it strong. Do you want some to take with you?"

My heart felt a sudden light at the prospect. Then I remembered I was stretching my money and didn't know if I'd be able to feed the brew to keep it alive.

I shrugged. "I don't much like taking care of things beyond myself anymore."

She nodded as we sat to eat. The stew was delicious and the beef melted in my mouth. I hadn't had such a meal since the Chateau. We were quiet for a long time while we just enjoyed it, washing it down with the bottle of red wine I'd brought.

It turned out Salanave hadn't done half bad for herself.

She explained, "After the trial I knew I couldn't go back. I had packed a bag that morning when I left. I did what I had to do, and it was the right thing, but that didn't stop me missing my life at Louveciennes. I even missed the Palace. It was a shock to the system, you understand, having a place to be that was my entire life one day and then the next having nothing."

"But you had been planning it? Preparing for it?"

"I knew I would do it but that makes no difference to the body; it goes into shock when everything it knows is suddenly different. At least you had your friends in Paris–I had lost most of mine long ago. I only had my family and suddenly no money coming in. And a few people in town calling me names when they saw me. Some of her maids bad-mouthed me to the townsfolk. But the townsfolk didn't understand what it was like.

They didn't know. I've never been the religious sort, but it did something to me knowing we threw away more food in a week than most people could afford in a month. I come from working folks, near to eating rocks to survive. All that excess at the Palace and Chateau didn't sit right on my soul. No matter how nice it was to eat well and see fine things, when I went home my neighbors were starving."

"I know you were smuggling food, Salanave."

"Well, I carried as much as I could and spread it the best I could. But when everything started to break up and the nobles hated the poor folk and talk of a revolution started–I knew what side I had to be on. She was spending our money to get those nobles out of the country and the poor folks had to stay here in the dregs of the mess the king and people like her made. It wasn't fair."

I couldn't have said it better myself. "I didn't know you felt that way. You might have let me in on your participation."

"Well, unlike you, I could keep things to myself. But you, even if you didn't say anything, your feelings were always written on your face. You couldn't hide any of it when Gaspard was around. And it just got worse over time. Worse, the more you went into Paris and started getting all that confidence. We knew something was happening with you, though no one imagined you'd become a Jacobin. And then... Gaspard hurt you and I couldn't do anything. I know you felt I turned my back on you, but—"

"—Stop, Salanave. I was wrong for lashing out at you. I was hurt but you know I understood, eventually. I don't blame you for making a choice I would have myself."

"It wasn't a choice. My family would eat or they wouldn't, Zamor. Nothing I did would have helped you but something I did could send my family to the bread line. No choice."

I nodded.

The potatoes melted as easily as the beef. "Now tell me, how did you end up here out in the country? This is a nice home. Your kids?"

"Grown and gone, married with their own babies and grandbabies. I'm a *great* grandmaman. I put the emphasis on that *great* part, makes me feel more regal and less old." I smiled at that. "After the trial we came here to my parents' home. Eventually, the kids moved out and it was just my husband, and then just me. I cook for the church and for some people who can't cook for themselves, and they pay me in what they can. I'm satisfied with my life. Except I had that one thing I was sorry for. That I didn't protect you that day."

It occurred to me that it was strange what people held onto. I had done everything in my power to forget that day, but Salanave had carried it with her well into her elderly years.

"Let's not talk about that, Salanave, it was a long time ago."

"If I had grabbed a knife or a hot iron... anything."

"We would have both ended up in the back room. There was nothing you could do."

"And then you run poor Véronique off. It's like I watched your life crumble right in front of my eyes..."

"Let's not talk about that, Salanave." I winced. "It was partly your fault, anyway."

"Mine? How do you figure that?"

"You told me to be small, small, small. You told me that to stop them from taking I had to stop myself from having anything good for them to take. But *you* had a family and people who loved you. You had at least that much. All I had was you and her. Then you abandoned me. And deep down I thought, if anything happened to her it would be because of me... my greed to have her in my life. Feeling like, eventually, they would take her and it would kill me. So I pushed her away so I could stay small. You were wrong to teach me that."

Her chin came up defensively. "It kept you alive."

"It kept me breathing. Not alive."

"Well, it was all I knew to give you. I gave you what I could to help you deal with Madame. And that... well, I thought for sure one of her wealthy friends would have saved her from the worst. I thought she'd be able to charm her way out of it; it wasn't like she was Marie Antoinette, she was French! I know when you were very young, you clung to her like she *was* your mother until she showed you otherwise. I'm sorry, Zamor, for how they forced you to free yourself."

I looked at her sharply. I had never told her about my freedom. But Salanave wasn't stupid; she would have figured it out.

"What is it with people always wanting to rehash what's done?" I snapped. "I only wanted to catch up with you, I didn't come for your opinion on how to live my life or to talk about ancient history. I'm an old man now, don't you see all the silver in my hair? I'm way past needing your approval on my life choices."

She sniffed indignantly and sat back in her chair, face pinched with irritation. "You could have a whole head of silver, but you're the same annoying hooligan you've always been. Still an ungrateful, arrogant little pissant."

I stood and leaned over to kiss her cheek. "I missed you, Salanave."

Her pale, wrinkled skin flushed with pleasure.

"I missed you, too, petit," she said, patting my arm grudgingly. "Even today, I can't look at a tub of rat poison but for thinking of you."

She cut me some blooms from her bushes and wrapped them in wet burlap for the trip home. I slipped a few coins on the table when she wasn't looking and told her I'd visit again. But as she watched me climb onto my horse and head out, we both knew the story of the cook and the child slave was best to end that way. I tilted my hat toward her as I rode away.

Chapter Fifty-Three

When I wasn't waxing nostalgia and tying up loose ends, I worked on the book I always dreamt of writing. It would be my *Social Contract*. I would be even bigger than Rousseau. It turned into a compilation of my thoughts about government and slavery and freedom. It held all the bits that never made it into the *Declaration of the Rights of Man and of the Citizen*. It held pieces of my own story and past. It was honest and brave and took four months to write. All the while, I searched for a printer, even before I was finished. They turned down my book one-by-one. Over and over.

But I still needed to eat.

"I can write about anything," I told one of them. "The clown that scares the children down the street. Man with the three-legged mule who always ends up walking the mule and carrying the load himself. The baker and the bread everyone knows is three parts bad meal to one part good. The weather, anything..."

His brow furrowed and he cupped his chin in his hand, torn. "I could use another writer, that's for sure. But you... you're known around here. You couldn't write under your name. No one can know it's you writing for me."

My shoulders sagged a bit, but I agreed.

I took these small writing jobs even as I continued my search for a printer with enough of a spine to allow me to write under my own name.

I bought the Chartreuse I'd been missing, as well as some tins of caviar, crème fraîche, and fresh bread. I'd missed them dreadfully. I hid my groceries in the sack I carried over my shoulder or they wouldn't make it back to my apartment. The food situation in Paris was slightly better than when I left but there was no point in tempting fate.

I would soon make sure that no matter what, I always bought caviar and Chartreuse, stockpiling it to supplement my main diet of soup and more soup. Some people might think caviar wasn't a good meal but smeared on a baguette with crème fraiche was a bit of pure heaven.

Finally, one publisher agreed to read a portion of it. By that time I had finished and left the full thing for him to read for a week. When I returned, he was waiting for me. His gruff face hesitated and then he smiled, his face folding into a thousand wrinkles. "This is magnificent," he said. "A pleasure to read. I'm publishing it."

***

The sound of the cork popping and the cheer that went up at our table at the tavern echoed the celebrations taking place in the streets, but for many different reasons.

Sebastien and Valentin sat with me, looking truly happy for me that my life's work would be realized. Sebastien took the bottle from the barkeep and filled our glasses with champagne.

"Good news for one of us is good news for all of us. And it only took—"

"—He's back!" came a yell from outside the window, interrupting us. We looked at the face of a party-goer from the crowd outside, which disappeared when he slapped the front of the day's paper against the window. The headline was bold:

Napoleon Bonaparte Returns to his Empire!!!

Shrieks of celebration and happiness went up outside.

Some people loved the emperor who had returned and taken the government in a coup the day before. Seeing it in print and hearing the revelry solidified that we were once again under an Emperor, I looked at Valentin's dejected face.

"Oui, oui," Sebastien groused with a frown as the paper disappeared and a smiling face grinned before running off, hooting like a fool. This earned an obscene hand gesture out the window, but he was already long gone.

"I suppose the King will put up some sort of fight," I said.

"Louis XVIII?" Valentin frowned into his drink. "He will fight whoever stands in his way from getting out of Paris. He doesn't want the same fate as his brother. With an open attack, he didn't dare take a chance of what Bonaparte might do. I heard he snuck out of town last night, along with several family members. They knew to get out before dawn."

"Crooks. They're all crooks," Sebastien said. I could feel the heaviness of their depressed spirits in the air and decided it was time to divert back to my news.

"Back to my good news!" I sipped my drink as their eyes rose to me.

"Yes!" Sebastien perked up, his face breaking into a bright smile. "Your name's going to be spoken about along with Rousseau and Voltaire! Imagine, one of us is going to go down in history. Just imagine!" He reached over and jogged Valentin's shoulders to inspire mirth.

"Okay, okay," Valentin said, loathe to praise me but with a grudging smile on his face. "I didn't think you'd ever get it done, but you did it. Santé..." That was high praise for him.

"That's right." I stood up and grabbed him with two hands behind his neck to fake-strangle him. "Santé!"

"What's going on?" asked the bar keep. He was an old school Jacobin. I couldn't remember his name.

"One-ear!" Valentin called out. Oh, yes. "We've got good news. Zamor's publishing a book. It's going to print as we speak."

The man smiled and looked at me. "Is that right, Governor? Good for you. I always knew it would happen, someday. All those years ago when you spoke at the club, I'll never forget how you played the Marseillaise on that violin. It brought tears to my eyes. And then, that speech. I never even considered women *at all* until you started going on about them and their rights. We probably should have let them in our club meetings. Good for you, Governor."

"Probably. Thank you." I nodded. "You can call me Zamor, though. What is your real name, by the way?"

"His real name is One-Ear, asshole," Valentin said.

"No, it's not, *asshole,*" the man responded, indignant. "My *real* name is Remy."

"All right." I raised a glass. "Join us in a toast, Remy. The Jacobins rise again!"

Our hooting earned the attention of a tableful of young men who began laughing at us, one of them standing up to say, fully within our earshot: "Someone tell the old-timers it's past their bedtime!"

Instantly we were on our feet.

"—Who are you calling old-timers?"

"—Still young enough to beat your ass!"

"—Come over here and let me show you how old I am!"

The youngsters laughed and put down money on the table before leaving the building. "Drunk old Jacobins…" one of them said on his way out.

Remy sat down at our table, looking tired.

"Every year they get younger and more disrespectful. They think they're something. Here, Zamor, I know this is what you like." He leaned over and poured me some Chartreuse from a bottle in his hand.

"Oh, that looks putrid," Valentin declared.

"*You're* putrid," I came back. "Thank you, Remy." I took a sip. "You know what I'm thinking? There are four of us here. Why don't we do something to put things right. We can still make a difference in this world. We still have time for a last success."

"Like what? What do you mean?" Valentin asked, suddenly interested.

"I don't know. It's just that Paris seems a bit sad. Remember when the club was young—how happy everyone was just to have someplace to go to talk about things? So people don't feel so alone? Maybe we should start the club again."

"For Bonaparte to shut it down and throw us into jail? No thank you," Valentin said.

"Well, maybe we call it something new. Maybe our goal could be helping people. Helping the poor."

"We *are* the poor, you fucking idiot," Valentin said, cocking a stare at me.

"Well, then, maybe we just talk, how about that? We invite common people, men and women alike, and just talk. Or just get together like the old salon parties."

"Maybe. That doesn't seem like such a bad idea," Sebastien said. "Socializing. That never hurt anyone. It doesn't have to do with the government at all."

"I think the old members would like it. The ones left. To talk to each other."

Sebastien looked thoughtful. "Maybe we could do something at my house. A gathering. Men and woman alike. Or at the park. Just something fun. The old group back together. But all of us this time. Not just the men."

"Not just the White ones," I said. "All the people. Liberté, Égalité, Fraternité, and all that. How did the first revolution start, friends? It started with words. It started with ideas. France still has work to do. Once my book is released, we can start there. Maybe then, start a club with new meaning for this modern world. How about that?"

"A club to sip tea," Valentin groused.

"Or wine, it doesn't matter," I said.

"He's right." Remy shrugged. "It was all words that made us think differently. We didn't even know how we felt until we started talking to each other. Didn't realize we all had it bad. We just get so used to things being one way, we don't even think of other ways. The revolution was good before the Reign. It can be good again."

"It's not a bad idea," Sebastien said. "The thoughts first. No need for trouble, just ideas. I like it."

"When can we get a copy of this book of yours?" Valentin asked. Just him asking the question was tacit approval. I smiled and held up my glass.

"Ça ira!" I toasted.

"Ça ira! Ça ira! Ça ira!" they responded with raised glasses.

Chapter Fifty-Four

The view of the Place de la République was different now that the beast was removed from it. From where we stood on the Pont Neuf bridge we could easily see the Palace of Tuileries, the Concierge, the Louvre–all those spots where we'd spent so much time.

"Are you still building?" I asked Sebastien. "I didn't smell sawdust in your house?"

We leaned over the rail, looking down into the Seine. The breeze was cool coming off the water and swirling up where we were, feeling on top of the world. Beside Sebastien I felt like the last couple of decades hadn't passed at all.

"Argh," he gruffed, rubbing his hands against each other. His knuckles had become knobs that must have been painful. "I do odd jobs here and there, but these hands don't want to do much more. I can manage enough to keep fire in our oven and food in our bellies. It's easier to eat these days–with the regulation on the grain and the kids gone. We even have meat sometimes."

"The air smells better out here."

"I should hope so, no more bodies left to rot in the open air."

"Did they build another cemetery, then?"

"A cemetery would require things like a church or a priest or something related to religion. We went through that whole period where the police were driving by cemeteries making sure grieving families weren't making too much of a spectacle. No open grieving, they said. And then they just wanted the bodies gone so nobody was reminded of the tribunal."

"It's inhumane to expect people not to grieve or want a religious ceremony."

"The people with money and private family cemeteries didn't have that problem. It was the poor ones who had no choice. And you know the republic didn't want religion to have prominence in anything for a long time. The rest of us go to the other place where they buried most of the people killed during the Reign underground. Come, I'll take you there."

We walked through town and came upon a building with a small line of people waiting at the doorway.

"The Catacombs? This building isn't new, is it? What was it before?"

"I don't know. Maybe it was the same, but sometime afterwards they went in with shovels to dig it deeper and wider. I'd never been inside until around 1795 or so, when…"

I thought it was sad that the people in line had to come here to visit deceased members, but they didn't seem at all distraught.

"No one seems upset here."

"They're not family members." At my look, he continued. "They're people come to see the underground resting place."

"Why?" That seemed ridiculous to me. There were mausoleums and tombs all over the country, I was sure. "Is someone important here?"

"It's not the person; it's the layout and structure. You'll see."

The dank smell of the place signaled that we were underground, hitting my nose when we finally got to move forward. A man thrust a torch our way to light the space that, once we descended, became pitch dark. Our feet sounded against the ground as we scuffled along, following those before us in a line.

"Just a little further on," Sebastien said.

I squinted my gaze in the darkness and waited to see the wall change to white stone or marble, like other mausoleums I'd seen. There were entombed spaces and crypts in many churches and so I looked out for the grandeur of the structure, my gaze elevated, until I felt Sebastien's hand hit my arm.

"Here we are."

My eyes followed his shadowed gaze and outstretched hand as he pointed to a wall. At least, it seemed like a wall at first. But the bricks were strange, some round and some thin. I had stopped walking, and people were going around us, annoyed by us, excited to move deeper into the tunnels. I squinted and after a minute or two, with my eyes adjusting to the low light, I finally realized I was looking at a wall made not of bricks but of bones. The long, thin ones with knobs at the end were leg and arm bones. The round ones, on closer inspection, I saw the sunken eye holes and the gape of where a nose would have been.

I jerked back so quickly I almost knocked Sebastien over.

"Sebastien, what is this place? What am I seeing?"

"What I told you. This is where most of them were buried. Hey, don't look so frightened, I didn't mean to spook you. I told you it was a burial spot. It's a perfectly respectable place. Come on, there're some benches up ahead."

We kept moving and the walls separated into divergent tunnels, the passageway widening at one point to allow for a center columnal structure comprised of bones made to allow people to walk all the way around it in a circle. On the outside walls there were benches. Sebastien gestured and we sat.

"I'm sorry, I didn't think this would affect you this way," he said. "I come here sometimes. Just to speak to our friends. The Girondins."

I looked at his face. I hadn't realized how the death of Brissot had impacted him, but now I was seeing how great the impact was surrounded by death.

"But there aren't even markers or names. They are stacked atop each other just as if it was a mass grave."

"It is a mass grave, Zamor. Yes, they are stacked but at least they are placed and not thrown. At least there's some order and design. At least there's some grace."

"Grace? Look at those people over there snickering and poking at them like juveniles. Where's the grace in that? Where's the dignity?"

"As opposed to allowing them to rot in the sun, the smell of them a cloud of death over the city? Many people died without a name. You remember the blood in the streets? The endless, constant death Max unleashed? It would have been impossible to keep up with all those people even if we'd had a functioning government. All we were left with after the Terror was the bodies. Yes, in a perfect world each of them might have had a true Christian burial. But with this place, at least can pay our respects. At least we can talk and even cry down here, if we want to, if we don't feel comfortable doing it above ground."

I didn't like it. But, looking around, I was now able to pick out who was there to gawk and the few faces that were somber and serious, like Sebastian's, here to visit deceased friends.

"Come, let's see a little more and maybe you'll start to see beyond what is obviously horrible to you. The beauty. Perhaps, even..."

Beauty seemed a stretch, but I followed him through the space. At one point we came upon a curve in the wall. There was a skull that was particularly shiny and bright, like it had been polished to pick up the gleam from the torch. It caught my attention with its bright smoothness. That's when I heard it.

"Zamor, you came to see me. I knew you couldn't stay away. I knew you'd never forget me."

I lurched back from it as my blood curdled.

"Hey, are you alright, friend?" Sebastien asked.

"Did you hear that?"

"Hear what?"

Indeed, no one was speaking at a normal volume down here, all of us whispering at various decibels as if this was a church in session. But the voice had been as clear as if had whispered directly into my ear.

"I told you we were meant to be together forever, you and me. And now you've returned."

It was Madame's voice. It was Jeanne du Barry, née Jeanne Becu. My benefactress. My jailor. My nemesis.

"It's her," I whispered.

"What?"

"Right there," I pointed at a white, shiny thing. "It's the Comtesse. It's her."

"It's impossible to know who is who. I see that you think you know..."

"I don't *think*, I know. *I know*. It's her. She's here. She's right there. And she's..."

"Your friend doesn't share our bond. He's a stranger to me, but you're like my very own son. And you're finally home..."

I pitched backward and almost fell on my own two feet. A strike of lightening froze the cavern in bright, blinding light–everything growing still and freezing people in motion. It was bright, blindingly white like the Labyrinth, but instead of the stone fox, it was that skull illuminated in front of me. That skull glowed vividly. I waited for the horror of seeing her, even though I'd never really believed in such things. But I didn't see her.

Suddenly, I felt her beside me, felt her breath as she leaned in to whisper in my ear.

"It's so good to see you, Louis-Benoit."

I'd never been able to break out of my frozen state in the Labyrinth on my own, but I broke myself out of it by mumbling in a litany... "No, no, no..."

Suddenly I was back in the catacombs and Sebastien was in front of me, clutching my arms, shaking me.

"Get a hold of yourself!"

I couldn't get out the words so instead I broke from him and headed down the tunnels, asking for instructions to the exit along the way, nearly running to get out. I felt her behind me in the coldness, following me. Chasing me. She chased me until I reached the stairs, and I took them in threes, as fast as I could, to get out into the open air and daylight.

Part V
CHANGE OF FORTUNE

Gilded Orange Books

CHAPTER FIFTY-FIVE

Dear Citizen,

To this day, I am sure, it was that visit to the Catacombs that changed my fortune. Somehow, being around all those bodies had unleashed her. Just by being there I had, accidentally, awoken her from the slumber of the dead.

And it changed the trajectory of my life.

—Zamor, 1820

***

Three months after his return Napoleon was ousted again. Louis XVIII returned to his throne, and we were once again ruled by the House of Bourbon monarchy, albeit this time a constitutional one.

Napoleon's second removal came with another wave of violence, though not from the government.

It was the royalists, *again*. In power now, groups of former aristocrats and nobles who lived, or had returned to France after the revolution, came for revenge against the old revolutionaries and the Bonapartists.

Though I understood the bitterness of those whose relatives were sent to the guillotine, almost immediately after Max was put to death the government had begun giving the property and wealth back to the nobles.

Émigrés who had fled came home and moved back into their castles. Descendants of those put to death (rightly or not) were handed back their inheritances with apology. Slave owners were given money to make up for the slave labor lost during the brief abolition.

While, on the other hand, the poor people never received any form of restitution after the storm. They never had money in the first place. No art. No fancy homes or decadent wardrobes. They were simply poor, as they always had been. It seemed to me if anyone had a right to lingering antipathy, it was the poor.

It was a chilly day to walk along the Seine and the street was sparse of people. Looking up, I saw a group of men in a carriage pull up ahead. They had drawn alongside a small group of people plastering fliers on a wall with a little pail of paste. Then, the group in the carriage began climbing out.

It happened so quickly, I almost didn't know what was happening when I saw it. The men pasting fliers had no weapons. The men in the carriage came out waving swords, slashing in a frenzy. Blood flew. I stopped in my tracks.

Though I couldn't see the victims from the crowd of attackers I saw the blood that spread on the ground beneath their coats. Then, when one man dropped to his knees and tried to crawl away between their legs, one of the nobles calmly pulled out a gun and shot him in the head. He fell prone, onto his face on the hard ground.

The gunshot caught attention like nothing else could, and a passersby began scurrying away quickly, like I should have been doing. But I was stunned as, just as quickly as they'd climbed out, the group of men all climbed back into the carriage, the driver striking the horse with a whip, not at all in a rush to get away.

I stood for a long moment while the carriage rolled down the road, staring at the pile of humans on the walkway, waiting for even the slightest movement. Instead, someone brushed beside me and said under his breath as he passed… "Should have known better, putting up signs of support for Bonaparte… Anyone with a brain knows when your leader deserts you, you're a fool to continue shouting your support."

He kept walking, sparing not more than a glance at the pile of dead men, hands in his pockets. I turned as well and walked in another direction, hearing my heart beating in my ears.

My legs kicked in automatically, moving me away from the scene just as quietly and quickly.

My good spirits at arriving in Paris had taken a steady supply of beating and I needed good news.

I headed to the printer to get an update on when my book would be published and, turning a corner, I saw smoke billowing from the building. My heart beat in my ears as I approached, the building in flames with a line of people passing along buckets of water from God knew where. I ripped my jacket off and jumped in the line closest to the building, tossing water into the open door.

Heat from the fire drenched my face in sweat. "More, we need more water!" I yelled. But then, a window exploded and the group of us on the street nearest to it ducked and backed away to avoid the flying shards of glass. Someone yelled at us to stay away, that it was too far gone now. The bucket slowed along the line as we watched, and then activity picked up again, with the water going to the building next to it.

"No, no," I said to them. "We can save it. Keep sending the water…"

"It's gone," someone said. "We're just trying to save the block now!"

I swiped at the bucket, but they jerked it out of my reach. They didn't understand. Looking around, my eyes captured the owner, his face was covered in soot. He stood as if frozen, and I bounded through the crowd over to him.

"What happened?" I asked. He didn't move. I took him by his arms and shook him awake. "What happened?"

His eyes focused on me and finally saw me. "What do you think happened? The royalists! Here, this was pinned to the door with a knife. It's your fault. Yours." He lifted his arm and pushed his fist at me. A balled-up piece of paper dropped out and I scrambled on the ground for it, reading it in a crouch.

In beautiful script, the message was clear:

I never found my friend at the Port at Le Havre and he never returned to Paris. His family had him declared dead. But after I returned to Paris, I remembered where I heard your name.
No printer in Paris will ever publish anything by the traitor Louis-Benoit Zamor or they will burn, too.

No signature, of course. It was the man from the town near the Port finally getting revenge on me. I had expected he might try to kill me, eventually—and maybe he still would. But this was worse. He couldn't have hurt me more if he *had* plunged a dagger into me. I should have killed him back at the town and now look – he'd gone and destroyed my life.

My eyelids began blinking fast. I stood up. My only copy of my book was in that building.

"It's gone? It's all gone?" I ran over to the printer. "Give me the key. I'll try to go in the back way."

"There is no back way, the back is engulfed in flames. My business and your words, it's all gone. And all the copies I had printed ready to go out—it's all gone. All of it. I never even got one out the door."

Not even one.

But it was my work of enlightenment to rival Rousseau. It was my vision of France from the eyes of the peasant who loved it. I'd poured my soul into it. *It was my life!*

I could never recreate those words. They were gone. And I was erased. How would anyone know me now? How would anyone know me beyond the insulting portraits of my supplication strung up and around Paris. The paintings that showed me serving *her* café. Over and over again. Always serving *her. Mocking me.*

My fingers began to shake. My eyes began mad blinking to keep the darkness from taking me.

He was saying it was all over. All my life's work was done. All of my purpose... gone.

I stumbled away from him, taking a last look at the building that devoured my words. Feeling as if I'd been in the building along with them.

I found my way into a tavern planning to order a Chartreuse to stop the quiver that had attacked my hand when I saw someone I remembered from the old days sitting on a stool, drinking beer. I swiped soot from my sweaty face and walked over to sit beside him, trying to blink the ash from my eyes.

"Bonjour. Do you remember me?" I asked him, feeling a bit desperate for the answer. *Does anyone remember me? Who will remember me now?*

He squinted at me through drink-soaked eyes but when the memory hit him, he smiled. "Ah, the Black Jacobin! It's been a long time!"

"Yes, yes." I quieted my voice, feeling my jumpy skin calm down as I sat beside him. "A long time. You've aged well."

"Lost everything," he said with a swig of the drink.

"What?"

"I said I lost everything in the revolution. My sister and son both." He pantomimed a slash across his neck. "We were supposed to be pulling the nobles off their high horses. Tell me, why did so many sans-culottes get the blade? Those nobles are out in the street right now, looking for someone to punish. A few of them died. Hundreds of sans culottes got the blade, maybe more, but they're running through the streets for revenge. They, *the ones who caused it*, because they couldn't tolerate the notion of paying taxes. They'd rather see the whole country starve than have to pay taxes on inherited money! The never even had to lift a finger and it's right back to that again." He gestured out the door and then went back to guzzle his drink. His drunken eyes didn't seem so clueless anymore.

"Everybody seems like they forgot," he said. "You know what I do? I take a visit every once in a while to London to that Madame Tussaud's to see my friends. You know she made wax of them all. Right off their dead bodies. Even that Madame of yours—the pretty one—got her face just like she was still living."

My stomach turned. It seemed a macabre thing to me, but it might be safer than the Catacombs; far removed from the place where the dead bodies rested.

"I went to Tussaud's and saw Max," he continued. "When they weren't looking I spit on his face. They saw it was wet, and I swore they had a leak in the roof." He cackled. "I talked to Max and the King, too. I told the King what a sorry pissant he was for trying to leave us high and dry. I hate the sorry bastard and I told him to his stupid wax face. And I'll visit again to tell him again. You're damned right, I will."

"If it makes you feel better, and all that," I said.

"Makes me feel like a drink." And drink, he did. The barkeep came over and filled his cup again. "We did the work. Whatever good Paris, France is today—*we* did the work. They don't have to worry about being snatched off the streets and thrown into the Bastille because of the work *we*..." he gestured madly between us, "...*we* did that work, people like you and me. And lost everything to do it! Vive la République!"

"Ça ira," I mumbled. *It will be alright*. My hand holding the drink was shaking as I looked down into its depths. The words meant nothing to me now. Everything I touched turned to merde. But I felt moisture clog my throat as he repeated the phrase with sudden fervor.

"Oui. Ça ira. Damned right!"

"Yes," I mumbled, head down, as the futility of my life crumbled around me. "Ça ira... and all that."

CHAPTER FIFTY-SIX

I spent three days in my room. Two of them I only left my bed to use the chamber pot. I went through a full bottle of Chartreuse and half a bottle of wine. I ate small bits of caviar off a spoon when my stomach began to grumble. I lay in my dirty linens without bothering to wipe myself down until my own stench motivated me out of bed. I opened my windows to allow the city air and city sounds to fill the space again. Finally, when I got up the energy to wet my face and body with a washcloth and go out seeking life, it didn't turn out well.

Someone was following me. And badly.

I hunched my shoulders and pretended not to notice. Every step, his grew firmer, almost like he wanted me to hear him. His boldness signaled to me that he was, in fact, a threat this time.

I wasn't in a mood to deal with this man. I hadn't slept in three days from sadness over my lost work and worrying about the Catacombs and where my brain would go the second I fell into sleep. And this man was following me.

It was daytime and the streets were heavy with people walking to work, walking from bars, hanging out on the streets. There was so much activity I might lose him, I thought. If I wanted to.

I was walking down one street and took a corner to see if I could shake him. I waited for the sound and after a short delay, I heard his footsteps had continued behind me. The street was more of a seedy alley and there was a man on the ground, drunk and pulling at my leg as I passed to beg for money. I kept going and heard him asking the same of my follower. I heard a loud "umph!" and suspected the beggar got a boot to the face. The idiot man couldn't even be bothered to try to muffle that altercation.

I was tired of dealing with people but this man was forcing me and a little bit of a flame fired itself up in me, starting to heat me up from within. The insult of indignation could fire up other things in me. My feeders were getting hungrier every second. At the end of the street I took another turn, quicker this time, hoping he would get bored and give up. Soon after I heard his steps more boldly. And then the flame filled me, and anger puckered from within.

I walked down a street that led under a bridge I knew which led to a deserted area in the shadows of the buildings and slums in a poor section of town. It was an area with dilapidated buildings where no one would voluntarily go, day or night. The ground was uneven with pieces of a fallen structure, stones and bits of wood of all sizes on the path and view of it mostly hidden by the skeletons of dead buildings. I spied a wooden plank with a nail on the end and stopped to pick it up, weighing its heft in the other hand. It felt good. Then I turned around and started walking directly toward him. I could now see it was the man, Roland. He stopped, seeming surprised to see me approaching, then stood his ground, dropping the paper beside him, chin coming up and one hand going into the spot under his coat where his waistband would sit.

I stopped and looked at that hand. It might hold a gun or a knife. Moving his coat a bit, I caught the glint of a knife. His face held a tiny, satisfied smile. Now that he'd been found out he seemed happy to show me he'd gotten the drop on me.

"Monsieur, le Page, Louis-Benoit Zamor," he drawled lazily as if with bored amusement.

"Bonjour, Monsieur Roland. Lovely day."

"It certainly is. Now, what is that you have there, old-timer? Some sort of stick?"

"Oui, it's a plank," I said.

"Come now, you mustn't hurt yourself."

"Want me to keep myself healthy so *you* can hurt me, is that it, young-timer?"

"I don't like hurting anyone, much less a gentleman such as yourself."

"I'm a gentleman today, am I? I thought I was a... what was it you called me..." I tilted my head in thought to find the memory. "Oh yes, a 'short little renegade slave' was the term."

"Wonderful memory for someone your age. As I was saying, I don't like hurting anyone but sometimes we're left with no choice. Those old rags you're wearing don't fool anyone. You are still the noble sympathizer. We were prepared to embrace you, but you refuse to submit to the cause. We offered you brothership on a platter, but you spit in our faces. So this is of your doing."

"No, Monsieur, I refuse to submit to *you*. And that's the problem, isn't it? I refuse to bow down to the oh, holy leader you think you are. Or any other aimless, purposeless idiot who thinks he has a cause. We served under an absolute monarchy once; that age of kings is done." *Sort of.*

"Keep talking, old man. I might have held pity for you but you're proving why that's wasted. The more you talk the more I feel you need to be put down. With respect."

That made my lips quirk up a bit and I nodded, jovially. "Respect taken." Inner fire boiled in me but some bit of me remembered my father's words. Maybe things didn't have to end badly, today. Maybe reason would win. The latent bit of decency in me decided to try. "What do you imagine will come of this little exercise? Will this solidify your power among the ranks?

Some Jacobins were equally as eager to gain power and most of them lost their heads over it. What they never told us, that I will tell you out of generosity of spirit, is that the ranks shift, you see! They move like a boat on untamed waters. One day you're in the groove and at the very top and then the next moment, without shifting your feet at all, you suddenly find yourself in exactly the wrong place at the wrong time. Because you were too focused on the carrot in front of your own nose to see the tide come in. Ask our Jacobin leaders. Ask Max. You see, true power doesn't come in the number of bodies you collect, it comes here," I tapped a finger against the side of my head. "Might will never overcome the power of a good plan, Monsieur. I assure you, the more blood you take the more likely you will be taken away by the same. Because the world shifts, Monsieur, and then you're right back where you started. Or worse." I smiled.

He looked at me for a long moment. I thought, perhaps, he was listening. Perhaps he would turn and walk away. But his next words proved me wrong.

"Good of you to try to portion out wisdom, Monsieur le Page..."

"Citizen Zamor, to you."

"...*Citizen Zamor*, I don't need your advice or protection. I don't need your old man wisdom. I can take care of myself and my group."

That made me smile out right. "Protection? Monsieur." I slapped the board into one palm. "Is that what you think I'm doing? Protecting you?" I was protecting myself, or trying to. I could feel where this was headed and knew it would be another mark against me in God's giant ledger. Mark or not, this man had it coming.

Rotten bag of scum. All I wanted was to take a walk and this miserable pissant had the nerve to follow me, track me to do me bodily harm because I wouldn't join his little group. Like his group offered anything of value to me. After all I'd been through. I would have given that stupid group some credibility and because I didn't want it, they thought they'd take me out. They might, but not without a fight.

Though my voice was calm, by this time I was seething. My hands weren't shaking but they were on fire from inside. I think something of this burning must have showed in my eyes because I saw in his brown ones a flicker of something. Doubt, awareness, confusion? I couldn't tell.

"Monsieur le—pardon—*Citizen* Zamor," he said, reaching into his waistband to finally pull out that knife. It glinted in the sunlight and the primal thing in me shifted.

I felt a lick of excitement. Something in me was happy to see that bit of metal for giving me a reason to lash out. A logical mind would have been cautious. I wasn't running off logic. I wanted to engage.

The man continued. "All we wanted was the proper respect. You can still change your mind and join us. After I give you a proper punishment and after a sincere apology, of course."

"So, a beating and then I'm to get on my knees to apologize, huh? Garçon..." *Boy...* "That's not going to happen." It was an ugly, emasculating term that was normally reserved for people of my hue. His eyes flickered with anger at the derision.

His voice hardened. "I'd advise you to change your tone."

"You advise nothing. I'm not one of your followers."

"Then you give me no choice but to give you a lesson in broad daylight."

He took a step forward. My lips began to quiver with anticipation, my eyelid twitching with excitement. I could see the exact spot in his neck where I was going to plant that nail. I could almost feel it ramming into him over and over. The thought of it made my blood rush.

My tongue darted out and quickly licked my parched lips while one of my hands gripped the board tightly. I looked at his knife and at his stance, and then up at his face.

"Let's put this matter to rest once and for all," I said, making an effort to keep my voice as calm and pleasant as possible. No point in being a brute about the fire raging inside me.

It was at that precise moment he glanced around him at our surroundings.

I could see what he was thinking in his movements. He'd been following me and had thought himself incredibly lucky to trap me in a desolate location with no one around to witness him. But now he was wondering if I'd baited him. Now he was starting to think he was the one trapped. Of course he was. As a long time survivor of the hunt, of course I knew the tricks of the hunter. I was already planning what to do with the body. Out here, I could bury it in plain sight and no one would notice. Or care.

"*S'il vous plait.*" *Please*, I said nicely. I tried to keep the plea out of my tone—didn't want him to hear how much I wanted this. "Step forward, Monsieur, our conversation has run its course." Both my hands now gripped that board hard on both ends and I felt it shaking from the force. He looked at the board and then up at my face.

Once again, my eyes must have given me away. I don't know what he saw in them, but he stopped in his tracks. He stopped, straightened, and began backing up.

A rush of panic suffused me. "Please, Monsieur Roland," I pleaded openly this time but instead of staying, he fumbled the knife back into his waistband.

"You're not worth the trouble. I won't bother you again," he said, backing up.

"Monsieur, don't go."

But he had turned and was walking and jogging away from me. Running. And once he was gone, I wanted to cry from the lost opportunity to vent some of what was building in me. Disappointed, I went to toss the board onto the ground, surprised when it stayed in one hand. I looked down and saw why; I had gripped the board and failed to notice the nail plunged into my own hand, blood running down in a river to pool onto the ground.

Later, I walked back to my apartment building and upon entering I heard the voice of the landlord's wife call to me.

"Is that you, Monsieur Zamor?"

"It is, Madame."

"Oh good. I wanted to ask." She leaned forward from where I knew she was sitting on a small settee, reading. "I wondered if you might want to go on a morning walk with me sometime?"

"Walk?"

"Yes, I know you've only been back in Paris for a short while and thought, perhaps, you haven't had a chance to re-acquaint yourself. The city is so beautiful in the morning at sunrise. I can't rouse my husband up that early and the kids are still in bed... it becomes my own special time. But you are such a pleasant tenant. My husband and I were speaking about how polite and kind you are. He says if I can get you to walk me, he would not even be jealous."

My hand flexed to keep any blood from my handkerchief-wrapped palm from dropping onto the floor. "Very kind of you Madame. A very lovely offer. I shall consider it one of these mornings. But, alas, I may be more like your husband, sleeping through the best part of the day."

She nodded and sat back, out of sight. "The offer is open if you change your mind."

"Oui, merci, Madame." I went to my room and cleaned the blood from my hand.

Chapter Fifty-Seven

I am a new man, I kept saying it to myself.

I tried to start again; thought I'd re-write my book. Tried again to write the words that would last under my own name. Words of meaning and substance. But life quickly reminded me of my mother's words about God laughing at our plans. I was tired all the time and began to feel an ache inside me like a muscle cramp that never seemed to leave. My age was catching up with me.

Then, not a year after my return to France, Sebastien dropped dead while haggling over the price of a cantaloupe with a market vendor in the middle of a Paris street. They carried him to his wife's house and sent for the doctor who determined he had been dead before he hit the ground. His heart. Valentin's pounding on the door of my little apartment was the beginning of a period of mourning, the likes of which I hadn't felt since burying my father.

I helped Élise bury her husband. After the small ceremony, I stood with her outside their house after Valentin walked home in the cold.

"I regret my long sojourn away from home and the time I lost with him," I admitted, lips cold.

"Don't. It might have been God had kept him alive as long as he had because you were gone, then gave him an additional year to be with his friend. For the two of you to make amends. A year for you to laugh like young men again, to play cards, to seal your friendship—remind you of the goodness of people. A year to forgive each other. You bought me twenty years with my husband, so thank you for staying away," she said, tears on her cheeks as she smiled in the cold winter air, her graying ginger hair blowing in her face. "Here, I have something for you." She dug into her bodice and pulled out a folded cloth, pressing it into my hand. "It's not my place or my understanding. I just tell you, a friend gave this to Sebastien and he told me years ago if anything happened to him I should give it to you. So, it is yours." She patted my hand that held it, and I kissed her on both cheeks.

She was moving out of the country to live with her son, his wife, and their kids in America. Élise rode away on the back of a carriage, her legs hanging down, holding her coat closed against the cold with one hand and looking how I felt, scared and alone. I waved and put on a false bright smile for her. When the carriage turned the corner, I let my hand and smile fall.

Back at the apartment, unfolding the handkerchief caused something as light as air to float out.

I looked down to where it landed on the floor and bent to pick it up, my body groaning as I squinted to see. When I pinched it between my fingers and held it to my eyes I recognized it was a dark, curly lock of hair. I rubbed it between my fingers and realized I recognized this hair.

Véronique. He'd left me a lock of her hair. Perhaps she'd given it to him to give to me all those years ago. Maybe she had wanted it to remind me of her?

But that was over twenty years ago. Anything that existed between us was dead now. I didn't know why Élise had felt the need to open old wounds. I folded it back and put it on a shelf next to my tins of caviar and Chartreuse and tried not to let grief overtake me.

My money from small writing jobs was running out. I earned more by playing violin at parties. I still played well. Surprisingly, the nobles who hated me any other day of the week loved it when I played. Standing in the rooms at fancy parties, with people like me still serving them, in whatever capacity, seemed to delight them. Almost made them feel like we were back in the old age of kings.

I truly tried to re-write my masterpiece. But my words ended up as drivel in the trash can and then the fire. Paper and ink cost money so I refused to write unless I felt my words were valuable enough to warrant the cost of recording them. There became fewer and fewer times that anything made it onto paper. I spent more time staring at the paper than writing on it.

And yet, somehow, whenever I was walking through town and had the misfortune of forgetting where I was, I'd sometimes have a jolt when passing the doorway of the Catacombs. During certain hours of the day people would line up but when it was closed to the public, after dark or early morning, the opening was a quiet, dark, yawning maw that was as compelling as it was horrifying. And every time I passed, I heard the silky, unmistakable voice of Madame.

"Zamor, come to me, my darling. Come to me my son, Louis-Benoit, we were meant to be together forever."

It was her voice, as clearly as if she'd never met the blade. Her voice that echoed throughout my limbs. *Was she why I'd been prodded to return?* I wondered. Did God want me back here to take my place beside Madame, just as she'd always predicted?

No matter my mood on arriving, whenever I passed the Catacombs, I'd leave that area fast with a cold sweat on my brow and a feeling that it wouldn't be long until her premonition came true.

Three years after returning to Paris, my optimism was finally well and truly dead. It became impossible to keep my hopelessness to myself. I was finally to that point of lonely that my father had spoken of.

I made friends with a woman in a tavern just to have someone to talk to. She seemed to enjoy my company but when she found out I wouldn't even try to please her she settled for keeping me company in return for gifts and money. I knew she didn't want me, but I didn't want to be alone. I allowed her to take the little I had just so there was someone for me to speak to or share supper with, occasionally, at the end of the day.

***

To pay my modest bills I started to tutor children in the neighborhood. I taught history and math and violin. I would like to say I was good at it, but I was a cranky instructor, as opposite Barnier as I could have been. It gave me just enough money to keep a roof over my head, Chartreuse in my glass, and tins of caviar on my shelf. It wasn't like I was spending it on other things.

I took to scolding my group of thirteen-year-old students on their lack of interest in the recent history. I explained to them how lucky they were to even have an education—that public education had been a direct result of the revolutionaries. But they didn't care, of course.

One day, my frustration came out in the worst way that it could. The children were always mischievous, but on this day, when I turned to the board one of them threw something at my backside. They all erupted into laughter. I should have ignored it—like I ignored all the other sleights and insults—but my temper gave way.

"That's funny, is it?" I asked the offender, a boy whose face was so gleeful you'd have thought my humiliation was inherent to his happiness. I jerked him from his seat by his arm–you'll recall my arms are the strongest things on me—and I proceeded to undo my belt and swat him on his backside. His friends laughed even harder which caused him to cry in embarrassment.

I let go soon enough but they were afraid of me now, hadn't expected the crouched over old Black man to be so quick or strong with his grasp. I wasn't as old as I looked.

Soon the word got around that I was mean to the children, and I lost all my students.

At some point I recognized that I was ill. I had a cough that was stronger and deeper by the day. The pain became bad enough that I sought out a doctor who came to my apartment and ordered me to take off my clothes for an examination.

"Is that really necessary?"

"I will get paid whether you get a thorough examination or not. You might as well get your money's worth. Unless you don't want to know what's wrong with you."

I, begrudgingly, disrobed. I did it with my back turned. I had no mirror in my apartment and didn't miss one. I hadn't looked in a mirror, on purpose, in quite some time.

"Sit down there," he said as I finished. I moved to sit on the bed and the slice of pain caused my breath to catch. He did a quick look over and his eyes betrayed surprise as he took in the roadmap of a lifetime of abuse that was now clear to him. His gaze stopped at my torso and swooped lower. "What happened there? You are mis-figured."

I flushed with embarrassment. "I can piss."

"But not much else, I'm guessing. Were you born that way?" My facial expression gave him the answer. "What happened to you?"

"The old regime and its tentacles. Fucking slave owners."

"You aren't from here, then? There are no slaves in France, haven't been for hundreds of years." If I heard it once I'd heard it a thousand times. He continued. "That looks like a scorned-husband injury." I looked at him in confusion. He softened his delivery, " I only mean often cuckolded men and scorned husbands tend to attack other men's privates—out of jealousy and spite. And cheated on women, too, sometimes, but I don't need to explain that. What was used? A poker?"

"A boot."

"Ah. I hope you got the woman, at least."

"Please finish your exam."

He did. For almost forty-five minutes he continued, finding areas of interest all over my body. I played an opera in my head and allowed him to do his work, only noticing the expressions of alternate wonder, horror and sadness on his face.

"Why, even to move must be long, slow torture," he said. "I feel broken bones improperly healed. I feel pockets of calcification in the wrong places. Even from the outside, I feel two of your ribs caved in or disintegrated, I can't tell. And that cut ... my, my. But you said it was your inside organs causing you pain. That's what you told me. Not these other things?"

"I'm used to the other things," I said. "It is down inside that causes me concern. Where I can't reach."

"You said you piss. What color is it?"

Of course, it was red. I didn't want to say it out loud. "Do you think it's a growth? Can it be cut out?"

He shook his head. "I can't be sure. The surgery itself, in your state, would kill you just to cut you open to see. And it would be excruciatingly painful—not unlike what gave you that the first time," he nodded toward my mid-section and I blanched with quick memory of that pain. "I wouldn't even know what to look for. Hours, open on a table with nothing but brandy to ease the pain... I know it's been done but I won't do it, ethically, speaking. No one else who's not a madman or sadist will do it, either. No one who's legitimate and not just wanting your fresh parts, anyway, if there's anything good left. You live here with a woman, correct? See if she will be kind to you and feed you hot soup. Tell her to make you comfortable."

"Ah, yes, yes. Hot soup, that'll fix things." I grinned. She'd send a bowl of hot soup flying at my head if she were around and I asked her. As if hot soup would make one dent in what was ailing me.

His eyes looked concerned and the sudden pity in them was arresting and unwanted. I wasn't one to take other's words as gospel and would have laughed him off had I not felt the truth of his words in my own body. Something insidious was within me. To get it out of me would kill me. To leave it in would kill me.

I went about my life and pretended I'd never gotten the diagnosis. Winter came and with no money to pay for heat, I layered clothes on to keep warm at night. I never realized how cold Paris could be.

I reduced my meals to bits of stale bread when I was hungry, letting a hard piece soften on my tongue so I wouldn't break a tooth trying to chew it right away. And I pretended my body wasn't growing weaker and colder and tighter every day.

I searched for something to hold onto even as my tins of caviar dwindled and the bottles of Chartreuse on my shelf became scarcer. I started to sip them instead of drink outright. I woke up each morning thinking it wasn't possible that this was the ending for me. Not the cunning, wily page who survived all manners of abuse and a revolution that took the strongest and weakest in all the kingdom. Not the boy whose mother called the greatest thing God ever made; the boy who had inspired the creation of a song and influenced the most powerful people in the most powerful nation. It wasn't possible that this would be the end for me, was it?

But my body didn't seem to care at all what my mind was screaming. I was dying, and it was amazing I had lasted as long as I had.

I began writing in my journal because, soon, that would be all that was left of me. I didn't have the energy to be as prolific as my masterpiece had been, but I could be straightforward and get my story of my life out. Maybe, someone would find interest in my journals after my death.

We make our plans.

Chapter Fifty-Eight

Dear Citizen,

Despite my state of mind, I'm a realist, not a pessimist. A piece of me wanted to believe that God brought me back to France to do more than punish me for my mistakes. Otherwise, I would have thrown myself into the Seine and been done with it.

I eyed that river longingly every morning when I saw the sun rise and sparkle on its surface. The Seine. It occurred to me that the old river was the only constant thing in my life since I was ten years old when its water bubbled up in the fountains at the Palace. That river was my friend.

—Zamor, 1820

***

"This small section of the Palace was the original hunting lodge. Then, the Sun King had all the rest added to the space to make it the wonder it is today. And yes, Napoleon did spend time here, as well."

The small crowd *ooh-ed* and *ahh-ed* as we stood in the front courtyard of the Palace of Versailles. We were a tour group for all sorts of people (from France and beyond) who had heard of the magnificence of the space. Their eyes were wide as they looked up and around.

As the guide informed us, the kitchen was demolished. Salanave would be heartbroken to see the pile of rubble that stood growing moss and grass where her kitchen used to be.

Most of the furniture had been sold, the animals in the menagerie shipped off to God knows where. The Palace walls had been stripped of all fleur-de-lys–looking bare without them.

Of course, while the guide was going on about the gold that used to adorn the walls I veered off at first chance. I slipped out of the house and walked away fast, towards a particular spot in the gardens. Looking back to make sure no one was watching, I awkwardly got down onto the ground and sat.

"Hello, little Jean," I said to the child who lay buried in the ground beneath me. "This is the proper place for us to speak, not in dreams or nightmares like you like to do. You haven't been by to see me so I came to say goodbye. I'm sorry I haven't been here sooner, but I'm here now."

Silence was punctuated by the occasional bird song in the air. The peaceful serenity swallowed me and my eyelids drifted closed. Immediately, in my mind's eye I saw the little boy as I had seen him the first time, tugging on my coat as a chubby-faced cherub, eyes large and eager to see me. I looked down and, for once, broke into a large grin to see his happy face. For once, I gave him the smile that filled my insides whenever I saw him. Bent down, to wrap him in the hug I'd always longed to but never did until after his soul had left his body. It felt sweet and special.

I opened my eyes. The sky was still blue, the birdsong still sweet, even without seeing him there in person. I reached into my bag. "I brought you something," I said, pulling out a croissant. It had cost precious coins at the viennoisserie in Paris. More valuable than flowers to us. I laid it on the ground beside me. "For old times' sake."

I only stayed a few minutes. Then I found the places where I'd disappeared to—or hidden in—as a child, remembering my overwhelm on first arriving. Sneaking off to the back rooms behind the theatre, I dug around in the spot where Barnier had found my violin. There were cubby holes throughout the palace if you knew where to look. Maybe I was hoping to find another violin, for what, I don't know—the dead don't play—but I found something better. There, among the discarded costumes and props for the many Versailles performances I found a box of yellowed papers.

It didn't take me long to recognize it as the music I'd used to learn. I snuck the box out the back way, much the same route that I'd used so many years ago in my aborted escape attempts. I looked a fool to the casual observer, shuffling along with a box of paper scraps, but I took it anyway and climbed onto the tourist carriage with it and waited for the others to return.

No one even noticed the box until it was time to depart and I reached under my seat and pulled it out. The tour guide bit his lip, wondering what to do and where it had come from. While he was thinking I walked past him with the box on my shoulder, weighing me down. And leaving, I carted it all the way home.

I was near to certain the music was that of my deceased friend, Josephe. Bonaparte wouldn't destroy everything of him like he had Dumas, if I had any control of it. I looked like a turtle hauling a boulder, but I managed.

The next day I sat on a chair at Remy's bar. It had become a regular haunt for me because it was close to home and Remy knew me. As I sat, he hit my arm as he passed by. "My boy over there will take care of you, I've got to get home. My wife's mother is visiting. Are you going to see Carne off?'

"What?" I asked.

"Carne. Valentin."

"What? What's happened with Valentin?"

"Didn't you hear? He's set today." He drew his finger across his neck. "Secret societies are not so secret and the new government doesn't much care for any of them. Especially ones plotting to kill the king. And on his birthday, the day of love!"

Valentin was named after the holiday, a romantic gesture that had plagued him all his life.

It had been months since I'd even spoken to Valentin. Beyond the republic, we didn't have much to talk about and without Sebastien—the only real link between us—I had no reason to stay in touch.

I went to where I'd heard the guillotine had been moved and there it was–though in a much more discreet place behind a building. The crowd was only a smattering of people. It seemed Paris had grown tired of bloodshed even if the beast never tired of being fed.

I watched as a group of men were pushed along to the edge of the stage and looked for the blond-haired man, not spying him.

"Carne!" A man moved forward, and I could see why I had missed him. I forgot they shaved everyone. His hair was gone and where it stuck out in patches was gray. He shook his head by habit—a lifetime of shaking his hair back off his face—and when he made the movement I saw him clearly. Shrunken with a face covered in lines and hollows, it was Valentin. When his eyes scoped out over the tiny crowd they saw me.

Valentin and I had never been the best of friends. But we had both held dreams for this country. We had both lost people. We both loved France.

"Fucking Jabobin scum!" a man up front yelled, spitting at Valentin even though he was well short of his target. Valentin winced at the words but lifted his chin.

"Lay down on your stomach," the executioner said. Valentin looked at me again. I nodded in acknowledgement. It was the least I could do, being that looking around the crowd I saw none of the people I'd seen in that hovel of a space that held his secret society. Too secret to show their faces, none of his new friends were there. His eyes flickered for a moment out of fear or gratitude. Then he took the position, and the platform tilted so his face was now to the ground, unable to see me or anyone.

I developed a bit of the palsy at that point. I don't know where it came from or why I should shake so. After all the death I'd seen, and all the years away, I couldn't imagine why Valentin's should cause me to shake. Anticipation of the *hush... swish...* causing my bones to quake.

"Chantez votre chanson, Sanson!" called a voice to the executioner.

Sing your song, Sanson! The song of death. The song that was so popular up to the Reign.

It seemed a lethargic, lazy ode back to the time of the Reign. Unwanted and unacknowledged by the others for whom death was no longer seen as sport.

I had pulled the hood of my cloak over my head so no one would notice how I was starting to shake, drawing my gaze upward to where that angled blade was perched.

I remembered the little toy on the table at the Palace. The King Louis XVI, and even Dr. Guillotine himself, had all been equally fascinated by the toy. I remembered the grape that spewed sweet juice when the blade of the toy came down.

They were both sacrificed to the monstrous life-size reproduction, along with some nobles and many, many commoners. My eyes watered with the dread of what came next. The sound. The horrible sound. And then a voice broke the inevitable...

"Valentin Carne!"

My eyes blinked involuntarily at the interruption of the ceremony, and I looked to find the source of the voice, as did the others. I saw Valentin's head still at the sound.

The executioner stopped, the chain in his hand, as a group of men entered the area and walked up onto the platform. Were they going to save him? Were they from his club here to save him? My eyes widened on the scene.

"This is a government-sanctioned execution," said the man holding the chain, holding the blade. "It shall not be interrupted, by law."

The man who was first pulled a sword from its case and pointed it towards the executioner, a devilish smile on his face.

"I do so hate to interrupt your work. But we must. I see there are three of you from the government. There are six of us, here with the swords of our ancestors. We will cause you no trouble nor harm if you give us what we want. We only want Carne."

Hope flooded through me. Valentin's friends had come for him!

"No, no..." I almost didn't know where that sound came from but realized it was Valentin.

"*No?*" I whispered to myself, confused. "But why—" And then I realized the group of men weren't his friends at all. That must mean...

"You're outnumbered," the leader said. "Fight us, Monsieur Execution-er, and there's no telling who might have to die with him. Release him, and we'll be on our way."

Those of us in the crowd were still, afraid to move a muscle. Afraid to even breathe. These men were members of the White Terror, come for their pound of flesh.

The executioner secured the chain and walked over to unlatch the board holding Valentin's neck inside the cradle. At the sound of the wood moving, he began to speak.

"No, don't," Valentin pleaded softly, cranking his neck to the execution-er who looked stricken.

"I'm sorry, I'm outnumbered."

"Please, just do it, quickly…" Valentin said, reaching for the board to try to place the brace over his own neck, reaching for the chain to try to whip it out of its holding place. He wasn't even all the way into the brace, it could take off half his head! No, no, no… not like this…

"Valentin Carne!" The leader of the group walked toward him, pointing his sword at him. Valentin continued to reach for the chain and the man struck out against the wood, an inch above Valentin's reaching hand. The hand stopped and the whole of him seemed to sag against the wood in defeat. The man continued to speak. "…Of the southern Carnes. Noble by blood turned Jacobin. And today, working-still—against your brothers in blood. A traitor to your class. A traitor to your people. A traitor to a noblewoman who loved you from childhood. A traitor to King Louis XVIII."

While he spoke, two of the members of the group had moved forward to grab Valentin up and off the beast, his hands still bound behind his back. They jerked him to his feet and one of them held him from behind with a hand clutching the front of Valentin's neck. The leader continued.

"Look and see, everyone. This man was noble-born. Bitter from losing his fortune. Though if his family lost it so easily, perhaps they never should have had it in the first place." Some of his friends laughed. "This man was a willing supplicant to Max Robespierre, murderer of nobles across this country. Then, somehow, he survived being cut down like the rest of the Mountain. But did he learn his lesson? Was he grateful? No. He's still plotting against the people of his blood. Your new friends turned you over, Monsieur le Duc Carne. They don't want you *either.*" He reached up and took Valentin's lower face in his hand, speaking into it. Valentin's eyes were red and watery as he stared the man in the face. "You're part of a secret society devoted to slaughtering all of the noble class."

Valentin shook his head furiously. "It's a lie… Just the King."

"What?" the man put his head closer to him. "What was that? Just the King? I heard you wanted to get rid of us all out of revenge for your family fortune."

"It's a lie. It's a lie. Just the monarchy. Only the monarchy."

My eyelids floated shut for a momentary sense of dread. Valentin thought the fact that he only wanted to kill the King made it better.

The man pulled away as if thinking it over and then turned away, and then turned back, quickly, to punch Valentin in the ribs. The sound of the crack echoed through the space. Valentin heaved and coughed.

"Valentin Carne," the man yelled, "you've been tried, convicted, and sentenced to death by the tribunal of the Sons of Noble Blood. Any last words? Any other Jacobin scum here today want to put in a word for this man?" Then, the leader turned and passed his gaze over the crowd.

Moisture popped out on my forehead as a piece of me struggled to stop myself from speaking up. *Shut up, Zamor!* my brain said. *Valentin isn't your friend!*

No, he had never been my friend, not like Sebastien. But we'd been through a lot. I'd known him from my earliest days in Paris when he was young and handsome and cocky and mean. I'd known him through the horror of the Reign. He'd helped free me when I was set to die. And today, there was no one to stand for him.

I was tired of being selfish. Tired of watching others die. As I looked around, I saw no recognition or concern on the faces of anyone else in the crowd.

"Anyone?'

He was an asshole, but he had gotten me out of prison once.

"Anyone?"

My eyelid twitched and I made a tiny movement, maybe my finger twitched.

Like a Jacobin of old, on the platform, Valentin must have seen the small movement because his eyes flickered to me, and—looking up in the air so as not to give me away—he gave a slight, imperceptible shake of his head: *No.*

I was panting through my nose as the leader of the group searched for Jacobins in the crowd.

I was dying already. I couldn't say why something in me resisted.

The leader's gaze floated over me. It was like in the time of kings. He saw me, but the fullness of me was invisible to him. He looked away, satisfied he would have no argument. Only then, did Valentin's eyes stray to mine as the leader declared, in a pleasant tone, his apology for the rude interruption. And then they were leading Valentin off the platform and out of the area, the sound of their steps echoing through the space.

Frozen for a long moment, the executioner gestured to the two guards to proceed with the others. But when he opened his mouth to announce the next one's name, the sound of a garbled scream rang out from beyond.

We all held still and quiet for a long time. Waiting, it seemed, for another horrible sound. As if what was happening here wasn't already horrible.

Then, the executions started again, and though I wanted to escape the *hush... swish...* I was petrified to leave. I stayed there, long after the executioner and his guards had packed up with their buckets of heads and bundles of headless bodies. Long after the other bystanders had drifted away. I stayed there, until I had no more logical reason to be there. Then, I walked out of the area and around the corner to the quiet and peaceful night. But quiet, sweet nights could be deceptive.

Since it was twilight, torches had been lit to brighten the streets and there were several couples meandering, arm-in-arm. I almost forgot it was Valentine's Day. There was a chill in the air and the trees glistened with something wet and pink. They glistened with white and peach.

I put my head down and walked, hands in my pockets, trying not to see or hear the stillness of the night as passersby stepped gingerly, fear etched on their features.

Keep walking, I told myself.

Up ahead, a nicely dressed couple walked arm-in-arm, maybe from an evening at the opera or theatre.

Keep walking.

Across the road, two dogs fought over something that they passed back and forth as they tried to wrest it from one another.

Keep walking!

The couple looked, curiously, until they were close enough to see. And, as I knew it would, her scream rang through the night and he clutched her in fear, pushing her along and away from the thing furiously.

I didn't have to see what the dogs had got to.

I kept walking as the pink and red and peach and white wetness dripped from the leaves of the trees, glistening bits of Valentin falling from the night sky like pink diamonds on his very special day.

Chapter Fifty-Nine

After witnessing the evidence of Valentin's murder, I walked the Paris streets to get rid of the shakes. I walked until my bones were sore, knowing I should go home. But I didn't want to bring the shakes home and walked more. And sometime while I was out the sun rose but was soon covered by the clouds.

I sat on a bench on the city street as lightning cracked the sky and it began to rain. I was looking at the ground before me but when the next lightning strike hit, for a split second I thought I was in the Labyrinth at Versailles. I blinked away the confusion. And then when the next strike hit, I realized, directly across from me in sharp relief, was the doorway to the Catacombs.

The palsy was worse now as I stared at that doorway, dark in the darker night. I could feel her calling to me, as real as if she was standing alive before me. Fear infused me and I rose up off that bench.

On my pained legs and back I walked through the rain, water trailing over my features. Walking through town I passed a painting on a storefront of me serving Madame with a smarmy, sneaking smile on my face. I recognized the work of the artist. Long ago, presented to Madame at the Chateau, I destroyed the first one. This second one was worse.

It was perched high off the ground so I couldn't tear it down if I wanted to. It was only one of at least three I'd seen in the city. Painted to mock and belittle me. Painted to put me into my place, as effectively as a ghost. I continued walking until I was home, grateful to wrench open the door to my apartment building.

"Is that you, Monsieur Zamor?" my landlady asked.

"Oui, Madame," I squeezed out, as politely as I could.

"Have you thought anymore of a walk as sunrise, Monsieur? I have noticed your color is not well, it might help you feel better. Perhaps tomorrow."

"Thank you for your concern, Madame, but I think I shall sleep tomorrow. I was out all last night and this morning, I think I could sleep a week."

"I was speaking to a friend who told me the Palace was particularly beautiful at sunrise. That the Sun King had arranged for sunrise to strike the grounds just so. Was that the case? Was it magnificent living in the age of kings?"

"It was horrible, Madame. As were the people! I hope they all burn in hell!" I sputtered before I could stop myself. She was quiet. I got a hold of myself. "Do forgive me, Madame, I have no idea where that outburst came from. I have bad memories of the old age of kings but that has nothing to do with you. My apologies. I think I shall sleep in tomorrow."

"My apology for opening a wound, Monsieur. Sleep well. The offer stands when you're ready."

"Oui," I said, taking the stairs, gasping and hurt.

The woman I spent time with was there.

I didn't want to talk to her, but I didn't want to be alone. She was heating water on the little stove.

"You need to get more water from the water man," she said, not a hint of softness in her. She'd grown tired of my dwindling finances and charming, acerbic wit. She constantly thought, with the way I spoke, I was mocking her lack of education. She grew tired of being seen with me and dealing with the occasional person who would recognize me in public.

Now, tonight, she stirred the hot water over something in a bowl.

"I don't have money for water," I said, lips still trembling, turning away so she couldn't see how shook I still was from the day's events.

"If you'd stop spending money on that green crap you could afford water. Do you have money for me, then? I told you I want to buy a dress."

I didn't lift my head, avoided her eyes, and peeled off my coat to hang. "If I don't have money for water what makes you think I have money for a dress? Oh, yes, you can't spell or add so you wouldn't understand that, would you?" Unnecessarily abrupt, I admit.

Over a bowl of oats tossed at my head she yelled at me: "You think you're so smart, why are you living in this craphole with the rest of us idiots?"

I explained, "It's because I'm so smart that I'm *still alive* to be in this craphole with idiots like you!"

She left, furious.

After she left, I went to bed and slept, hard, the rain putting me to sleep.

I woke up, blinking away the sleep, my body protesting as I sat up. I hadn't slept well—I dreamt of the sound of that damn machine.

The room was quiet and still. I noticed the wrap she normally left on the chair in the corner that was there when I went to bed was gone and knew she'd been there. I looked around the room and it didn't take long for me to realize that she'd rifled through it. The few drawers I had were open, my clothes spilling out. Her things were gone. And the worst thing... *the very worst thing...* was that my violin was gone, too.

I imagined the smirk on her face when she did it. It would fetch her a decent amount of money, I was sure. She could buy that dress with the money from my violin.

Her companionship hadn't been worth my violin. Taking it hurt me many times more than it was worth to her. I suppose that was her point.

I stumbled out of bed and my knees hurt.

I remembered then that Valentin was gone. All my friends gone. I wondered at God's plan because it was so different from mine.

God was compassionate. Isn't that what they said?

God loves you. Does He really?

We make plans.

Was God laughing? Was He laughing at me?

"Stop!" I yelled out loud, the voices ringing in the small room. I brought my hands up to hold my head which ached from the sound. "Stop! Please stop!" I dropped to my knees and hardly noticed the pain as I cried out, sobs racking me as I clutched handfuls of the blanket in my hands. Sliding down to the floor I curled up into a ball, my voice winding down to a wordless, wide-mouthed scream.

Chapter Sixty

I managed to fall asleep on that floor and, as was my luck, was visited by the Well-Beloved, Louis XV in my dreams. We picked up on that walk through the botanical gardens at the Palace as if all the time in between the last dream—years—was but a moment before.

"I have a secret," he leaned down to whisper in my ear. "You are our favorite thing…" he insisted, his brow furrowed even more so, as if his words should mean something to me. "Maybe, someday, you can share the information with Madame if she needs it. This story might give her comfort. "It's a mystery, where the thing is! Maybe you'll be the one to solve it. After all, you are the Governor of Louveciennes!"

Even dreaming, I felt compelled to tell him the truth. My young self looked at the serious, powdered face of the king with his painted red lips sweating profusely and staring at me as if what he was saying was of most importance.

"Your Majesty," my ten-year old self told him, wondering if the news would get me strung up in the palace dungeon. Perhaps left to rot down there with a mask covering my face so no one would ever know who I had once been. A mask covering the face of the favorite thing that had no name.

Still, one is bold in dreams. "Madame du Barry is dead. I helped kill her. Don't you see her where you are?"

His forehead creased in worry and his hand went to his mouth as all of his many years of life were coming upon him at once. His eyes filled with tears, and I looked down to avoid his stare, trying not to notice the way his hand wobbled and shook.

"I didn't want to deny her," he said. "I had to. I had to, to get into heaven," he pleaded his case to me. As if heaven would ever require one to denigrate someone as cost of entrance. I looked at him again.

"Is that where you are, your Majesty?"

"I... well..." He looked around the Palace grounds and at that moment the blue sky darkened as if the sun was suddenly blocked by something large. He looked up and around, panicked, as the scene he knew so well slowly became overwhelmed by darkness working its way down over us.

I wasn't afraid that darkness. I knew what it was and what to expect. Seconds later when a thunderclap filled the air everything went dark until... one... two... three...

A lightning strike suddenly brightened the world and the two of us were frozen in its glare. And then, I heard the faint call of a familiar voice.

"My love... is that you..."

No, no, no...! Now, I was afraid.

The Well-Beloved disappeared and all went still.

Then, I was sitting on a bench on the grounds of the Palace, the tall trees disappearing as snow blanketed the ground and opened up to a white expanse of the green carpet of the Palace. The cold caused my breath to come out in tufts of smoke between my lips, and I was wearing my worn cloak over a threadbare top and pants. The cold snow-covered ground radiated iciness through the hole in the bottom of my shoe.

I knew then when a dark figure developed like an apparition before me, the snow falling so I could barely see, what was coming. As it approached, the shadow of it melted into the figure of her. Jeanne du Barry approached, dressed in one of her white ball gowns, looking like she had the first day I saw her. The cold didn't seem to touch her at all.

Her face was bright and beautiful, happy to see me. I looked down towards the ground, shoulders sagging. This was to be it. I would die in a dream, and she would take me, as she'd always promised.

With my eyes no longer on her, suddenly I felt her beside me and saw her hand reach over onto my lap to take mine. I allowed mine to lay in her cold palm, limp. I looked up at her and her eyes were wide, affectionate, her gaze caring.

"My lovely Louis-Benoit, it's so good to be so close to you. You've been avoiding me for so long, I thought I'd never get this chance."

"I'm not long for this world, you had only to wait a day or two and I'd be sitting right beside you in hell. Why come now?"

She smiled prettily. "Silly boy, if I had waited I wouldn't be here at this precise moment. Don't you remember? I told you that someday you would be alone and starving on the street and you'd be sorry. And look at you! Just like I said. Rags on your body and stomach rumbling from hunger without me. Aren't you sorry now, that you betrayed your Madame? I'm the only person who ever loved you. Even now, after everything you've done, I still love you. And I forgive you."

"I don't want your forgiveness."

"I will mark it down as a temporary bit of madness and forgive you, I said."

"I don't want your forgiveness. I never asked for it and I never will. I'm not sorry for what I did. You gave me no choice."

"There's always a choice, love."

"Oui, and you had a choice, too. You chose to keep me captive when you could have let me go. You chose to take my freedom when you could have let me be."

Her lips pressed closed in annoyance. "Come now, don't make me angry, my love. People say things they don't truly mean and I understand that. But you know, it will forever be you and I. Madame du Barry and her Page. That's what we'll always be."

"I never asked to be a part of your life."

"You were blessed *to be a part of my life," she seethed through thinning lips. "Don't you understand by now? It doesn't* matter *what you want. You have never been anything without me. And you'll never be separate from me. We will never be apart. Never. Never."*

I woke up, my eyelids flying open in the dark room, my heart beating loudly in my chest. I put a hand over it to slow it as moisture squeezed from within my eyelids and I panted myself to normal breathing.

I didn't want that. *Dear God, don't send me back to them again.*

CHAPTER SIXTY-ONE

Valentin's death hit me harder than I expected, considering we weren't really friends. The finality of it on top of all the recent events, crept up on me gradually, much like my inside pain. Where before it had been an ever-present ache, now it was becoming a greedy maw of burning fire that would send strikes through me, on occasion, painful enough to double me over.

I'd accepted my impending death but I was afraid of the pain. I started to wonder if I should help death along? Maybe cause my own demise before the pain became too great? It seemed a prudent idea.

I had the bright idea to throw myself off Pont Neuf into the river. When the time came to do it and I tried to lift my leg high enough to get over the stone I realized it wasn't as easy as it would seem. My joints did not like to move like they once had. My thighs resisted the stretch. Even my most reliable arm muscles, instead of pushing me up so I could catapult myself, they clutched onto that stone cold bridge like we were lovers. I can't imagine how odd I must have looked to passersby, launching one leg that barely left the ground, and holding onto the railing with all my might. I snorted with mirth at my own stupid idea right out in the open on that bridge. I barely earned a glance of concern.

Though dramatic, the bridge thing had been too ambitious. Simplicity was the best route when one couldn't accomplish acrobatics. The next day, I woke up with a better idea.

I walked outside my apartment door, shutting it behind me. Standing on the landing, I looked down at the many, many stairs and decided this was the thing to do. Old people died by accident on stairs everyday; surely, me pitching myself on purpose would do it.

Because my vision wasn't as strong anymore, I squinted to make sure my aim was straight. It wouldn't do to be off and be saved by a wall or left hanging off a broken edge. No, I had one chance.

I took a deep breath. I backed up a step or two for leverage and then did as much of a leap as I could in my condition. But half a second later, both feet off the ground, eyes wide with anticipation, a single thought streaked through my head out of the blue.

Like they weren't part of me, first one arm, then the other, reached over, grappling for the rail. And, once again, there I was, my arms clutching for solidity while my feet floundered.

"*Oomph!—*" was the noise I made as my body came down and made contact, landing like a sack of potatoes in the middle of the stairway. I landed sideways, one foot half-on, half-off a step, and on my hip on the side closest to my traitorous arms.

From beyond the closest open doorway, my landlady must have heard the impact, and called out to me, sight unseen.

"We're not getting any younger, Monsieur Zamor," she called to me, pleasantly, as I pulled myself up on groaning knees.

I almost laughed. No one told me age came with a body suddenly having the ability to fight itself.

"Oui, oui, Madame..." I croaked, getting to my feet. The sprained ankle took issue as I dragged it, and myself back into my room.

The third day I dug around in my things to find a tiny handkerchief I'd folded long ago revealing dried-up belladonna leaves and berries. I got excited. I took some water and boiled it on a stovetop to steep the tea with the leaves. Then, looking at the brew in my cup, that looked less-than deadly, I fished a mortar and pestle from my cupboard and ground up the shriveled black berries as best I could, tossing all of it into my cup.

I looked at the muddy brew, hesitated only a second, and then drank it down, chewing on the bits and pieces that didn't dissolve, Swallowing with a grimace. It certainly tasted like poison. Drinking that tea, huddled in my room on a chair, my cloak draped over me, one though persisted...

So, instead of thinking, I took myself to bed and lay there, waiting.

I rolled around in bed with a stomach ache that night and fell asleep. The next morning, I opened my eyes to the ceiling.

"F---," I croaked.

Poison. Bah! Too bad I had no rat poison in the house.

Chapter Sixty-Two

A knocking rattled at my door. I sat up, feeling my insides clench with resistance. Lifting a fist to wipe the moisture that fell from my mouth onto my rank, wrinkled clothes I shook myself to.

Bang, bang, bang. Someone was persistent.

"Oui," I called out with a hoarse voice. "One minute." My muscles and the insides of me groaned as I stood. I stumbled over to my washbowl, dipping a rag into the water and running it over the bare parts of me and behind my neck. Dropping it, I hobbled over to the door, jerking it open. I blinked to clear the confusion from my eyes. A woman was standing before me, a little purse on her arm.

"Sara?" It was my friend from the little town near the Port at Le Havre.

"Will you let me in or are we to speak in the hallway?" she asked pleasantly. I waved her inside and she stepped in gingerly, the slight twitching of her nose picking up the smell of alcohol and sickness and an insufficient wipe-down with the cleaning cloth. "My, what do we have here?" Her eyes went up, down, all around.

"What are you doing here?" I tried to tuck the front of my shirt into my pants and continued to wipe my eyes with my sleeve. She walked over to the single chair in the single room and sat down looking at me, expectantly. Confusion filled me until I jumped slightly.

"Oh, can I get you something? I can put on some water for tea or café?"

She smiled. "I would no more accept something to drink that you make from that little space than I would stick my hand in an open oven. Besides. I see no oil or wood. Or water. But thank you for the offer."

I looked at my own little space. She was right. I had no water left in the bucket on the floor by the stove and the can that held wood only had a sad stick that had splintered off from a piece of long-used lumber. Clothes spilled out of drawers and I had sponged already from the wash-bowl—half-empty with a ring around the inside.

"It's February," she said. "It's cold in here. You must be cold, non?" she said, more gently. I shrugged.

"I don't feel it much."

"I've come at a bad time?"

"Not at all, I just had a difficult night. How about..." I went over to my cupboard. I had a dirty little glass which I wiped out with one thumb, noticing the look of revulsion crossing over her features. "Don't worry, this one is for me." Then, I pulled out my bottle of Chartreuse and poured some in the glass. I walked over and handed her the bottle. "You drink from that."

She took it and looked at it dubiously, picked up the edge of her skirt to wipe around the rim. Then she glanced at me and put the bottle to her lips while I sat on the floor in front of her to drink.

"Mmm," she said after tasting. "Tastes like grass, mint, herbs of the field. Not bad."

"What are you doing here? How did you find me?"

"Well, that's quite a story so I'll start with the easy answer. I walked into the first printer I found—because I was sure you'd be writing—and he told me that no printer who wanted to keep his shop from burning to the ground would publish anything from the traitor Zamor. That's when I realized that people here don't like you much. I thought you said you had friends!"

"I do. I mean, I did. All the others, not so much. They can't get over Jeanne du Barry."

"It isn't her they can't get over, it's the fact that a Black man dared to consider his own life over a White woman's. By their way of thinking you should have, happily, sacrificed your life for hers. If you had, they'd be calling you a saint right now. But you'd be a dead saint … where's the worth in that?."

She wasn't wrong. Perhaps, I had always known I was supposed to be the loyal servant from Voltaire's play, from which I'd been named. That was always to be my true purpose – to serve until the end.

"Then…" she continued. "I asked around in bars and a tavern owner just down the street with one ear lobe told me where you live and here I am. Not a bad place, I imagine, when it's clean."

"You came all this way to criticize my housekeeping."

"Someone has to."

"I don't care about it, at all. I don't care about much anymore. " My eyes dropped from her and I looked down into my glass, having difficulty looking into her face. I blustered to hide my shame. "Yes, well, it turns out I'm a failure as a writer, or at least a published one. My masterpiece was destroyed in a fire along with all my hopes and dreams. Now, I dabble. So, bon santé, oui?" I toasted her, mirthlessly. The drink tasted good. I'd long since stopped feeling the burn from it but the flavor was still nice. I looked at the glass that was empty way too soon. She reached over and topped me off.

"Self-pity doesn't suit you, page. Well, maybe I'll go ahead and tell you why I'm here," she said. "It's quite a surprising story. You see, I was having tea one day and happened to look out the window over to the tree." She said it as matter-of-factly as if she was speaking about stopping over to the neighbor's house.

"The *dead people* tree?" I asked.

"Oui, only this time it was my dear, sweet Sissie."

"Sissie?" I was confused. "You swore you didn't..."

"I didn't!" She looked insulted. "I would never hurt *my sister!* That's why it was such a surprise to see her there at the guilty man tree. Anyway, I went outside to the tree to ask why she was there. And she spoke to me."

"Like, with her voice?" I snorted with disbelief. I was one to balk, hearing Madame's voice all around Paris.

"Like, when you're standing someplace minding your own business and a thought just enters your head. Like that. She said I should check on you."

"What is it with people always claiming dead people are around concerning themselves with us. Dead people are dead and that's that."

"She said I should check on you and I decided I would. Because I owe you."

"You don't owe me anything. You never asked me for anything."

"No, I never asked, but you gave, anyway," she acknowledged. "Luc is very important to our community, I'll have you know. He has become a brave, honorable man. He has this innate sense of responsibility that extends to those around him. He is this strange combination of good and kind. And selfless. It's the oddest thing; sometimes I just look at him and wonder how he was made from the circumstances from which he sprung. And then I think of you and what you did. What *you* taught him. So now, everyone loves him and they have come to love me, too. In their way. They think that because I raised him perhaps being a murderess isn't so bad."

"He was a grown man already fully formed when I met him. I could hardly teach him anything that wasn't already in him or taught to him by you." I laughed a little though it rattled up inner pain in me and I winced, succumbing to a coughing spell that sounded loudly in the room until I finished, fumbling in my shirt for a handkerchief to wipe my mouth, trying to hide the red stain it made, folding it and slipping it into my shirt pocket. She caught the movement.

"Is that from too much drink last night or something more?" she asked knowingly.

"It's from what will finally do me in." I smiled wryly. "Promises to be a long, slow death. And no matter how I try to hurry it along, it seems I have a stubborn determination to survive, even when faced with my own efforts. Every night I pray to die and every morning I wake up again. The pain... is bad. I thought I'd spare myself the ordeal and put myself out of my misery so I tried tossing myself into the Seine. I even pitched myself from the top of the stairs and all I did was sprain my ankle. My hand wouldn't let go of the rail."

"None of that is funny."

"I wasn't joking."

"Well, that's it, then," she said, exasperated. "That's what Sissie was telling me. You need me to take care of you. Come now, pack up. I'll take you home."

I smiled. "No. Not a chance."

"What do you mean? You're dying. Why die alone when our community will help you through it? Why not go where you're loved?"

"Sara, I'm a vain man. I can think of nothing worse than going back to that place of admirers for them to see me like this..."

"But we want to be there for you."

"Sara, Paris is my home. It's where I printed my first words and where I first met people who knew me and loved me as I am. Aside from you, of course. I became a free man in Paris and I will die here."

Our visit was short after that. Sara felt helpless and I loved her for caring how I died. At the door, saying our goodbyes, she took the sides of my neck and leaned her forehead against mine.

"Mon-*sieur* ...?" she whispered in the way and fashion she taught me as a child about to receive another beating from not learning French fast enough. It was the word I couldn't grasp until she told me the trick. My eyes filled as I completed her lesson.

"Mon-*sieur* ..." I said softly. "... the second part like a whisper..." I repeated her instruction.

"You always were a good learner," she smiled though tears were in her eyes. "Adieu, mon petit frère,"—*Goodbye, my little brother*—"Adieu."

I didn't tell Sara everything.

It had occurred to me there was a very real and obvious reason I couldn't die. I had unfinished business. It hovered over me like the feeling when you leave a fire burning in the stove, forgetting to put it out before you leave. Or forgetting your keys in your trouser pocket.

I sat down on the chair and picked up the bottle of Chartreuse, putting it to my lips.

Three times I tried to do myself in, and every time just one thought went through my head just before I stopped myself: *I wish I could see Véronique one last time.*

I did, indeed, harbor that selfish desire that I didn't deserve on my best day. But, also, I owed her. I owed her the answers I had always been too afraid to give. I owed her the truth of who I was and what I'd done throughout my life. I owed her the right to tell me to go to hell, with a full understanding of me. I didn't *want* to hear her say those words to me, I just owed her the chance them. They would break my heart, but still ... it had been broken before and I survived.

And then, of course, the fact that I longed to see her was always in my mind. It was the one good thing about enduring what was sure to be a painful experience.

I had given her up and had no rights to her. I would ask nothing of her. But I wanted to see her more than anything in the world. Loving Véronique had been the purest, most honest thing I'd ever done in my life.

Well, every man deserved a dying wish and this was mine. It was penance, but it was also the last request of a dying man. If it was a mistake, it wouldn't be my first. Oui, I would see my love one last time.

The decision made, resolution of it settled on my heart. It felt right. I sipped my green drink and, for once in my life, I was absolutely certain I was doing the right thing. Even just a glance at Véronique would give me the courage I needed to leave this world.

Chapter Sixty Three

"Bonjour, Madame," I called to the wife of my landlord as I stepped out of my apartment building the next day.

"Bonjour, Monsieur Zamor, wrap that cloak tight. There's still a nip in the air."

"Oui." I clutched my collar closed with my hand as instructed because there was a cool draft of wind that I knew from experience could settle into one's bones quickly. Shuffling off down the street, I used some of the last of my coins hidden under my mattress. A few minutes later, I was sitting on a seat behind a rented horse that seemed even older than me. We headed off to the west of Paris.

On the way through the countryside I passed a field of wildflowers and slowed the horse to stare at it a moment. I remembered dancing with Véronique in the fields. I remembered Lightning. I even remembered laughing with Sebastien and Valentin, Josephe and Thomas. I remembered little Jean. All these things passed through my thoughts and I smiled. Despite everything, I had known love. I had given it and received it. I had lived life and enjoyed more than I would ever admit.

That's when a thought struck me so profoundly, I wondered how I'd never considered it before: All those years ago Salanave had warned me not to give Gaspard something important enough to take. As I told her, making myself small hadn't stopped me from feeling pain. But now I knew it was even more than that. Just as my father had admitted that finding me in a plantation in the United States would have rooted him there. At the time it seemed a bleak notion, but now I saw it for what it was... a testament to his love for me. A life without things important enough to fear their loss–why, *that was not a life at all.*

One should be grateful if they have something that makes their heart clutch thinking of its loss. And I had that with Véronique Clair of the East.

I'd lied to myself for more than twenty years. The one thing I had hoped would die never did. My feelings for one person had survived the Reign, survived world travel, survived old age and, alas, would survive even me.

I took my time traveling to Croissy-sur-Seine. I led my horse to the house on the street that overlooked the river at the point where the jagged edges of the Seine meet. It had been twenty-six years since I'd seen Véronique.

My cloak had thinned too much to compete with the wind but it was the heaviest thing I owned. It was not that frigid of a day, but my bones felt every chill.

There were flowers around Véronique's house even in the cool air. The house was so well kept it hardly looked the same place with its paint and well-tended lawn and those bursts of colors in the garden. She so loved bursts of color.

A placard out front said "seamstress". Questions roamed through my mind, like, how could she comfortably announce her profession? I walked up to a window and peered inside. The little place was just as full of flowers and plants. A dog ran around in circles and then darted up to two children, maybe ten and twelve years, who promptly began chasing the happy dog around the house. I smiled though my eyes were suddenly wet. She had children and she must have married! I winced with that thought.

I caught a glimpse of her from where she was occupied at the far side of the living parlor. She'd barely aged. Her hair was only a little grey above her ears, like time had stood still, and she had an expression of something I could only describe as contentment on her face. Her determined brow had relaxed; there were no lines on her forehead that I could see. No worries for her, not anymore.

A thousand questions flowed through my brain, all questions I had no right to ask, but wanted to ask for the man in her life: *Are you kind to her? Do you pay attention when she speaks? Do you touch her gently? Is there a name you call her and keep for her ears alone? Are you romantic with her and make her blush? When she cries do you hold her tight to make her feel safe? Does it make you smile when she gets that determined look upon her face? Are you in love with the slightly crooked front tooth? When she took her headwrap off for the first time did you touch her hair like the most precious spun silk? Did you let her clutch your hand when she brought your children into the world? Do you pray for her? Do you thank God for her? Do you make her feel like she is the most special thing on earth? Do you love her?*

The sound of someone humming a familiar tune tore me from my reverie and I wiped a hand over my wet face, stepping quickly away just as a young Black woman came into view from where she had been around the back of the house. She looked at me, surprised.

"Oh, bonjour," she said. "Did you need some darning work? Don't feel shy to interrupt; there's never a moment of silence in the house. But always time for another customer."

"Bonjour, Mademoiselle," I replied. "That tune, what was that you were singing? It sounds very familiar."

"Just something that pops to mind when I'm gardening or taking a walk." She looked at me like I had missed the more pressing question. "Don't be shy, Monsieur. I can see that coat of yours can use a bit of work. Her prices are reasonable, I assure you."

I looked at my cuffs and they did, indeed, need some work but the number of patches it would take to repair it would cost the price of a new coat. "I admire your keen perception, Mademoiselle, but I'm not a customer. I am new in town and was happening up the road when I saw this spot."

"Oh, forgive me. I promise it wasn't a slight, only an observation from someone used to looking for things to mend."

"You have worked for the Madame for a long time, then?"

"All my life." She smiled at my confusion. "Though the sight may not suggest it, she's my mother. The children with boundless energy, my siblings. I know you will notice the age difference so I will tell you. Their papa is mine in all the ways that come with raising a child, except for blood. He married my mother when I was already in the world. It is a testament to the type of man he is that he loved another man's child. Especially knowing my own father was her true love."

"Your own father?" I felt the coldness that comes slowly when the blood begins to drain.

"Maman has never loved anyone as much as him, it doesn't even offend papa. He can't be jealous of a dead man. My blood papa was one of the many lost in the Révolution. My mother always told me to be proud; my father gave his life to give France its future. Standing up for what he believed in. For many years when I was young, she was still very angry with him for choosing his circumstance over her. But she said that, in retrospect, she realized he gave up everything he had, even her, to fight for his dignity. To fight for his rights as a Frenchman. He was a Jacobin and master orator during the very forming of the republic. Can you imagine? I know some people blame the Jacobins for the Reign, but I think they did quite a bit of good and didn't get a chance to finish. My papa wasn't a madman like Robespierre. He spoke for the rights of Black men and women to be citizens. He was a true hero and proud son of France. Who qualifies more for the right to be called a son of France than one who has suffered its indignities. Vive la Républic, oui?"

My lips had gone numb, but I gave a quick nod as I took quick glances at her from under hooded lids. I couldn't stop looking at her, but I didn't want to make her uncomfortable.

She straightened and adopted a mischievous look as her chin went up and she began to recite something:

"'...For equality to mean something it has to work for everyone, or it means *nothing*. We want a France that shows the world what equality truly means...'"

As she said the words I had spoken to the Jacobins, I felt like I had so many years ago when looking at the ceiling of Saint-Chappelle. At that moment I could see in the lovely young woman a small, tiny bit of me. And I recognized the song she had been humming as my lullaby. I had forgotten it, after all. Véronique had not. Just as she hadn't forgotten my words.

I could still see Véronique in the hall, watching on as I delivered the speech that I'd hoped would change the world. The speech that had made me feel for one moment like I was at the top of the world. That I had re-discovered the greatness my mother had seen in me from birth. Véronique had been right there with me. She must have saved the papers from the fire, understanding how much that moment meant to me.

The young lady was speaking my words but the sound of them fell away as I watched her, my eyes struggling to keep focus and keep the moisture at bay. Tears would only mar and block this vision and I needed to see. I needed to look at my child!

All the years I'd been so obsessed with seeing my words in print, in being an orator, in having my words printed with my name. And yet in this moment, the young lady before me meant more than anything I'd ever done, anything I'd ever said. On this day, I'd come to this place dead, and now I was reborn.

She finished the passage and blushed... "I'm sorry. There's more but you didn't ask to hear all that. I tend to feel compelled to recite my father's words. Words are such an important thing to leave, don't you think? More valuable than all the money in the world. Words are legacy and I always want to do his justice. I feel close to him through his words, even though I never knew him."

"I'm sure your father would be more proud of the legacy *you* are to him than his words," I said over a throat I had to clear. "The blessing of having such an intelligent young woman as his daughter means more to him than any words. The miracle of you... I'm sure, he would say."

"But I imagine you know all about the Révolution," she continued. "You must have children my mother's age?"

That was how old I looked, that my child thought I was decades older than her mother, when we were practically the same age. I wouldn't correct her. Thinking I was ancient was a good disguise. The young woman might have seen herself in my face were it not covered with a grey beard, pre-mature wrinkles, and the ravages of time and bad living. The ravages of age and pain and regret had taken me over.

"What did you say your name was, Mademoiselle?" I asked.

"Marianne," she said. Of course, Marianne: the name of the symbol of France's freedom, the symbol of the republic.

"That's lovely," I said. "And do you stitch, also, or do you have other plans? You seem to be an intelligent young woman."

"I'm so happy I seem so to you, Monsieur—it would break my heart if I thought I disappointed a kind stranger," she smiled.

I picked up the sarcasm, immediately, and a burst of laughter popped from me, which caused her to do the same. She obviously had her mother's brains and my wit. My biting tongue. Though, Véronique could be equally as sharp. Maybe she was a combination of two people who couldn't hold their tongues.

"If I didn't know better, kind stranger, I would think my parents put you up to question me, but please know I earn my keep. When I'm not helping my mother by tracking down customers in the street, I'm teaching. Like my grandmother."

Like your father.

"And I don't have to marry to teach so, no offense, if you're seeking to yoke me to an eligible grandson or great nephew, don't bother. My parents have tried. I'll have none of it. It's no longer my mother's day when women had no choices. I will teach and write until this country observes all its people, even Black women, as citizens. Maybe soon, I'll leave this place to strike a new path of my own."

The defensiveness in her tone was all Véronique. The determination. The small frown on her brow. I smiled.

I could clearly see what was happening here. Her mother was keeping the girl close. I couldn't blame her. Véronique had been young and brave once, too, and what had it gotten her? Pregnant and abandoned, at her most vulnerable, in the midst of war. Forced to find a way to survive for herself and her child. She must have been so frightened and hurt. I winced.

Oh my love, please forgive me. The words came from my heart as if she was standing there to hear.

The fact that Véronique was holding Marianne close made perfect sense to me but I saw something in the young woman's eyes. Fire and wanderlust. Desire to find her own moon. Yearning to unearth her own greatness. Even with quick, furtive glances at her I could clearly see the restlessness that drove youth and spurred revolutions of mind and spirit. I could see the fire and cunning intelligence tempered by her sweet countenance and gentle manners.

Love for her mother was likely the only thing that was keeping Marianne tethered to Croissy-Sur-Seine this long, but something told me it wouldn't keep her for much longer. This girl—this *woman*, Marianne—was the perfect storm of her mother and me.

Oh Mon Dieu, I thought, as I fought to keep my lips from turning in a smile, turning feverish with glee. What an incredible human being stood before me. Marianne would be a wonder in this world! She was surely the greatest thing God put on earth.

I nodded, picking up the strings of our conversation that I'd managed to hold while scoping her mind. "You don't have to do anything you don't want to do, don't let anyone tell you otherwise," I said, speaking quickly. Feeling protective of this child I'd only just gotten. "It is still difficult for an unmarried woman in many ways but, perhaps, like your mother, you will find a friend you can tolerate who will give you a safe life."

"Tolerate? Safe? Your words confuse me, Monsieur, but I'm sure you mean no offence. My mother loves my papa, even if he is not my father."

I bit my tongue to silence myself before making another mistake. "Of course, of course, I meant no offence."

"And my mother's life has been anything but safe. My mother was a sans-culottes in one of the women's groups that popped up in the church near where she worked. Don't let her status today fool you. Along with mes tantes Salanave and Élise" – *her aunts*— "they did their part to champion for women. Now it's my turn, and I'll continue my parents' work for freedom and citizenship for our people. I'll continue the fight for the rights of women."

Salanave and Élise? They knew! Of course they did. Now, all the unspoken words and clipped comments made sense, if I had been paying attention. Salanave reminding me of how I'd treated Véronique to prompt my guilt, perhaps to send me her way. Élise stopping Sebastien every time he... Sebastien knew too! Mon Dieu. I should have known!

I wanted to hop up and down with excitement. Véronique and Salanave had always been close and now I knew why. Now I understood so much more. I'd been such a fool. Such a fool.

"But," she sighed, "as you say, perhaps I'll find a friend I can 'tolerate' who's as splendid as Papa. Or, maybe, I'll find a man I love enough to sit a burning candle in the window every night. If I can't find the latter, I will settle for the former."

"Candle...?" I breathed.

"Oh," she swatted at the air. She pointed, haphazardly, to the window. "It's nothing. Just my mother imagines that candle will put my father's soul to peace. She lights that candle in case he's looking down or up, she says. I truly think it's just a story she tells me to make me feel better."

I looked to the house and, perhaps because it was daytime and I'd been so set on seeing her, my eyes had skipped right over the little candle in the window. It was our sign to each other! My heart swelled and Marianne went on, never knowing how every word was growing that heart.

"Maman used to tell me my father was driven and haunted—that he needed someone on this earth to love him. And though she was angry at him she said she wished him peace of soul and spirit because giving her up to fight for the republic was likely the worst regret he would have in life, he loved her so. Maman is modest."

Laughter popped from me at her sarcasm again, surprising her; the sound of it seemed to humor her as I quickly got myself under control.

"Because true love never dies, not even when our flesh does. Love is like water, she says, it flows to all the places we can't reach. It soothes the deepest thirst. Love is the gift God gives us to sustain us even in the worst of times."

She seemed to come to herself, shaking her thoughts of her dead father. "All this talking I'm doing I've forgotten simple manners. What is your name, Monsieur?"

"My name…" How I longed to reveal myself to my child. I didn't imagine Véronique had told her my name if she was pretending I was dead. I didn't imagine she would tell her my name, regardless.

My Véronique didn't hate me. That was all that mattered.

In my quietest moments over the years, I'd often wondered if I'd made the right decision. Despite my bluster and claim to the contrary, leaving Véronique had scarred me. I knew now she loved me even more than I'd thought—and was stronger than I guessed. And that I loved her even more than I dared acknowledge.

Perhaps I could have made her happy, somehow, even with the damage done. It could have been me, Véronique and Marianne sitting in that little house; close enough to Paris that I could get over to see Sebastien and take in theater. But with a wife and child at home to hold and care for and love. A family. It was all I'd ever wanted, really. It was the reason I so wanted to be respected, so I could be worthy of something as basic as a family.

For the greatness in me could only truly be seen by those who loved me, after all. Try as I might have over the years since being torn from my parents, no amount of gravitas or accolades had ever made me feel as special as the words of someone who knew me. And loved me.

Questions about Véronique rolled through me and I would never hear the answers from her lips, but I didn't need to. She saw my truth when I couldn't. She saw my desperate need to be something special, my obsessive need for validation from people who would never validate my humanity. She saw my head-long and steadfast drive to do anything, even sacrifice myself, to prove something to people who had never held me in any esteem; to get them to acknowledge my manhood. To be *someone* in the eyes of the people of the highest in society. All so that I could prove to myself that I deserved more than to be treated like a thing. Prove to myself that I was more than they said I was.

She saw all that and didn't hate me. Her actions were all the answer I needed.

And now, I realized that all along she was giving me all that I wanted. *More* than I deserved. She did the difficult thing, too, and in doing so left me my dignity. Because of her, in my child's eyes... I was the hero I always wanted to be. Marianne probably imagined a father with the stature and grace of Josephe or Thomas. She wouldn't even be looking for someone like *Zamor*. It wasn't fair that I should get off so cleanly.

Long ago I told Véronique that people can't really love for a lifetime. I was wrong. A fool. I loved her then, and I loved her still. I loved her, always, and I would love her for eternity.

But no matter how much I wanted to reveal myself to my child, I would not undo Véronique's work for all the world. Not even for Marianne. And I couldn't take the chance that Marianne would recognize my unique name. I'd been given enough of a gift today, I wouldn't be greedy.

In France, you couldn't walk two steps without running into a Louis, so I kept it simple. "My name is Louis," I told her. "It is so nice to see a young person such as yourself taking an interest in your country's history. It was a truly amazing time to live through. Though, as you suggest I, too, lost much during the Révolution. Still, it was worth it. But I have something here." I reached into my pocket and pulled out something I had carried with me for years.

It was truly ironic that over the years I had given much money and gifts to people, many I hadn't even cared about. I'd done niceties for people I barely knew but all along I'd had a child in the world who I was sure needed things. My Véronique must have needed many things finding herself with child and alone. I felt a slice of hurt for her at that moment, and the position I put her in. Without finding the man, she might have lost all. I would go to my grave with that regret and gratitude for a man I didn't know but made me burn with envy. My envy did matter. God had stepped in and protected those I loved when I didn't.

Now, I didn't have much more than the coat on my back, except for one thing. I hadn't known how I would give it to Véronique but giving it to Marianne was a better solution than I could have imagined. I held it out and explained when she took it in her hand. "A momento a friend of mine thought was pretty. I never had a chance to give it to her but perhaps you would like it."

She held the small porcelain dancing figurine that her mother had saved from sure disaster so many years ago. She held it up to the light. It was still intact and well cared for, cherished second only to my lost violin. As unrealistic as it was, I had given Véronique so little in our time together I hoped if I ever saw her again I could bring her *something* she loved, something to remind her of our best time.

"Oh, it's lovely," Marianne said, turning it around in her hand. "And it looks expensive. I couldn't possibly."

"You must," I insisted. "To make an old man happy. I have no one to give it to and it would be a shame if it were lost."

"Let me get my maman and papa and show them, I know they'd love to meet you." She looked ready to call out but I stopped her. No matter how much I wanted to see her mother, I would not be any more selfish than I already had been. I would not intrude upon her happiness. But my heart was lighter than it had been in years. I would not push my luck.

"Actually, I must go." I waved a hand as if suddenly I was in a rush. "I forgot I am to meet a friend. You have brightened my day more than you know. I bid you farewell, lovely Marianne." I leaned forward and kissed her gently on both cheeks.

"I will see you again?"

"I—" I was distracted by sudden movement in the window and saw her passing by. Just a quick, passing glance at the woman who owned my heart. A glimpse of her waist in a modest green dress, and her hands holding a small vase of flowers. Not Madame's flowers—but her own. She held them the little jar with careful reverence. She had always so loved even the smallest beautiful things... had always lit up with joy even though her face might be stoic. My heart beat like a drum. *Get a hold of yourself, Zamor!*

"I-I must go. We'll meet again, someday, I'm sure of it."

"All right. Farewell, Monsieur. It's been a pleasure."

I walked away from that place as fast as I could just in case Marianne ignored me and called out to Véronique. Though my body hurt, I couldn't stop the smile that spread across my face as I walked away like a busy crab.

My future had not been taken from me. Where I fell another sprouted, stronger and smarter and braver. They would keep coming even stronger, smarter and braver. They would do more than I. *Be* more than I.

But I was a stepping-stone for the progress that would be my child and all from her, and that gave me more joy than I'd felt in a lifetime. More joy than I'd felt since lying in the arms of Véronique, more joy than I'd felt playing music to her on the violin, more joy than riding on the back of Lightning as we flew through the night air with the cool breeze of freedom on our cheeks.

It was worth it, after all. I would do it all again for the blessing of a young woman named Marianne made by the grace of a humble, beautiful servant woman with a determined face and a beautiful smile.

God brought me back to France, and now I knew why.

Chapter Sixty-Four

Transformations sometimes led to unfinished business. Now that I unearthed the mystery of what mine was, I knew I still had more to do.

It came to me on the ride from Croissy-Sur-Seine: My child was going to leave home soon, of that I was sure. And when she did, I wanted her to have something. She needed money!

I was hot, sitting on that carriage seat, even though it wasn't hot outside. The sickness in me was burning within. But I had another kind of fever. I had the fever of knowing I was running out of time. I had to help my daughter!

When I should have gone east on the road to Paris, I went west, using the reins to kick that sad little horse into a little more speed on the road towards the town of Louveciennes and Chateau du Barry.

The once-manicured grass along the road had grown high and was threaded with weeds and wildflowers. It made me smile. I had been a wildflower once among the manicured gardens of the Palace, too. I had been the scourge there and the same here.

I once thought Madame was the devil, but I could now acknowledge she probably thought the same of me. After all, I had upset the Chateau du Barry and ousted its queen.

Back to the scene once again, I took in the appearance of the abandoned home as I pulled up front. It had been so beautiful to hold so much evil. Climbing down, I secured the horse, and walked up to the front door which was already ajar, glass on the floor in the foyer. But instead of exploring the house I went back outside. It was abandoned so I was free to walk the length of it, sitting beside my old tree until the sun began to leave for the day. Even with the overgrowth it was beautiful. How I would have loved to be there as a free man. That would have changed everything.

Then, I walked to the Pavilion and looked out over the edge to where the Marly Machine still chugged on along the river bank; still turning as long as there were men to work it and water to be carted to the Versailles fountains, running for the tourists' pleasure.

Back at the house all of Madame's portraits, art, and most of the busts with her likeness were gone. But, lo-and-behold, hanging on the wall, my portrait stared back at me from my youth. I was in white satin with a slight smile on my face as if I knew something the world didn't. Ah, the confidence of youth, I thought. I couldn't have convinced the man in that portrait that things would end this way for all the world.

Of course, the house was further ransacked. As my shoes crunched glass underneath, the staleness of the air and the dust motes that flew up at every step told me this place hadn't been inhabited for years, even.

Walking through the house was like a fever dream; it looked a shell of what it once was, but I couldn't tarry. Pain was deep within me but so strong I felt my limbs wanting to curl me up and lie me down.

"Not yet—" I hissed to myself. I had work to do!

I went to the study first and began yanking open the drawers of the desk that weren't already askew. I ran over to the podium with the hidden compartment that once held her statue and opened it, finding nothing. Then, I ran over to the silk drapes and, as I'd seen Madame do that last day we lived together, I began tearing them open at the seams between the lining and the dusty satin. I felt like crying when they were empty.

Running to my old room I pushed aside the frame of the bed that had been stripped, it's mattress likely never to be seen again. I got down on the floor, my coat scooping up all the dirt and dust from years gone by so that it would look gray when I left here. But it didn't matter. With my hands I clawed at the loose floorboard where I had kept my treasures all my years living here, only to find two coins. I had taken everything the night I left.

With a sigh, I sat back on my haunches, moisture welling in my eyes as my torso clenched in a spasm. There had to be something. *Anything.* I cried out as the spasm overtook me for a good ten seconds.

Suddenly, the stone-cold fox that had been gone for years came back with shocking clarity—before me and staring into my eyes like a lover. I knew what it meant. I knew my panic had brought it back. My panic and this place. My desperation, and this place. My pain... and this place.

Come away with me! it screamed at me. *Save yourself!*

But now I understood, the fox that had saved my mind when I was a young, desperate boy, would as easily kill me now, if only to save me from more pain. And I couldn't die yet. I had more to do.

"No," I said, waking. "*...Not ready...*"

And, as if the sound of my voice was its command, my body stirred in response.

During those few seconds I had fallen onto the floor and lost my senses. Waking, I had to unclench my hands and blink because my eyes were dry as if they'd frozen open. I gasped deeply, knowing I must have stopped breathing to suck in air so deeply.

I had seen something, briefly, quickly, after the fox disappeared. A glimmer of a thought so fleeting I might have missed it if my mind wasn't suddenly so sharp. A memory and a dream.

The memory was Madame on trial.

***

"And were the stolen jewels your only jewels or do you have more? Perhaps hidden away?" Grieve had asked her.

"Yes, I do sometimes choose to hide my valuables, likely near the greenhouse or the ice house."

***

But that wasn't all. It had always been a badly kept secret among those of us who would wander outside at night. During the nighttime, Jeanne du Barry would bury jewels under the cloak of nightfall. Sometimes, the moonlight would shine on her hair as she dug into the earth to make space for a small packet.

She had offered up jewels in exchange for her freedom, but how much did they find? Because she'd been burying jewels all of our lives on these grounds.

Suddenly, a memory of a dream came sharply and poignantly. It was the one that kept coming back. The dream of the memory that I hardly ever thought of when fully awake. It was one of those memories that you forget so deeply, when you dream of it you imagine it is fantasy. It was a memory that meant nothing to me, usually.

It was Louis XV and I walking side by side in the gardens as pointed words of his made their way through my brain. This time, we weren't at the Palace; we were here, at the Chateau.

***

"Look, pull out the pocket watch I gave you. When you look at the face of a clock you won't only see the time of the day. You'll remember the signs of the Zodiac, won't you? You'll remember there are twelve. I have a secret."

A secret!

He leaned down to whisper in my ear. "At the Chateau at Louveciennes I had the gardener plant bushes around the property in a circle. One for each Zodiac. Twelve bushes in a circle, with the house as its north star at midnight... and a thirteenth bush to represent the three of us and our love for each other. He gave me a mischievous grin. "It's a mystery, where it is! Maybe you'll be the one to solve it. After all, you are the Governor!"

***

And the pieces of the puzzle came together. I knew what I had to do and at that moment it seemed impossible. In response to even the thought of it, pain centered in my gut and I saw the fox before me. It stared at me in my mind's eye, calling me insane.

Every fox must *survive its own hunt, Louis-Benoit Zamor... and all that!* it said, throwing my words back at me. Telling me to go its way and escape the pain. Telling me to save myself. But, for once, I was going to save myself by going through the pain. To save the ones I loved.

My face twisted in a grimace that was a smile.

"No," I said to the stone fox. "I don't need you now. I need to finish"

In my mind's eye, the stone creature disappeared. He'd done his best. I would be left with my own pain now.

As my vision cleared, I knew I didn't have a lot of time. My episodes of pain would lead to my demise, and I would be lucky if I lasted until daylight. But I still had work to do! Getting air back into my lungs I got back on my knees and stood up, grinning like a fool. It wasn't time. Yet.

A few minutes of staggering to my feet, I gained some strength back. I used it to stumble through and out of the house, across the yard and over to the gardener's shed. Cobwebs glistened in the midday light streaming through the windows. I scavenged until I found what I wanted. Two mismatched leather gardening gloves of the same hand would have to do. And one shovel.

The weeds were high, but I could see the remnants of the once-manicured rose bushes. Seeing two of them helped me find the others. I began to dig. That odd bit of strength in my arms moved me along. Fabien's advice about moving through pain kept me going. My arms hurt and my hands began to blister as February ground was hard. I threw my cloak off because I was sweating through my clothes and kept digging. And then, after the twelfth rose bush proved fruitless, I fell to my knees, laboring to breathe.

I didn't understand. I'd dug up all twelve bushes. All twelve!

I looked around the now-wild grounds and my breath slowed as I spied the one bush along the perimeter that was out of place and all alone, almost hidden back in the trees. Almost. The bush that was unique and represented change. The bush that could both heal or kill. The bush that no one in their right mind would ever think to even touch.

The moon was lighting the sky and its rays lay upon that last untouched plant in that God-forsaken garden.

I smiled and, with my shovel, headed toward the small bush of dreaded belladonna. The Devil's Berries. The unkempt bush among the beautiful, manicured gardens of strategically placed rose bushes. It was a shrub, really, almost hidden, behind the tree line where no one but the most wretched ever ventured. The wild plant with its small black, poisonous devil's berries that he'd chosen to represent me.

Of course.

Chapter Sixty-Five

My arms hurt so that it was difficult to hold the reins. My legs wobbled, the nerves jumping on their own steam—refusing to obey me any longer. I kept the horse going slow so I wouldn't fall off. I was exhausted but I still had more to do. Just a little more and I could rest.

"You all right, old-timer?" Someone called out to me on a horse going the opposite direction as I passed.

"Oui, oui, merci," I said with a wave of my hand in the air, trying to infuse some vigor in my voice. But that sad horse was keeping me atop his back by its movement, one hip at a time. One trot at a time.

"My sweet Louis-Benoit, I can't wait to have you back."

Madame's voice rang in my head.

At that moment, I had another epiphany as I sagged atop that poor horse. All this time I'd been thinking she was haunting me. I had never felt guilty about what I'd done—she'd set it up so I was forced to, after all—but I did feel some bit of responsibility. Over the years, maybe had wondered if there were other options. She was right about one thing—we all have a choice. I choose to live in the only way I could find.

But the fact that she kept coming back confused, confounded, and—yes—frightened me. At least it had up until this very day as I sagged against the poor horse carrying me. Maybe digging up treasures at the place that used to be my home had unearthed some answers, because now they came to me with clarity.

I wasn't afraid of *her*. I was afraid of being connected to her for all of eternity. I was afraid that I'd only be known as Du Barry's Page; never more than the bauble or toy of a pampered woman. It was how I came to France, after all. To them, I was only her thing. It was why I hated the posters so much. It was why she still plagued my dreams. She wasn't haunting me. The thought of never being free of her, was.

Upon that horse, my lips quirked with irony. The journals, and a splendid child who didn't know me by name, were my only legacy. France may never consider me as a person of my own right. There was nothing I could do about it now, and so there was no more need of haunting.

"My dearest Madame Du Barry," I croaked to the night air. "You may keep waiting in hell. I was never yours to have. And never will be…"

The cool, quiet air met my words and a response never came from Jeanne du Barry. The night was as still and cool as a stone fox in a winter's garden.

That horse carried me into Paris sometime in the deepness of the night and I, gratefully, turned it in to where I rented it, happy they always had someone on shift to collect and loan horses. Then, I walked through town to my neighborhood. I was slow, but I was grateful Remy's bar hadn't closed its doors when I arrived, though it must have been close to eleven in the evening. I was crouched, but my cloak covered me so I simply looked like another old, stooped Parisian. He looked up when he saw me approaching and then quickly looked again.

"Mon Dieu, you look like hell. Face is as green as your favorite drink. Sit down before you fall. Have you seen a doctor?"

I pulled myself onto a chair as he poured me a glass of Chartreuse. He didn't know I was one foot in the grave; I never could see the point in sharing that bit of news. I took the glass in a shaky hand and drank the drink down quickly.

"No cure for old age, I'm afraid," I said. "Listen, I need to speak to you..."

"Ugh, is that smell coming from you?" he asked, grimacing and covering his nose with a towel. "What have you been doing..."

"Listen, Remy!" I hissed, the air coming out of me broken with the stagger of lungs that wanted to shut down. The sound of me gasping caught his attention and his face softened as he looked closer at me.

"Hey, what's wrong? What's the matter? Are you sick, then? Are you bad?"

"I need you to promise me something. I need you to keep this." I pulled a box from under my cape that I'd shoved my things into. It wasn't big—it was the best I could find in the empty chateau. I shoved it across the bar toward him and leaned in. "I need you to keep this and hide it."

"Why, what is it?"

"Nothing bad and nothing anyone is looking for. It's a box and a cloth bag on top. If anyone should come here—say, a nice-looking woman..."

"You know *another* nice-looking woman. I just sent one your way a few days ago..."

"...If a different nice-looking woman—a woman with a tiny frown between her eyes named Véronique—if she should come here, can you give her the box? I wouldn't ask but you are... you are the only friend I have left. If she doesn't come in a year, everything in that box is yours. Would you please?"

Remy shuffled like he was slightly uncomfortable but then his face softened even more. "Well, of course I will. You're my friend, too, non? My last one. I'll do whatever you need. Is it bad, your illness, then?"

I darted a quick glance his way. It wasn't in me to lie at that point. I shrugged. He gave a sober nod.

"Hand it over, then. I'll keep my eye out for the nice-looking woman."

"She's beautiful."

"All the more reason for me to look out for her, then," he said. "I don't know how you get so many beautiful women in your life." He refilled my glass of green brew and then filled a second, holding it out for us to clink glasses together. "Santé." We then nodded at each other and drank. He grimaced and it made me laugh weak pops from my chest.

"And one other thing: That cloth sack on top, that's for you."

"I don't need your money, batard." *Bastard*. He thought I was insulting him.

"Listen to me," I said. "I don't have anyone else I trust. You know that in this city far more people hate me than even know me. Portraits up all over Paris mocking me, determined to keep me the servant to a woman I never wanted to serve. I never had a choice in that and I don't have a choice in what they're saying about me now, but I have a choice in how I treat my last friend. Let me do this one thing. One last thing, please."

His face was stubborn but his eyes shone wetly. He nodded roughly, as if to hold in tears. "And what should I do now, with all my friends gone? I must be truly cursed to be the last of the Parisien Jacobins."

"Last of the Jacobins?" I croaked with a smile. "Jacobins never die. Vive la Révolution. Ça ira." *It's all good.* I raised my glass, and he broke into a grin, parroting my move.

"Ça ira, Governor. Ça ira."

Chapter Sixty-Six

I returned to my apartment building on the Rue Perdu. Though it was well past midnight I saw the light of a candle in the little room off the front hall.

"Is that you, Monsieur Zamor?" It was the landlady...

"Oui, Madame. You are up late."

"My husband is sleeping loudly tonight. I thought I'd take the opportunity to read this novel."

"Any chance to spend time reading a good book as a chance well spent, Madame," I said, heading toward the stairs.

"Monsieur, might I convince you to share that walk with me in the morning?"

I stopped at her words. It only just occurred to me that I had seen my last daytime. I had breathed my last chestful of Parisian air. I would go to my room and never come out.

And, though I longed to make sure I was found, I wouldn't ruin her morning for all the world. She had been kind to me.

"I don't think so, Madame, I think I might sleep in tomorrow."

"Oh, well, maybe another time."

I breathed a sigh of relief. "Oui, another time."

If she were to see me, she would see me doubled over, practically crawling up the stairs, but I continued. "Madame, you-you have been most kind to me. I do appreciate it more than I can say." I was being sincere. I couldn't have asked for a kinder person to find my body.

"Oh, goodness, it is nothing," she said, and I could hear pleasure in her voice. "I would be happy if all of our tenants were as pleasant. Bonsoir, Monsieur Zamor."

"Adieu, Madame," slipped out of me by accident. If she noticed my use of *good-bye* instead of *good-night,* she didn't say anything.

Pain roiled through me and my organs spasmed inside me, but I managed to make it upstairs. Once inside, I shrugged out of my cloak, allowing it to fall to the ground. Then, I lit a candle. It had been almost a day since I'd eaten but I was certain I couldn't hold anything down. That made it all the better that I was out of bread and caviar, and Chartreuse. I had a dusty bottle of red wine on a shelf.

I started to pour a bit into a small glass and then said "to hell with it", and drank straight from the bottle. The fiery brew went down smoothly, immediately relaxing some of the tension in me.

I wanted to crawl into bed but I had one last thing to do. I sat at my small table, took out a quill and ink and two sheets of paper. I wrote two letters and put them into one envelope. I wrote as my wrist shook and my eyes blurred. I wrote out my heart. I wrote out my soul. And then, finally done, I folded the letters and put Véronique's name on the envelope.

Next, I went through my journal entries, scribbling out Véronique's name. If they were published I wanted no one to trace them back to her. My child was free of spirit and free from any negativity associated with me and I wanted her to remain that way.

By the time I finished my last journal entry, the quill shook in my quivering fingers but I was grateful I managed this far, dropping the quill pen on the table and spilling the bottle of ink. I wanted to clean the mess but my vision was so blurred by now—there was nothing to be done about it. I proceeded to lay the papers and envelope on top of the box of Joseph's music. Hopefully, when they found me, they'd find my story and his through his music.

Lurching to my shelf with empty caviar tins, I felt around with my hands until I found that tiny bundle of Marianne's hair wrapped in cloth, clutching it to me as I panted in gratitude.

My insides convulsed so I clutched myself, helping my own body to the bed. It felt as though it was no longer mine, this body. I crawled into bed with it, wrapping myself in a blanket, holding the little bundle to my chest.

Pain was a clenched fist shaking my body like a rag doll. But even the pain couldn't take away the happiness I felt. The bed was cold, cold, cold, so I wrapped tighter in the blanket. When all was said and done I was sure I'd be found curled and as small as I was when I came into the world.

Lying on my deathbed, the room cold and lit only by a single, sputtering candle on the table beside me, it occurs to me that I've become a cautionary tale. An example of a life lived, wrongly.

But then again, it wasn't *all* bad.

I remember the night after a late gathering while the nobles were carrying their wine-soaked bodies through the trees back to the Chateau, Véronique and I went to the backside of the Pavilion where the landing overlooked the Seine River and as the sun climbed light blue before burgeoning into light of day, we danced. The servant and the slave danced nature's ballroom under the pink sky as the birds began to sing and no one was there to watch but God. We danced under His gaze as He blessed our love. Dancing under the heaven and into the sweet light of day.

As I lay there, knowing that the next time I closed my eyes would be the last I thought of my Véronique and me. I thought of our wonderful child. Mon Dieu, I was wealthy with things my enemies would love to take. What a wonderful thing. Too bad for them they never would.

Once again, my lips twist with sick humor. My vision finally fails me, completely.

I imagine I am, once again, in that silk and velvet-lined golden carriage and feel my face contort into a grimace of a death mask as my life plays out in the dark space behind my eyelids, one last time.

***

And now, the strangest thing happens. As my conscious thoughts drift away and my eyes drift closed, it's not the stark, cold light of a lightning strike in a Labyrinth that I see. It's not the blond woman who calls herself my mother, arms stretched out to me with a toothsome smile and sparkling blue eyes.

I see two sets of brown eyes. I think ... yes ... I see my parents here to greet as they were when I was about seven, just before I was taken. First, my father, but as a strong, vibrant man. And then I look beside him and tell myself it can't be ... I can't remember my mother. But oh yes, this isn't merely a memory, returned. They are here and suddenly coming into focus.

She has eyes like warm milk, soft with her love for me. Her hair is brown and along the edges, in the summer, pieces of it go lighter brown in the sun. Her skin is smooth and dark, and when she presses her cheek against the top of my head, the feeling of safety melts my inside and causes me to sigh.

Her lips curl in a smile for me and her voice—though I'm not hearing the words—opens the doors to a flood of feelings of all she was to me. Memories of her holding me at night, rocking me in her arms, serenading me with her special song that made me love music. Holding out her arms to me as I run into them. Laughing with me as I eat porridge all over my face. Clapping for me when I take my first steps. Holding my face in her hands.

"My sweet boy," she says, her voice as clear and honest as the sun; her eyes shining with pride as she looks into my face. "You are the greatest thing God has ever made."

I watch her lips as she says those words, my eyes greedy for the sound of them from her own mouth. She looks at me with pure love. Together, my parents look at me as if I'm a precious gift. In their eyes, I can see it! I am the greatest thing that God ever made. I believe it because it's true to them! They didn't lie to me. I have value. I am important. I am loved.

I'm buoyant with happiness.

My twisted death grimace loosens and the muscles in my face relax. There's no more pain. And now, I'm lifting from the bed from the light heaviness of their love.

The sound of the hooves of the horses of death ring in my ears but instead of the comfort of a carriage with the fleur-de-lys, I feel the hard bumpiness of being in the back of a lumbering, loud, ragged wooden cart. Just like the one that carried me away from Chittagong. I'm back in that cart but instead of taking me away, it's carrying me up to where my parents seem to be lifting into the sky. Up, up, up...

I start to smile and feel the haunches of one particular horse underneath me; the familiar body of a royal steed that has become accustomed to the signal of my every move. It is my beloved Lightning! Underneath me, she knows I recognize her because she whinnies, loudly, in triumph and throws her head back in glory. She's young again and free.

I feel movement in front of me and look down upon a small head with tight black curls. Small brown hands reach forward, each to rest on the back of mine, holding the reins. Little Jean twists to look up into my face, his cheeks shining with the thrill of the ride. "We're going home, Monsieur Zamor. Where you go, I go," he says, a smiling cherub anxious to end the long journey. It's not a question this time.

It's so bright I look up to see what has happened to the roof. Instead, I see the ceiling of Sainte-Chappelle Cathedral I love, with its stained glass mosaic of colored light raining colors of heaven down and around us. Like a bazaar. Like a celebration! It opens to a beautiful sky and Lightning carries us both, up, up, up...

The feeling of my body falls away like a sodden coat, dropped off me, and I breathe a sigh of contentment. Peace. Finally, I can stop fighting.

I can't help but giggle at my cleverness: I've somehow tricked God into thinking I deserve to be in heaven!

But I'm not going to correct Him. I'll just let the light take me where it will ... and sleep the deepest sleep, with love washing over me like the sweetest, sweetest bath.

It is a fitting end, I think. C'est la justice poétique.

Poetic justice... and all that.

Epilogue

Dear Citizen,

This is my last journal entry and my final words to you…

A relationship amongst adults—a "relationship" contract of sorts—must be mutually agreed upon for it to be real, which is only possible amongst equals. It is impossible to love one who has stolen your freedom. It is impossible to betray someone with whom you've never had a contract.

Freedom is as essential as food and water and air to breathe. There is no amount of privilege that can take the place of it.

My loyalty was owed to no one but myself and my goal towards freedom. Anyone who would argue that point must face God and explain that to him.

I love France with all my heart and soul. Anyone who would argue that never knew me.

I once labeled myself a pragmatist. But as I lie on my deathbed I tell you that's changed. I no longer only see things as they are. I'm now seeing things as they could be. My eyes have been opened and oh my, how excited I am for the future I will not see! It changes my outlook a bit.

Oui, un renard doit survivre à sa propre chasse. A fox must survive its own hunt … and all that.

Yes, this undignified death may be the way I deserve to go: la justice poétique pour moi.

All true.

But let me be a lesson for this reason: something always lives beyond the hunt. It is the greatness within us that drives every human being to want to thrive beyond survival, even in the face of our own mortality.

I must pose one last question to you: What if the greatest thing a country can produce is not its powerful leader? What if a country's greatest thing is, in fact, the being or beings upon which it heaps its discontent? Upon whom it burdens with the most shameful of its abuses. Upon whom it stares in the face and chooses to deny its very existence? What if the being that experiences all manners of indignity is the very being who loves that country the most? Would that being not, dear Citizen, truly be its greatest thing? Is that the truth no one will ever admit?

I want my last words to mean something beyond what will be found in this bed in the morning. If you read nothing of my journal and choose to skip to this last page, let these words stay with you:

L'espoir fait vivre! Hope springs eternal!

I die with a smile, knowing my love is happy and my child will thrive. I die with hope for others on my mind and happiness for their potential in my heart. I die knowing, without a doubt, that my brethren will someday be free. I die, knowing that, someday, France will fulfill the promise of what it can be.

Forgive my poor penmanship. I must go now, eternity calls.

Dear Citizen of my beloved France ...

I love you. Vive la France and Ça ira!

Sincerely, Louis-Benoit Zamor,

Citizen, True Son of France

February 6, 1820

Adieu

Fin

This historical fiction trilogy is an unusual representation of Jeanne du Barry and Louis-Benoit Zamor. My version of their story portrays her as less than kind and him as just less than evil. I feel the need to explain my thought process.

Descendants of enslaved people in the U.S. know what it's like to be spoken of as if we aren't full human beings: Being told our ancestors enjoyed slavery, being depicted in art and media in ways to dehumanize us, listening as slavery is trivialized as something to get over rather than an open wound that's never been addressed. We are used to the PR spin, so I recognized it when reading the accounts that presented Zamor as just evil with no redeeming value.

Without denying the reality of Zamor's part in the death of Jeanne du Barry, I wanted to know the story beyond the spin. I wanted to find the answer to the mystery of why this man would turn on a woman he had been close to for over two decades. Simply assuming evil intent is a lazy fallback to the notion that Black people aren't real human beings with feelings, thoughts, intelligence, and reasoning capability.

By this point, you know I believe turning on du Barry was the only way available to earn his freedom. I came to this conclusion for several reasons.

- We know Zamor was bought by/for Louis XV. Yes, it's possible he was freed immediately upon arrival in France as a child, but there are no records of that.

- All accounts suggest he was abused terribly as a child and treated more as a pet than a person.

- After the death of Louis XV, Louis XVI enacted provisions prohibiting enslaved people from petitioning for freedom for any reason, I believe done so while Zamor was still under his roof at the Palace.

- Into adulthood, while living with du Barry at the Chateau at Louveciennes, her doting was met with disdain and contempt.

- Zamor was a follower of Enlightenment writer Jean-Jacques Rousseau, who wrote on equality of men. Becoming a Jacobin reflected these beliefs and directly contradicted values of the ancient regime.

- The first thing he did after du Barry's death and his imprisonment was disappear from Paris.

- Zamor's death certificate listed him as a freed man.

All of these factors led me to believe, he was still enslaved at the start of the revolution and had been, for all intents and purposes, trapped in his relationship with Du Barry. And if he was enslaved, all bets were off on what he was willing to do to gain his freedom.

All accounts of Jeanne Du Barry presented her as kind-hearted. The prevailing theme is that she was loving towards him. How is it possible for someone to have such a reputation and be the complete opposite in reality, Was mine a fair depiction?

Back when I was in school some teachers would tell me, with a straight face, that some slave-owners in the U.S, were kind. They meant it. But everything is relative. Is it possible that Du Barry was considered kind by her peers in comparison to them? In comparison to other slave owners who treated their enslaved people atrociously? From the standpoint of the enslaved, captors appear more as varying degrees of evil. Relationships are never as loving as the captors represent because the uneven power dynamic makes a normal relationship impossible. So, two things can be true at the same time: Du Barry could have been considered kind by her peers while also being a slave owner and source of unending pain to him.

Once again, this is all conjecture. My frustration is knowing that if Louis-Benoit Zamor had been a White man, his life story would have been recorded, just as with his revolutionary peers. He wouldn't still be presented with all the depth of a cartoon character. Even though there is now controversy even over his ethnicity, I suggest ethnicity can be revealed by the treatment of the subject. I believe he was a Black man and the portraits previously attributed to him are true.

My hope is that historians decide to crack open all the records I couldn't find or didn't have access to, even if only to refute my fictionalized account. I welcome full and thorough research on this man! I'm anxious to discuss the controversies and contradictions that linger today, even as his (given) name has almost been lost to history.

As I end this journey with a character I have come to love, I say this: If Zamor's name must be linked to Du Barry, forever, let him also be linked to the survival spirit that sustained him while embedded in a hostile society, and through a revolution. Let him also be thought of as intelligent and resourceful. Let him also be remembered as a lost child of the slave trade who just happened to end up in France.

Thank you for reading this story and spending time in my mind. I love to speak to book clubs—reach out to me if you'd like to talk at patti@gil dedorangebooks.com.

I'd be so grateful if you would leave a review with your favorite book-
seller.

***

GILDED ORANGE BOOKS
www.gildedorangebooks.com

Resources

As I mentioned at the end of Book Two, for those interested in this time period I'm listing some videos and resources. This is not an exhaustive list— there's plenty out there about the revolution.

Below videos are the sources previously cited. Once again, I tossed a wide net and used everything from internet chatter to academic texts to provide broad context. Please do not blame any of the writers or filmmakers below for my stories; they had no idea when they wrote their pieces that I would get to them and do what I did for the sake of my art.

Dramatized Re-enactment Docu-Series:

- Marie Antoinette: The Trial of a Queen, directed by Alain Brunard, 2018

- The Rise and Fall of Versailles (dramatized re-enactment), directed by Paul Burgess, 2009

Resources & databases:

- Wikipedia

- Researchers at the Bibliothèque Nationale de France, BnF (The National Library of France), and the BnF research database, Gallica

Articles:

- Zamor, the slave boy from Bengal played a major role in bringing down Bastille during French Revolution, Get Bengal, December 30, 2021: https://www.getbengal.com/details/zamor-the-slave-boy-from-b engalplayed-a-major-role-in-bringing-down-bastille-during-frenc hrevolution

- How an Indian man taken to Europe as a slave played a role in the French Revolution, Bose, Arghya, July 14, 2020, Scroll.i n https://scroll.in/article/967343/how-an-indian-man-taken-to -europeas-a-slave-played-a-role-in-the-french-revolution

- In Paris, Offspring of the Revolution, Mikelbank, Peter, Mary 16, 1989, Washington Post

Books:

- Venus Noire: Black Women and Colonial Fantasies in Nine-teenth-Century France (Race in the Atlantic World, 1700-1900 Ser.), Robin Mitchell, University of Georgia Press, January 1, 2020

- African Europeans: An Untold History, Olivette Otele, Basic Books, August 29, 2023

- "There are no Slaves in France": The Political Culture of Race and

Slavery in the Ancien Régime, Sue Peabody, Oxford University Press, September 26, 2002

Plays:

- L'Escalavage des Noirs, ou L'Heureux Naufrage, MMe Olympe de Gouges, performed Dec 1789, La Comédie Française (translation by Hannah Palmer)

- Alzire, Voltaire (translation by William F. Fleming), First Start Publishing e-book edition, October 2012

Academic journals & papers:

- Bishop, Cécile. "Seeing Race, Seeing Ghosts: Zamor, Ourika, and the Specter of Blackness." L'Esprit Créateur 59, no. 2 (2019): 56-71. https://doi.org/10.1353/esp.2019.0016.

- Brixius, Dorit. 2020. "From Ethnobotany to Emancipation: Slaves, Plant Knowledge, and Gardens on Eighteenth-Century Isle de France." History of Science 58 (1): 51–75. doi:10.1177/0073275319835431.

- Hammersley, Rachel. 2015. "Concepts of Citizenship in France during the Long Eighteenth Century." European Review of History 22 (3): 468–85. doi:10.1080/13507486.2015.1036231.

- Mccloy, Shelby Thomas. 1945. "Negroes and Mulattoes in Eighteenth-Century France." Journal of Negro History 30 (July): 276–92. doi:10.2307/2715112.

- Parrish JN, Leary JPO. The French Revolution and the Rise of Surgery. The American SurgeonTM. 2000;66(1):94-95. doi:10. 1177/000313480006600120

- Sarti, Raffaella. 2022. "From Slaves and Servants to Citizens? Regulating Dependency, Race, and Gender in Revolutionary France and the French West Indies." International Review of Social History 67 (1): 65–95. doi:10.1017/S0020859021000432.

- Schreier, Lise. 2016. "Zamore 'the African' and the Haunting of France's Collective Consciousness." Nineteenth-Century Contexts 38 (2): 123–39. doi:10.1080/08905495.2016.1135290.

www.ingramcontent.com/pod-product-compliance
Lightning Source LLC
Chambersburg PA
CBHW070300310726

48976CB00005B/1504